I[illegible]TH . . .

T[illegible]ast, a Spitfire was streaming smoke.

He banked sharply. Now he could pick out the identification number. It was Sergeant Bill Kinsella of Caton's Yellow Section. He called over the R/T as he followed it down.

'Are you wounded, Bill?'

'No! No! I'm OK, sir. But I've got no oil pressure.'

There came more black smoke from the engine cowling as Kinsella attempted to boost the throttle. The undercarriage was down, but the wheels hit too hard. Yet, somehow, Kinsella managed to keep control and the aircraft was hurtling over the rough terrain until it hit a line of rocks where it tipped sedately up on its nose. Taylor had expected Kinsella to leap out, but he didn't. And, seconds later, the aircraft exploded in a sheet of orange flame with the boy still inside . . .

Also by Matthew Holden in Sphere Books:

SQUADRON 1:
SONS OF THE MORNING

SQUADRON 2:
THE SUN CLIMBS SLOWLY

SQUADRON 3:
SCRAMBLE DIEPPE

Squadron 4: Desert Spitfire

MATTHEW HOLDEN

SPHERE BOOKS LIMITED
30-32 Gray's Inn Road, London WC1X 8JL

First Published in Great Britain by Sphere Books Ltd, 1980

TRADE
MARK

Set in Monotype Times

Printed in Great Britain by
William Collins Sons & Co Ltd
Glasgow

Chapter One

With dawn the sandstorm eased and as the troops crawled from their foxholes with eyes inflamed, ears and nostrils choked with swirling grit, they glared accusingly into a yellow-tinged sky in which the sun was already threatening the heat of the day. They got stiffly to their feet, rubbing their chilled limbs, stooping to snatch their blankets from the shallow holes they had scraped in the sand. Those with desert sores picked painfully at the rims of the abscesses, brushing away flies and wiping off the sticky grit with rolled corners of grimy issue-handkerchiefs.

Here was another dawn. Another day with just the possibility they might live to see another sunset, another night of penetrating cold, before the whole bloody miserable demoralising routine began again.

Those in the front line, with the forward reconnaissance elements of the Afrika Korps five hundred yards – or five miles – beyond the Rahman Track to the west, stood down from makeshift defences strategically sited across a plateau of brown rock and sand.

By sections they dismantled their Bren-guns, using long lengths of 'four-by-two' to ease the sand from the barrels, pistons, cylinders and cocking mechanism. Later, they would have to empty the magazines, mop them out with oil and reload.

This was a procedure which took place every morning after stand-down, for every night the desert wind whipped up the sand into a dark murk as impenetrable as a London pea-souper. It followed that only when they had completed their chores could the infantrymen being to think about their stomachs. Eventually, the cooks would come forward with pieces of cold, tinned, bacon; hard-tack biscuits; a spread of butter; and, if they were lucky, a seven pound tin of jam to share amongst a full company.

In the armoured units there was more work to do for the swirling grit penetrated air-filters, quickly transforming engine oil into a heavy abrasive paste which could wear out a Rolls-Royce tank unit within hours. Furthermore, armoured units, like aircraft, had to be instantly mobile on call: operational and dependable. In consequence, a trooper's lot was very much secondary to the maintenance of the reconnaissance cars, tanks and self-propelled guns.

But the ground forces did have one morale booster in the knowledge that conditions were as bad for the enemy – worse in some instances, for most of the day the Germans had to screw their eyes into a blinding sun which, so far as the Allies were concerned, conveniently rose in the east. The desert was a unique battleground, for here there were no civilians to confuse the tactical planners, no refugees, no towns, no buildings and few natural strongpoints. It was as though the desert were some great arena, ideally chosen by two great, highly-mechanised, armies where they could kill and mutilate each other to their hearts' content.

Territorial gains were of little significance. Success could only really be measured in degree of annihilation and the destruction of supplies and weapons.

There was nothing else! – only an unchanging panorama of undulating dunes, rock and scrub; the violent heat of the day when metal parts of vehicles and weapons would blister flesh. Fresh food was unobtainable and the troops swallowed ascorbic acid tablets to compensate, but these did little towards healing their sores. Water was strictly rationed and after washing and shaving it was re-cycled for vehicle radiators and the cooling jackets of Vickers machine-guns.

Veterans who had served with the desert army since General Sir Archibald Wavell's initial successes against the Italians in 1940 – incredibly ex-factory workers and shop assistants from places like Blackburn and Reading – had taught themselves to tolerate the desert; that and no more! But to recruits coming west across the narrowing distance from Alexandria, it was a living nightmare from which they would ultimately find escape only in death.

To the rear, the Desert Air Force fared little better. Conditions on makeshift airfields with a scattering of sun-bleached tents at one end were only a marginal improvement on those of the infantry in the forward positions. And what the airmen escaped in hit-and-run raids they paid for in an increasingly aggressive bombing and strafing programme from the Luftwaffe and, occasionally, from the Regia Aeronautica. Only when the pilots were airborne with the cockpit canopies open were they able to breath freely and release some of their pent up venom against Axis pilots.

The British fighters, mostly Hurricane IIs and Curtiss Kittyhawks, had problems identical to those of the armoured vehicles and had to be fitted with special air filters which caused drag and a lowering in performance to give the Messerschmitt Bf 109 a disproportionate superiority. Also, machine-guns and cannon became clogged with sand and they frequently jammed, even during take-off, whilst windshields rapidly became scored to create every pursuit-pilot's nightmare – poor visibility.

Aerial combat was fast becoming too much of a gamble. The Axis had recently begun to use Macchi 202s of the Regia Aeronautica and Messerschmitt Bf 109s at upwards of the 22,000 ft operational ceiling of the Hurricanes and Kittyhawks. From such height advantage they would 'sit' and swoop to peck at fighter escorts rather than risk themselves in attempting to break through to the bombers. Tactically, this was far from ideal, but despite the Axis pilots' unwillingness to engage in whirling dogfights, the growing losses of Allied aircraft at a time when air-superiority had to be maintained, was disturbing.

An immediate answer was to reinforce the Desert Air Force with the Mark VB Spitfire which, though reaching obsolescence on the Channel front against the Focke Wulf 190, would more than hold its own in the desert against the Mc 202 and Bf 109 on performance, manoeuvrability, and operational altitude.

The problem was that few Spitfire squadrons with battle experience were available for transfer to the Middle East. But General Harold Alexander, who had recently assumed command for Forces in the Middle East from General Auchinleck, had, as a priority, exerted some pressure in this respect upon the War Cabinet in London.

This, not unexpectedly, had immediate effect. And amongst those UK-based Spitfire squadrons detailed for the Middle East was Piper Squadron, now commanded by the recently promoted Dominic Taylor and still reeling from their involvement in the Dieppe operation on 19 August 1942.

The 30th of September turned out to be a black day for the German Luftwaffe in the Western Desert for, on that day, they lost their hero, their Golden Boy, their 'Star of Africa': Hauptmann Hans-Joachim Marseille.

In under two years, Marseille, at the time of his death commanding I/JG 27 Staffel, had claimed an incredible total of one hundred and fifty-eight victories over Allied aircraft. These ranged from the early Gloster Gladiator biplanes to the newest desert fighter, the Mark VB Spitfire.

Marseille was a slightly-built, likeable, happy-go-lucky young man in his early twenties and had always sworn that no Allied pilot would ever shoot him down. And that day he died proving his point.

Ironically, he was flying a new Messerschmitt Bf 109 G and leading an escort to a Gruppe of Stuka dive-bombers over El Alamein when an oil pipe fractured and his aircraft caught fire. He used his skill to glide the burning plane westwards over his own lines, but when he rolled it over on to its back for him to bale out he hit his head on the tailplane which knocked him unconscious. As a result, his parachute failed to open. Pilots of his Staffel gasped in horror as they saw his slim body plummet to earth. This was the end of a legend.

In a lesser way, that date was also memorable for Piper Squadron, for it marked their first operational sortie with the Desert Air Force.

At 15.20 hours the whole squadron was airborne, flying at 24,000 feet as top-cover for four Blenheims and a close-escort of Hurricane IIs heading for Tobruk with targets detailed on the build-up of armoured formations within the northern defensive perimeter.

From that altitude – high enough to engage Mc 202s or Bf 109s standing by to pick off the close-escort fighters – Piper Squadron looked down upon a desolate landscape of flat brown scrubland with the iridescent emerald green of the Mediterranean to the north. The Squadron was flying in the formation they had applied successfully in the UK and over the Pas de Calais: 'finger-four' – widely-spaced pairs and none weaving. This formation, as also recently adopted by the Luftwaffe, was the only one which could possibly work in such conditions where the sky was always blue; where the sun always shone; where there was rarely sufficient cloud coverage in which to hide; and where a weaving aircraft could be spotted miles away. Also, in combat the 'finger-four' formation enabled the leading pilot of the pair to commit himself knowing that his wingman could be relied upon to be behind him, guarding his tail.

In the leading Section, Squadron Leader Dominic Taylor dipped his wings first to starboard and then to port, clearing blind spots and to get a glimpse of the Hurricane close-escort formation below.

Piper Squadron was going to find things very different here. They'd need no brief to emphasise that point! By chance, flying was easy today for it was simple enough navigating parallel to a clearly defined coastline. But how about when they flew south-west? How could they navigate accurately over endless miles of rock-strewn desert and smooth, undulating dunes? There, there were no roads, no railways, no towns. Just barren emptiness! But the tactical dispositions of the opposing armies did present one advantage compared with Northern France for, on the outward flight, anyway, they would always have the sun behind them and if anyone was going to be bounced at 24,000 feet it was a fair bet that it wouldn't be Piper Squadron.

Below and to starboard the huddled buildings of Tobruk and a scattering of half-sunken ships beyond the harbour could be clearly defined. Taylor glanced to starboard where his Number Two, Mike Norling, caught his eye and grinned; his long fair hair blowing in the slipstream from his open canopy. Taylor pointed vaguely towards Tobruk at which Norling nodded; he, too, then dipping his starboard wing to widen his field of vision.

'Hello, Piper leader! Hello, Piper Leader!' A sharp voice broke over some desultory chatter amongst the Blenheim pilots. 'Bandits! Bandits! Bandits! Ahead and high. Now let's see what the Spits can do for us!' Then to the close-escort Hurricane squadron. 'You heard that, Beta? Beta? Beta?'

Below, Taylor watched the Hurricanes, some two thousand feet above the square formation of the Blenheims, move methodically into a defensive circle. As he acknowledged to the Blenheim leader, Joe Caton leading Yellow Section up five hundred feet and behind, spotted the enemy.

'I got 'em, Piper leader. Starboard beam. About same Angels. Nine or ten of the sods!'

'OK, Joe!' Taylor acknowledged, then: 'Stay with it, Piper Squadron. We'll play their game until they make up their minds. Up a little. Follow me! Keep between them and the sun.'

The six newcomers to the Squadron – five of them Sergeant Pilots – gripped hard on their control columns with faces tense. Some had experienced limited action over Northern France, but they felt no more confident than those about to face their first battle.

Now the Squadron was closing rapidly with the Messerschmitt 109s – a couple of miles! . . . less . . . Christ! Already they were over the target area . . . the Bf 109s would help keep the flak down, anyway!

Crash! Crash!

That was no flak! The Blenheims were unloading their bombs and below, way down below, tanks and self-propelled guns were bucking on their tracks, seeking cover by pile-driving at speed through the walls of buildings.

Crash! Crash!

As the formation of Messerschmitts dipped into their attacking dives the light flak which had been bursting amongst the Blenheims ceased abruptly.

'Down they go! Follow me!' yelled Taylor and he kicked his rudder bar, rolling to the left with Norling not a dozen yards behind him, whilst Orange Section under Jimmy Easton followed by Caton's Yellow Section, fell into the pre-arranged attack pattern. Now, secure in their pairs, they were diving for the line of descent of the Messerschmitts.

'All bombs gone!'

This was the Blenheim leader; but the information was of no consequence to the pursuit aircraft. The Hurricanes were still in their circle above the bombers, their pilots with their thumbs on their firing-buttons ready to engage if the enemy tried to break through to the bombers.

But Piper Squadron caught up with the Messerschmitts with less than five thousand feet to go and at upwards of four hundred miles an hour. For a split second, Taylor had their leader in his sights and he cursed volubly as his squirt ripped along the black cross of its port wing; then slipping to port on the chance of catching the wingman, but they were both gone banking above and away from the Hurricanes.

Caton's Yellow Section had caught the tail-enders, but could get none in their sights. On his port beam, Caton saw Johnnie Kitchen fire a long burst and when he glanced below he saw a Bf 109 on its back and pouring glycol.

Now the action had dropped beneath the Blenheims and two of the Hurricanes had joined the running, diving, battle on the chance that it might develop into a whirling dogfight. Taylor's altimeter was registering less than three thousand feet and below he could pick out burning vehicles and the minute figures of running men attending fire appliances.

Where the hell were the 109s? He glanced in his mirror and saw Mike Norling, as dependable as ever, on his tail. Then there came an explosion below as one of the Messerschmitts ploughed into the scrub – maybe Johnnie's kill – followed by the sudden angry chatter of small arms fire from infantry positions on the perimeter of the town. Taylor hauled his control column hard back into his stomach and climbed steeply under a savage boost of power, but only to see the Bf 109s chasing westwards. To the east, a Spitfire was streaming smoke.

He banked sharply. Now he could pick out the identification number. It was Sergeant Bill Kinsella of Caton's Yellow Section.

He called over the R/T as he followed it down.

'Are you wounded, Bill?'

'No! No! I'm OK, sir. But I've got no oil pressure.' There came more black smoke from the engine cowling as Kinsella attempted to boost the throttle.

'Won't she come up?'

'No! I'm going to have to land. Not enough height to bale out!'

Taylor cut back his speed, anxiously watching Kinsella's aircraft, with engine firing erratically glide lower and lower.

'Christ! Keep her nose up, Bill!'

It struck him that this had been a hell of a short war for the young sergeant. He continued to watch. The undercarriage was down, but the wheels hit too hard. Yet, somehow, Kinsella managed to keep control and the aircraft was hurtling over the rough terrain until it hit a line of rocks when it tipped sedately up on to its nose. Taylor had expected Kinsella to leap out, but he didn't. And, seconds later, the aircraft exploded in a sheet of orange flame with the boy still inside.

Back at the airfield, north of the Alam al Bedir ridge, Taylor learned that Johnnie Kitchen's success had been the only enemy aircraft shot down, but that Jimmy Easton and

Sergeant Jean-Michel Ferre – one of the two Free French pilots temporarily attached to Piper Squadron – both claimed Bf 109s damaged. It appeared that the rear Sections in the attack had had the only chances to engage and that made Taylor wonder if he had gone into the attack a fraction of a second too early.

On the other hand, and regrettably, the Squadron had suffered its first casualty in the Western Desert. A young man's life had been sacrificed. An irreplaceable piece of equipment destroyed.

In the tent which Bill Kinsella had shared with his co-sergeants, Ken Harris and Charlie Reed, Joe Caton perched contemplatively on the edge of Reed's bunk and stared across the short stretch of sand-strewn floor to the neatly made-up bed which had been the dead man's.

Kinsella's relatively pointless death had brought home to Caton once again the fact that he was the sole survivor of the original Piper Squadron which had been formed under Teddy Perowne at the time of the Dunkirk evacuation in 1940. Since the tragic loss of his close friend, George Barclay, during the trauma of Dieppe – Operation Jubilee – six weeks earlier, the question of his own survival had been something which he had not allowed to dwell on his mind. Whenever his thoughts had turned in that direction, or to the death of George, he had taken up his newly acquired responsibilities as Second-in-Command of the Squadron and lost himself in routine administrative work with the ageing and recently appointed Adjutant, Flight Lieutenant Len Jupp, DFC.

But during those endless nights when the United States giant carrier *Wasp* had lurched through the U-Boat infested waters west of the Bay of Biscay he had repeatedly asked himself why, for Christ's sake, had he not jumped at the chance of a staff-appointment with Headquarters Fighter Command, Stanmore, Middlesex?

Why? Why? Why?

He'd done more than his share of ops. Far more! And that

hadn't made it easy for him to convince the CO that he was determined to continue operational flying. He was fit and he was a competent and experienced pilot, he had argued. Damned good! His records were there for them to see. Yes! he'd certainly had his chance to escape, for the CO had even attempted to pressure him. But he hadn't changed his mind because he knew, that deep down inside him, he just couldn't let go. Besides, he could never have faced Sue, knowing that he'd chickened out!

In retrospect he had often wondered why he had taken so long in asking Sue to marry him. And the fact that he had taken her to bed on a couple of occasions before he had done so still twinged his conscience now and then. For he knew perfectly well that ever since that day eighteen months ago when she had helped drag his injured body from his crashed Spitfire, she had been his bulwark against the terrors and dangers of aerial combat.

But, as he prepared to collect Kinsella's assortment of personal things arranged tidily about a framed black-and-white print of a plumpish smiling girl in a wide-brimmed straw hat, he knew that personal vanity had also swayed his decision. But now there was no chance of second thoughts. No escape! He had well and truly burned his boats.

There could be no dashing off from this airfield to spend a couple of hours with Sue at the farm. There would be no telephoning her whenever he felt lonely and vulnerable.

He could die, dammit, and she wouldn't know a thing about it for weeks! She would go on writing him letters and telling him of her love for him and all that time he could be a rottingcorpse in some wind-blown patch of rock-strewn sand.

How different it would have been had George Barclay survived to share these new trials with him. But even George, the cool, methodical, and brilliant flyer who had believed himself impregnable had perished amongst the blazing ruins of Dieppe.

Resignedly, he began to drop Kinsella's things into a large brown envelope. He was a bloody fool! He should have gone to Stanmore when he'd had the chance.

Jimmy Easton's Orange Section, the only one to remain 'on-state' after the squadron's early afternoon sortie, was scrambled shortly after 17.00 hours on a hurried brief from Group to operate in a low-level army-co-operation role supporting infantry and light armoured units which had come under heavy pressure east of Deir el Munassib.

But after the tensions over Tobruk and the seemingly pointless death of Bill Kinsella, all four members were glad to be airborne again. Not only was an opportunity of immediate action likely to be a test of their nerves; but there was every advantage in getting to know as much about the desert as they could in the least possible time.

They flew in pairs in the adopted 'finger-four' formation with Jimmy Easton and Chris Fenton forward and Johnnie Kitchen and Charlie Reed a little higher and behind. Conditions were identical to those of the earlier sortie: clear sky with some heat haze lifting from the sea. But this time they headed south-west towards the northern rim of the Qattara Depression, hugging the bearing which Group had fed them, but not too worried about navigation because there would be no problem identifying the action when they got close enough.

The Section climbed steadily, Easton with his eyes on the clear sky seeking enemy aircraft which might be sitting high, waiting, looking for the flash of sunlight on the leading edges of their wings and canopies.

He glanced into his mirror and saw Johnnie Kitchen doing the same thing. It was more than a bit dicey – this roaring along at fifteen thousand feet, their aircraft spotlighted against the brown desert, sitting ducks for any marauding enemy skilled enough to dodge their air search.

They reached the Allied lines in what appeared to be a lull between enemy bombing raids. The command sections, which were deployed amongst the rocks on the rim of the Depression, appeared very vulnerable with most of their camouflage cover gone. A half-mile or so farther forward were what looked like 3·5-inch medium artillery emplacements undergoing a concentrated fire programme. The belch of flame and the recoil of the long barrels were clearly visible from the air and they were shooting in rotation through the battery – an impressive sight!

Easton flicked his R/T switch to 'Send'.

'Here we go, Orange Section. We'll start our descent . . . Now!'

Ahead, they could make out the shell-bursts from the guns over which they had flown only a few seconds earlier. Easton glanced at his altimeter. One thousand five hundred feet – he must assume that those shell-bursts were close to the German forward positions . . . the British infantry would be dug in and, being much smaller targets than the guns, would not be easy to identify.

He switched his R/T back to 'Send.'

'Orange Section! Down another five hundred, but for Christ's sake watch out behind, Johnnie!'

He switched back to 'Receive' as Kitchen's voice came back at once with a touch of good-natured humour.

'Sky clear so far, Orange Leader!'

The four aircraft sped westwards in a widely spaced diamond formation, the pilots now and again risking a glimpse at the activity on the ground.

There were machine-gun emplacements snugly hidden beneath camouflage netting with only the snub barrels of the Vickers visible, spitting tracer. There were light tanks racing across the Front with their guns swivelled to the enemy and with giant cones of yellow dust pluming from their tracks. There were heavier tanks dug into hull-down positions amongst the rocks, firing intermittently with their turrets open and beflagged antennae bending to the desert wind.

Then they came upon the infantry. They could pick out the up-turned faces of the soldiers clutching their rifles, Bren-guns and mortars. Those in slit trenches waved enthusiastically, but others were running in what seemed to be pre-arranged formations. Here and there, some fell, throwing up their arms mid-stride, stumbling face down in the sand.

It was like watching a clip from some wide-screen extravaganza from which the sound track had been removed, leaving only the roar of their own Merlins in their ears. Now the infantry were going into some sort of attack for more soldiers were climbing from their foxholes to form a line in depth before an open space which could only be the beginning of a minefield.

Beyond were the Afrika Korps; their positions as clearly defined from the air as those of the Allies. Occasionally, the sun would glint off a helmet or a bayonet, but it was the muzzle flashes of their automatic weapons which gave them away.

Orange Section dived on them from less than two hundred feet, Easton opening fire first at a range of three hundred yards and he saw his bullets ripping into the forward trenches. A Spandau machine-gun tilted crazily on its tripod as the gunners slumped across it. As he pulled out of the shallow dive he had time to glimpse Kitchen's fusilade whipping up the sand around the German forward flank positions. He hoped the Spitfires were giving the Allied infantry the kind of boost to their morale they needed, though he wondered what the hell they planned to do when they reached the minefield.

'Orange Leader!' This was Charlie Reed up at the rear, showing his tension. 'Bandits to starboard and behind! Looks as though they're bombing the artillery!'

Easton swung round his head to see Fenton and Reed already peeling away to starboard. On the ground, bombs were bursting amongst the medium guns which were still maintaining their rate of fire.

'Climb! Climb! Climb! Orange! How did those bastards get there?'

He hauled back his control column and kicked on the rudder bar climbing steeply towards the enemy aircraft at full throttle, at once identifying them as Bf 109 adapted fighter-bombers. There were four and it looked as they had completed their bombing run. Now they were going to get themselves a dogfight, whether they wanted one or not.

No problem here of deflection calculations – converging at a relative speed of upwards of five hundred miles an hour. He spotted Fenton almost level on his right; Kitchen and Reed would be on their tails. It was now or never – so long as Charlie didn't panic and held his fire until Fenton and he broke away.

The leading Messerschmitt opened up too soon and tracer sped well below them. Easton set his jaw, feet poised on the rudder bar, hands loose on the control column, his thumb taking what amounted to first pressure on the firing-button. His eyes focused through the ring and bead sight along his engine cowling. His acceleration was still increasing and when the leading Messerschmitt appeared in his sight for that fleeting fraction of a second he pressed the button with a cool detachment. Simultaneously, it seemed, most of the Bf 109's starboard wing floated away. On reflex, Easton broke away to port and, as he did so, there appeared a second Messerschmitt sideways on and, along with Kitchen, he squirted at the black cross along its fuselage. But, miraculously, the Bf 109 survived, spinning free in a tight barrelled aileron turn.

'OK behind, Jimmy!'

This was Kitchen still on his tail and fast becoming the perfect wingman and Easton levelled to see the remaining Messerschmitts banking westwards and climbing fast.

Below, and not a hundred yards from the artillery positions, he watched the Me he had hit churn into the ground. Without wings, the fuselage went on bouncing and turning over in the sand interminably until it exploded in a sudden ball of flame.

Easton looked over his shoulder and saw Fenton and Reed coming back into formation. Everything suddenly appeared detached and orderly as though nothing had happened at all – just like another clip from that same movie; but this time with sound.

He switched his R/T to 'Send'.

'Good show, lads! Pity we let them drop their eggs. Best go home! We're too low on ammo to chase!'

Later that evening and despite Kitchen's and Easton's successes that day, there was an atmosphere of troubled introspection in the marquee which served as an anteroom to the officers' mess.

Dominic Taylor and his five officers were hunched in uncomfortable field chairs at one end of the big tent where the sidewalls had been rolled up to provide a through draught and an outlook over the northern end of the landing strip. There, under guard, the aircraft were dispersed against probing enemy ground patrols as well as strafing Luftwaffe.

Most of the pilots were sipping whisky, for there was little beer available and Mike Norling had summarised their reactions to the squadron's first casualty – the loss of Bill Kinsella – with the oft-used phrase: 'Bloody bad show!'

The fact that the day's score was two to one did nothing to compensate for Kinsella's death; but the boy had died and there was nothing anyone could do about it. Yet, that didn't alter the fact that somewhere in a Wiltshire village there was a young woman who'd become a widow before she'd had chance to become a wife.

At her parents' home, wedding photographs would still be on the sideboard with a noticeable hesitancy in the smiles of the guests as though they might already have been anticipating the worst. A haphazard pile of cheap wartime presents; a pair of flannels, bought on coupons for the honeymoon, neatly stowed away in a new wardrobe ready for the next leave. Now only heartache, unfathomable grief.

Dominic Taylor sat broodily staring across the endless desert, his eyes slitted and troubled, his swarthy face as dark as any Arab's in the fast-fading light. As yet, he hadn't fully absorbed the sudden changes which Fighter Command had thrust upon Piper Squadron. Even the limbo of the voyage and the hair-raising take-off from the carrier's flight-deck north of Algiers, followed by three days of bombardment in

Malta, had done little towards helping him to adjust.

Gone was the CO, Canadian Lee Hillas, with a DFC to mark his exemplary leadership of the squadron during the Dieppe raid, and now to take command of a recently-formed Commonwealth squadron in the West Country. Gone, too, were the irrepressible Yorkshire pair, Lawson and Shaw, promoted to Flight Lieutenants and posted as Flight Leaders to a squadron of No. 9 Group, Lancashire.

So, with George Barclay and Clive Ralston dead and Danny Watson a prisoner-of-war after he had baled out over Dieppe, half the Piper Squadron of less than a month ago had disappeared in what seemed overnight! His own promotion to Squadron Leader together with a Mention in Despatches for subsequently snatching Lee Hillas out of Occupied France* had given him some satisfaction. And, as a result, he had wasted no time in bumping up Joe Caton and Jimmy Easton to Flight Lieutenants and Flight Leaders, whilst after twelve months' service as Pilot Officers, the promotion of Mike Norling and Johnnie Kitchen to Flying Officers had been automatic.

After that, all he had been able to do was hold his breath until the arrival of the five reinforcements which would bring the squadron strength up to overseas establishment. As he had anticipated, four of the five had turned out to be NCOs: Sergeants Reed, Kinsella, Ferre and Ordenneau – the latter two Free French, ex-Aviation Militaire who, a year earlier, had escaped through Spain to Gibraltar and were the only members of the reinforcements with combat experience.

The fifth was Lieutenant Stewart Maclellan of the United States Army Air Force – a typically extrovert, noisy and frequently infuriating young man who had also joined Piper Squadron on a temporary posting. He had had some experience flying Spitfires and Group had eventually decided to give him an opportunity to use that experience with a British combat squadron before joining 57th Fighter Group.

* *Scramble Dieppe*, Matthew Holden.

In Taylor's mind there was little doubt that the influx of such a high proportion of unblooded pilots could not be good for the coming operational commitments of the squadron. Half the pilots skilled flyers and battle experienced, the other half a positive risk and spurred only by their dedication.

He was also going to have to ensure that the recruits wound down some; otherwise they would disappear, one by one, in much the same way as young Bill Kinsella had died that morning. Besides, in the desert, Mk VB Spitfires were far too valuable pieces of machinery to risk on the impulse of some youth who still believed there was glamour in flying pursuit aircraft with the RAF.

On a vastly broader canvas, Lieutenant General B. L. Montgomery from his caravan Headquarters north-west of the Alam al Halfa ridge, had put forward his plans for the forthcoming attack from the El Alamein springboard which he had code-named Operation Lightfoot.

For an operation of such magnitude and importance this was a relatively simple plan – intentionally so by the restriction of the width of the Front across which it was to be launched.

Between the Qattara Depression and the Mediterranean Sea at El Alamein, a distance of some twenty-five miles, infantry of the British 30 Corps, supported by massive artillery concentrations, would cut two corridors through the enemy's defences which they would then widen in what the General had described as a 'crumbling' action in a methodical annihilation of the German holding troops.

It thus followed that Field Marshal Erwin Rommel would be compelled to commit his already depleted armour which would be destroyed by the might of the recently reinforced British tank regiments now equipped with Crusader Mk III tanks with six-pounder guns and with American-manufactured General Sherman tanks armed with 7·5 mm guns. Then, with the German armour out of the battle and British air superiority guaranteed, the speedy rout of the entire

Afrika Korps was a certainty.

On the face of it, Operation Lightfoot might have appeared as an optimistic and over-ambitious plan, but this was not so for Montgomery was relying mainly on weight of numbers, which during the past months and as a result of London War Cabinet priorities, had grown to unprecedented proportions. These could be measured by the fact that at the start of the offensive the British 8th Army would have over one thousand tanks available for battle with two hundred in workshop reserve, whilst Rommel would have no more than two hundred and fifty tanks fit for action and these to be divided between the once crack 15th and 21st Panzer Divisions.

Also, the Allies had almost double the artillery of the Germans, totalling over one thousand pieces including the highly mobile American 105 mm self-propelled gun, devastating in its fire power.

But, probably most important of all, was the increased strength of the Desert Air Force. In direct support of the ground troops there would be upwards of seven hundred and fifty aircraft, mostly fighters but with a high proportion of bombers and fighter-bombers. Two thirds of these could be put into the air at any one time – more than double all the aircraft which the Luftwaffe and the Regia Aeronautica could muster together.

In his brief to senior commanders, General Montgomery summarised his battle tasks:

> 'Methodical progress; destroy enemy part by part; slowly and surely. Shoot tanks and shoot Germans. He cannot last a long battle; we can! We must therefore keep at it hard; no unit commander must relax pressure; organise ahead for a 'dogfight' of a week. Whole affair about ten days. Don't expect spectacular results too soon.'

The date specified for the launch of the attack was the early morning of Saturday, 24th October. Meanwhile, in the three weeks waiting period, armour, infantry and the RAF would combine in systematically wearing down the enemy. As a combined operation they would constantly and unremittingly sap his strength so that when the massive bombardment of the night of the attack hit the enemy positions he would already be demoralised.

Chapter Two

The wind built up about midnight. And with the wind there came flying sand which tore against the sides of the tents as though they were being rubbed by abrasive pads. It found its way under the tent walls, between the end flaps and through the ventilation ports. The men awoke, switching on electric torches, watching it drift like snow inside the tents, already sensing it in their mouths and nostrils, their eyes beginning to smart.

They bundled themselves into their clothes, throwing on greatcoats against the cold of the desert night, buttoning them up to their necks and putting on goggles to keep the sand from their eyes. The lucky few who could have slept through the pandemonium were roughly shaken awake. Personal comfort came a long way down the list of priorities – a long way down after aircraft, weapons, ammunition, water and food.

Dominic Taylor, Len Jupp the Adjutant and George Romain the Intelligence Officer, who shared a tent, were the first to brave the storm pausing only to stamp the tent pegs harder into the ground and check the rocks piled over the main guy lines. Then they split up, intending to get the rest of the pilots moving, but they came upon the whole eleven of them congregating outside the NCOs lines and preparing to dash the couple of hundred yards to where the aircraft were dispersed.

They set off together, shoulders hunched, heads bent against the stinging grit, hands cupped over mouths and nostrils, thanking God and the Quartermaster for the goggles and yet wary of losing their way in the dark.

But soon they reached the single strand of wire before the

half-completed blast walls and followed it along to where the ground crews were working on the Spitfires which were bucking at their anchor ropes like frightened horses.

The found the ground crews had wasted no time. Ropes had been secured to the under-carriages and looped round Dannert wire stakes screwed their full length into the ground. Stabilising guys had been fastened to wing tips. Flaps had been secured. Cotton waste had been stuffed into exhaust ports. Groundsheets had been lashed over the perspex canopies for the sand would have scoured them opaque within minutes. Tailplanes had also been lashed to Dannert stakes and most of the men were now standing by their planes, breathing hard, checking the doped cotton over gun and cannon ports, re-plugging air-intakes, fuel ports and joints in the engine cowling and canopies.

The time was 01.15 hours and the wind was getting higher. There would be drifts across the runway which would take hours for the squadron bulldozers to clear. Even if it slackened before dawn there would be little chance of flying next day.

Taylor went back to his Adjutant and Intelligence Officer.

'You two had better get back to the R/T,' he shouted. 'Tell Group that we can cope. Our biggest problem is that we've no perimeter defence!'

'The infantry will be still dug in due west!'

'I was thinking about German armour! Right now it's easier navigating an armoured car than it is walking!'

Jupp and Romain set off back to the administration lines, agreeing with Taylor's comments. The Afrika Korps were unlikely to heed the elements. Rommel had once remarked that only camels burrowed down in a sand storm – not the 15th Panzers!

But, on the other hand, Piper Squadron had neither weapons nor trained men to reinforce the infantry screen and they doubted whether the soldiers would welcome any interference. The infantry would be coping, too. Not happy, but coping; eyes and guns attuned to an all-round defence system; their own patrols probing as far as the Rahman Track.

Dawn seemed late that morning, for all that happened was that the darkness gave way to a luminous yellow haze which did nothing to increase visibility beyond a few yards. But, at least, the men were able to see the aircraft and recognise each other! They grinned and shook their heads at the sorry sight they presented whilst the wind still shrieked and the sand still flayed them.

After stand-to, Taylor told the NCOs to split the men into two groups and send one half back to their lines for food and rest. Until the gale slackened and work could begin on the aircraft and runway they would operate in two shifts.

A little later the pilots also went back to their lines for there was nothing more they could do. During the long night their presence had helped boost the morale of the ground crews and, when possible, they had put their weight to guy lines or hung on to wing tips and tailplanes. Ironically, it was a good thing that the wind was still high for none was in condition for operational flying after such a night.

So the officers and the sergeants went directly to their own messes, the four NCOs happy to get from under the COs direct supervision though most of them considered it petty having separate messes under such operational conditions. After all, they were all doing the same job, taking the same risks in the air and, as there was only one cookhouse on the airfield, they all got the same food!

The American, Lieutenant Stew Maclellan, with the USAAF in mind had been very outspoken on this subject which hadn't pleased Dominic Taylor and had ended with a strong but private admonishment when the CO had been able to catch him alone.

In the officers' marquee, askew but still withstanding the buffetings, the full complement of squadron officers – less George (Tommy) Handley, the Engineering Officer, who was still with his ground crews, were sipping a mixture of coffee and grit and waiting for the Mess Sergeant to arrive with the usual breakfast of tinned bacon, hardtack field biscuits and a half-pound of marmalade for them to share.

Stew Maclellan peered round the gathering, taking in the bloodshot eyes; the grey, tired, faces; hair and ears caked with brown grit.

'Jesus!' he commented. 'But you look as though you been to bed with camels!'

Johnnie Kitchen, sitting next to him, stretched an arm to ruffle the American's hair so that sand cascaded into his coffee.

'Kitchen! You rotten bastard . . .'

Johnnie ducked, half-expecting to have Maclellan's coffee poured over his head. But the American paused with the mug held high to cast a dubious eyes at Dominic Taylor who was watching him moodily. That caused him to turn to Joe Caton, shrugging. 'I was only kidding, y'know Joe! Honest, I was!' And, as Johnnie Kitchen relaxed, he shot out a hand as quickly as he had done, laughing uproariously as sand poured from Kitchen's hair into his coffee.

He placed his mug firmly on the table then.

'Listen, you guys,' he began, 'I'll tell you something that happened to me when I first came over to Somerset . . .'

His voice tailed off and his blue eyes widened as there came another sound above the buffeting of the wind and the drum of sand against the canvas. The rest of them froze, faces tensing. It was a sound which most of them had heard before. It had started with a low distant hum, growing rapidly into whirr-whirr-whirr, a high-pitched whistle and then . . .

CRASH!

'Bloody shells!' Norling announced calmly and the others looked at each other speculatively, not wanting to be the first to move.

But Dominic Taylor got to his feet.

'SP guns!'

Again there came the distant hum. They counted: One. Two. Three . . . CRASH!

Taylor strolled nonchalantly to the tent flap, pulling it

aside and letting in a blast of sand. But he dropped it back into place almost immediately and rejoined the group.

He shook his head hopelessly.

'Squadron drill is that we go to the slit trenches,' he said gruffly. 'The fire-platoon assembles outside the Operations Room and the guards stand-to both here and in perimeter defence around the airfield. But what the hell? The slit trenches are filled in and the rest of the squadron will have heard the shells for themselves. So what to do we do? We've no communication other than by . . .'

As though waiting for the cue, the field set link with the Orderly Room buzzed. George Romain made a motion of standing up, but Taylor waved him down and strode to the set.

'Yes? CO here!'

He listened intently, a finger closing one ear against the gale, acknowledging impatiently before dropping the receiver back into its metal container.

As he did so there came again the whirr-whirr-whirr in the sky followed by the explosion; but it was impossible to tell whether it was within the airfield perimeter or not.

'You fellows can please yourselves what you do,' he told them as he came back to pick up his cap and goggles. He grinned. 'If Jerry happens to drop one on you I suppose somebody will let me know eventually. Anyway, I'll be in the Orderly Room.' He glanced at Jupp and Romain. 'OK, you two! We might as well make the most of the opportunity to catch up with our clerking.'

The three of them were preparing to leave the mess when another shell landed and this time the blast of the explosion merged with the scream of its flight. The marquee billowed, tearing pieces of shrapnel sliced through the canvas and one, the size of a meat cleaver, glanced off one of the poles peeling off a splinter of half its thickness. The pilots threw themselves to the ground, hearts thumping, faces beginning to pale. Those who had survived the Battle of Britain and experienced the German blitzkrieg against fighter airfields were more shaken than the rest. To the others this was a new dimension to the war and one from which they could not escape by a boost of throttle at upwards of three hundred miles an hour!

From the west the persistent and measured bark of a quick-firing anti-tank gun added to the din. The pilots strained their ears, listening for the rumble of tracks. It could be that British forward infantry or armoured units were engaging. They lifted wry faces to grin nervously at each other. Thank Christ for the poor-bloody-infantry! Those lads had wasted no time . . .

CRASH!

The tent billowed and more shrapnel tore through the canvas.

'This is getting beyond a bloody joke!' Taylor was angry now and he pushed himself up on to his elbows, eyes flashing.

CRASH!

The measured, unhurried, thud of the quick-firing gun persisted. Perhaps, now, there were more. There seemed to be others to the north-east. Then, from somewhere very close there came a piercing, agonising, scream.

'Stretcher bearers!' someone yelled. 'For Christ's sake, stretcher bearers!'

Taylor sprang to his feet. 'Come on, you lot!' he shouted. 'Up off your bellies!'

But they got up warily, not knowing what to do when they got outside and scared of what they might see.

Joe Caton was first to the flap and he dragged it aside roughly, screwing up his eyes and clamping tight his mouth against the grit. He followed the sound of shouting men and towards him, through the yellow haze, there came a lone stumbling figure. The man's hands were clutched about his stomach and blood was gushing from between his fingers as though someone were emptying it from a bucket. Caton halted in horror whilst Jimmy Easton pushed past him to grab the man's shoulders, lowering him into the sand where he lay still with eyes wide open filling with grit.

As Easton straightened up he turned ashen-faced to Caton.

He was shaking, unsteady on his feet, holding out his hands which ran with blood.

The wind dropped at midday. The sand began to settle and within half an hour bulldozers were clearing the drifts which had formed in broad, undulating, lines across the runway. There had been a rush of telephone calls between squadrons and Group Headquarters and it was evident that more than one airfield had been under fire from German 7·5 mm self-propelled guns.

Piper Squadron had lost three ground crew killed and two wounded, ironically caught in the open by the last shell of the salvo as they had made a belated attempt to reach the slit trenches. As the light improved the blood-stained sand was dug away and transported in buckets to the perimeter whilst the bodies were draped in sheets, loaded into ambulances and taken to the rear.

To Piper Squadron the events of the early morning had been a foretaste of what was to follow. It was evident that with the Desert Air Force there would be little respite. Here, they were almost as much in the firing line as were the forward infantry units and it followed that when the Luftwaffe couldn't get at them, then assault patrols of the Afrika Korps would make damned sure they didn't rest. To the pilots the artillery bombardment had been yet another jab at their morale – what was the point of being an airman if some bastard was going to knock you off before you could get off the ground? But, in the desert, everyone was in the same boat. Gone were the days when, after a couple of sorties, a pilot could spend an evening in a country pub. Here, with darkness, they were more vulnerable on the ground than they were in the air.

By early afternoon the airstrip had been partially cleared, at least sufficiently to allow a few aircraft a reasonably safe take-off. And, as though waiting for the signal, two Spitfires were immediately scrambled to intercept a reconnaissance Ju 88 which was reported to have swung south from the sea at a point east of the Rahman Track. Taylor detailed Joe Caton who had had his share of experience with these 'schnell-bombers' over northern France – a medium bomber with the speed of a fighter. In turn, Caton had detailed his wing-man, Jean-Michel Ferre to go along with him.

Whilst the urgency of the interception had come into Group's 'flap' category, Caton insisted on double-checking his aircraft before take-off. He recalled instances in the past when, after a night's blitz on the home airfield, he had taken up his Spitfire to find the guns had not been cocked and only when he had wheeled into a dogfight had he found himself unarmed and helpless. On other occasions he had found that the bulb in his reflector sight had fused which left him with only the basic ring and bead sight along the engine cowling. Such omissions, which could have led to the death of a skilled pilot and the loss of an aircraft, were inadmissible on the part of groud crews. Even so, it is not easy for a man to work on a complex piece of machinery such as an aircraft when he is having to dodge shrapnel and machine-gun bullets whilst doing so.

This thorough check cost them a minute of valuable time and whilst Caton was sure that the CO would be getting hot under the collar, he didn't let it worry him. If the Junkers was still approaching from the sea, then it would be all the deeper into Allied territory when the interception was made.

Caton gave Ferre the thumbs-up sign as he began to taxi delicately over the rutted ground to the runway with the Frenchman then following at about thirty yards. When he boosted the throttle during take-off he became airborne without trouble and climbed for height above the airfield with Ferre hard on his tail. He set course on the bearing which Group had passed over the R/T, still climbing. But when the altimeter registered 12,000 feet he levelled out.

Seconds later, Group Control came back.

'Hello, Piper Leader! This is Zeta! Take bearing, figures: three, six, four. I say again: three, six, four. Bandit eye making run fifteen miles south of coastline between Ruweisat and

Alam el Halfa ridges. He'll probably turn before you intercept.'

'OK, Zeta! Message understood. Please keep me informed!'

Momentarily he throttled back and Ferre drew level, not more than thirty feet or so beyond his starboard wing tip. He grinned across at him as he spoke over the R/T.

'You heard that, Jean-Michel?' he asked, at which the Frenchman nodded energetically. 'OK! We take new bearing now!'

They spotted the Ju 88 suddenly and simultaneously; below them at about 10,000 feet.

'We'll go straight in Jean-Michel! I'll lead astern and then pull the plug. Try and come in from the sun to quarter-attack. Go!'

'Oui! Oui! Oui!'

Caton grinned, guessing that Ferre might be anticipating his first kill in the desert.

The distance between them and the Junkers closed rapidly and they could now see that this was not the Ju 88 as specified by Group but the Ju 388 photographic-reconnaissance adaptation: yet, easily recognisable by the engines protruding far from the leading edges of its wings.

The German crew had been quick to spot the Spitfires, even as they dived from the sun, for the Ju immediately changed course north-west, climbing steeply in an attempt to take impetus from the dive of the attacking fighters.

Caton and Ferre broke wider, wary of the punch which the Junkers carried in its lively all-round defence of twin 20 mm and twin 30 mm MK 103 cannons. It had reached a speed in excess of two hundred and fifty miles an hour when Caton struck from above and astern. He opened fire at approximately three hundred yards with the Junkers' cannon shells streaking low and beneath him; the German fuselage gunner evidently expecting him to break away seconds before he did so. But Caton ran his eyes along the lean fifty-foot fuselage, from the tailplane to the bulbous 'greenhouse' nose, and then pressed his firing-button on a merciless, jarring, seven-second burst. He sensed he had hit the fuselage gunner for he glimpsed the tracer shells suddenly shoot high and to starboard. Then he pushed forward his control column and boosted his throttle into a steep dive, making way for Ferre's quarter-attack.

Ferre wasted no time. As Caton broke away he threw his aircraft expertly into a full deflection attack from above and to port, opening fire in a long burst at between two hundred and two hundred and fifty yards. Then he, too, 'pulled the plug' into a screeching dive and levelling to join Caton who was trying to climb across the path of the Ju, now in trouble, with its port engine streaming a plume of black smoke.

It seemed that whatever the Germans had gathered in their film cans, they were determined to dump in the sea rather than lose them on a forced landing in Allied territory. The Ju also seemed to be flat out at upwards of two hundred and seventy miles an hour even though the smoke from the port engine was beginning to thin.

Ferre switched momentarily to 'Send'.

'I do not believe it, Joe! I saw pieces drop away from that engine!'

Caton throttled harder into his climb.

'We'll try and turn the bastard!' he said as though thinking aloud. 'They can't have much gas left. Same attack, Jean-Michel. Astern and to port. Wait my signal!'

They climbed above the Ju with the sun on their starboard side and glinting distractingly off their airscrews and engine cowlings. Caton lifted his starboard wing tip so that it partially covered the sun and cut out some of the glare. Then they throttled back at a thousand yards, out of its effective range, positioning themselves for the repeat attack.

'Bandits, Joe! Twenty, *peut-être*, high and to port!'

'Oh, Jesus!'

Ferre hadn't let the heat of the chase divert him from his elementary air-search drill. Caton glanced up to see the formation of dots, unidentifiable at that range. Then, as though with a great sigh of relief, the Junkers 388 altered course to head towards them.

'Ignore the sods! Same attack, Jean-Michel, Go! Go!'

The words jumped from Caton's mouth under their own volition and he jammed his foot on the rudder bar and threw his aircraft into a tight turn as though Ferre might have been an enemy fighter on his tail. At the same time he boosted his throttle to full power to dive at the stern of the Junkers, his thumb hard on the firing-button. More pieces flew off it, but then he noticed a concentration of tracer from his own guns which indicated that his ammunition was almost spent. Thank God the fuselage gunner was out of action! The Ju crew would have at least one dead man to take with them wherever they were going in the next few minutes!

Ferre followed, holding fire until he was within less than two hundred yards; but, as he closed, the Ju swung expertly away to starboard and it was too late for Ferre to adjust his deflection. He recalled the fighter pilots' creed – never hang about when you're low on ammunition – and thrust forward the stick into a dive with rocking turns to left and right. His heart raced as shells from the Ju's forward cannons streamed past his port beam. But then he was clear and diving after Caton. There was nothing they could do now but run for home.

As he joined Caton at about 9,000 feet and close to the coastline, Caton's voice came over the R/T with more than a hint of relief.

'Kittyhawks climbing into the sun, dead ahead!'

Ferre scowled into the glare and saw a group of dots develop wings as the passed overhead. Now he knew why the German Gruppe had not sent fighters to dive on their tails. He continued to watch the Curtiss Kittyhawks and counted – probably a full Wing of them. It looked as though the troops below were in for a few minutes of lively entertainment!

'Let's go home!' Caton said laconically. 'Surely one out of that lot will have the sense to see to the three-eight-eight!'

When they came within a mile of the airfield they found another Section was being scrambled. Two aircraft were already airborne and throttling back, waiting for the others to join them. As they drew closer they put names to the identification numbers: Taylor, Norling, Maclellan and Harris.

This wasn't good! Six Spitfires hanging about over the airfield, pin-pointing its position to enemy aircraft and artillery gunners who could be on the lookout.

When Taylor and his Section were clear, Caton waggled his wings in acknowledgement, switched his R/T to 'Send' and said: 'Good luck, fellers!'

Then, temporarily 'off-state', Caton and Ferre left their aircraft with their ground crews for re-fuelling and re-arming and made their ways back separately to their tents.

Ferre sought out his friend, Robert Ordenneau, gave him a brief resumé of the morning's combat and told him of their bad luck with the Junkers Ju 388.

Ordenneau had been non-committal at the time, only sleepily interested in flying when the heat of the day was at full bore.

This was the time when a great lethargy struck those not employed on some active squadron duty. Not only was the heat unbearable with rivulets of sweat trickling through the fine sand caked on the mens' bodies; but, with it, there also came the flies. There were millions of them which sought out the putrescence of the latrines, desert sores, kitchen waste and then returned to implant their bacteria around the eyes and mouths of those who did not keep moving.

The two Frenchmen, naturally acclimatised to the Riviera sun, were probably the only two to venture from their tents. They stripped to shirt and shorts and wandered alongside the runway towards the perimeter, pausing now and then to watch the heavy bulldozers still working on the runway and churning black diesel fumes from exhausts which danced in the heat haze.

They both agreed on one thing – it was far better for a French pilot to fight in the Western Desert than on the Channel front. Too many times during their first few months of combat service with the RAF they had taken part in fighter sweeps over Northern France and seen their countrymen and women die as a direct result of their involvement. They had watched ammunition trains explode from their cannon fire. They had seen loaded German motor transports lurch from the road to go careering amongst French civilians when the Wehrmacht driver had been killed by their bullets. They had seen crippled aircraft of both air forces explode amongst farmsteads, blocks of flats and even school playgrounds. From the remoteness of 20,000 feet it was impossible to draw a clean line between the occupying forces and civilians. The margins were too narrow. Innocent French people had to die along with the enemy.

But, here in the desert, the Boches were isolated and vulnerable. Here, there were no French people, no civilians to get in the line of their bullets and cannon shells. Here, they were able to meet the Luftwaffe in the clear desert skies without interference or restraint.

At the outbreak of war both Ferre and Ordenneau had been officer cadets with the Aviation Militaire and would have qualified as pilots but for the military reversals of 1940. Even so, had it been possible for them to get to the Channel coast from their station at Limoges, they would have risked Dunkirk. But there had been no chance. Later, in 1940, when their training unit was disbanded and the cadets had been detailed for forced employment under the German-inspired Relêve scheme, they had joined a band of RAF aircrew who had baled out over France and were making their way 'down the line' back to England. They passed through Toulouse and Perpignan by way of a series of Resistance detachments and safe-houses, then crossing the Pyrenees to Figuras in Spain from where they were taken to the British Consulate in Barcelona. Three days later they were flown to England from Gibraltar. Within a week they were posted to No. 3 Initial Training Wing, Hastings, from where on a clear day they could look across the Channel to the coastline of their beloved France.

They progressed on 'above-average' ratings through Cranwell and No. 5 Service Flying Training School where they flew Hind, Audax and Miles Master – their first retractable under-carriage monoplane. But their fighter-pilot education had only really begun at No. 5 Operational Training Unit, Aston Down, Gloucestershire, where they flew Battles, Defiants, and eventually Spitfires. There they also practised formation flying, formation attacks and dogfights piloting the Spitfire with its eight machine-guns.

Then, and only then, did they know they had finally made it – the long, long, trek from the damp cellars of the French Resistance to the operational squadrons of the Royal Air Force. Initially, they requested to join one of the Free French squadrons but, at that time, the Air Ministry was unwilling to risk too much emphasis on national involvement – a lesson learned after some experience with the Poles. As a result they were posted to a Spitfire squadron operating on the Channel front from Deal. There they had more than pulled their weight. In the space of six months Ferre had chalked-up two kills and Ordenneau three and a half. But they had both bucked at Dieppe. Plaintively, they had spread out their hands in typical French fashion and asked their CO how they could be expected to strafe a French town which was already being shelled by the Royal Navy and bombed by the RAF? Could he have flown with Aviation Militaire and helped destroy Worthing – *par exemple*?

The Squadron Leader had understood and so had the Wing Commander and so had the Group Captain and, as a result, the two Frenchmen had been held in Group-reserve during the course of the Dieppe raid. But, in so doing they had also become sitters for recruitment to Piper Squadron already reforming for immediate service in the Western Desert. Dominic Taylor, the Squadron's new CO had readily agreed to their posting and Ferre and Ordenneau had jumped at the chance of meeting the Boches on neutral ground.

Now, in the blazing heat of the afternoon they reached the top of a rise in the endless stretch of sand, rock and scrub.

There they sat down, mopping their brows, easing their limbs and creasing their eyes against the glare. To the east, the bulldozers were no longer in sight and Ordenneau took a ground compass from his pocket and took a bearing on the line of their footprints to find that they pointed back due east to within a couple of degrees either way. They were to be congratulated!

'Shall we go farther?' he asked his friend who shrugged as he got to his feet.

'Why not? I have known it hotter in Antibes! Let us see what there is over the next crest.'

'Germans, probably!'

Ferre laughed.

'Not so close, surely . . .'

But before he could finish his sentence the sand, a few yards to their right, began to spurt. For a moment Ferre stared at it as though he were experiencing some unique kind of mirage. But then, the chatter of a machine-gun travelling over the distance from the ridge ahead caught up with them. On reflex they threw themselves flat in the sand. They were in the open, there was no cover at all within half a kilometre. They looked at each other with anger as well as apprehension in their faces. Was this how it was all to end? Out here in the scorching desert? Unarmed? During a stroll beyond the end of the airstrip? Had all their work been for nothing? Were they to die here in this wilderness or spend the rest of the war in some German prisoner-of-war cage?

The machine-gun was still firing intermittently, seemingly on fixed lines for its bullets were churning up the same stretch of sand. By lifting their heads a fraction they could make out its muzzle-flash from the rocks to which they had been heading.

There came the sound of a motor engine at full revs at which the machine-gun intensified its rate of fire. The Frenchmen turned at the new danger to see an armoured car approaching at speed. Sand was billowing from beneath its wheel arches, leaving a widening plume of yellow dust in its wake.

'Afrika Korps!' sighed Ordenneau, but Ferre was shaking his head.

As far back as the autumn of 1939 he had learned to recognise the square outline of a Daimler 'Dingo' scout car.

They stood up together, hands high, even though the covering machine-gun was still firing.

The scout car jerked to a standstill not a couple of yards from them. The commander, a lieutenant perched high in the tiny turret, waved an arm to the machine-gunners and the firing ceased at once. He glared down at the Frenchmen, the hair protruding from beneath his black beret thick with sand, anger distorting his sunburned face.

'What the hell are you doing here?' It was an obvious question they had anticipated. He was a young man, about the same age as the sergeants.

Ferre pulled a face, already recognising the divisional flashes of the 7th Armoured.

He spread out his hands. '*Nous sommes Français! Nous ne parlons pas . . .*'

'Oh, for Christ's sake, don't give me that! You're RAF, aren't you? What are you? Free-French?'

'Yes, sir!' Ordenneau decided it was wise to become regimental. 'We were enjoying a walk.'

'A walk?'

'Yes, sir. We do not fly our Spitfires all the time. There was a sandstorm. Afterwards we were shelled. Now we cannot fly today.'

'Don't you know you almost got yourselves killed?'

'We expected you to be facing the other way. To the west.'

'There's such a thing as all-round defence here on the ground . . .'

'And so in the sky!'

The lieutenant's face relaxed; but he pointed back to the rocks from where the machine-gun had been firing.

'You caused a hell of a flap just now,' he said more calmly. 'There's too much heat shimmer to take chances. I'm sorry, but I don't think my CO will let you get away with it.'

'Do you mean we are to be your prisoners? Prisoners of the British?'

The lieutenant shook his head and found himself smiling.

'Maybe not this time. But don't you do anything so bloody stupid again. Do you understand . . . ?'

'We understand!'

'Then I'll need to know your squadron.'

Ferre shrugged resignedly.

'I have a feeling that our CO will not let us get away with it either,' he said.

Shortly after Joe Caton and Jean-Michel Ferre had taken off to chase the Junkers Ju 88, the rest of the squadron was placed on 'Available' and then, within minutes, on 'Readiness'. It appeared that the sandstorm had brought along with it other priorities.

A quarter of an hour later, One Section had been scrambled on a vague Group brief to strafe the coast road west of Sidi Rahman where considerable movement of enemy transport columns had been reported. Group HQ had added that it was imperative that the Afrika Korps should be denied re-establishing supplies following their heavy losses during the Battle of Alam el Halfa a month earlier.

Taylor decided to lead his own Section of Norling, Harris and the American, Maclellan; leaving Jimmy Easton and his Orange Section still 'on-state' in the Dispersal 'Hut'.

Easton had pulled a face at the news and when Taylor had stared moodily at him he had shrugged and observed: 'I suppose somebody's got to look after the old homestead' – letting Taylor know that Orange Section would willingly have volunteered.

He watched Taylor and his three pilots dash across the sand to their aircraft to hurry through their pre-take-off procedure. At that moment there came the sudden roar of aircraft engines in the sky to the west and when Easton spun round he was horrified to see two dots approaching low and at speed. He was about to yell to his own Section to scramble when he identified the aircraft as Spitfires – of course! Joe Caton and Jean-Michel Ferre returning.

What was the matter with George Romain, the Intelligence Officer? he asked himself. Why hadn't Taylor and he been informed that Caton was due? This was the kind of balls-up which could easily have ended in tragedy – as though there wasn't enough of it about!

As Taylor led his Section into the air he, also, was curbing his anger and as he picked up Caton's 'Good Luck' call over the R/T he was just as aware of their vulnerability as Caton was. It wasn't like Romain to slip up on anything so routine . . . that was something else for him to think about when he got back!

But as the Section headed northwards in their widely-spaced pairs with their canopies open and the slipstream from the airscrews corkscrewing around their engine cowlings, much of his anger evaporated.

This was the first time he and his Section had been airborne since escorting the Blenheims to Tobruk the previous afternoon and, as with Caton and Ferre, it was a relief to escape from the heat, the dust and the flies. He settled down in his cockpit, glancing at Norling about a hundred yards distant on his port with the sun glinting off his canopy, the boy's head moving slowly and systematically in an all-round air search.

To the rear and a couple of hundred feet higher, were Maclellan and Harris, equally widely spaced and neither weaving. The long noses of their Spitfires were angled upwards as they maintained the ascent; together looking all the world like an illustration in a pre-war RAF recruitment advertisement in some glossy magazine.

He found himself wishing he was out on some training jaunt, with nothing else to do but practise a few combat aerobatics and then return to a well-appointed mess for drinks and lunch. Why the hell had they to fight when life could be . . . he pulled himself up sharply, amused at the direction in which his subconscious had been turning. For a moment it had been as though he were back in his hospital bed with his dream fantasies of flight through a clear and endless sky where no danger lurked.

'Hello, Piper Leader! Aircraft on port beam and heading west. Looks like bombers with a hell of an escort.' This was Mike Norling.

Taylor checked before acknowledging.

'Yes! OK, Mike! I've got 'em!'

What was happening to him? He'd been day-dreaming! He shook his head and blinked his eyes as though jerking himself awake. It just showed what a night without sleep could do to a man!

Now, the formation to port was taking on three dimensions, Taylor checked his altimeter. Close on 24,000 feet. He switched to 'Send'.

'All One Section! We'll level at Angels Two-Five. Wait for instructions.'

Now the pilots could identify the aircraft. Eighteen or more Bostons and six Baltimores were trundling along at about 19,000 feet with an almighty escort of between thirty-five and forty Curtiss Kittyhawks.

The bombers were flying in depth in a compact formation with twelve of the Kittyhawks in close-escort position about half a mile astern and a thousand feet higher. The other two fighter squadrons were a further 5,000 feet or so higher and equally spaced on either side of the bombers. It looked as though there was going to be a hell of a party somewhere and Taylor grinned to himself at the idea of this armada dropping its bombs on the coast road west of Sidi Rahman . . . not much chance of that, worse luck, but it was certain there was going to be some congestion over his Section's target area.

He adjusted course and found that the bombers were doing the same and, in consequence, the Section was beginning to close the distance between them. He throttled back, at the same time conscious of their increased vulnerability from pecking enemy fighters which might be somewhere up in the sun shadowing the bigger formation.

He screwed round his head, checking that Maclellan and Harris were still in position as rearguard, momentarily undecided how to handle the situation. If he got too close there would be an immediate outcry from the Kittyhawks. If he dragged, the Section would be out on a limb.

He became aware of a tingling sensation creeping from his finger-tips. The control column unaccountably turned to jelly in his hands. His lips dried and there came a darting, blinding, pain which spanned his temples causing him to momentarily close his eyes tight. But when he re-opened them, the pain was still there and his stomach began to churn as though he might vomit. There was an ice-cold perspiration forming on his cheeks and he began to shiver. He lifted a hand as heavy as lead from the control column and it took all his concentration to stretch his fingers so far as the R/T switch.

'New bearing!' He formed the words through numb lips. 'We turn north-east.'

'North-east?' This was Norling, incredulous.

Taylor came back with none of the venom which Norling had anticipated: 'We'll clear that congestion in front!'

He switched to the new bearing as he spoke watching Norling closer now on his port beam, who seemed to hesitate before banking parallel. Ahead, now, the sky was clear and he could look over the arid desert below to where darker lines zig-zagged north to south marking the Allied support positions.

The pain across his temples began to ease. Some of the nausea also left him and he gripped hard on the control column as the feeling slowly returned to his fingers. Whatever had hit him a moment ago was passing, thank God!

He boosted his throttle on the new bearing, fixing on the green line of the Mediterranean now on his quarter beam. He nudged northwards a further couple of degrees, then another couple, and a little more until the Section was heading directly towards the sea which looked dull and lifeless with neither tide nor surf. Immediately ahead, at about two miles, was the coast road to the Allied side of the Rahman Track, deserted, for the Allied trans-shipment point was several miles to the east.

He switched his R/T back to 'Send'.

'We'll turn here and run parallel to the road. Due west!'

This time there followed no comment and the Section, in its pairs, banked to the new bearing. Far ahead was the large bomber formation, now little more than dots in the sky with the black puff-clouds of flak patterning the blue beneath them. They were too high to be at my serious risk from anti-aircraft fire; the German gunners using their shells to pin-point the path of the bombers.

Taylor looked down on to the coast road, seemingly as deserted as it was on the Allied side. Where had Group got the idea there were motorised columns on the move? Or had the bombers and the escort Wing scared them off?

He was feeling fine again. The pain in his head had gone. The perspiration on his face had dried and the sun had begun to burn his cheeks again. They would go down and have a closer look, though it could be dicey, for in the desert a pilot couldn't put pieces of the countryside between his aircraft and an alert enemy. Here, there were no tall trees and buildings to hide behind. Here, the enemy could plot the line of attack from the moment a formation left the sun. Still, it was a fair chance that the enemy columns were hiding beneath their camouflage netting and somewhere close.

'One Section! We'll go down to Angels One-Three, and see if anything's stirring.'

He dipped the nose and began a shallow descent towards the road, coming upon a squadron of Allied scout cars deployed as though for battle. But the Section swept over them at upwards of 15,000 feet.

At 13,000 feet they had reached the road, which stretched endlessly due west beyond the minefields; but there were still no signs of enemy movement.

Taylor hesitated.

Now they had reached the German forward positions and there came a flurry of machine-gun fire. Tracer floated towards them, but arcing away before it reached their altitude. He looked ahead in the direction in which the Boston formation was heading and there was still no indication of any Luftwaffe attempt at interception. Heavier flak from medium pom-pom guns began to pattern the sky around then, starting as slowly as the tracer and racing past ahead at an incredible speed. A tight group of shells suddenly exploded dangerously close and the instant change in air-pressure caused his aircraft to lurch.

Instinctively Taylor adjusted and, as he did so, back came the blinding pain to his temples. He was aware, too, that Mike Norling had drawn closer. He was staring at him across the distance of a couple of wing spans, doing a mime and pointing earthwards.

Taylor knew what he was suggesting and shook his head sufficiently emphatic for Norling to see. He switched to 'Send'.

'One Section! There's nothing doing down there! We might as well go home!'

'Home?' This time it was Stew Maclellan sounding as incredulous as had Norling a few minutes earlier. 'Godammit! Can't we have a bash at the gooks with the big guns down there?'

But Taylor, with nausea again fogging his senses, didn't have the will to reply. Instead, he put pressure on the right rudder bar and banked the full hundred and eighty degrees in a wide, wide, sweep. And, as he did so, the pain across his temples and the nausea in his stomach suprisingly began to ebb away.

That evening there was much speculation amongst the junior officers concerning their CO's strange behaviour over the Sidi Rahman coast road.

Stew Maclellan, in his typically brash and outspoken way, had pulled no punches.

'He chickened out! Sure as I'm standing here!' he exploded. 'Maybe that goddam Boston show un-nerved him.

But that's what he did! He chickened out!'

Caton, who had only had a sketchy report of the sortie from Ken Harris by way of Jean-Michel Ferre, had sensed his anger rising at the American's accusation. He'd seen Taylor in action at Dieppe and the man's courage had never for one moment been in doubt. Hadn't he won himself a Mention in Despatches? Yet, he had said nothing about it to Maclellan but, when the opportunity came along, he sought out Mike Norling. Surely something, somewhere, must have gone wrong? It wasn't customary for a full Section to return to base without firing a shot in anger!

But Norling had been unable to add anything constructive. He had shaken his head, as bewildered as Caton.

'You tell me, Joe!' he had said by way of reply. 'When the CO altered course north-east I thought he'd made a mistake. But when I queried it he just ignored me.' He shrugged. 'What can a feller do? For me, I'd have gone along with Stew and had a go at the Jerry gunners!'

'Maybe Stew can talk too loud, Mike?'

'But he had a point, Joe! Before we turned for home we were running on to the German forward artillery positions. We could have hit them, even from a couple of thousand feet!'

'Even so,' answered Caton, patiently, 'a man can't go around claiming that his squadron leader has chickened out of a battle.'

But Norling was not so quick in agreement as Caton had anticipated he might be.

Dominic Taylor had asked himself that very same question: had he chickened out of the attack against the German artillery? Had he taken the easy way out and run back to base when he'd found that Group's initial brief was no longer valid?

The possibility worried him – as did the reactions he'd experienced at the time: the blinding headache; the loss of feeling in his finger-tips; the nausea and the sweating. Could these be symptomatic of a stress he hadn't known existed – something which had been lying dormant in his subconscious since that July day a year ago when he had crashed his Spitfire into the Hampshire wood?

The possibility didn't bear thinking about and he attempted to shrug it off by telling himself that bacteria was rife in the desert; that contaminated food and water and a deficiency of green vegetables had given him a dose of what the USAAF labelled 'Montezuma's Revenge'.

He had a couple of large whiskies in his tent and the spirit eased his stomach immediately which helped convince him that he had indeed, picked up one of the desert bugs. Even so, it wasn't going to be easy facing the boys in the mess tonight! They weren't so green as not to guess that he'd run for home rather than risk a skirmish with the ground troops.

He was just on the point of leaving his tent when Len Jupp, the Adjutant, came along with news of the two Free-French sergeants' exploits with the 7th Armoured Division.

Jupp, who had flown with the Royal Flying Corps back in 1918 and was old enough to be the father of most members of the squadron, smiled tolerantly.

'Young Ferre had just done a sortie with Joe Caton. And dicey, too, I hear. He decided to go for a stroll with his pal, Ordenneau, to wind down. They were both 'off-state', of course.'

'A stroll?' Taylor came back at him with a vehemence which surprised him. 'The stupid, bloody, French halfwits! A stroll! Would you credit it?'

And with that he jammed his cap on his head and strode furiously out of the tent. His anger was helping him. He was aware of that! But, nevertheless, now he'd a point to make. At the same time, he'd have a few words with George Romain concerning that pantomime on take-off.

Meanwhile, farther east, at GHQ British 8th Army, preparations for the launch of the forthcoming Operation Lightfoot were progressing according to plan regardless of sandstorms and persistent enemy interference.

Troops, armour, ammunition, fuel, supplies and rations were pouring into Alexandria and Suez at an unprecedented rate.

Reserve camps were hurriedly being laid out to accommodate reinforcements before being pushed westwards to join regiments for the initial assault through the German minefields and defences along their Rahman front.

The Desert Air Force was also being reinforced. As with Piper Squadron, some came by aircraft carrier as far as Algiers from where they took off the flight-deck for Malta on a dicey flight of some six hundred and sixty miles, navigating on Bizerta and the two Italian held islands of Pantelleria and Linosa.

To make this flight, the aircraft – mostly Mk VB Spitfires – were fitted with ninety gallon slipper tanks, the weight of which was compensated by loading only two of the four cannon with sixty rounds in each magazine.

Thus, unwieldy, low in fuel and under-armed, they had to run the gauntlet of patrolling Axis fighters. Yet, surprisingly, there were few losses and the subsequent flight from Malta to Alexandria was comparatively trouble-free, for the farther east they flew the more they came under the protective umbrella of the established Desert Air Force.

Less fortunate reinforcements came the long way round by sea by way of Durban, Johannesburg and Suez – a journey lasting eleven weeks. Yet, these too, were arriving on schedule.

Chapter Three

The following morning the squadron was roused at 04.00 hours and put on 'Readiness' which meant that they had to remain in the vicinity of the aircraft, be wearing flying gear and be capable of becoming airborne within five minutes of the order to scramble.

So, at 04.05 hours the pilots were grouped outside the tent Dispersal 'Hut' enjoying that brief spell of the desert day when the chill of night was giving way to the first touch of warmth. These were also the precious few minutes before the wind began whipping up the sand and before flies, in their millions, began to torment.

Taylor had checked the 'state' cursorily, then strode over to the mechanics who were starting the engines, warming them up and checking before switching off.

The pilots watched him as he paused now and then to speak brusquely with members of the ground crews. His face was hard and uncompromising, his body powerful and erect, his dark brow creased in a fixed frown.

Mike Norling turned blandly to Jean-Michel Ferre who was standing beside him.

'Somebody sure upset the "old man", yesterday!' he observed with a straight face.

Ferre shrugged, not sure how to take the comment. He was very conscious that he and his friend were still NCOs amongst commissioned officers. Of course, everyone had heard about their 'stroll' the previous afternoon. It had been a good laugh. After all, it wasn't everybody who could put a brigade of the 7th Armoured Division on full alert! Later in the evening, Norling together with Johnnie Kitchen and

Stew Maclellan, had taken a bottle of whisky over to the Sergeants' Mess and made the most of the chance of a party.

But now, not four hours after the event, and still with a sore head, Ferre could only shrug unhappily. It would be some time before Ordenneau and he would live it down.

Taylor was on his way back to Dispersal when the line extension from the Orderly Room 'phone rang. He sprinted the fifty yards and snatched the handset from its cradle. As he listened, the pilots zipped up their Irvin jackets, put on their leather helmets, checked their gloves and goggles. Leather jackets, gloves and goggles could be the most important pieces of a pilot's flying gear if an aircraft caught fire. Without them they could be blinded, fried alive and, even if only the fingers of their left hand were burned, they would still die because they wouldn't be able to pull the rip-cord of their parachute.

Taylor dropped the handset back into its cradle.

His dark eyes roamed critically over his pilots.

'OK!' he said shortly. 'We're to scramble, but let's not panic about it!'

He pointed to the large-scale map pinned to the top of the barrack room table at the far end of the tent, impatiently brushing away sand and then jabbing a finger over the red circle which marked the Luftwaffe airfield at El Daba.

'We go as a squadron to El Daba and strafe installations. There's a report that new Bf 109s are expected and we want to make things as difficult as we can for them when, and if, they arrive. We fly usual formation, two secs of four and one of three stepped up astern.' He shot a glance at Joe Caton. 'You will bring up the rear this time with Yellow Section, Joe, and see you keep a sharp lookout. We'll have the sun behind us, but the Luftwaffe could be up and amongst us as soon as we show up on their radar screens.' Then, louder: 'OK. Any questions?' He glanced over the group. 'Right! Let's move!'

When the pilots reached their aircraft the ground crews had already started the engines. They strapped themselves into their cockpits, checked their instruments and the bulbs in their reflector sights and began to taxi towards the runway, automatically forming themselves into Sections, leaving the way clear for Taylor and his Section to take off first.

Yellow Section watched the rest of the squadron become airborne, already vulnerable in the clear sky with the sun at an awkward angle as they throttled back, waiting for them. Then Caton led his Section to the runway and, in under three minutes, the full squadron was forming into its Sections, line-astern and heading west and fixing on the distant coastal railway line which would lead them directly to their target.

Taylor came on the R/T.

'Hello, Orange leader. Hello, Yellow Leader. Both acknowledge!'

'Hello, Piper Leader! Orange OK!'

'Yellow, OK!'

'Climb Angels twenty-two. Figures, Two-Two! We'll by-pass target fifteen miles to south and attack from west. Single sweep with all three Sections and straight home. Orange left! Yellow right! We'll take care of the centre. Sections will attack line-abreast. No need for top-cover. We'll be in and out before they know we've hit them! Above target we go down to one hundred feet and open fire at four hundred yards. After attack climb due east.' He let a few seconds pass. Then: 'Acknowledge, Orange Leader!'

'Wilco, Piper Leader!'

Easton's voice had its usual calm confidence. After all, he thought, this was basic strafing procedure though he'd have been happier with a Section remaining high as lookout and top-cover – and if he still didn't have doubts following the CO's questionable sortie with One Section yesterday afternoon!

'Acknowledge, Yellow Leader!'

'Wilco, Piper Leader!'

Joe Caton sounded reasonably happy though at the back of his mind, as with Easton, Taylor's recent strange behaviour still nagged. But he didn't think twice about the lack of top-cover. As Taylor had outlined, the squadron would be in and out before the enemy knew what was happening. The use of high top-cover would have reduced the impact of the attack and trebled the length of time above the target. Besides! It was good to get high in a clear sky once again with the heat, the flies, those bloody flies! and stinging sand way, way, down below. He pulled back his control column and watched the long nose of his Spitfire tilt upwards as he increased the angle of ascent to correspond with Easton's Orange Section some four hundred yards ahead.

'OK, Piper Squadron.' This was Taylor again. 'Follow me!' A pause, then: 'Yellow Leader! Climb another thousand when squadron reaches twenty-two. Keep your eyes skinned behind, Joe!' Another pause. Then: 'Watch for flak above the Rahman Track in about four minutes!'

Two minutes passed, then Joe Caton came on the air.

'Hello, Piper Leader! This is Yellow Leader. Clouds building up over the sea. Looks pretty black!'

Taylor sounded impatient as he acknowledged.

'Yes! I've got 'em, Joe! That's all we need now, bloody rain! No more chat now! Radio silence until target area. All check that you stay switched to receive.'

Caton pulled a face at Taylor's irritability. Whenever he'd led a patrol, he'd always been glad to find his pilots sharp and on the lookout. A leader had a lot of things to do: navigation, assessment of the target area, planning the attack. He couldn't always be relied upon to be the first to spot either enemy aircraft or other hazards. There was no doubt that something was troubling the CO and he began to wonder if Stew Maclellan's outspoken criticism had somehow reached his ears.

The clouds were certainly building up to the north, dark ominous patches of cumulus occasionally broken by savage streaks of forked lightning which stabbed earthwards. For a moment Caton believed he had heard thunder but then he saw the orange flashes of airbursts to the right, brilliant, and awe-inspiring in a way, against the black clouds. But it was sporadic fire interlaced with small-arms tracer which arced below them, already spent. He glanced at his altimeter. Close on nineteen thousand and still climbing. It would take him a little time to settle above the squadron at 23,000 feet. In the meantime he would keep his fingers crossed that there were no Bf 109s lurking in the sun, above and behind them.

Ahead he could make out what little could be seen of the German front line which ran more or less parallel to the Rahman Track from east of Tel el Eisa in the north, through Dier el Munassib and Himeimet, to the rim of the Qattara Depression. It crossed his mind that the Afrika Korps camouflage was pretty good. Only here and there on flat stony stretches of ground could he make out vehicles and tanks beneath their netting and, even these, would not have been discernible from such an altitude but for the interlacing of their tracks in the sand. This all went to indicate why marauding patrols of the Luftwaffe forced Allied bombers good and high.

He noticed that Taylor's leading Section was shifting five or six degrees to the north. Caton adjusted, looking to his left and catching Jean-Michel Ferre's eye as, momentarily, they drew level. Ferre lifted a hand and pointed to the dark cloud mass, pulling a face, and Caton knew just what he meant. The squadron was going to stand out a mile, highlighted by the sun against such a background. He turned in the other direction and glanced at Robert Ordenneau who, according to standard air search procedure, was twisting his head to look upwards and to the rear, squinting into the sun. He obviously had no time to worry about his Section Leader and Caton wondered if he, too, was troubled by the clouds.

Dominic Taylor at the point and with his mind and eyes concentrated on the job in hand had now left the air-search to his Section Leaders and their teams. They had crossed the German front line and were probing deep into enemy territory though there had been little more than sporadic interference from anti-aircraft batteries. Obviously, the squadron had been seen and their course would now be being plotted; visually and by radar. Yet, there had been no sign of enemy aircraft, no Messerschmitts up high and poised to intercept.

Thank God, anyway, he seemed to have got that desert bug out of his system. His impulsive abandonment of yesterday's sortie could have done nothing for his image in the squadron – but he'd put that right today!

He glanced at his wristwatch. It was still only a little after four and the Afrika Korps would still be standing-to in their positions, hence the concentration of small arms fire and tracer just now! But he mustn't let himself get complacent. It was a certainty that the Luftwaffe weren't going to let him shoot up their airfield without a fight. Counter-measures in some form or another would be there waiting for them.

Leading Orange Section, Jimmy Easton sat easily in his cockpit, going systematically through his air-search procedure as relaxed as he had ever been and beginning to think he might grow to enjoy his new job in the desert – providing he could operate from some airfield a little closer to Cairo. Jesus! But wouldn't that be something? He should have volunteered for Bomber Command – 160 Liberator Squadron, for instance, for they had an extended operational range coupled with vulnerability on the ground which, together, warranted more lavish accommodation and all that went with it! During the past eighteen months he'd been operating from Kent airfields he'd never given the desert a single thought. Now it was going to be a hell of a job ever to forget it. He pulled a wry face and, as his air-search took his eyes to the starboard beam, they dwelt for a moment on the dark, handsome, profile of Johnnie Kitchen. Johnnie and his buddy, Mike Norling, would miss their two WAAFs and the afternoons the four of them had spent together in the caravan parked on a farm adjacent to the airfield. The desert didn't provide that kind of diversion!

The sky to the north-west had darkened and lightning flashes were becoming much more frequent, momentarily brightening the perspex canopies like a photo-flash.

Dominic Taylor re-checked their position. Now, he calculated, they must be roughly due south of El Daba. The sun was still bright behind them in a clear sky which contrasted dramatically with the cloud coverage ahead. It was difficult picking out detail on the ground, but he could make out an indeterminate group of small buildings which evidently comprised the village and justified its marking on the map. This was also reported to be the terminus of German rail traffic from Sidi Barrani and Tobruk where supplies were transferred to motor transports for the last leg of their journey forward.

He maintained an unchanged course and altitude for a further ten miles and then banked north-north-west in a wide sweep with the squadron maintaining formation. Now they were almost amongst the clouds and there splattered on their canopies drops of rain the size of half-crowns which immediately broke up into tiny droplets which raced to the rear under the corkscrew slipstream from the airscrews. The pilots cursed. They would have forfeited what little element of surprise they had hoped to achieve for clear visibility.

Taylor was holding the wide arc of the 'U'-turn. Now the sea was directly ahead and they could make out the railway line and the movement of loaded tank-transporters along the coastal highway beyond. These, alone, would be a prize worth seizing. But Taylor maintained altitude until they had completed the full circle and the squadron was heading back due east.

The pilots switched their firing-buttons to 'Fire' and eased themselves in their seats ready for action. In a line-abreast attack they would cover the full width of the enemy airfield and its buildings in one single sweep – as Taylor had said, 'We'll give 'em all we've got and head straight for home.'

Joe Caton smiled to himself at the thought. Despite all his arguments and scathing criticism before Dieppe six weeks ago, here was Taylor doing exactly what Lee Hillas would have done under similar circumstances. It had been Hillas who had originally introduced such hit-and-run tactics to Piper Squadron. Could it be that the man was trying to prove something?

The rain had begun to beat down heavily when Taylor eventually broke the wireless silence which mattered little, now, for the squadron was sure to have been spotted visually.

'All Piper Squadron! All Piper Squadron!' His voice was studiedly matter-of-fact. 'Here we go down to Angels Five. Section Leaders watch your positions. The rest of you keep searching. Out!'

Through his misting windshield Caton watched the leading Section tilt into a shallow dive. Then, as Taylor reached the lower ceiling the Section throttled back to allow Orange and Yellow Sections to move forward into the full line-abreast attacking formation. Now they could make out details of the airfield some five or six miles ahead, the sun still shimmering off the sharp angles of the blast walls as they closed rapidly.

'All Piper Squadron!' Taylor again, but this time with a distinct urgency in his voice. 'Here we go! And good luck!'

The Sections launched themselves into a steep dive, boosting their throttles to level out at upwards of three hundred and twenty miles an hour at between a hundred and a hundred and fifty feet. It wasn't easy maintaining close formation with the rain streaming along their canopies. And the flat ground, now a dirty brown and swimming with water, just below them was racing past at what seemed an impossible speed towards the muzzle and tracer flashes from a concentration of guns in sand-bagged emplacements around the airfield perimeter.

On his port beam, Caton glimpsed one of Taylor's Section rapidly lose height until it was tearing along at an acute angle only feet above the ground. Then, its port wing dug into the ground and the aircraft began to cart-wheel, shooting flame. Caton caught his breath. The American! The noisy, loud-mouthed, likeable, Yank! Stew Maclellan! There came a vivid flash from farther to port. Somebody else had been caught by the Spandau machine-guns even before he had had a chance to open fire. He fixed his ring sight on a group of buildings directly ahead and pushed his thumb hard on the firing-button and held it there, at the same time aware of the crash of machine-guns and cannon from the two French boys at either side. These lads took their war very seriously but, then, they had cause to! His aircraft thumped and juddered and his vision blurred with the vibration. With that and the streaming rain he realised how easy it was to lose the vertical as young Maclellan must have done. But he held his position in rigid formation, watching his shells raking the workshops ahead. Taylor had picked a good line of attack for they were speeding parallel to and between the blast walls. He saw men being hurled bodily from their shelters under the concentration of their fire, their bodies then flopping limply into the mud whilst others panicked towards slit trenches which were already crammed with people.

Only seconds passed before the squadron was clear and Taylor glancing from side to side to confirm that his Sections were still with him. He had begun his climb when Easton's voice rang over the R/T.

'Bandits! Bandits! Bandits! Twelve o'clock and high!'

The squadron climbed savagely, banking into a defensive circle as Messerschmitt Bf 109s dived, line-astern, amongst them from the sun.

Caton swallowed hard as he pulled back the control column and boosted his throttle to get into position. What would they have given now for top-cover? Here they were below 5,000 feet, miles behind the enemy lines and with most of their ammunition gone. He watched a couple of Me109s hurtle past the other side of the circle and saw the lines of their tracer shoot wide. Then he turned back to his own side, but could see nothing but sky. There came more tracer ahead and he saw that two of the squadron were engaging from their side of the circle. He screwed his head round to the rear for he could see nothing in his mirror and then he realised that the clouds had covered the sun – just seconds too late!

'Hold formation!' This was Taylor at last forsaking his R/T

procedure. 'Don't break until the command!'

Jimmy Easton smiled sardonically. As though anyone would be so crazy! But it appeared there were only three Messerschmitts up with them. If the squadron hadn't been out of ammunition they'd have made mincemeat of them! As it was, the bastards would probably risk a second run . . . he noticed that Chris Fenton, about forty yards ahead, had begun to stream smoke. Had it been so close? Jesus! Chris had a hell of a way to nurse his Merlin! If he dropped out of position in the circle, ten to one the Me 109s would peck him off. He glanced in his mirror seeking Johnnie Kitchen behind him, but there was only empty space. Where the hell was Johnnie at a time like this? The Me 109s might risk another dive through the formation, but one thing was certain: they wouldn't dogfight in these conditions. Besides there was no telling how long they had been airborne and waiting. Maybe, with a bit of luck, they too could be getting low on fuel and ammunition.

With the loss of two of his Section, Stewart Maclellan and Ken Harris, Taylor sensed some of yesterday's tension returning. He'd noticed, too, that Jimmy Easton was swanning about without his wingman which probably meant that Johnnie Kitchen had also bought it – though he hadn't seen Johnnie go. On top of that he'd let his squadron get bloody-well bounced!

His heart began to race as his vision blurred and there came again that creeping numbness from his fingertips. Cold perspiration began to form in great beads across his forehead and that same blinding pain returned to span his temples like some violent electrical discharge between two poles.

Oh, Jesus!

Nausea gripped him as he tried to speak into the R/T, deliberately hardening his voice.

'All Piper Squadron! We'll risk a break and head home. Take Orange Section to the point, Jimmy!'

But Chris Fenton came on the air before Easton could throw his switch to 'Send'.

'Hello, Piper Leader! This is Orange Three!' Fenton was keeping his cool. 'I've got a misfire. I doubt if I can keep up in a break!'

But Easton came back immediately.

'It's OK, Chris! We'll cover you, but you'll need height over the flak. Nurse her along for Christ's sake, Chris!'

But Fenton did not make it back to base. He began losing height over the crucial Rahman Track with a flurry of air-bursts spreading around him. Yet, somehow, he managed to hold his revs and when Jimmy Easton went down with him he saw that the boy was grinning and pointing towards the Allied forward lines. At least, he would be with friends.

Easton throttled back, keeping pace with him down to a couple of hundred feet and, when he saw him make a copy-book landing on the rock-strewn sand, he hauled on his stick and climbed to rejoin the squadron.

Chapter Four

Dominic Taylor sat alone in the big tent which served as an Operations Room. The squadron had just been put on 'Available' which meant that the pilots should remain in the vicinity of their aircraft and be within easy range of loud-speaker or telephone so that they could hurry to their air-craft on call. He had told Joe Caton to pass on the order to the pilots and had remained in the Operations Room poring over the large-scale map of the vast stretch of desert between Alexandria and Benghazi and, in particular, the area of the morning's sortie.

There was some movement on his left which he caught from the corners of his eyes and he looked round irritably to see George Romain's red and peeling face poking round the tent flap. The Intelligence Officer appeared nervous and was smiling apologetically at his intrusion.

'Dominic! Group's on the wire. The Skipper! Alan Harcourt himself . . .'

Taylor nodded resignedly. Group Headquarters had already taken his preliminary verbal report and it must have been passed directly to the Group Captain.

'All right, George,' he said evenly, 'put the call through here and keep everybody else off the line!'

Romain nodded, still nervous, and disappeared. Taylor pulled his cigarette case from his breast pocket and carefully selected one, determined not to hurry. He was being equally casual when the telephone rang; though it seemed to him to sound unusually harsh and aggressive.

'Yes? Squadron Leader Taylor here!'

There followed formalities with some clerk or other. Then

there was complete silence for the best part of two minutes before Alan Harcourt came on the line. Taylor had only met him once before and that had been for a hurried quarter of an hour's discussion when the squadron had been officially welcomed to the Group.

'Ah . . . Dominic!'

'Sir!'

Taylor could picture the dapper little man with the round, red face, keen blue eyes and central parting in his carefully brushed dark hair.

'Um . . . yes! The . . . er . . . draft of your verbal report on your show this morning has just appeared on my desk together with some pictures from Tactical Reconnaissance . . .' Taylor scowled tight-lipped, staring through the half open tent flap with face hard and uncompromising. He was damned if he was going to help Harcourt make his rocket any easier. So he said nothing and waited for the Group Captain to continue, which he did, more positively now: 'Yes! The pictures didn't show very much, I'm afraid, but I believe you reported the hell of a storm blowing at the time. Couldn't really be blamed for not brewing the whole damned place up under those kind of conditions. Huh?'

Taylor's eyes flashed. The attack had been as good as any other squadron in the Group could have made it. 'We raked the entire airfield and emptied our magazines into the service bays and . . .'

Harcourt cut him short.

'But you say in your preliminary report that there were no enemy aircraft on the base. Didn't it cross your mind to ask yourself where the hell they were?'

'There was no time to play around with tactics! Visibility was down to a minimum and we were committed before we could identify!'

'Yes! Yes! I appreciate that; but that's not the point I'm making Dominic! The thing which really worries me is that you evidently launched what amounted to a blind attack without top-cover and then, when you pulled out from your dive, you got yourselves bounced by three Me 109s. Three! Only three against . . . how many, do you say? Nine?'

'Yes, sir. Nine!'

'And as a result, you lost two?'

'Yes!'

There followed a long silence during which Taylor tapped angrily on the table top with his still unlit cigarette. Then Harcourt came back: 'Bit of a bad show that, isn't it?' Now there was a distinct edge to his voice. 'There's also something else which arrived on my desk this morning; a signal from the 7th Armoured Division! The brigadier claims that two of your sergeant-pilots were found wandering in the desert yesterday afternoon. Quite irrelevant to the job in hand, of course, but isn't there something lacking somewhere in Piper Squadron, Dominic?'

Taylor wanted to tell the little man that there wasn't a damned thing wrong with his squadron which time and a little more experience in the desert wouldn't put right. That it was easy enough for some pompous sod to squat on his arse in some great luxury hotel and criticise the operation and discipline of a squadron which he'd not even found the time to visit. But he fought down his flare of temper and said: 'I'll send you in a written report later today!'

But Harcourt dismissed the suggestion with another question.

'Tell me! Do you have a reliable second-in-command with you?'

'Yes, I do!' Taylor replied shortly. 'A fellow named Caton who happens to be the sole survivor from the original Battle of Britain team.'

'Good! Good! Good!' Harcourt began to relax. 'Then I'll tell you what you can do, Dominic! Put him in command for the rest of the day and you grab a jeep and drive over here. I think it might be better if you and I had a little, man-to-man, chat.'

Shortly after Dominic Taylor had left the airfield the squadron was scrambled and briefed to intercept bombers heading due east, south of the Qattara Depression. There were reported to be up to twenty bombers, as yet unidentified, and as many Bf 109 fighters in close-escort. Two squadrons of Hurricanes had already been scrambled and it was anticipated that interception would be made roughly from the centre to east of the Depression, itself.

Piper Squadron, now reduced to six aircraft and under the command of Flight Lieutenant Joe Caton, became airborne in under four minutes and was flying on the old formation of two vics of three: Section One – Caton, Ferre and Ordenneau, Section Two – Easton, Norling and Reed.

They reached 20,000 feet in under nine minutes, heading directly on the bearing which Group had given them over the R/T.

Mike Norling, up and behind Two Section, spotted the action first: 'Ahead at two o'clock, Piper Leader!' Without Taylor, R/T procedure had relaxed. 'Christ! Look at 'em, Joe! Dozens of the sods!'

'OK, Mike!' Caton acknowledged calmly. 'Hold formation, Piper Squadron, until we can see a bit more.'

He re-checked his reflector sight and switched his firing-button to 'Fire', then settling himself down in his seat as he had a few hours earlier above El Daba, prepared to join the whirling dogfight ahead.

The last thing Caton had expected was to be in command of the squadron that day though, at the time, he had no reason other than to accept on its face value, the straight-forward explanation which Dominic Taylor had given him: 'Sorry, Joe, old chap, but I've to leave you holding the baby for a spell this afternoon. Seems I'm wanted for a special briefing on God knows what . . . maybe Alamein! Anyway, you'll be all right, of course!'

Caton had nodded. He had been on the point of remarking that the squadron was down to half strength, anyway, and that during the past two years he'd had plenty of practice leading section sweeps over Northern France where the opposition had been far greater than they were likely to come across in the desert.

But he said: 'Lucky man!' And then, with a grin: 'Where's the briefing? Cairo? I'd hoped I might have had a look in at Shepheard's myself, before the big flap starts.'

Taylor had shaken his head and Caton had noticed the hesitancy in his eyes which, at the time, he had interpreted as reaction from the morning's traumatic sortie.

'No such luck!' Taylor had forced a laugh. 'Only so far as Group HQ. Should be back by nightfall.'

So Caton had wandered back to his tent with a thoughtful expression on his face; but he had had little opportunity to ponder on his CO's preoccupation for, with half an hour, the squadron was scrambled.

Now he glanced in his mirror as though half-expecting to see Jean-Michel Ferre on his tail. He hadn't liked abandoning the proved 'finger four' formation, but with only three aircraft in each Section he had had no alternative.

They were closing the distance at just under three hundred miles an hour and it became easier to pick out the dogfights at roughly their altitude. The sky was buzzing with aircraft which appeared like scores of angry gnats whilst, two thousand feet below them, a sharp vic of bombers was doggedly maintaining a north-east course above the rocky terrain of the Depression.

'Hello, Piper Leader! Hello, Piper Leader! This is Tango Leader! Tango Leader! Do you hear me?' There was urgency in the Hurricane Wing Commander's voice.

Caton replied, unflurried.

'Hello, Tango Leader! This is Piper Leader. Loud and clear!'

There came a short laugh of relief over the R/T.

'Good! Thank God you've arrived! And just in time! You'll see we're pretty busy, but we're coping. Hell of a party! Can you look after the bombers? We make it sixteen! Figures, One-Six. Over!'

'Hello, Tango Leader. Great! We'll take care of the bombers. Over!'

'Good! Buy you a pint, some time! You're in for a treat! Good hunting!'

'All Piper Squadron! All Piper Squadron!' This was Caton to his pilots. 'You all heard. Nice an' easy now! We'll have a good look before we engage. Await my orders!'

He changed course to head directly towards the vic of bombers, though still maintaining the high altitude. Then, once again, Norling shattered the silence, his voice lifting in his excitement.

'Look, Joe, for Christ's sake! They're Stukas! They're bloody Stukas! Oh, Jesus, fellers! Just look!'

And he boosted his throttle to draw level with Jimmy Easton, pointing forward to the now clearly defined Junker Ju 87Bs, labouring on at their flat-out speed of two hundred miles an hour. No wonder they'd got such an almighty close-escort!

When Caton acknowledged there was none of Norling's exhilaration in his tone.

'All right! Calm down, lads! Like I said, nice an' easy! This is a chance we can't miss. But we'll have a closer look, first.'

The Wing Commander commanding the two Hurricane squadrons had been reasonably accurate in his assessment of the enemy bomber strength, even though he may have had no time other than to take a couple of quick glances in their direction.

There were seventeen Stukas in all: eight flying at either side of a flight-leader and now easily recognisable by their angular construction; fixed undercarriage and wheel spats; their long perspex canopy with the second crew member facing astern and clutching a single 7·9 mm MG 17 machine-gun.

Joe Caton experienced the same twang of sympathy for these very vulnerable German airmen as when the squadron had bounced similar Stuka formations over the Channel, even though they had been on their way to bomb London. These now obsolescent aircraft had little or no chance against MK VB Spitfires which could almost double their speed. Also, they had little manoeuvrability and despite guns fore and aft, were completely blind from a low, quarter-attack.

What had the Hurricane Winco said?

'You're in for a treat?'

Caton smiled sardonically, wondering what the Ju 87 pilots were thinking now they had the Spitfires in their field of vision.

In the early days, such formations had endeavoured to break on contact with fighters but, recently, they had abandoned this drill because their escorting Messerschmitts were far too fast to maintain close support even in a dive. Yet, it had taken a long time for the hard-headed Germans to accept the fact that they were less vulnerable so long as they maintained formation or wheeled into a defensive circle.

As the squadron lost height, Caton looked up at the dog-fight. There were two aircraft plummeting earthwards and a third was pouring smoke, but all three were too far away to tell whether they were British or German. Undoubtedly, the Hurricanes were playing a great tactical battle, forcing the Messerschmitts farther and farther from the bombers and leaving the sky clear for the Spitfires.

'Hello, Piper Squadron. All Piper Squadron!' This was Caton, again, with his assessment of the situation made. Now he would commit himself and the depleted squadron irrevocably. 'Synchronised attack from the sun! Number Three Attack! Repeat, Number Three! We shall attack starboard beam of formation only. One Section will make the quarter-attack. Two Section from the stern. We've done this Number Three many times together, Jimmy. Leave Charlie high on guard! OK? Watch your distances, then pull the plug when you break downwards!'

As they closed, Caton at the point, boosted his throttle, kicked his rudder bar and along with his Section, now in line-astern, half-rolled into position to launch an attack from ahead of the bombers and pass some six hundred yards to the flank. Easton led his Section, also in line-astern, slightly below the starboard line of the bomber formation, wary of the rear gunners. Then, as the turns were complete, both Sections automatically moved into line-abreast.

'Great, Piper Squadron!' This was Caton again, still unflurried. He had seen the beautifully executed move of Easton's Section and young Charlie Reed breaking to climb astern. 'Right! Now we'll take the whole damned lot on their starboard side. One Section! Number Three Attack! Go!'

He shoved his thumb hard on the firing-button and his aircraft bucked and juddered through the impetus of his dive and the vibration from the four Vickers and twin Hispano cannon. With Ferre and Ordenneau in line-abreast, they raked the eight starboard Stukas without a shot being fired at them in retaliation, then shoving forward their control columns into near-vertical dives as Easton's Section roared in astern of the bombers.

High above, watching the sky for any Messerschmitts which might have come chasing from the dogfight, Sergeant Pilot Charlie Reed looked below with eyes widening in incredulity. He counted as he watched the Stukas go: One. Two. Three. Four. Five! Five of them were already spinning down, pouring smoke. One lost its port wing. Another disappeared in a blinding flash of orange flame. Christ! He felt a lump rise in his throat. Five! And the rest of the formation on the port side were beginning to panic, endeavouring to break.

Piper Squadron had reformed and was climbing fast, heading away to turn against the port flank of the Stukas. Caton remained grimly silent until they had climbed into their Section formations for the repeat attack. His voice, then, reflected none of the emotion of victory.

'Same drill as before, lads! But come in sooner if you can, Jimmy. We missed the forward three!'

Easton pulled a face, but acknowledged: 'Roger, Piper Leader!'

He would have needed a Mark IX to do what Joe had asked of him!

'What about that clever bastard in front, Joe?' This was Norling remembering Johnnie Kitchen.

But Caton, sensing the danger of personal emotion controlling impulse, cut him short.

'All right, Mike! No chat! Repeat Number Three Attack. One Section. Go!'

Again came the boost of throttle; the half-roll with the Section in line-astern; the automatic spread into line-abreast. This time it was an even smoother attack for both Sections came within range within split seconds of each other. They opened fire together, too, but now the Stukas were breaking, diving with their sirens screaming, jettisoning their bombs as though they were launching themselves into one of their own copy-book attacks. But three more failed to pull out of their dives and another climbed away to starboard pouring glycol.

'Eight!'

Joe Caton, still on 'Send', spat out the number without knowing he had done so. Then: 'All Piper! Great show! The bastards are scattering. We'd best go home unless you want to fight without ammunition.'

He spun his head round sharply to see an aircraft diving on his port beam. Charlie Reed from his guard position with his magazines full. He went down and down and down and the rest of the squadron watched his guns blaze and tracer rake the full length of the Stuka flight leader as he tried to marshal his shattered formation. The aircraft exploded before Reed had pulled out of his dive and there was nothing left to see but a few parts of burning Stuka floating down to earth.

From his position on Easton's right, Mike Norling glanced at his Section Leader and nodded gravely. He said aloud: 'Couldn't have done it better myself!' But Easton couldn't lip-read and Norling's R/T was still switched to 'Receive' as it should be.

'Hello, Tango Leader! Hello, Tango Leader!' This was Joe Caton seeking the Hurricane Wing Commander.

Nothing happened.

Caton switched back to 'Send.'

'Hello, Tango Leader! Hello, Tango Leader! This is Piper Leader!'

'Hello, Piper Leader. This is Tango Leader! Sorry! I was busy! We just don't believe our eyes up here. How many for Christ's sake?'

'Nine! Plus three or four damaged.'

'Nine! We should have met you fellows earlier! We got us two Bfs, but we've lost two. The rest of them broke away when they saw what was happening to the Stukas. We're going home. Thanks, Piper Leader. I'll make that two pints!'

Caton acknowledged quietly.

'Thanks, Tango Leader. It's time we went home, too. Roger and Out!'

Back at the airfield, the pilots left their aircraft with the ground crews for refuelling and re-arming and made their way to the Mess for lunch with their spirits high. Incredibly, the depleted squadron of six aircraft had put at least twelve enemy bombers out of action and nine of them permanently. Equally important, not a single German bomb from that formation had fallen on an Allied position. The occasion was certainly one to celebrate and, to a man, the pilots rushed to buy Joe Caton a drink. But he shook his head, grinning, and hurried away to make an initial report by telephone to Group Headquarters.

'Don't forget we're still on "Available"!' he warned them. 'Better keep off the booze and your ears pinned back for the next scramble.'

The information deflated them a little, but as they crowded round the bar with glasses of tonic water in their hands, there were smiles on their faces. Mike Norling, too, had found satisfaction in that the death of his friend a few hours earlier had to some degree been avenged. Yet, no one spoke of the three men who had died on Taylor's earlier sortie. It was sufficient that they had survived to fight again as a team and, as a team, they had done a worthwhile job.

'Joe laid on the hell of a show, Jimmy!' commented Mike Norling and, from him, that was praise indeed.

And Easton smiled and nodded. He had enjoyed the very orthodox Number Three attack and the whole of the plan spelled out before the squadron had been committed. Yet, he knew that it would have had little success against faster bombers – Heinkel He 111s, for instance, with a top speed close to that of the Spitfire. But it seemed that at last Joe Caton was finding maturity, though it had taken the desert to bring it out! It was also a fact that neither Dominic Taylor, nor Lee Hillas could have put on a better show than this morning. They would have gone buggering in at the head of the squadron, broken the Stuka formation like a triangle of snooker balls, and left every man to himself. They might have totted up as many kills, but the attack would have lacked the kind of finesse which Joe Caton had demonstrated!

That afternoon the squadron was again scrambled to provide high top-cover to half a dozen Blenheims attacking Sidi Abdel Rahman just south of the coastline. They were intercepted by seven or eight Messerschmitt Bf 109s, supported by a couple of Italian Macchi 202s which seemed to have come along for the ride. But their interception was a desultory, half-hearted, affair.

Caton's Number One Section had a couple of squirts at the 109s but it was evident that the enemy was unwilling to be goaded into a free-for-all dogfight. And, as a result, the Blenheims had no difficulty in dropping their bombs from a reasonably high level and without much threat from coastal flak.

From their high position at close on 24,000 feet, Piper Squadron were unable to make out what degree of damage to installations the bombing had caused; but, on the other hand, the Blenheim leader subsequently reported seeing a Messerschmitt on fire though he was not able to confirm whether or not it had crashed.

When the Blenheims turned for home without having a really determined attack thrown against them, the Messerschmitts also broke away to follow the two Macchis which were already leading the run back westwards.

The two Piper Sections returned separately. Caton's Number One Section, low on ammunition, went first whilst Easton's Number Two Section remained as high rearguard for a full minute until they were clear.

Much later, that evening, when Mike Norling came into the Mess with Jimmy Easton, Caton was already there making the most of the squadron being place on 'Released' and buying drinks all round.

'Ah! Mike! Jimmy!' He greeted them appearing happier and more relaxed than he had in days. 'What'll it be fellers?'

Easton looked at him from under his eyebrows and whispered hopefully: 'Beer?'

Caton laughed as he spun round to the barman.

'Show 'em, Willie!' he said, and the barman stooped behind his makeshift counter to straighten up again with a wooden crate cradled in his arms. Caton pointed to the label. It read: '36 x John O'Keefe's Real Canadian Ale.'

'Present from Group!' Caton announced. 'And, special delivery! I suppose that it isn't every day that half a squadron bags nine!'

He dug into the crate with both hands and pulled out a further half-dozen bottles. 'Oh, yes, and there's something else!' he went on. 'We're on "Released" until midday tomorrow.' He passed round the bottles, grinning, then pausing to look at Jimmy Easton as a new thought struck him.

'Hey, Jimmy! How about calling in Charlie and my two French lads? We can't have 'em hanging about a sergeants' mess after a day like today, can we? Bugger the discipline!'

It was about an hour later that Chris Fenton rejoined the squadron. He burst into the Mess with his round, boyish, face flushed with health.

'Hi, fellers!' he greeted them as they clustered round to thump him on the back. 'Why'd you start the party without me? Supposing I'd decided to go home!'

Jimmy Easton thrust a bottle of John O'Keefe's at him. 'Get this down Chris, boy!' he said. 'We've got news for you!'

Shortly afterwards, Dominic Taylor returned from Group Headquarters, but he had already heard of the squadron's Stuka 'party'.

Shortly after breakfast the following morning, when the pilots had briefed their ground crews on priority maintenance tasks, Mike Norling had sought out Joe Caton.

Norling had drunk far too much the previous evening. But they had all learned that, in future, John O'Keefe's Real Canadian Ale should be treated with greater respect. John O'Keefe's was, undoubtedly, strong stuff!

'You got a minute, Joe?' Norling asked. He looked pale and tired and Caton wondered whether he had slept.

'Yeah! Sure, Mike!' he replied at once, pointing to the open side of the big tent. 'Are we all right here, or do we go for a walk?'

'Maybe we can sit in the shade, huh?' He smiled wanly at Caton's expression, then adding: 'I mean under the blast walls.'

They crossed the three hundred yards of sand to where blast walls of empty eight gallon petrol tins filled with sand were in the process of being erected between stacked crates of rations, ammunition, fuel and aircraft and vehicle spares. At the far end a makeshift bunker had also been constructed for personnel as a passive air defence priority. Norling pointed, at which they plodded through the loose sand to its shaded side.

They sat down and Caton took a cigarette pack from his shirt pocket and passed it to Norling who took one with his brow clouded, his hand then grabbing nervously at Caton's wrist as he struck a match.

'It's about Johnnie, Joe,' he said quietly.

Caton did not look at him. Or course! He had guessed. He

blew out smoke, staring through the rapidly thinning haze to the open desert to the north.

'I've kept thinking about you and George Barclay since Johnnie bought it,' Norling went on. 'You an' George were as close as any two mates can be until he caught it at Dieppe. Well! I don't need to tell you about Johnnie, do I? We'd been mates since Number Five OTU.' He took a deep breath, seeking words, his eyes lifting to the empty sky. Then he shook his head. 'I just can't get it that he's gone, Joe! Yesterday, when we were knocking off the Stukas, I kept glancing in my mirror, expecting to see him on my tail. You know we both came from Newcastle? On Tyne, that is! * We shared all our leaves. We knew each other's parents. Dammit! We'd planned to marry those two WAAFs we used to run around with in Kent!' He smiled sadly as Caton turned to face him for the first time. 'It's true, Joe! You never thought we were serious, did you? Well, I guess war makes a feller that way! Jesus! How can I face Johnnie's Sally ever again? Joe! You've been through it all! How the hell do I make out, now?'

But all Caton could do was shake his head. Yes! He'd been through it himself! Many times! Through the Battle of France, the Battle of Britain, Greece, Dieppe, and now the Western Desert; and he wasn't any wiser than when the whole circus had begun in 1940. But he'd caught it harder than Mike Norling, for George Barclay had been his buddy through the whole of those long years until Dieppe had cut him down.

'There are no answers to your questions, Mike,' he said, eventually. 'Johnnie's gone just as George has gone along with all the other lads we've seen shot out of the sky. How old was Johnnie? Twenty? Twenty-one?' He jerked a humourless laugh. 'We get old before our time in this business, don't we? You ask me what I did when old George bought it as though I'd found an easy answer to our daily routine of killing and being killed. But I haven't, Mike! God knows I've found nothing! I'm just as raw, just as scared and just as emotional

* See *Squadron 3: Scramble Dieppe*, Matthew Holden.

as I was on my first sortie. Maybe yesterday, when we hit the Stukas, I was kidding myself that the lads we knew are still around somewhere. That's not too difficult when you're in the air! Like you just said, you half-expected to see Johnnie still on your tail. Soon you'll be asking yourself if he'll be in the Mess tonight. That's how it goes, I guess!'

Chapter Five

Dominic Taylor had returned from his visit to Group Headquarters unimpressed and unrepentant.

Group Captain Alan Harcourt had not kept him waiting, but had had him ushered into his presence immediately upon arrival. Taylor had stalked stiffly into the room with shoulders back, head high, and saluted with the perfection of a Guards' Regimental Sergeant Major. And that, to some degree, had taken Harcourt aback. From his deep leather chair he had acknowledged the salute with the casual lift of the fingers of one hand; but he had not missed Taylor's powerful body; the deepset, impenetrable, eyes; swarthy face and strong line of jaw.

During the two hours since his telephone conversation with Taylor he had taken a second look at Taylor's confidential file and there was no doubt at all that it was very impressive. Regular RAF officer. Cambridge rugger blue. Cambridge squadron. Cranwell and an 'above-average' rating. Battle of Britain and, then, a terrible pile-up in a Hampshire wood when he had screeched a few feet above a sleeping village to plough deep amongst the trees where his fuel tank had exploded and the whole wood had become a conflagration. Yet, despite a cracked spine, a stomach gushing blood, and the wood ablaze around him, Taylor had miraculously survived. That had taken courage, Harcourt conceded, for during the following months of pain and surgery Taylor had continued to look to his future as a fighter pilot when nine out of ten would have resigned themselves to living out the rest of their days as hobbling cripples in a home for incurables. And, true to his word, and with a dogged determination which had impressed all who had come into contact with him during his twelve months' convalescence, he had eventually proved himself fit again for operational duties. Not only that, but he had volunteered to join Lee Hillas's squadron for the Dieppe raid. Squadron Leader Lee Hillas of all people! The screw-ball Canadian who had been one of Taylor's own rookie pilots way back in 1940!

Now, as he looked across at the man and his personal file containing all that impressive data on the desk before him, Harcourt began to wonder if his approach during their earlier conversation had been the right one. Could be that he had been a trifle too impulsive . . .

He pushed himself to his feet to shake hands as Taylor relaxed.

'Ah! Dominic! Good of you to come so soon!'

'Sir!'

Harcourt indicated a chair at the corner of his desk.

'Please sit down, Dominic. There are cigarettes if you'd like to smoke.'

Taylor shook his head, waiting.

Harcourt forced a smile, deciding to abandon the harsh line of criticism he had been formulating in his mind during the past hour. He must take it easy with a man of Taylor's stature . . . he began ad-libbing immediately.

'Ah, yes! Very pleased to see you again! We hardly got time to know each other the last time we met. Trouble is that everything and everyone here seems to be flat-out all the time. Particularly with the big flap on the cards . . . !' He shrugged as though dismissing his own problems, then going on more spiritedly: 'I really asked you to come along here because it's so easy for people to get an entirely wrong impression over a telephone. Particularly a field-line! Could be you considered me over-critical on your handling of your show at El Daba this morning. Well! Perhaps I was! But you will understand that I can only interpret those reports as I visualise the incidents in my mind. After all, I wasn't there, though I did have some worry about that top-cover business . . .'

Harcourt went waffling on until, a few minutes later, an orderly arrived with coffee. And whilst they sipped from the thick and heavy mugs he switched his tack and began to expound on the Group's involvement in the forthcoming Operation Lightfoot.

There came a knock on the door and it opened immediately and a fair-haired officer wearing Squadron Leader rings and walking with the aid of a stick came into the room.

Harcourt paused, mid-sentence, looking up.

'Sorry to worry you, sir,' the newcomer said quietly, 'but a signal has just come in which I think you might like to see, particularly as,' he turned to smile bleakly at Taylor, '. . . Squadron Leader Taylor is still with you.'

Harcourt nodded, taking a single flimsy sheet of message pad.

'Yes! Thanks! Leave it with me, Peter,' he said at which the officer nodded briefly and left the room.

Taylor watched as Harcourt read through the signal. When he had done so, he smacked it down forcibly on the desk with the palm of his hand.

He looked at Taylor quizzically.

'This morning, you did tell me that you'd a reliable Second-in-Command, didn't you Dominic?'

Taylor's eyes narrowed. Challenging almost. His voice was curt. 'Yes, sir. I did!'

To his surprise, Harcourt was grinning.

'Then I'd say you're not a bad judge of character. You won't know, of course, but this fellow Caton and what's left of your squadron bagged nine Stukas this morning!'

But, during the drive back to the airfield and despite the nagging after-effects of the morning's recurring bout of nausea, it was an entirely different subject which Taylor had at the back of his mind – the question of replacements.

It wasn't that there were no experienced pilots in the Desert Air Force. On the contrary, there were more than enough and most of them anxious to exchange their clapped-out Hurricane IIs and Curtiss Kittyhawks for Mark VB Spitfires.

This fact amused Taylor, who, looking back no more than a few weeks, was able to recall the kind of comments which Lee Hillas had thrown around the Mess concerning the squadron's obsolescent Mark VBs. The trouble was that on the Channel front these aircraft were no match for the recently introduced German Focke Wulf 109s and the pilots had been wanting to get their hands on the new Mark IX Spitfires which were being distributed to tactically-sited squadrons as quantities became available.

The difference in the Western Desert was that the Luftwaffe had no Focke Wulf 109s and that, in consequence, the Mark VB Spitfires were operationally superior to the Messerschmitt Bf 109 and the Italian Macchi 202s which, generally, were in a worse condition that the out-dated Hurricane IIs.

One thing was certain, Taylor mused. When the squadron did get its replacements he would have to make sure they were desert experienced and had done their hours on Spitfires.

So, with the interview with the Group Captain behind him and forgotten, he drove back to the airfield in a much better frame of mind than when he had left it.

But, contrary to his beliefs, he had not had things go so much his way at Group Headquarters. For, after he had left, Alan Harcourt had opened the confidential personal file in front of him and thoughtfully pencilled a large question-mark against Taylor's name.

Taylor's heart began to pound when he suddenly found he had no revs and had begun to lose his position in the rear vic of the squadron. Smoke began to stream from somewhere down below the starboard exhaust ports and he guessed that the Me's bullets had gone in there. The two forward pilots were pulling away rapidly and John Clarkson throttled back at a wing-span distance to turn an anxious face to him. But all Taylor could do was point dumbly to his smoking engine. Even the R/T had died!

Taylor also throttled back and then gave the engine a few sharp jabs which picked up some of the revs. But they were insufficient to maintain his altitude. Now the Bf 109s had realised he was straggling and a couple of them dropped back from formation for the easy kill, preparing to run quarter-attacks from astern. Desperately, Taylor pushed forward his control column and with the two Messerschmitts still on his tail dived in a tight, aileron, turn to about ten thousand feet.

His stomach heaved and he shook his head helplessly as he again glanced in his mirror to see them still coming astern. Again, he pushed forward his control column and built up as many revs as he was able and the squirt of enemy tracer split the sky a couple of feet above his canopy. Then, as another line of tracer missed him by inches to port, he flung the Spitfire hard to starboard.

This must be the end! – he told himself. It had to be for there could be no escape from these two, relentless, Me 109s intent on their kill. Somewhere, high above and still hammering at the formation of Dornier 217s, the squadron would have neither the time nor the opportunity to come to his aid. Even John Clarkson had been absorbed into the dogfight.

The second Me flicked across his mirror and he jabbed at the rudder bar, breaking farther to starboard with more tracer flashing to port and behind . . . it could only be a matter of time! He pulled back the stick, desperately seeking more height from his wounded Merlin, but what little response he was able to coax from the motor only brought him back into the path of the first Messerschmitt. He jabbed again at the rudder bar and slewed savagely to port with the wooded and undulating horizon turning and twisting across his vision as he floundered into what he had meant to be a half-roll. He shot a glance to his mirror again to see the Me still there with flashes bursting from the cannon in its airscrew boss. He flung the Spitfire into a near-vertical dive wondering whether he would have the power to pull out of it; and, as he attempted to do so, there came a hail of tracer which snicked the top of his canopy without going through and leaving burn-marks in neat, parallel, lines along the perspex. More bullets slammed into the armour plating behind him and he jerked back the control column in a reflex action rather than in an attempt at finer evasion. And, as the long nose of the Spitfire tilted upwards in a slow and laboured climb with the Merlin spitting back from most of its exhaust ports, glycol began to stream over the canopy, obscuring his vision. He levelled as best he could, praying for the few seconds grace he needed for the gylcol to clear. But it really mattered little for very soon, with the coolant gone, the engine would begin to seize. He looked earthwards for the first time since he had been hit because, at that moment, sideways was the only direction in which he could see from the cockpit. To his starboard was rolling Hampshire countryside, semi-wooded with farms and clusters of small houses here and there, a village pond and a spread of sward. Amongst that typically-English pastoral scene people would still be curled up in their beds, sleeping; none of them knowing or caring about the life and death struggle being fought a few thousand feet above their heads.

His only hope was that soon the Me 109s would have to give up their chase to rejoin the returning Dornier formation – but that meant that their kill had also become an urgency. Yet, miraculously, even with a dicey engine he was still flying! But then, as the glycol cleared, the grey shape of a diving Me appeared in a head-on quarter-attack. Taylor broke to port as its guns and cannons blazed. For a moment he thought he had escaped, but he began to sense a cloying warmth spreading about his waist.

The Me was banking away in a steep climb . . . maybe, please God! he'd played them out for time. But as the possibility entered his mind, so the second Me attacked in an identical quarter-dive to his port side. More bullets tore into his engine, more tracer squirted over his head, striking his tail-plane.

The warmth about his waist was spreading and when he pushed his hand inside his Irvin jacket it came away red and sticky with blood. There was lots of it now, gushing from his stomach and spreading over his thighs in a red film which splattered to the metal floor of the cockpit. He grabbed his oxygen mask and began to breath deeply and, almost immediately, the red curtain which had begun to drop before his eyes, lifted. Surprisingly, he felt no pain and when he looked up into the sky there were no grey shapes of Bf 109 Messerschmitts either above or behind. At last, the bastards had been compelled to rejoin the Dornier formation before it reached the Channel!

He throttled back, speed no longer important: he would clear the village and the hillside beyond even if he had to do so with the airscrew windmilling. The Merlin, despite brave attempts to keep turning, was beginning to seize. He tipped the nose fractionally. Below was a road, but it was full of bends. There was also a meadow of about four acres, but there were irrigation ditches running across it. There were more houses, Godammit! Another small hamlet he'd never even suspected.

Now, the Merlin was stalling and he used what few revs remained to lift over the thatched cottages, but he had not sufficient to clear the wood. Incongruously, he put down the flaps before the Spitfire struck the treetops and went hurtling through the branches, snapping them off as the airscrew churned into the foliage. Then he was only feet above the ground, skidding through bracken and leaving a yellow, leaping, path of flame behind him. There were flames in the cockpit, too, and the Spitfire was ploughing through soft woodland earth with them roaring like a pressure stove around his head. He began to scream . . .

'Dominic! Dominic! For Christ's sake!'

Taylor jerked awake to find Jupp and Romain at his bed-side, shaking him, slapping his face, gripping his shoulders.

His screams subsided to a whimper and then he was still. The two officers, wearing only the shorts in which they slept, stared at each other questioningly; then Jupp leaned over Taylor and began to mop the sweat from his forehead with a handkerchief. Taylor still looked shaken, eyes wild, face a ghastly pallor beneath his tan.

A full minute passed before he swallowed hard and did his best to force a grin.

'That bloody nightmare!'

'Sure! Sure!'

'I was burning in that damned wood, again.'

They released his shoulders, breathing hard. It had not been easy holding down a man of Taylor's strength and size. Jupp pushed a half-full tumbler of whisky at him which Taylor grabbed and downed most of it in one. His face then began to relax and he breathed a great sigh as he stretched himself beneath the single sheet.

'I suppose I've woken up the whole, bloody, airfield!'

But Jupp shrugged.

'We all get nightmares now and then, Dominic,' he said quietly. 'No one's going to ask who was having this one.'

Taylor nodded, then glancing at his wristwatch. It was half-four – just about the time he'd crashed into the Hampshire wood that morning.

The following morning, Dominic Taylor drove the thirty-odd miles back to Group Headquarters.

He had told Jupp he was to attend a further operational conference with Group Captain Alan Harcourt at which Jupp had nodded discreetly and said: 'Very good, sir,' and left it at that. Neither did he nor Romain, who also happened to be in the Orderly Room tent at the time, make any reference to his early morning trouble.

From his point of view Taylor attached little importance to the fact that Jupp and Romain had witnessed him shaking with terror. As Jupp had said at the time – most men in the front line of battle whether they be navy, army, or air force could repress their sub-conscious indefinitely. It had a nasty habit of creeping up on a man and stabbing him in the back at a time when he was least able to resist – when he was lost in a deep sleep of exhaustion.

But, nevertheless, Taylor was worried that the unexpected recurrence of the same nightmare which had sapped his strength during the first months of his convalescence might be directly linked with the physical reaction he'd recently experienced when things had got tough during aerial combat. He'd dismissed the possibility of some bacterial stomach infection for he'd found that, on the ground, his usual healthy appetite had not been impaired. In fact, there had been times in the mess when one or two of the pilots had commented that the desert air seemed to be agreeing with him!

During the two hours he had lain awake turning the recurring nightmare over in his mind, he had decided there was only one thing he could do about it, and that was to risk an off-the-record chat with the Group Medical Officer. Then armed with an expert opinion, he'd take whatever action he considered best for himself and the squadron; and, after all he'd been through before joining Piper Squadron, that might not be easy!

He left the squadron mess after an early breakfast, then making his call from the Operations Room when he had no trouble in fixing an appointment with the Group MO who, over the line, appearred to be a pleasant enough fellow and not at all surprised at Taylor's forthright and even aggressive request.

'You too?' he commented with a laugh; and that helped Taylor who wasted no time in handing over the squadron command to Joe Caton and climbing into a jeep.

The MO turned out to be a young doctor who had had neither time nor opportunity to operate a civilian practice, but had volunteered for the RAF direct from a teaching hospital. He was a tail, lean, fair-haired young man with an easy grin and keen blue eyes; all of which did much to dilute Taylor's rising tensions. His name was Bowers and he took over the interview from the moment Taylor had sunk into a chair opposite him. He prodded that same personal file which Taylor had last seen on Alan Harcourt's desk.

'I ran through this,' he said blandly, flicking over the cover. 'No point in wasting time!'

He looked meditatively across the desk, taking in Taylor's broad shoulders; close-cut jet hair which fitted him like a skullcap; dark piercing eyes and the strong line of the jaw. Then he added: 'You know, you don't look like a psychiatric case to me!'

Taylor pointed to the file.

'I've got those bloody nightmares back!'

'How many?'

'One!'

Bowers smiled. 'I get 'em, too! Quite frequently, in fact! I caught the blitz. Twice. Coventry and Exeter. Doctors haven't time to sit in shelters, either.'

Taylor's expression softened. He was beginning to like this outspoken young man.

'That's not all,' he said more easily. 'I've also started having reaction during combat. Yesterday I took my Section home when I should have engaged. This was the second . . .'

Bowers raised a hand, cutting him short.

'Wait. Wait.' he put in gently. 'Please don't be so quick to commit yourself. There might well be other reasons . . . I mean reasons other than your crash which could affect your metabolism under acute stress . . .'

And from that point, with infinite patience, Bowers went on to outline the causes and effect of battle tension: a change of environment from the relatively peaceful, off-duty, social life of an English airfield to the inhospitable and uncompromising desert; the frustration generated by an enemy who struck from behind and could rarely be called upon to fight in the open; boredom; a lack of mail and communication with home; the heat and the all-enveloping desert which was more restricting than a prison cell; the stark possibility of a sudden and savage death; the grinding and unrelenting responsibility of command.

When he had finished, Taylor smiled ruefully and asked: 'Are you telling me in a roundabout way that I'm wasting your time?'

Bower shook his head.

'No! Not a bit of it! I'm saying that I've known many senior officers, squadron leaders and others much higher up the ranking scale experience identical symptoms. But I have also learned that time and adaptation can heal quickly and invariably does.'

'Then what should I do?'

'Do? Go back to your squadron. If you find youself tensing in combat, then think on what I have told you.' He tapped the personal file. 'So all right! You've had your problems in the past, but my belief is that you'll soon acclimatise. However, if you ever get the idea that you might be risking either lives or aircraft, then you must come back here at once. All right?'

When Taylor returned to Piper Squadron, thoughtful and only partly convinced by what the Group Medical Officer had told him, he found the squadron on 'Readiness' and the pilots clustered in and around the Dispersal 'Hut' with Joe Caton in command. He at once accelerated to his tent where he hurriedly threw on his flying gear and then drove back to Dispersal to join them.

He glanced at his watch.

'Twelve-thirty!' he remarked to no one in particular but Chris Fenton, with his mind on food, told him that lunch was on its way and should be arriving at any time.

But before the dixies of M & V rations, hard-tack biscuits, and tea could be delivered the telephone jangled.

Taylor snatched up the receiver as the others began to put on their helmets, goggles, Irvin jackets and gloves.

Seconds later, Taylor slammed it back into its cradle with face grim. This must be his last chance! He recalled how they'd got away unscathed from that panic break from the defensive circle east of El Daba! Could it be an omen that they were bring scrambled again for that same target area?

He briefed his pilots in short, clipped, sentences. This time the squadron was not going to El Daba alone, but as part top-cover with twelve Kittyhawks of 4 Squadron, South African Air Force; six of 250 Squadron; six of 112 Squadron and twelve P-40 F Curtiss Warhawks of 66 Squadron United States Army Air Force. This strong fighter cover was to escort no more than four Bristol Blenheims which would obliterate the El Daba airfield. At the same time, they would be acting as bait to lure up enemy aircraft which would then be engaged by the large covering force of Allied fighters.

Thus the objective of the 'circus' was twofold: to destroy enemy aircraft on the ground and in the air; and, secondly, to put the El Daba airfield out of action during the remaining few vital days of the build-up to the Alamein attack.

The eight aircraft of Piper Squadron in two Sections each of four: Taylor, Norling, Fenton and Reed; Caton, Ferre, Easton and Ordenneau, were airborne in under four minutes and heading to the rendezvous with the South African squadrons before flying north to join the main formation which was assembling above Alam el Hafla.

The formation had circled once to give the close-escort and escort-cover squadrons time to take up their positions.

Now, the Blenheims were flying at 15,000 feet with six Kittyhawks at either side as close-escort and a full squadron of Kittyhawks behind and a thousand feet higher. Stepped-up behind were twelve more Kittyhawks which made up the escort-cover squadron. Then, high above the bombers and their close-escort at 26,000 feet were the twelve P-40 F Curtiss Warhawks of the USAAF and the eight Spitfires of Piper Squadron. This top-cover was positioned to engage any Luftwaffe fighters which might either peck at the close-escort from the sun, or come up to intercept the bombers.

The formation moved north-west at the speed of the Blenheims – a little in excess of 260 miles an hour, through a clear sky and with the sun now overhead and casting little shadow amongst the wadis and rock outcrops below.

To Piper Squadron this was the first show of force of which they had been a part since their arrival in the Western Desert and did much for their morale. On his part, Dominic Taylor settled himself in his cockpit with only the job in hand foremost in his mind; the traumas of the nightmare and his cap-in-hand visit to the Group MO thrust determinedly to the back of his mind. Now it was up to him! Bowers had helped, without any doubt, and now this crucial sortie would prove the doctor right or wrong.

From 26,000 feet he could make out little of the finer detail on the ground, but had no difficulty in recognising the El Daba airfield which Piper Squadron had strafed a couple of days earlier.

It was still under water from the heavy rains and the Wing Commander, commanding the 'circus' who had been meticulously briefed on the situation by Tactical Reconnaissance, intended to make the most of this opportunity to destroy it.

But as the formation closed the distance, and by sheer coincidence, a close-escort of fourteen Messerschmitt Bf 109s had just take off prior to linking up with a Stuka formation which was assembling to the north and were quick to spot the Allied bombers approaching from the east. Immediately, twelve more Bf 109s were scrambled, making a total of twenty-six which wasted no time in coming up to intercept the Blenheims and their close-escort of Kittyhawks.

Perhaps they were too confident in their numbers that they never saw the Spitfires and Warhawks lurking in the sun, for they launched themselves into a vicious line-astern attack at close-escort height and, for once, not well positioned to operate their climb, dive, fire and continue-diving-through-the-formation-routine. Even so, they struck hard at the high rear of the close-escort and six of the Kittyhawk formation wilted and three went down under their initial bursts. The Messerschmitts, spurred by these easy kills, followed through in shallow dives, still in line-astern, intending to bank sharply and pick off more fighters from the rear of the formation before the escort-cover squadron could adjust. But the Spitfires and Curtiss Warhawks came hurtling from the sun and caught them at their most vulnerable angle – as they were beginning to climb from their shallow dives.

At the point of the top-cover, Dominic Taylor had expected the Me 109s to continue through to the bombers, but they had not done so and the Blenheims were already unloading their bombs on to the flooded airfield and its buildings. Next moment he was roaring into the attack with Piper Squadron stretched behind him, guns and cannons blazing. He caught an Me in his sights for a fraction of a second in a perfect deflection attack and fired on reflex, seeing the bullets rake the port wing and the rear of the fuselage as it climbed clear. He spun round his head, looking for the wingman, suddenly finding himself enjoying the chase. The problem was identifying friend and foe. The similarity between the Warhawks and the Messerschmitts was too close for comfort and most pilots needed to see the black crosses before they dared open fire.

The enemy had now broken formation under the unexpected attack from the sun and the sky had become a whirling mass of twisting and turning aircraft, tracer and smoke; with all attempts at any prearranged patterns of attack forsaken by both sides.

Movement on the port beam caught his eye and he glanced up to see three Me 109s diving towards him. Savagely, he jabbed at the rudder bar and pushed forward his control column into a steep dive; but then he noticed that they were not heading for him but maintaining their dive to the close-escort group which was about two miles ahead by this time. He was about to shout a warning over the R/T, but the amount of chatter pouring through the earphones made it impossible. But, now, the close-escort had spotted the 109s and Taylor, without time to check whether Mike Norling was behind him, swung after them. As they opened fire on the

Kittyhawks he dived on the tail of the rear Messerschmitt and pressed his firing-button. Pieces flew off it from tail to nose and it burst into flame even before he had reached it. He was barely into his breakway dive as it exploded.

'On your tail, sir!'

Jesus!

This was Norling, who had been trying hard to keep up and had got in a burst as the Me had attacked.

Taylor plunged into a barrelled, aileron, turn as tracer sped within feet of his port wing. He then threw the Spitfire into a barrel half-roll farther to starboard and whilst the aircraft was on its side he pulled the stick back firmly and pushed the rudder bar into another steep dive with more aileron turns.

The Me had attempted to dive with him, but now it was way to port with Norling still chasing.

Taylor glanced in his mirror and saw only empty sky, then twisting again to starboard and looking up into the sun before banking tightly to get behind Norling.

Suddenly he felt buoyant. He'd got a kill, dammit! He'd got a kill! His first since he'd knocked out the couple of Stukas above Dieppe. He'd got a kill and that after the bloody nightmare and the crawling he'd done that morning at Group. Christ! He should have waited!

About a thousand feet above he picked out Chris Fenton and Charlie Reed, together on the tail of an Me which was already streaming glycol. Further to the west were more Spitfires. Four of 'em, thank God! Caton and his No. 2 Section were also still in business.

Few statistics were issued by Group Headquarters following the 'circus' over the El Daba airfield; but, subsequently, it transpired that all in all the Desert Air Force were to fly over 200 sorties against that same target. It was evident that General Montgomery needed the airfield neutralising and meant what he said!

Dominic Taylor did, however, learn from general uninformed chatter and the Group 'grape-vine' that the Luftwaffe had lost nine of their Bf 109s that day. The Blenheims had patterned the airfield with bombs and all four had escaped unharmed. But six Kittyhawks and one Warhawk had been lost.

Yet – and this was the thought which warmed Taylor's guts at the time – Piper Squadron had come through the battle victorious and unscarred. Norling and he had confirmed kills. Caton's Section had reported three Bf 109s damaged and two of which they would have finished off had they not got too close to the air-defence machine-guns of the Afrika Korps at the airfield perimeter.

It had been a good day, Taylor thought, and he'd come through his own, private and crucial test with flying colours. And when the pilots left their aircraft with the ground crews for re-arming and re-fuelling, he walked with them to the mess for a belated lunch, joking with them for the first time since they had arrived in the Western Desert. He even let Mike Norling buy him a drink.

But Joe Caton thought it would have been a happier and more appropriate occasion if Stew Maclellan had still been around to buy it!

During the mid-afternoon the first batch of mail reached the squadron since they had arrived in the Western Desert. Its arrival might also have caused some problems, but Post-Corporal Wilf Marsh, who was long experienced in the subtleties of his work on southern airfields during the Battle of Britain, had removed those letters addressed to pilots who had recently failed to return from operations. These he sealed in a large envelope which he sent to the Padre at Group HQ who would decide whether to destroy them or return them to the senders in due course with a suitably worded note.

Joe Caton probably got the biggest batch – eight letters. There were seven from Sue written on alternate days, consecutively numbered, and bearing the Maidstone postmark. There was also one from his father, the Cumberland country vet.

He gripped them tight like a small boy who has unexpectedly received a surprise birthday gift and hurried from the mess to seek the solitude of the blast walls where he had sat earlier with Mike Norling. There, he settled himself down in the warm sand and, with the war suddenly a million miles away, he opened his father's letter first.

As he had expected, there was no more than the customary single sheet written in a bold but not clearly decipherable hand. He read through it rapidly. It was as good as ever this time of year in Millbeck – as though he didn't know! Besides, autumn was always a slack time, but his father hadn't troubled to take a holiday away from the valley. It was no joy travelling in wartime with service men and women cluttering up the trains! This was typical father, Joe thought, still unwilling to accept the war as fact. As ever preferring to lose himself amongst the hills and fells around Skiddaw. The war was into its second year and there was still no sign of him ever changing his head-in-the-sand attitude. Joe smiled wistfully at the mental picture of the burly frame of his father in corduroy slacks and tweed sports coat, leaning on the cottage gate and looking mildly down the long paddock to where a line of elders marked the meandering path of Nether Brook. He would have given anything to have taken Sue up to Cumberland for a few days whilst the autumn tints were at their loveliest – how did they compare with the Western Desert? The letter ended with the usual 'Look after yourself, Joe, and Good Luck, lad – Dad.' No mention of the war. No mention of Dieppe. No mention of the desert. No grumbles about rations or clothing coupons. Just; Good Luck, lad!

He stuffed the sheet back into its envelope and picked up the others, arranging them in their consecutive numbers. Then, carefully, he slit open the first one which had the original RAF post-coded address he had given her during his embarkation leave, and took out the pink notepaper with its usual subtle hint of *Jolie Madame* he had come to know so well.

'Joe, my darling.' A warmth suffused his body which had nothing to do with the heat of the desert.

The Kent harvest had been and gone and it had been a bumper. The neighbours had been helping with the last of the hay and they'd had a party afterwards – oh, Joe! If only you'd been there! Gilly Bowers – you remember Gilly? – had turned up with her boyfriend who'd unexpectedly arrived home on a long furlough. He's in submarines. My! They're far worse than Spitfires, Joe! What a nice foursome we could have made together if only you'd had a little longer leave. They'd been miserable, hadn't they? Only four days before embarkation and I've still no idea where you are, love. You'll write, won't you, as soon as you can . . . but it really was a heavenly leave, wasn't it, darling? . . . (it struck him that she may intentionally be avoiding mentioning George Barclay) . . . Mum is showing me how to make a rug! I'll put it in our bottom drawer and, later, she says I'm to make a patchwork quilt. Remember the one at the Compleat Angler in Marlow?'

How could he ever forget the Compleat Angler and the first bitter-sweet night they had spent together, each dreading the morning and yet another parting.

'With all my love, forever, darling . . .'

He opened the second. More local news about the farm. More hopes for their future together. Some hopeful chatter on reported Russian victories . . . counting the days to your next leave – whenever that will be. Wish I'd some idea where you are!

So ran on more letters, most of them family stuff about the home and the few trials of wartime which managed to seep into that sequestered spot.

His father had written to her. That was surprising for she'd always believed that Bill Caton shied from putting pen to paper – didn't the number of his debtors prove as much? Didn't the fell farmers around Skiddaw owe him a small fortune – just because he never got around to sending them bills?

He didn't really want anything. Just to say how pleased he'd been at the news of their engagement when Joe had called in for a few hours after the Dieppe affair. He hoped they'd waste no time in coming up to Cumberland again soon. After all, there was no reason why Joe shouldn't qualify to take on the practice when the war was over. How about that? asked Sue. She'd never really thought of him having to work for a living. Would he like to be a country vet? Could they really live on Skiddaw? What a lucky girl she was – going to be a vet's wife!

Later, towards the end of the pile, he found the envelopes had been addressed to a Middle East Forces postbox which meant that she must have already received his first letters from the desert. That also meant that her letters could not have been written more than a couple of weeks ago! Great! No longer would they have to write to each other into the blue, as it were.

Yet, Sue wisely asked few questions of life in the Western Desert, restricting herself to inconsequentialities such as was it very, very, hot? Do camels have two humps, or are they dromedaries? She could never remember. And . . . oh, yes! He wasn't going to be a dad! Not just now, anyway. She'd been a little worried . . . no, apprehensive, perhaps, over the past week, but now everything was all right. After those four days it must have been a near thing, she supposed. Of course, she wouldn't have minded, really, but it would be best to wait a while, wouldn't it, darling? After all, if they were going to have children it might be as well to wait until they were married and could enjoy them together . . .

Later that day, Dominic Taylor summoned Joe Caton to his office.

Joe, who had spent the whole afternoon answering Sue's letters, strode jauntily across the stretch of sand to the

Orderly Room tent. In the heat of the day the whole of the lee side was rolled up and he saw Taylor in discussion with Len Jupp, the Adjutant, long before he reached the tent.

Taylor looked up as his shadow crossed the entrance. He indicated a canvas chair.

'Come and crowd round this table, will you Joe? We've got some quick decisions to make and what I really need is your confirmation and support.'

Caton looked into the Squadron Leader's dark eyes, the beads of sweat on his forehead, the damp black hair, the moist smudges around the armpits and collar of his tropical shirt. Whether he, Caton, approved the ideas or not would be of little significance for he was sure that Taylor would not be deflected from his own assessment of the situation – whatever that might be.

'These bloody replacements, Joe!' Taylor exclaimed irritably when Caton had drawn a chair up to the table. 'We need four, right?'

Caton nodded.

'I like the spread we've got now,' Taylor went on, 'over the two Sections. Me, Norling, Fenton and Reed. You, Easton, Ferre and Ordenneau. And that means that if we're to get four replacements to bring the squadron up to operational establishment, then I plan to insist that we get us a complete and competent Section which Jimmy will take over eventually.' With that he paused, seeking agreement.

Caton nodded.

'Fair enough!' he said, but then hesitating before he continued.

Taylor's temper showed.

'Go on, for Christ's sake, Joe! Bloody well say it!'

Caton took a deep breath. He hadn't wanted to appear as though he were knocking at Taylor, but now he'd already committed himself and Taylor knew, as well as he, that there was no way in which he could be gentle.

'I was thinking that we've already lost four pilots and five brand-new Spitfires,' he said quietly. 'Trouble was those boys weren't ready for the kind of action they found themselves in and none of us did a good job on that first crack at El Daba because we were looking out for them and losing our concentration at a time when we needed it most. My guess is that was how Johnnie went!'

Jupp turned to nod his endorsement and Caton knew that Taylor, like everyone else in the squadron, had a lot of time for Len Jupp – an officer who had seen it all before they were born!

'The point is, Joe,' Taylor resumed less harshly, 'that Group, as ever, will be seeking an easy way out.' He pointed roughly in a north-easterly direction as though indicating just where Group HQ lay. 'Literally, they'll have dozens of experienced volunteers wanting to change over to Spitfires. So all right! Let's be having four of 'em here! Give the rookies, when they arrive, a chance to find their feet on Hurricanes first. We want none of 'em at Piper Squadron and that's for certain!'

Caton found himself grinning.

'As your Second-in-Command, what do you want me to do about it?' he asked.

Taylor prodded a sheet of pencil notes on the desk in front of him.

'Do, Joe?' he echoed. 'I don't want you to do a bloody thing! You've already done it!'

'I have? Done what?'

'You've agreed, haven't you?'

Chapter Six

To the eastern side of the Rahman Track, which marked the width of no-man's land between the British 8th Army and the German Afrika Korps, Allied GHQ was trying not to appear unduly worried at the positive increase in enemy activity along the Front. To them it was evident that Field Marshal Erwin Rommel, the Desert Fox, had more than a strong suspicion of what was going on, for German fighting patrols, both armoured and infantry, were persistently probing Allied defences and snatching prisoners whenever a small detachment could be isolated which, in that kind of terrain, was not uncommon.

In consequence, Allied retaliatory raids were intensified, not so much to seek Intelligence, but to try and dissuade the Germans that any Allied operation was imminent.

For the first time in that theatre of war, Allied strength was superior to that of the combined Axis Powers. Reinforcements, arms, ammunition and supplies were still pouring into Alexandria and Suez at an undiminished rate. Amongst these were 300 Sherman tanks equipped with the new and devastating 75 mm gun which President Roosevelt had promised Winston Churchill at the time of General Auchinleck's withdrawal and which would add immeasurable striking power to the Allied divisions.

As yet, the troops who were to fight the forthcoming battles knew little of these preparations. Most units had had a personal visit by the new Commander of the 8th Army, General B. L. Montgomery, who, together with his aggressive training programmes and plans for the future had attempted to boost their flagging morale by airily stating they were soon to be given an opportunity 'to knock Jerry for a six out of Africa!'

This was good, strong, fighting talk but initially it made little real impression upon the frontline troops who, during the past two years had endured the repetitive, daily grind of 'stand-to', weapon cleaning and constant look-out, enlivened too infrequently by an occasional skirmish under the searing heat of the desert day. And, as darkness fell, they would huddle in their foxholes under a single blanket, shivering from the bone-piercing chill of the desert night until dawn and another 'stand-to.'

Sooner or later, a piece of flying shrapnel would hit either them or their buddies and their blood, as thin as water, would drain into the sand, often before medical help could reach them.

So what difference would one more big push make? they asked each other. The scale of the operation was of little significance because no matter how devastating the barrage, how vicious the air-strike, or how many tanks they had in support, ultimately, success or failure would be funnelled down to several thousand isolated mêlées – a handful of chaps from Manchester scrubbing around in the sand with a few fellows from Dortmund. Eventually, they would find themselves on a new stretch of sand on a new spot on the map. But the view would be the same and the whole boring, strength-sapping, existence would begin again.

In the air above the battlefields – Spitfire against Messerschmitt, Warhawk against Macchi – fighting would be even more detached; pilots rarely having to face more than one opponent at a time and probably never even glimpsing his features.

Then, if the Allies were successful, Rommel's Afrika Korps would chase back to Tobruk or even Benghazi; but there would be no end to the desert war. No matter what this feller, Montgomery, said, it would go on for ever and ever!

The pilots of Piper Squadron, one-third below operational establishment, were already beginning to feel the increasing pressure and those amongst them who had survived the Battle of Britain recognised a growing similarity in the routine. The eight hours on and four hours off 'state' could be a punishing involvement depending exactly when the periods dropped. For instance, sleep would usually be possible during the midnight to 4 a.m. stint; whereas, during an afternoon they were able to do little other than lie on their camp-beds streaming with sweat and longing for their next duty turn and the rush of cool air against their faces at 20,000 feet. So far, the squadron had flown no night sorties. Nevertheless, pilots were compelled to stand-to on the chance of enemy strafing from the air or the kind of long range shelling from self-propelled guns which they had experienced during their second night at the airfield.

During this period there had been an increasing number of sorties by the Desert Air Force against the Luftwaffe base at El Daba which, to the pilots, appeared to have a charmed life. But, on the other hand, they unbegrudgingly paid tribute to the resourcefulness of the German ground crews who managed to keep the airfield functioning on a day-to-day basis.

As the days passed, pilots of the Desert Air Force – fighters, bombers and reconnaissance – became increasingly alarmed at the mounting total of Allied losses over El Daba to such a degree that the sorties became collectively known as the 'Daba Prang.' At higher levels, questions were raised as to whether such an expenditure in aircraft and pilots warranted the involvement. Yet, pressure was maintained on El Daba as on other Luftwaffe bases and on the coastal railway along which came most of the Afrika Korps' supplies.

A mid-October issue of the Allied Fighter Command Intelligence Summary, issued down to squadron leader level, reported the Desert Air Force to have destroyed in excess of 110 Bf 109s on the ground at El Daba and damaged as many more, whilst some forty-odd had been shot down in combat. What the Summary did not say, however, was that the toll of Allied aircraft over the target was approximately the same.

But GHQ, Cairo, had the satisfaction in knowing that the Axis Powers, with their supply lines stretched to dangerous limits, could least afford such losses.

Piper Squadron had been quickly absorbed into this routine and, as the days passed, their acclimatisation to the desert, its hardships and its unrelenting inhospitability, improved. They flew their sorties stolidly and without too many complaints and their aggression in combat compensated the boredom of life on the ground. And, despite such involvement and the steadily rising pressure whether flying in two Sections, a single Section, or even in pairs, they had surprisingly only one casualty – Chris Fenton.

This happened on the morning of 18th October when the squadron had, along with the rest of the Desert Air Force, been briefed on the commencement of a new air offensive in strength against Axis ground troops as part of the build-up to the Alamein offensive.

At 11.00 hours on that day, the eight Spitfires of Piper Squadron were scrambled to provide top-cover to an independent group of six 'Bombfires' briefed to strafe German armour. The target selected was west of the Rusweisat Ridge where the German 21st Panzer Division hinged on the Front with the Italian Ariete Division.

The 'Bombfires' were Mk VC Spitfires which had been modified and tested in Malta where they had been fitted with improvised bomb racks and used to attack Axis airfields in Sicily. The Spitfires had been selected to replace the Hurri-bombers because the Luftwaffe, very much aware of the questionable performance of the Hurricane II against the Messerschmitt Bf 109, had not hesitated to send up their fighters to intercept. The Spitfires, which had two 250 pound bombs slung beneath their two outboard cannons, were an entirely different proposition. For, even with their bomb loads, and discounting a slightly reduced rate of climb above 19,000 feet, had all the advantages of the Spitfire VB against the Bf 109.

So far as Piper Squadron were involved in the 'Bombfire'

sortie they also had the reassuring knowledge that the pilots of these aircraft were a highly-experienced and courageous group of individuals who had already proved their worth against the Luftwaffe and the Regia Aeronautica over Italy and Sicily as well as the Western Desert.

Piper Squadron rendezvoused with the 'Bombfires' at 11.10 hours thirty miles east of the Rusweisat Ridge. There they adopted a pre-planned formation: two vics of three 'Bombfires', each vic escorted on either side by a pair of Spitfires and, from the ground, appearing together as a formidable group of fourteen Spitfires hell-bent on trouble.

The 'Bombfires' began their climb to 18,000 feet, circling at plus-4 boost, taking twenty minutes to reach this height with maximum 500 pound bomb loads. Piper Squadron maintained formation during the climb, observing that their adapted sister-aircraft seemed to handle normally and beginning to wonder what all the fuss had been about during the briefing. Now and then they would glance across at the 'Bombfire' pilots with the query in their eyes. But the 'Bombfire' pilots were invariably going through their standard air-search routine with relaxed and even languid expressions. To them, obviously, this was just another day!

Forward, with the leading vic of 'Bombfires', Dominic Taylor on their port side and with Mike Norling farther to his port beam and a hundred yards behind, felt the same kind of anticipation at this new experience as did the rest of the Piper Squadron pilots on this sortie. It was going to be interesting watching Panzer tanks being pin-pointed by 250 pound bombs from 10,000 feet. It was also going to be interesting seeing what the Luftwaffe planned to do about fourteen Spitfires trespassing into their air-space! The problems of only a week earlier were becoming less and less significant.

With the rear vic of 'Bombfires', Easton and Ordenneau of Two Section flying wide apart and above and behind Caton and Ferre in a top-cover role were also relaxed, continuously glancing rearwards into the sun. If there was going to be an attempt at interception, then that was the only direction from which it could come.

Below, now, were the Allied artillery positions, visible only because the heavy guns were involved in some form of counter-battery action – could be the 9th Australian Division Taylor guessed, recalling the brief. That meant that within minutes they would reach the medium artillery, infantry, armour and reconnaissance and then the wide stretch of minefields between the opposing German reconnaissance and infantry.

But where the hell was the Luftwaffe? Where were the German aces whose names were becoming legend throughout the Western Desert? Names like Werner Schroer of I/JG 27 Staffel and Hans-Arnold Stahlschmitt of III/JG 27 Staffel? Where these characters too canny to pitch their reputations and their Messerschmitt Bf 109s against the immensely superior Spitfires? Or . . . or, were they already somewhere up in the sun, still climbing whilst they built up an overwhelming strike-formation? That was something for the raiders to think about and the possibility was printed indelibly in the minds of the pilots. What price a few Panzers, anyway?

Flak began to spread ahead of them, pin-pointing their course to any ground batteries or intercepting squadrons which might be interested. This was heavy stuff. Filthy black puff-clouds which polluted the clear azure of the desert sky and the German gunners were making no attempt to traverse, waiting for the Spitfires to fly into their shrapnel. Very soon they were amongst the mushrooming explosions which caused changes in air pressure which the pilots compensated by rudder and stick, the stench of cordite seeping through their part-open canopies.

'Hello, Piper Leader! Hello, Piper Leader! This is Sigma Leader confirming procedure! Strafing attack begins now!' This was the Squadron Leader commanding the 'Bombfires.'

'OK Sigma Leader! This is Piper Leader. Proceed on plan!' This was Dominic Taylor, quietly relaxed, acknowledging. 'Roger and out!'

Piper Squadron throttled back, allowing the 'Bombfires' to

move into a single echelon of six aircraft, line-astern.

Seconds later their CO again came on the R/T. 'Hello, Piper Leader! Targets ahead, clear and distinct. Procedure continues. Out!'

Piper Squadron boosted their throttles until their eight aircraft, now in line-astern formation, were on the port side of the 'Bombfires' maintaining speed and position.

Taylor came on the R/T to his pilots.

'Hello, Yellow Leader! Break Yellow Three and Yellow Four to top-cover!'

Caton answered immediately.

'OK, Piper Leader! Wilco!' Then, to his Section: 'You heard that, Jimmy? Robert? Go up to Angels Twenty-four. Two-four! Break now!'

And, without acknowledging, Jimmy Easton and Robert Ordenneau angled the long noses of their Spitfires into a steep climb at the same time banking in a wide enough circle to take them beyond the target area from which they would be heading back east by the time the 'Bombfire' attack went in.

Caton, with Ferre behind, checked his speed at around 320 miles an hour holding position. Now the whole formation had become two parallel lines of Spitfires, each of six aircraft in close line-astern formations.

Below, the target as defined in the Group brief, was looking very vulnerable. There were three columns of heavy tanks ploughing doggedly through a stretch of loose sand which rose from the churning tracks into a thickening, pluming, fog. Yet, even from 20,000 feet it was still possible to follow the path of each armoured vehicle, no doubt with its commander too intent on keeping pace and maintaining position in the column to worry about air attacks.

Caton counted, dipping his port wing a fraction to widen his field of vision: there were sixty of them, maybe! Three columns of twenty some ten miles behind their own front lines and heading north-west. He wondered whether Tactical Reconnaissance HQ had also got a fix on them.

'Bloody Ities!'

This was Mike Norling, as impatient as ever for the action to begin. And, on this occasion, there came no snarling rebuke from Dominic Taylor, who was also taking a long look. They were Italian, all right! There was no doubt about that and probably heading to tighten the hinge-link between the Ariete Division and the 21st Panzers.

The shallow dive had taken the formation down to 18,000 feet. They were almost above the target and it seemed they had still not been spotted by the tank formation. Neither were there any signs of the Luftwaffe or the Regia Aeronautica coming up to intercept. Even the flak from the east had petered out.

'Hello, Piper Leader! This is Sigma Leader! Main attack imminent!' A slight pause, then he spoke to his pilots: 'OK, Sigma Squadron. Follow me down. Pair off to cover all three columns. We've all done this before! Attack begins . . . Now!'

At the word 'Now' he half-rolled his 'Bombfire' on to its back and dived vertically with the two aircraft of his Section hard on his tail which then echeloned to starboard. Immediately, the leader of the second Section duplicated the manoeuvre and with his aircraft also in line-astern plunged on to the tank columns at angles of eighty-five to ninety degrees.

Using their reflector sights as bomb sights, they released their bombs at 10,000 feet by which time the speed of their dives had built up in excess of 500 miles an hour.

Without such nose-heavy acceleration, Piper Squadron were unable to keep up, even though they 'pulled the plug', opening their throttles as wide as they would go. And the 'Bombfires' maintained their speed to a strafing altitude chasing after their bombs with machine-guns and cannons blazing through a scattering of light flak now being thrown up by the Italians. They were pulling out to re-form line-abreast by the time Piper Squadron was on the target and by which time, too, their bombs were bursting with devastating accuracy amongst the tanks. As Piper Squadron opened up with machine-guns and cannons, they caught fleeting glimpses of bucking and exploding tanks, men scrambling in panic through the leaping flames and then, in seconds, they were through and climbing into position alongside the 'Bombfires' to head back east.

Now they had an opportunity to glimpse the results of the swift attack which had caught the Italians so much off their guard. Smoke billowed from the formation which had halted and bodies, which had been thrown twenty to thirty yards from the column, littered the sand. Others, badly wonnded, crawled pitifully towards those who had been lucky enough to survive the attack. Twelve or so tanks were burning furiously, the dense columns of smoke snatched by the desert wind into long black streamers which floated eastwards towards their own forward infantry positions.

There was still no sign of enemy interception. The 'Bombfire' leader commented on this laconically: 'Looks as though we got away with this one, Piper Leader. You bring us luck! Maybe we should see you again, some time!'

Taylor came back.

'Bloody good show, Sigma Leader!' He even managed a laugh. 'We could use some of you chaps when you get fed up with the bombs.' Then, to Caton: 'Hello, Yellow Leader! Re-form Yellow Three and Four! We'll go home, now!'

It was on the return flight over the Italian forward positions that a derisory spread of flak happened to hit Chris Fenton's Spitfire.

He immediately switched his R/T to 'Send'.

'Hello, Piper Leader! Christ! But I'm hit again! She's pouring oil and I can't see a bloody thing through my windscreen. I'm dropping out of the way, below formation!' There was anger as well as frustration in his voice.

Taylor came back at once.

'Can you make it, Chris?'

'Not a chance, sir! It's getting hot in here. I'm going to jump before I have a fire!'

'Hold your bearing. I'm coming with you!'

Fenton eased back his throttle with the oil temperature

soaring and the Merlin taking on a harsher and what he would have termed a more expensive note. He throttled back farther as Taylor came alongside, holding position a wing span from his port beam. The CO was smiling encouragingly, relieved in the knowledge that Fenton was neither wounded nor pinned in his cockpit. He pointed due east in the direction of the Allied lines. If Fenton could eke out another few miles from his seizing Merlin the armoured divisions could be relied upon to send out a vehicle to pick him up.

'You're sure you can't put her down, Chris?' It would be better still to salvage whatever remained of the Spitfire.

But Fenton was adamant. 'Not a chance, sir!'

Above, the squadron had also throttled back, vulnerable, yet unwilling to leave either Fenton or Taylor as stragglers – a situation which could give heart to any Regia Aeronautica Macchi 202 pilots who might be lurking in the sun.

Fenton sat rigid, the control column tight in his hands, eyes fixed on the instrument panel. At any moment now the engine would seize. If he was going to jump, then he had to do it now!

He switched back to 'Send'.

'Now or never! Going now, sir!'

He braced himself, determined to show no panic, shifting his seat to the full 'up' positions, then sliding back the canopy to its maximum and locking it open. With stiffening fingers he began to unfasten his harness. For a moment he sat upright, perfectly still, holding his breath. Then, he grasped his parachute rip-cord with one hand, holding the stick firmly with the other as he rolled the aircraft over on to its back and dropped quietly into space.

Taylor watched him plummet a good thousand feet and when, seconds later, the white parachute blossomed he boosted his throttle and climbed steeply to rejoin his squadron.

That evening, the pilots of Piper Squadron were sitting down to their late meal when the sudden scream of air-raid sirens sent them leaping from the table and dashing to their aircraft. The first bomb landed seconds later, bursting short of the blast walls. This could have been a lucky break for the Luftwaffe – ten yards to the west and it would have landed smack on a reserve fuel dump.

Jean-Michel Ferre with Robert Ordenneau hard on his heels was first to his Spitfire, pressing the starter button and yelling: *'Vite! Vite! Vite!'* to a ground crew caught halfway through re-arming.

Three Heinkel IIIs swept overhead before the Merlin fired, the nose-gunners cannon shells raking the ground behind it. But, then, Ferre was moving, turning sharply on to the airstrip with his engine roaring, striving to get away. To his left a column of black cordite smoke mushroomed through an almighty explosion and for a fleeting moment he hesitated, scared that his friend had been hit. But then he saw Ordenneau's Spitfire alongside him, also building up revs as they roared down the runway line-abreast.

As the two Frenchmen became airborne, so Dominic Taylor reached the runway with more bombs dropping close and blasting great columns of sand high into the air on either side. Through this yellow fog, tore lumps of shrapnel varying from quarter-inch cubes to razor-sharp slivers over a foot long. He glanced up into the sky, seeing two Heinkels line-abreast, pulling out of their bombing-run with two Spitfires on their tails but losing pace rapidly. He hoped that Ferre and Ordenneau would give their attention to fast climbing rather that letting their hate for the enemy take precedence over common sense. Three pilots were safely off the ground, he told himself. With a little more luck the squadron would survive the raid for, in such an emergency, Len Jupp and George Romain would take up the stand-by aircraft though they would avoid getting themselves involved in any whirling dogfight.

But, as Jupp dashed the extra fifty yards to where the two stand-by aircraft were parked, he looked upwards to see the protruding glazed nose and twin engines of a Heinkel III at about 4,000 feet. As he watched, a stick of bombs detached themselves from beneath the fuselage to come falling untidily, but with unerring aim, towards the airfield. Jupp halted and, for a full three seconds, he froze transfixed amidst the pandemonium, his eyes on the falling bombs as they drifted towards him as though drawn by some invisible magnet. And, when he did move, the bombs landed astride the two stand-by Spitfires and they blew up simultaneously in one gigantic ball of flame which billowed high into the desert sky, scorching his face and arms. Now there was nothing he could do and he burrowed his face in his arms and lay still in the sand with the debris falling about him.

The steady bump-bump-bump of Bofors guns on the perimeter opened up as Caton and Easton taxied together to the airstrip, moving delicately around bomb craters. There came more bomb bursts and some cannon fire from a Heinkel fuselage gunner as the enemy aircraft climbed away. And, to his left, Caton saw a Spitfire slew over on to its port wing which sheered on impact whilst the aircraft tilted up on to its nose, the airscrew churning wildly into the sand.

Charlie Reed hadn't made it for one!

He wondered about Mike Norling who had always been amongst the first two or three to get himself airborne in a flap.

It was tricky taking off over the broken surface and after his wheels left the ground they touched again and he more or less bounced his Spitfire into the air under a mighty surge of throttle.

As he began to climb he clenched his teeth, hauling hard back on the control column. This could be as dangerous a moment as when he had been on the ground for the fast-moving Heinkel IIIs with a top speed almost equal to that of the Spitfire, could be a problem in any form of aerial combat. Their armament of five 7.9 mm MG 15 machine-guns; one 7·9 mm MG 17 machine-gun; and one 20 mm MG FF cannon which together formed an almost 360 degree field of fire, constituted a force which had to be respected. Even so, they could be very vulnerable to a Mk VB Spitfire with height initiative.

He tugged at the control column as he might have the reins of a hesitant horse before a difficult jump.

'Come on, damn you! For Christ's sake climb!'

The Merlin seemed slow to respond, as though unwilling to face the He IIIs. But when he glanced to his left he saw Jimmy Easton level and frowning into the sky to the west which was pock-marked with anti-aircraft bursts, as strategically placed batteries beyond the perimeter attempted to cut off the Luftwaffe's escape route.

Higher, and also to the west. Ferre and Ordenneau had linked with Dominic Taylor who had formed them into line-astern with himself at the point. They were still climbing in a tight circle, positioning themselves for an attack. But, from below, this looked a hopeless gesture for the Heinkels were coming out of their second and what was sure to be their last bombing run before turning for home.

Caton sensed movement in his mirror and for a fleeting second his pulse raced until he recognised the familiar frontal outline of a Spitfire which could only be that of Mike Norling. He wondered what had kept him.

He switched his R/T to 'Send'.

'Jimmy! Mike! We'll hold this formation! Maybe we can give the fellers up there a hand!'

But Taylor, even in the heat of the scramble had made a quick appreciation of the developing situation. He knew that the two stand-by Spitfires had been destroyed on the ground; and that Charlie Reed might well be dead and his aircraft probably a complete write-off. This was a hell of a set-back but surely, for Christ's sake, the early warning system should have prevented it! Somebody, somewhere between the Rahman Track and the airfield, should have picked up the Heinkel formation either visually or on radar. What the hell was Group HQ doing? Anyway, for once he'd have a come-back at Alan Harcourt! But, now, he remained clinically calm. Three Heinkels were already heading back west; but the other three, in line-astern formation, were only just beginning to turn away from the burning airfield.

He switched to 'Send' and his orders to Ferre and Ordenneau were curt and to the point.

'We'll all take the bastard at the rear and give him all we've got! Follow me!'

And, as he shouted the last two words, he swung his Spitfire into a quarter-frontal attack on the last of the Heinkels and tracer from the top fuselage gunners of the other two streamed past him at either side. There came to him the kind of elation which he had experienced during his early combat days before the crash. His thumb took first pressure on the firing-button. He couldn't really miss! The great bulk of the Heinkel with its fifty-four foot fuselage and seventy-four foot wing span seemed to screen him from most of the airfield. He ran in so close that he could see the prone body of the nose gunner, very vulnerable surrounded only by perspex; the the taut face of the fuselage gunner, contrasting chalk-white against his black flying helmet. As he fired, the wings of his Spitfire shook with vibration, jarring his vision at the vital moment; but he watched his cannon and machine-guns rake the enemy aircraft before he broke away to port under full throttle.

A split second later Jean-Michel Ferre, with heart surging at having the enemy at his mercy, duplicated the attack, eyes flicking across the bloody mask which had been the fuselage gunner's face, then sending in a long burst with devastating accuracy. The bomber heeled heavily on to its starboard wing, the pilot dead, the nose gunner miraculously unwounded and struggling desperately with his harness.

Behind, Ordenneau had only time to break away to starboard as the Heinkel exploded and pieces of it rattled off his wings and fuselage.

He glimpsed a body drop from the wreckage, arms and legs flaying the air and then, suddenly and apart from the steady throb of his own engine, all was quiet. The five remaining

Heinkels had gone. The Bofors guns beyond the perimeter had ceased firing whilst, above, the sooty puff-clouds of their air-bursts were quickly thinning in the desert wind. He pushed his throttle forward to catch up with Taylor and his friend, Ferre, who were flying low and line-abreast, assessing the damage to the airfield. To his starboard beam and still high were the three Spitfires of Caton, Easton and Norling. He hoped their buddy, Charlie Reed, would be all right . . . then his face creased in a wry grin as he recalled that, once again, Chris Fenton had missed all the excitement.

About a minute later, Taylor led the five Spitfires down, threading his way between black-rimmed craters and jolting precariously over bumps much larger than they had appeared from the air.

When he had taxied to Dispersal he remained in his cockpit until the rest of the pilots were down, gazing thoughtfully at the still-burning fragments of the disintegrated stand-by aircraft over which fire-crews were busy squirting foam. Then, as the pilots clambered from their aircraft he, too, jumped to the ground, scowling at the number of casualties and the amount of damage which had been none of their responsibility.

Len Jupp hurried to his side.

'George and me tried, Dominic!' he blurted in a rush as though he had been storing up those words. 'We did our best, but we just couldn't make it!'

Taylor forced a grin and thumped him on the back, then pointing to the pile of junk which had been the He III, now a tangled, smoking, heap scattered a half mile or so to the north of the administrative tents which, surprisingly, were still standing.

'Damn glad you didn't, Len!' he answered with feeling 'Another couple of seconds and probably I wouldn't be talking to you right now!' Then, more sharply, with his dark eyes again creased in a worried frown, he asked: 'How's Charlie?'

Jupp took a couple of seconds to consider the question.

'Charlie Reed . . . ? Oh, you mean after his take-off?' He pointed halfway down the runway where Charlie Reed's Spitfire was tilted on to its nose and it port wing lying in the sand beside it as though it had just dropped off. 'Oh, Charlie's OK! He climbed out and walked to medical with a cut arm. Bloody mad he was, though! But he said his Spit's OK if somebody can fix him a wing back on!'

They had reached the knot of pilots who looked up with apprehensive faces as the CO approached; not sure whether to voice their own anger at the lack of warning or to let Taylor do the talking. Mike Norling was just making up his mind to get his feelings off his chest when there came the roar of an engine from the direction of the administrative tents. They turned as one man to see a sand-camouflaged 15 cwt truck lurching over the pitted ground towards them.

It braked to a juddering halt and a fair-haired Flight Lieutenant, wearing khaki drill and a service cap, sprang from the seat beside the driver. He had a lean, deeply-tanned, face and the long hair which spread from beneath the cap was sunbleached almost white. He grinned amiably as he looked easily round the group, then pointing westwards and skywards.

'I say! Hell of a prang that!' he observed lightly. 'But one of you chaps certainly knocked spots off the old One-One-One!' Then asking: 'Any of you fellows happen to be the CO? er . . . Squadron Leader Taylor, they tell me!'

Taylor fixed him with his most malevolent glare.

'I'm Taylor!' he said.

'Ah . . . !' The newcomer looked him over for a couple of seconds, squared his shoulders and saluted smartly.

'I'm Penallen, sir! Flight Lieutenant Russel Penallen!'

'So?'

'We're your replacements, sir!' He grinned at Taylor's expression. 'Didn't you know about us? My three chaps are in the back of the truck with the kits . . . keeping out of the way until we find what the drill is . . .' His voice tailed off as Taylor, with a face like thunder, turned to his adjutant.

'Did we know about this, Len?'

Jupp shook his head emphatically. 'We knew just as much about replacements as we knew about the raid,' he said.

Penallen found his voice again.

'Actually, it was a bit of a rush, sir! We'd to make up our minds within the hour or we'd have been on our way to Malta.'

'Malta?' Taylor echoed, whilst the rest of the group became suddenly interested.

'Yes, sir! You won't know, of course, but we were some of the chaps on the sortie with you earlier today against the Itie armour. You remember! The Bombfires! Put up a jolly good show together, I thought. Anyway, Groupie gave us the chance to join Monty's show . . .' His face brightened visibly . . . 'We've an idea the balloon is to go up in a day or so. Is that right? Anyway, like I said, we jumped at the chance and here we are. After all, you did mention over the R/T that you'd like us! New Spits are being ferried from Suez in the morning.' He shrugged, having said his piece, smiling easily round the group, waiting reaction.

The frown had left Taylor's brow and he was looking hard at Len Jupp with the suggestion of a grin breaking the hard corners of his mouth.

He turned back to Penallen.

'Tell me, Mr Penallen,' he said quietly. 'How long have you been flying Spitfires?'

Penallen looked up into the sky, thinking, then asking: 'Do you mean me, personally, sir, or my Section?'

'Your Section!'

Penallen shrugged. 'Oh, I'd guess about eighteen months. Greece, Crete, Malta. You know the drill! We also did a tour over here in the early days with Wavell's show.' He smiled. 'We've all got gongs, you know, apart from poor old Couttsie, but we don't bother to wear 'em out here. But they do go down well with the girls at Shepheards, in Cairo.'

Taylor was actually smiling. He pointed to the 15 cwt truck with the airman-driver sitting patiently behind the wheel and no sign of movement from beneath the canvas tilt.

'Then you'd better introduce your Section, Mr Penallen.'

By way of reply, Penallen lifted his voice a few decibels. 'All right, chaps!' he called. 'This is it! Out you come!'

There followed the crash of the tailboard and three men eased themselves stiffly to the ground. They, too, wore khaki drill and service caps easing the cramp from their limbs as they joined their Flight Leader and assessing the assembled Piper Squadron pilots in much the same way as Penallen had done. Penallen wasted no time in beginning the introductions.

'Flying Officer Laurie Coutts, sir! He's from Edinburgh, don't you know. Then . . . er . . . Warrant Officer Davey . . . I mean, David Bennett, DFM and lastly, Sergeant . . . I must emphasise the rank! Sergeant George Leigh-Flemying DFM and Bar.' He looked back at Taylor, grinning, anticipating the kind of reaction he had witnessed on so many other occasions when he had presented this lean, aristocratic, young man. 'I believe, sir,' he added, attempting to keep a straight-face, 'that Sergeant Leigh-Flemyng is planning to be a Labour Peer one day! He's never been really keen on promotion though he doesn't mind the odd gong now and then. Anyway, you'll be getting all the gen from Group if they ever get round to sending you our documents.'

There followed handshakes all round, the pilots of Piper Squadron clearly as delighted as their CO at the unexpected arrival of such talent.

As Taylor turned towards the Orderly Room tent to make his initial report to Group HQ on the enemy air raid, he found Penallan at his side.

'As we're not expecting our kites until the morning, sir,' he said, 'perhaps we might volunteer to give the ground crews a hand tidying up the mess around the service bays. I mean we can't get to know these chaps too quickly, can we?'

But before Taylor could agree, a second 15 cwt truck appeared from the direction of the administrative tents, and as it sped towards them they recognised the 7th Armoured Brigade flashes painted boldly on the front wings.

The pilots halted, waiting developments. Then, those who knew him, cheered loudly as Chris Fenton stepped out. He paused only to wave his thanks to the trooper-driver before hurrying to join his friends, his eyes wide in disbelief at the sight of the bomb damage, the burning stand-by Spitfires and the disintegrated Heinkel.

'Why does everything always happen whilst I'm away?' he asked plaintively.

When he spotted the new arrivals he shook his head and shrugged helplessly.

To Dominic Taylor the day had been eventful, but not unsatisfactorily so. The morning's sortie with the 'Bombfires' had been very successful and, despite the havoc caused to the airfield in the early evening, the squadron had acquitted itself with honour. He had chalked up another kill and the remains of the Heinkel He III littered the desert half-a-mile away to prove it. Chris Fenton, who could have been lost, was very much alive and now he had a full-strength squadron to lead into the Alamein offensive.

Thus, Operation Lightfoot, now imminent, would cause him no problems for, unlike the lengthy preparations before the Dieppe raid, there were to be no involved and lengthy briefing sessions. Each squadron would operate on a specialised brief and so continue until countermanded.

Perhaps it would have helped the operation of the squadron if Penallen's Section of replacements had had some combat experience with the two Piper Sections but, under the circumstances, that was out of the question.

So, so far as he was concerned, everything seemed to be going well and he looked towards the morrow with optimism and some enthusiasm.

But, that night, his recurring nightmare returned in all its stark realism. The most terrifying thing about it was that the pattern of the dream unaccountably changed towards the end – something which had never happened before.

The beginning – the dramatic build-up to the horrifying

climax – was the same: the desperate, lone, battle with the two pitiless Bf 109s; his inability to break contact and the lack of help from the rest of his squadron.

Once again there came the splatter of enemy tracer through his wings and engine cowling; the immediate drop in engine revs and more bullets slamming into the armour plating at the back of his seat; the blood from the wound in his stomach; the endless series of tight, aileron turns; the uncontrolled dive he was sure was taking him to his death . . . all these were the same as they had been a hundred times before.

Then had followed the usual respite – the surge of hope before the awful crash when the two Messerschmitts had been compelled to forsake their kill. Then came the difference! To starboard there was no longer the rolling English countryside with its sprinkling of farms and hamlets. In this new ending to the dream there was nothing but the brown rock and burning sand of the Western Desert which stretched unbroken as far as he could see. And, this time, when his engine finally cut he did not lift the Spitfire's labouring nose over a sleeping Hampshire village, but over the snaking lines of Allied trenches around which men were lying, screaming, bleeding and dying. And the only flames he saw were those in his own cockpit which roared about his feet and legs. And, to add to the horror, his right foot was jammed between the rudder bar and the side of the cockpit.

As on previous occasions, Jupp and Romain shook him awake, stilling his screams, plying him with neat whisky. And, as before, Taylor took control of himself. But the dream was a severe set-back to his morale at a time when he was going to need all the courage he could muster.

Chapter Seven

At 21.40 hours – 'Zero' minus twenty – on the night of Friday, 23rd October, a thousand artillery pieces of the British 8th Army opened up along the twenty-five mile front between the Qattara Depression in the south and the Mediterranean Sea north of El Alamein.

The battle for North Africa had begun.

The barrage, the most tremendous used by any nation since the First World War, crashed and roared with a rising fury, breaking the darkness with bolts of orange-white flame and the quickening, jarring, jolt of high explosive. To the west, men of the infantry and artillery batteries of the Afrika Korps; the 15th and 21st Panzer Divisions; and the Italian Ariete Division, huddled low in trenches dug into the loose, shifting, sand seeking protection from the thunder of bursting shells. Shrapnel began to scythe over their positions, zipping through the air at a speed too fast for the human eye to catch, yet each and every piece promising bloody death.

But the barrage, despite its ferocity, held few real terrors for these veterans of the Western Desert. Long ago they had learned to heap themselves in the bottom of their slit-trenches, close their eyes against the flying grit and stuff pieces of field-dressing into their ears to muffle the pandemonium raging about them.

After the first five minutes or so, German gunners miles to the west, were aligning their howitzers and super-heavies on to prearranged defensive fire-tasks – the very areas in which the Allied assault troops were forming up.

Farther forward, medium and field-gunners were bracketing the strip of ground between the Allied front line and the eastern edge of the minefield. Here, they would put down a concentrated counter-barrage of high-explosive – one through which the Allied infantry and sappers would have to pass before they could start lifting the mines. Their problem would be deciding where the Allied creeping-barrage ended and the German counter-barrage began. At the best they would have to advance through one of them – at the worst, through both!

Thus, the scene was set for the most ambitious operation of the war, so far.

At 'Zero'-hour, 22.00 hours, Allied assault infantry: Australian, British, Indian, New Zealand, Rhodesian and South African, wearing shorts, bush shirts, and with steel helmets tilted over their foreheads rose with fixed bayonets from their foxholes to march stolidly into the teeth of the German barrage. And, as they did so, the Allied artillery lifted from the German forward positions to pre-selected targets farther to the rear, the fire-control now coming directly under the command of Royal Artillery forward observation officers moving with the infantry.

By this time, visibility had lessened under a thickening yellow haze of dust rising to upwards of 200 feet above the fury of the shelling from both armies.

The moon, dull and waxen from the ground, no longer cast long shadows over the undulating lines of distant dunes; but, in the clear night sky above the battlefield, it shone brightly along the leading edges of the wings and the sharper angles of the camouflaged fuselages of the Desert Air Force. More than seventy bombers and flare-dropping aircraft were already probing deep into enemy-held territory, bombing artillery positions and supply lines, turning night into day above the attacking Allied infantry.

Sortie had followed sortie with little initial interference from the Luftwaffe. Fires began to break out to the west as ammunition and fuel dumps were hit, boosting the soldiers' morale. Far to the south, there had been a lucky hit on a main dump and columns of flame-laced smoke were pluming

3,000 feet into the sky, a visible tribute to the persistency and courage of the bomber crews.

As more troops joined the advance, so light bombers flew low over the minefields laying down thick, curling, smoke-screens. Through these, sappers crawled on hands and knees towards the first line of mines to begin the hazardous task of clearing and taping the two parallel corridors through which the Allied infantry and armour were to pass. Then, as the light bombers turned for home to refuel, squadrons of Hurricanes manned by pilots trained in night-flying, could be heard roaring westwards to launch strafing attacks on Luftwaffe airfields as far back as Fuka.

Initially, the attack was considered to be progressing according to schedule; but, by midnight, it became apparent to Allied GHQ that much of the initial momentum had been lost. Allied assault battalions were still pinned down by withering enfilade fire on the wrong side of the minefield and crews of Wellington bombers had reported desperate battles being fought along the whole shell-splattered length of the Rahman Track.

It had also been reported that farther south, infantry divisions of British 13 Corps were also bogged down and, so far, had not secured their initial objectives.

With dawn, and the commencement of intermittent, darting, sorties by the Luftwaffe, it became apparent that the Allied advance had slowed almost to a standstill. British armoured divisions, which were to have broken through the outer screen of the Afrika Korps and 'crumbled the enemy from inside', had been halted and were sitting, vulnerable, in the middle of the minefields which had not yet been cleared. In consequence, there was no question of them swanning freely to the enemy's rear for some time and, as a result, the infantry divisions in support were also suffering heavy casualties.

Yet, Montgomery hung on to his original plan of opening up the two corridors even though his armoured divisions became increasingly harried by the Luftwaffe. But things were far from easy for the German pilots for, in low-level strafing attacks on tanks and armoured cars, they had more-or-less to fly directly into the concentrated fire from their guns and, at the same time, run the gauntlet with the Desert Air Force and flanking Bofors units and medium anti-aircraft batteries shooting over open sights. Their choice was the devil or the deep blue sea: either they risked heavy losses amongst their already depleted formations, or they left the Allied armour unmolested.

The Desert Air Force at once took steps to effect a quick annihilation of the Luftwaffe and from the early hours of darkness, when 73 Squadron had led the initial attacks in support of Allied ground troops, their fighters had inflicted telling casualties upon the enemy. But the Germans were far too astute to risk death in whirling dogfights, preferring to race for the safety of their own lines whenever Allied fighters appeared in strength. This was very frustrating to pilots of the Desert Air Force and it soon became evident to those in command that the biggest contribution to the success of the operation could be achieved by blasting the German infantry and panzers whenever they got an opportunity.

By the time Piper Squadron was committed – shortly after 05.00 hours on the morning of 24th October – the general brief to fighter squadrons had been revised. Depending upon Group HQ's appreciation of the current battle situation, squadrons would, wherever possible operate a series of what the Germans termed 'Freie Jagd' sorties. In rough translation, 'Freie Jagd' could be termed an overall licence to hit the enemy hard on the ground on the chance that such action could develop into aerial combat.

Dominic Taylor, still a little apprehensive by the changing and frightening sequences of his nightmares, faced that dawn with a troubled frown. But the rest of his pilots, including the four 'Bombfire' replacements, were in a lively mood and anxious to get a grandstand view of the Allied progress in Operation Lightfoot. Initial reports, so far circulated to squadrons from Group HQ, had been pointedly non-committal and those with earlier battle-support experience pulled wry faces in shrewd guesses that specific and vital objectives had not yet been taken.

They had breakfasted in the Dispersal 'Hut' with the full squadron on 'state', as ever enjoying that brief, cool, start to the desert day; and with the roar of gunfire carried from the west by the prevailing wind sounding no more than a dozen miles away. But they had no time to linger for they were scrambled before they got to the marmalade stage, racing to their Spitfires still chewing last mouthfuls of hard-tack biscuits and cold bacon.

The squadron was airborne within four minutes, flying in the standard formation of three Sections, each of two widely-spaced pairs and none weaving. This was something which the original members of Piper Squadron were happy to see re-adopted. The temporary, but unavoidable, return to vics of three with one high and weaving had caused them more than a little anxiety at times.

Dominic Taylor was at the point as usual with Norling, Fenton and Reed. Joe Caton, leading Yellow Section as top-cover had Ferre as his Number Two; Easton and Ordenneau as Three and Four. The replacement Section of 'Bombfire' pilots, now coded Orange Section, were on Taylor's starboard beam. All four pilots of this Section: Penallen, Coutts, Bennett and Leigh-Flemyng, as well as Chris Fenton of Taylor's Section, had new and only partially-tested Spitfires which had been delivered from Suez by ferry pilots twelve hours earlier.

At Taylor's insistence, Group HQ had granted the squadron a day's 'Release' to give the 'Bombfire' pilots an opportunity to adjust to Mark VBs and check out any minor faults; and, at the same time, to provide some leeway for the squadron to weld together as a whole.

In consequence, most of the day had been spent in the air a

couple of dozen miles to the east of the airfield above rough outcrop and sand where they went through the book from basic formation flying to ground strafing and aerial combat. All, including Taylor, were pleased by the results and the kind of close harmony which had been achieved between Sections within such a short space of time. In addition, off-duty periods in both messes had been brightened by the influx of new and extrovert personalities.

Now, flying at 20,000 feet and still climbing, there would be no problems so far as navigation was concerned for the squadron had, as a primary target, been directed to the area now code-named the 'Fist.' This was a salient, or bulge, which, through the night, had been forced into the German line by British 30 Corps to the north of El Alamein and a couple of miles south of the coast.

As a secondary target, farther south, was the strategic enemy strongpoint along the Himeimat Ridge which had still not been taken and was causing Allied infantry problems from German artillery observed from what, in the desert, amounted to a commanding height. Since first light the Desert Air Force had also concentrated much of its light-bomber and fighter-bomber force against this ridge.

Now, from what Piper Squadron could see from 20,000 feet-plus the amount of movement along the snaking support lines westwards was an inspiring sight. Lines of tanks, armoured cars, lorried-infantry and supply vehicles were moving forward in never-ending numbers, relentlessly closing the distance to the battle zones, feeding new life-blood through the vital arteries of the attack.

At lower altitudes, formations of Allied aircraft were instantly identifiable from their position in the sun. There were Hurricanes, Tomahawks, Warhawks, Beaufighters, Spitfires, all with the same intent of purpose to ease the lot of the troops on the ground either by direct support or by chasing enemy aircraft from the sky.

To the far west, surrounded by circling covering fighters,

and apparently unmolested by the Luftwaffe, Wellington bombers were high over their target areas. The explosions from their bombs could be seen clearly, despite the yellow murk of the sand haze which rose from the ground beneath them.

To those of Piper Squadron who had fought over Dieppe a couple of months earlier, the immediate battle situation appeared not unsimilar for, as they approached the front line, they came upon squadrons of Allied fighter-bombers and fighters circling high over the 'Fist' salient waiting to be committed to the action below. As with Dieppe, the 'Fist' was too narrow to contain the full power of the Allied air offensive. And, also as at Dieppe, the Luftwaffe had still not made its appearance in strength even though the Desert Air Force had been in action for over three hours.

There was little doubt that the Afrika Korps gunners would not understand what had happened to their air-support. And, with no Allied tanks to shoot at, they traversed their guns on maximum elevation and pumped shells up and amongst the strafing Desert Air Force which, to them, seemed to be having a field-day.

Most of this flak as well as that from anti-aircraft batteries astride the coast road, burst below Piper Squadron who had now reached 25,000 feet with most of the pilots trying to be first to spot pin-pricks of Bf 109s coming to do battle from the west.

Dominic Taylor was not one of these. The nightmare and a certain amount of associated tension during yesterday's practice runs had left him still a little apprehensive. He tried to convince himself that once the battle began – as, indeed, when he had engaged and shot down the Heinkel III over the airfield a couple of days ago – he would find himself not only able to cope, but as competent as he had ever been.

Stepped up a further 3,000 feet and to the rear, Joe Caton's Yellow Section breathed cool oxygen, now and then glancing down at their two sister-Sections on the lookout for trouble. Caton didn't mind being top-cover yet again for it was apparent that, under the critical eyes of the 'Bombfire' pilots and the squadron very soon likely to be in the centre of the arena, Taylor was laying-on this strike-attack strictly by the book. Sadly, there was no question at all of Yellow Section engaging ground targets and, also, they were unlikely to be committed to any kind of action unless the Luftwaffe attempted to intercept. Yet, under desert conditions a clear sky could be transformed within seconds into a whirling gyrating, display of roaring, spinning and diving aircraft.

Jean-Michel Ferre had been impulsively outspoken in his disappointment: 'The first time we have the Boches at our mercy and Robert and I have to stay up high!'

Jimmy Easton had grinned across the distance of a couple of wing spans, trying to catch Caton's eye and fully expecting to hear Taylor explosively bawling out the Frenchman for chatting over the R/T.

Taylor had heard, but he had not let the incident disturb his concentration for, as the squadron drew closer to the 'Fist' there was much developing on the ground to claim his attention. From that altitude the salient reminded him of pre-war Hollywood films of the French Foreign Legion besieged in remote desert forts. For here, too, the outline of the bulge was clearly visible, circling in a loop above the almost straight line of the Front which ran due south and parallel to the Rahman Track. There was a great deal of activity. The three sides of the salient exposed to the enemy were bristling with small arms fire whilst, to the west, Wellington bombers were making repeated runs over the German heavy batteries which were maintaining a concentrated fire-programme against the 'Fist'.

Taylor switched his R/T to 'Send'.

'Hello, Piper Squadron! This is Piper Leader! Looks too busy down there. We'll forget it for now and try the Ridge.' His voice was calmly confident. There followed a short pause then: 'Adjust to new bearing for secondary target. Figures: Two. Two. Four. Now!'

Caton watched Taylor's Section throttle back whilst

Penallen's Orange Section, on the starboard beam, banked south-west in a wide arc and accurately maintaining formation.

As the squadron approached the Himeimat Ridge it at once became apparent that, here, the battle was much more fluid. There were armoured units of both armies swanning about east of the Ridge whilst, farther south, a full-scale tank battle was developing. There, through swirling dust and the flat blast of exploding shells from Allied batteries to the east, Sherman tanks in widely deployed formations were storming Axis positions on the reverse slope of the Ridge where the minefield had evidently been breached.

'Hello, Piper Squadron!' This was Taylor again, assessing the situation. 'We'll give our tanks a hand! We go down now to Angels Five, Sections in line-astern. Joe! You stay up there with Yellow Section. Follow me, Orange! Here we go . . . Now!'

Caton flipped his R/T to 'Send'.

'Yellow Section. This is Yellow Leader. Keep your eyes on the sky, fellers! I'll watch what goes on down there.'

He glanced in his mirror and saw Ferre in position on his tail. The Frenchman must have seen the movement of Caton's head from behind for he gave him the thumbs-up sign which Caton acknowledged by the lift of a hand.

His eyes followed the two attacking Sections which had now levelled at the 5,000 feet specified by Taylor before dropping to a strafing height from which they would sight on selected targets. From above, the operation looked studiedly efficient but, below, fire from entrenched Spandau machine-guns was hosing around the Sections and uniquely dangerous by the sheer weight of its concentration.

Mike Norling roared behind Taylor at a distance of less than fifty yards with the lumbering bulks of Mark VI Panzer tanks intermittently flitting in and out of his reflector sight. Seconds later, Taylor's Spitfire shuddered as his guns and cannon roared and, below, one of the Panzers suddenly disintegrated into flame whilst a section of infantry, which had been advancing behind it, crumpled silently to the ground.

Norling swung a couple of degrees to port, pressed his firing-button and more men crumpled with the shells from his cannons ploughing up the sand around them. For one fleeting moment he could glimpse the stark terror on the faces of those who had not fallen as they panicked to cover behind their tanks.

Next came Chris Fenton and Charlie Reed, sensibly moving farther to port to widen the effective front of the attack. As they opened fire, Taylor was already climbing clear, but as Norling boosted his throttle after him, there came a sudden flurry of black airbursts which appeared ahead without warning as though haphazardly flung there by some mighty hand. Momentarily, his engine faltered as lumps of shrapnel peppered his port wing.

Brutally, he knocked his R/T switch over to 'Send'.

'Bloody SP guns a couple of hundred yards west! There's a wadi or something there! See it?'

Despite a sudden rise in heart-beat he had not been too shaken to spot the concentration of self-propelled guns dug hull-down beyond the Ridge.

He had expected Taylor to seize the opportunity to drive the squadron attack deeper, but Penallen came on the R/T from his Orange Section who were committed to their dive.

'Leave the bastards to me!'

It came as an order rather than a suggestion and Orange Section sped only feet below the steeply-climbing Fenton and Reed, diving into the bright chain of muzzle flashes from the self-propelled guns with machine-guns and cannons hammering. The gunners attempted to traverse to the new targets, but they were far too slow and Orange Section's shells struck the open hulls, sending shrapnel ricochetting around the inner, open-topped, compartments, scything and re-scything into the crews' flesh until it spent itself.

At the tail of Orange Section, Dave Bennett was just in time to see three of the guns explode simultaneously as, from the east, Allied armour taking advantage of the Spitfires' intervention, raced to drive home their attack.

Taylor continued to climb, watching Orange Section pull clear of the small-arms fire before switching his R/T to 'Send'.

'Good show, Piper Squadron!' he said matter-of-factly. 'We'll save the rest of the ammunition for the flight home. Just in case!' Then, to Caton's Yellow Section. 'What's it like up there, Joe?'

Caton came back immediately.

'Like a summer's day! Not a Kraut in sight!'

As the squadron reformed, Russel Penallen was thinking how effectively his Section could have used bombs against the self-propelled guns. The change from fighter-bomber to pursuit-fighter was going to have its limitations – particularly if the Luftwaffe continued to remain in hiding!

Flying eastwards and parallel to the coast they came upon an air battle over the sea where it appeared that a flight of Beaufighters were engaging a merchant ship escorted by a single destroyer, two Junkers Ju 88s and a Dornier Do 24 flying-boat. The pilots were at once intrigued for it was apparent that the merchant ship must be carrying a cargo of some importance to the Axis desert war effort for it to attempt to reach Tobruk at the height of the Allied offensive. It was also significant that no other Allied aircraft chose to interfere, leaving the Beaufighters alone with their target-brief.

By the time Piper Squadron was close enough to pick out detail, the merchant ship and the destroyer were both listing and smoking; and the Dornier 24 flying-boat, hopelessly outmanoeuvred in its bulk and restricting top speed of 200 miles an hour, had plunged in flames into the sea. Two of the Beaufighters had cut off the Ju 88's line of escape westwards, leaving the remaining five to position themselves for the coup-de-grâce. Piper Squadron watched them dive line-astern into a beautifully-executed frontal quarter-attack; and the Junkers, with their gunners scarcely firing a shot in reply, just keeled over and followed the flying-boat into the sea. As a parting gesture, the Beaufighter leader did himself a smooth victory roll before heading his formation back east.

Still high on top-cover, Joe Caton experienced that same twinge of sympathy towards those vulnerable German airman who had just died so horribly and so pointlessly, as he had at the time of his Stuka party a couple of weeks earlier.

But Dominic Taylor's reaction was entirely different, for the flames which had engulfed the Germans were the same kind of flames which had tortured him in the Hampshire wood and which still returned to him in the throes of his nightmare. Besides, his engine was beginning to spit back through the exhaust ports and that could mean either a fractured fuel or oil pipe – probably as a result of the small-arms concentration over the Himeimat Ridge.

Wasn't that what had happened to the Luftwaffe star, Hans-Joachim Marseille, on the day of Piper Squadron's arrival in the Western Desert?

Christ! Could it be that he, too, might burn up from such a piddling thing as a busted piece of coppper piping . . . ?

His vision began to blur and, once again, there came the tingling sensation to his finger-tips, the start of the headache. He throttled back and then, in an unpredictable surge of temper, savagely jabbed it forward again and when he looked back at his instruments he saw that the oil pressure was remaining steady. Thank Christ for that, anyway! Now, somehow he'd to keep his cool – at least until he got east of the Rahman Track.

Taylor did make it back to base and, in the brief respite which the squadron enjoyed during the process of refuelling and rearming, the pilots unanimously agreed that the strafing attack had, generally, been successful.

Certainly they had given a hand to the Allied armour struggling at the Himeimat Ridge as well as demonstrating to the Afrika Korps that the Desert Air Force had well and truly knocked the Luftwaffe out of the sky – for the time being, at any rate. That they would very soon be back and in strength was a certainty and a situation to which the squadron looked ahead with anticipation and some apprehension. In the meantime, the pilots would put their feet up; for today, undoubtedly, was going to be very, very, busy! But, during the squadron's short spell on 'Released', there arrived a signal from Group HQ of special significance. Len Jupp, who was the first officer to read it, at once smiled broadly, clamped on his cap and hurried to find Dominic Taylor. The CO, who had still not fully recovered from his attack of combat-nerves, was lying on his bunk endeavouring to regain his composure before making his initial report to Group on the early-morning sortie.

He looked up irritably as Jupp stooped beneath the open tent flap.

'Oh, Jesus! What it is now, Len?'

Jupp was smiling.

'Signal from Group!' Then, after a moment's pause. 'Shall I read?'

'Yeah! Yeah! If you must!'

'Joe's got his gong at last! DFC!'

At the news, Taylor sprang impulsively to his feet and the iron band which had been gripping his temples suddenly eased. He found himself smiling broadly as he crossed to the Adjutant, almost snatching the message form from him. He read and then looked back at Jupp.

'The Stuka party!'

'Yes! Nine down and three damaged. And all in under four minutes!'

Taylor reached for his cap.

'Come on, Len!' he said. 'Let's go and tell the fellers.'

During a scratch lunch the squadron drank to Caton's health and continued success in diluted orange juice. There were comments typical of the personalities of the pilots. These ranged from Mike Norling's brusque: 'Should have given you it eighteen months back, mate!' to Penallen's rather condescending: 'Welcome to the club, Joe! Though, of course, you won't be wearing it . . .'

Jean-Michel Ferre was clearly the most deeply moved, intensely and demonstrably proud of his Section Leader's success and the fact that the sortie in which he had flown wingman to him had been acknowledged in such a positive manner.

From Caton's own point of view, at last here was something worthwhile for him to tell Sue. When he got a chance – and the ribbon – he would have a photograph taken for her and also one for his father.

Later, he sought out Jimmy Easton who, true to his nature, had kept himself from the hub-bub of noisy congratulations, preferring to have a few quiet words with his old friend at a time when they could talk more freely.

He pushed out his hand as Caton approached with the same infectious smile on his face which Caton had got to know so well over the past twelve months.

'Congratulation, Joe, old chap!' he said quietly, then adding. 'Of course, as Mike put it, you deserved it ages ago. I really had thought about recommending you myself!'

Caton grinned, flattered to see a man of Easton's integrity so genuinely pleased.

'There's something else, Jimmy,' he said.

Easton lifted his eyebrows.

'Let me guess! You've got the VC but it's being kept dark for security reasons!'

Caton laughed aloud.

'How'd you know? But there *is* something else. When this flap's over I've to go to Cairo for the investiture.' He shrugged. 'GHQ Middle East. Probably Monty himself. Who knows?'

Easton nodded.

'But of course!' he agreed. 'You can't win a prize gong and expect it to come up with the M and V, can you?'

'No! Not really. I suppose. But what I was about to say was that there'll be a couple of days leave thrown in with it. In Cairo, that is, and I'm being offered a chance to bring along a colleague with me. Well . . . I was wondering if you'd like to come along, Jimmy. You know! For old times sake. You and I have been through a lot of rough stuff together during this past year. So how about it?'

Easton was smiling, clearly surprised and a little moved at the spontaneity of Caton's suggestion.

But he said lightly: 'I was always led to believe that it was dad who'd to stand beside the hero boy at an investiture. But, as I don't suppose he's likely to be passing through Cairo, the answer's a loud and resounding Yes! Sure I'll come along and see you made famous, Joe!'

There were eight more sorties that day, four at full squadron strength; two at Section strength and two with only a couple of aircraft scrambled to probe enemy defences to the south where the 13th Australian Division was still making heavy weather.

As yet, the Luftwaffe had still not appeared in strength and, certainly, seemed unwilling to commit itself to any form of aerial combat. Occasionally, Stukas escorted by Messerschmitt Bf 109s had had a tilt at Allied armour and infantry, but had called off their attacks and turned for home whenever Allied fighters had tried to intercept. There were no casualties amongst Piper Squadron that day though, as with Dominic Taylor and Mike Norling during the early morning sortie, several of the aircraft had been peppered by small-arms concentrations from Afrika Korps positions west of the minefields.

But Taylor did not let the pressure on the squadron interfere with Joe Caton's moment of glory which, come hell or high water, just had to be celebrated there and then.

He, therefore, cooked the 'on-state' roster to give Yellow Section a free evening and, whilst the rest of the squadron was grouped in and around the Dispersal 'Hut', Caton, Easton and the two French sergeants, Ferre and Ordenneau, had the run of the officers' mess and bar.

It was towards the end of the evening, when the creeping desert cold had begun to take the edge off the heat of the day, that Caton grinned tipsily at the wingman.

'You know, Jean-Michel,' he said confidentially over yet another tumbler of the inevitable John O'Keefe's Real Canadian Ale, 'I think you and I are getting to like this desert life!'

Chapter Eight

The following morning the battle situation had improved considerably but had, still, very much to be won. The Allied positions at the 'Fist' to the north of El Alamein had been consolidated and the salient driven deeper into Africa Korps territory which armoured columns were valiantly trying to widen both to the north and south.

Farther south, Allied infantry had taken the Miteiriya Ridge and strengthened their positions with what armour had fought its way through the minefields against the full weight of the 15th Panzer Division. The Germans were now reported to be bringing the 21st Panzer Division and the 90th Light Armoured Division to push home their counter-attacks against the Ridge. But these were being subjected to determined bombing attacks by Wellingtons which were still maintaining their pressure.

Since dawn, Desert Air Force Fighter Command had been at full stretch. Priority sorties were been flown repeatedly against the still-operational Luftwaffe airfields at El Daba and Fuka as well as against road-tanker convoys on their way from Sidi Barrani to refuel the hard-pressed Panzer divisions.

On top of these, the usual patrols and strafing attacks in support of Allied ground formations had to be intensified to help consolidate the rapidly developing military gains.

It was to this fluid and, as yet, indecisive battle situation that Joe Caton awoke with a sore head to find Yellow Section 'on-state' whilst Russel Penallen's Orange Section, which had spent most of the hour of darkness in the Dispersal 'Hut,' had a chance to sleep.

Caton, with his Irvin jacket over his arm and flying helmet

perched on top of his head, set off to the Dispersal 'Hut' with Jimmy Easton trudging sleepily through the loose sand, the chill of dawn giving way to a blood-red sun mounting the sand ridges to the east.

When they reached the 'Hut' they found Ferre and Ordenneau already there. Ordenneau was pouring fresh coffee whilst Taylor and his Section, which had been 'on-state' since 04.00 hours, were lolling uncomfortably in their field chairs.

'You like coffee, Joe? Jimmy?'

At long last the French sergeants had got round to addressing their officer colleagues by their christian names.

Both nodded and when Ordenneau passed them the steaming mugs they sank gratefully into adjacent chairs, cupping the mugs in their hands, anxious for the sun to climb a little higher.

A little later, breakfast arrived at which Taylor and his Section stirred themselves to munch broodily at the usual rations of tinned bacon and hard-tack biscuits. But none of Caton's Section appeared to be hungry and dug only into the butter and marmalade, frequently demanding more coffee. Presently, orderlies reappeared to clear away what remained of the food and the pilots sat frowning into the brightening desert, each with an ear attuned to the field telephone on the table at the back of the tent.

Still, nothing happened; but that did not surprise them for they had had no report on the overall progress of Operation Lightfoot and were unaware of Group HQ's programme so far as it affected their squadron.

Then, out of the blue, Wilf Marsh arrived with a bundle of mail. Immediately, their pensive lethargy was changed magically into cheerful good humour as they crowded round the short, burly, form of the post-corporal.

Ferre and Ordenneau both had letters - from their families in Occupied France! It subsequently became known that these had been smuggled out through the Confrérie de Notre Dame Resistance Group by way of a British Specia

Operations Executive agent. And now, the two French boys stood side-by-side in the rising desert dawn, clutching the envelopes in the handwriting they knew so well and with tears streaming down their cheeks.

As he had hoped, Joe Caton got a fistful. There were four from Sue and one from his father. But the one which intrigued him was from Sue, across the top of the envelope of which she had printed in bold, red, letters – 'Open this First!'

He grinned as he settled himself back in his field chair, lifting the pink envelope to his nose and sensing the faint aroma of *Jolie Madame*, the perfume with which she usual touched her letters to him. He opened the envelope, pausing momentarily to glance malevolently as the field telephone, thinking: 'If that bloody bell dares to ring now, I'll smash it to pieces . . .'

But it didn't ring and he took out Sue's letter which, to his surprise, covered only one side of a single sheet of notepaper. From the instructions on the envelope he had anticipated more.

He began to read and, as he did so, a smile touched his lips which spread warmly across his face.

> '*Darling*!' it began. And he could almost see the bright eagerness in her eyes; the sweet, impulsive curve of her lips.
>
> '*Darling!*
> *Guess what! Great news! We've the chance of the cottage at the end of the long paddock. You remember? We walked round there during your last leave. Watermill Cottage it's called. The old wheel is still there and it works when the race fills. Isn't that marvellous? Old Annie Jackson is leaving next month to join her daughter in Devizes and now Dad says we can have it. Say you'll like it, too, darling! Please! It means we can be together whilst you study in London and then, when you've got your degree, we can go up to Skiddaw as we'd planned. I was terrified that we'd still be apart for ages, even after the war is over, But now we can be together . . . forever! Please write quickly, darling. Straight away! This*

very moment! And tell me that we'll have Watermill Cottage. We've loads of old furniture stacked about the farm and I can start work brightening it up at once. We might even be able to spend your next leave there. Won't that be heaven? Please write now!

All my love, as ever,

Sue.'

Caton sat still in his chair with the open letter clutched in his hand, his eyes staring dreamily up at the apex of the tent. He was not seeing the drab stretch of sun-bleached canvas but the gentle slope down the long paddock to the brook and the ancient, stone-built, millrace alongside the bulk of the cottage which had once been a watermill. In his thoughts it was still summer, just as it had been during his last leave, and Sue was standing at the door waiting for him as he ran through the long grass to join her.

He found himself smiling at the soap-opera picture which his imagination had conjured up and, only then, did he notice that Jimmy Easton sitting in the chair beside him was watching him curiously.

Easton grinned as he stuffed his own letter back into its envelope.

'Good news, Joe?'

'Yeah! I'll say!' Caton readily. Then, impulsively, he pushed Sue's letter at his friend. 'You read that, Jimmy, and tell me whether or not it's good news!'

'Should I . . . ?'

'Yeah! Yeah! Go ahead!'

Easton took the letter and read through it slowly. And when he handed it back to Caton he, too, was smiling broadly.

'You're a lucky man, Joe,' he said. 'All this and a DFC!'

Caton laughed.

'Christ! Yes! For a moment I'd forgotten the gong!'

'Then hadn't you better reply?'

'What? Now? On-state?'

'Why not? The lady says you've to write back at once, doesn't she? Straight away. Well, this is straight away, isn't it? Right now!'

Caton nodded and pushed himself to his feet, crossing quickly to the field telephone table where he tore several sheets from the signal pad. He also took an envelope with which he returned to his chair, eyes on Easton who was nodding encouragingly.

He sat down and from his breast pocket he took a pencil and began to write as the words came to him.

'Darling Sue,

What super news! I just can't believe it. Really, I can't! Of course we'll have Watermill Cottage and, of course, I remember it. Wasn't it me who remarked that it would just be right for us? Thank your Dad, thank Mrs Jackson and thank you, my darling. Like you said, I'm wasting no time in writing back – hence the stationery. I'm on-state, would you believe it? and writing this in my flying gear with the sun getting hotter with every word.' He paused, then, seeking words which might give a reasonably cheerful account of life in the desert. Then, he went on to add that he was beginning to settle down a little better and that he still felt he had done the right thing in not taking an easy way out by accepting the posting to Stanmore. It would have been nice to have been close to her but, after all, people had to fight if they were going to win the war . . . He wandered on in the same vein for a few more lines and then signed in the same way as she had done –

'All my love, as ever

Joe.'

Only then as a postcript did he add:

'Oh! I almost forgot! I've got me a gong. DFC!'

He addressed the envelope and then turned to the rest of his correspondence taking up the letter with the Cumberland postmark from his father. He had just begun to slit open the envelope when the harsh jangle of the telephone broke his concentration, momentarily startling him as Dominic Taylor pushed roughly past to grab the receiver, making pencil notes as he listened.

Caton stood up, too, beginning to shove the envelopes into the side pocket of his Irvin jacket but then, on second thoughts, he took out the letter he had written to Sue and propped it on its edge against the telephone. There was just a chance that the post-corporal, or one of Penallen's Section, might come along and whisk it on its way. After all, Sue had been very insistent that he should waste no time!

Taylor dropped the receiver back into its cradle and turned wrily to his seven pilots.

'OK, fellers! We scramble! Jerry has counter-attacked on Kidney Ridge and he's throwing everything he's got against our boys. SP guns, flame-throwers and tanks. Our job is to attack his forming-up zones. Same drill as before, unless the Luftwaffe decides to put up Stukas and fighters!' His voice sharpened. 'Right! Let's go!'

It took the squadron seven minutes to become airborne for the aircraft had been widely dispersed around the runway perimeter in the event of more harassment from either the Luftwaffe or self-propelled guns.

They climbed to 18,000 feet six miles west of the airfield knowing there was no sudden-death urgency in this sortie. It was a matter of chance whether their arrival at the Ridge coincided with some tactical need for reinforcements or not. It was better to take time and formulate a plan as the situation developed.

As the two Sections climbed in their 'finger-four' formations, Taylor took time to rummage in the side pocket of his Irvin jacket to pull out an envelope he had received in the morning's unexpected batch of mail. From it he extracted a snapshot, very amateurishly taken. It was a blurred photograph of a young woman, elegantly posed in front of the distinctive radiator grill and long bonnet of a Rolls-Royce. She was smiling condescendingly at the camera, snooty, chin high. He turned the photograph over. On the reverse was written in a hurried scribble: 'Found this heap parked in Windsor. Couldn't resist! I'd a hell of a job setting the camera and then dashing back before it clicked. Best, as ever. Helen.'

Taylor grinned. Helen Morley! The girl Lee Hillas and he had shared since way back in 1940 and as crazy as ever. He recalled their last afternoon together in Henley, just before the Dieppe raid, and the things she had said about their long association. But now, if she were sincere, it seemed that she and Lee Hillas had finally lost touch. For good, she insisted. He wondered! It was no trouble at all for a girl like Helen to adjust the direction of her affections to suit circumstances. What was it she used to say? . . . 'when one car door closes another opens!'

He thrust the envelope back into his pocket, still smiling, then shifting himself in his seat, checking his instruments. As the altimeter hovered around 19,000 feet he flicked his R/T switch to 'Send'.

'Hello, Piper Squadron! This is Piper Leader! Alter course to figures: One-Eight-Seven. Now!'

Caton acknowledged and settled down with Ferre up and behind him, Jimmy Easton and Ordenneau on his starboard beam. He glanced to his left to see Taylor leaning forward in his cockpit as, at the same time, he tilted the nose of his Spitfire to give him a wider vision directly ahead.

'Bandits! Bandits!' This was Taylor with a rising exuberance in his voice. 'Directly ahead! Maybe they're above the ridge. Form in-line, Yellow Leader!'

Yellow Section throttled back with Caton and Ferre taking forward positions.

Now they could see there was some spirited action above Kidney Ridge as well as on the ground below where it seemed a full-scale tank battle was in progress amongst a swirling haze of yellow dust. Above, in the clear morning sky, was a confused mix of Messerschmitt Bf 109s, Hurricanes and Curtiss Kittyhawks. Farther in the distance, two aircraft which were unidentifiable were spiralling to the ground and streaming black smoke. As Taylor watched, a match-stick figure detached itself from one of them and, seconds later, the white canopy of a parachute billowed above it. He wondered whether the lucky man was friend or foe and whether his luck would hold to drift him behind his own lines.

He switched again to 'Send'.

'Climb Piper Squadron. Let's make it Angels Two-Five before we get there!'

As he spoke and eased his control column back he was wishing that his nerves were as cool as his voice had suggested they might be for, already, there were suggestions of the tingling sensations in his fingertips. He breathed a great sigh and lifted his eyes heavenwards as though in supplication.

Why, for Christ's sake? Why?

The crippling headache was bound to follow. Then the nausea, the impaired vision, and they weren't even in action yet.

He should hand over command of the squadron to Joe Caton, here and now! But how could he? What kind of a reaction could he expect if he were drop out of his responsibilities the moment an air battle became imminent? His teeth clamped tight over his bottom lip. Somehow he'd got to hold on and, somehow, he'd got to pull the squadron through whatever lay ahead. Jesus! If Helen Morley could see him now!

Below and ahead was the oval despression of rock and sand which had been named Kidney Ridge. And, though now little could be seen of the tank battle raging in the dust cloud, it was apparent that their approach had been observed for five or six Bf 109s had broken from the dogfight to climb rapidly. The original brief by Group to harass enemy forming-up zones could be forgotten; for, like it or not, Piper Squadron was going to be involved in a kind of aerial combat more in keeping with the Channel Front than the Western Desert.

'Bandits! Bandits! Bandits! More coming in from starboard at two o'clock!' This was Robert Ordenneau up at the rear of Yellow Section, voice rising in his excitement.

'Roger, Yellow Four!'

Taylor acknowledged with heart pounding and the first vicious stabs of pain bombarding his temples. Then adding: 'Maintain formation, Piper Squadron. Keep climbing fast!'

Now, the whole detail of Kidney Ridge was lost in swirling sand and dust, isolating the aircraft in a clean, pure, world of their own.

At long last, Caton thought, here in the morning sky above the desert, pilot would pit his wits, his skill and his courage against pilot. What was happening on the ground was no longer of any significance. He smiled grimly to himself at the thought as he pulled his control column farther towards him, matching his angle of ascent to that of Charlie Reed at the rear of Taylor's Section.

He glanced from one to the other of the approaching enemy formations. Neither was adjusting course or even trying to manoeuvre, each intent on presenting a minimum target. Inevitably, they would meet Piper Squadron in combined quarter-frontal attacks.

Seconds later, tracer drifted towards them from the flank formation which had fired too early. The bullets arced below at which Ferre instinctively lifted his aircraft a further hundred feet above Caton, thumb already on his firing-button.

'Don't break!' Taylor's voice was reflecting some tension now. 'We'll take the bastards ahead, first! Ignore the others! Follow me!'

He levelled out at a little above 24,000 feet whilst Caton and his Section continued to climb in preparation for a diving-support attack. With luck, they would have a couple of thousand feet height advantage over the enemy. Taylor had decided well!

More tracer and more flak and this time dangerously close as it floated towards them before accelerating overhead at an incredible speed. The Me 109s had corrected the gravity drop of their bullets.

'Go! Go! Go!' yelled Taylor and with the pain now

clamping tight across his temples he aligned the nose of his Spitfire on the leading Messerschmitt. The split-second it crossed the green dot of his reflector sight, at a range of no more than 200 yards and at a relative velocity in excess of 600 miles an hour, he pressed his firing-button in a three second burst.

He lifted his eyes from the sight, narrowing them in pain, shaking his head in an attempt to clear the spreading blind spots from his vision. And, through the haze he saw the tail-plane sheer from the fuselage and what was left of the Messerschmitt spin away.

Christ! But he'd got himself a kill, even in his condition! But now he could scarcely see, the left half of his vision had kaleidoscoped into a complex of brightly coloured lights. He shook his head yet again and hauled back on the stick knowing that he would survive only so long as he maintained height. The rest of the squadron must take over the initiative now.

'On your tail, Piper Leader!'

This was Mike Norling who, on Taylor's unpredictable action, had been thrown out of position; at which Taylor instinctively flung his aircraft into a tight half-roll and pushed forward his control column under a boost of power to launch himself into the near oblivion of a vertical dive. He held his breath, creasing his face against the pain, seeing only a confused blur below him. But there were no bullets thudding into the armour plating at the back of his seat, no cannon shells tearing the wings to ribbons. He'd managed to escape, thanks to Norling! He breathed his relief as he pulled out of the dive and began to climb again, risking everything with little knowledge of what was happening about him, seeking only height.

By this time, the action had caused the two Piper Sections to break and adjust to the new threat coming from the flank. Caton glanced in his mirror to make sure Jean-Michel Ferre was high on his tail. Already he had fired two squirts and missed with both. He banked sharply to port as movement below snatched at the corners of his eyes to see an Me 109 tilting a shallow dive at some unseen target. He kicked brutally at the rudder bar and thrust forward the stick and, momentarily, the yellow dust cloud on the ground screwed a full circle until the Messerschmitt was beneath him. He pressed his firing-button and then rolled to starboard with no time to see how much damage he had done, conscious of more movement about him and unable to risk even a split-second glance in his mirror. Hunching himself over his control column he twisted towards the new movement and a second Me 109 appeared in his sights. Again he pressed his firing-button, but the Me peeled away and he could not be sure whether he had hit it or not. Now, he did look into his mirror, but there was nothing but blue sky and more Messerschmitts. Where the hell was Jean-Michel? The Messerschmitts behind had switched to his port side with Jimmy Easton amongst them twisting and turning in desperate half-rolls before attempting to swing round to meet them head-on. Caton sensed a sudden surge of tension such as he had not experienced since Dieppe. For Christ's sake, Jean-Michel? Where are you? He shoved the rudder bar, half-rolling towards Easton who was still under pressure; but there came lines of tracer immediately across his front and he had to stall turn. But then he spotted Ferre pulling out of a dive far to starboard and a Bf 109 spiralling in flames beneath him. His eyes searched the sky about him, finding it near impossible to distinguish friend from foe, but it seemed that most of the action was above and to port. Taylor appeared to be still circling and he couldn't make out why. Ferre had levelled from his climb above the fury of Easton's involvement, looking for his Section Leader. Ordenneau was there, too, now! No casualties so far, Caton thought and he pulled back the stick, intending to climb towards Taylor who must be in some kind of trouble. His Merlin roared under the burst of power as Ferre's voice broke shrilly over the R/T.

'Piper Leader! Watch Joe's tail!'

Dominic Taylor heard the sudden cry and his hand jerked convulsively at his control column but, by this time, he was flying almost blind. He could see neither Caton's Spitfire, nor whatever was threatening it.

'Joe! Joe! On your tail!' This was Ferre again, beginning to panic.

Caton twisted into a barrelled aileron turn to port, then again, intending to attempt to face the enemy as Easton had done a moment earlier. But when he glanced to his left he saw a Bf 109 coming in hard, moving with him. He twisted again, but the burst of cannon fire which shattered his port wing came from the other side. There must be a couple of the bastards! Why hadn't Taylor come to help? Ferre had seen the CO four or five hundred feet above him just as he had. More tracer came from the port side as the starboard Me closed, then deliberately witholding its fire until the pilot was ready to break. Caton's face froze in disbelief as he glimpsed the cannon in the Messerschmitt's propeller-boss blaze and sparks suddenly began to fly from his engine cowling.

'Damn you, Taylor! Damn you!'

This was Jean-Michel Ferre still on 'Send' and close to hysteria as a second burst from the Messerschmitt tore into Caton's cockpit who stiffened as red-hot shrapnel cut across his chest. The Merlin spluttered into silence, its airscrew windmilling, and the Spitfire turned lazily over on to its back; and, to Caton, feeling as though it were floating away on some lovely, soft, mysterious cloud.

There was no pain and when he looked down to the jagged tears in his Irvin jacket he stared at them in bisbelief. Only when the blood began to ooze from them did it enter his mind that he had been hit. He felt neither anger nor fear, his whole body beginning to float in that same, lazy, abandoned way as the aircraft which had carried him so high into the sky. He sensed, vaguely, the chatter of the squadron in his earphones and, for a fleeting moment, he recognised Ferre's accent, but it had nothing at all to do with him. The squadron would take care of itself and his Spitfire would take care of him just like in the early days when his Spitfire had been his buddy who would make sure he came to no harm.

The aircraft had slipped into a steep spiral, but Caton heard nothing of the roar of the slipstream around his half-open cockpit as the acceleration built up. He was going to die. That was for certain; but death wasn't going to be a bit like he'd always feared it might be.

The hazy recollection of one of George Barclay's oft-repeated philosophies slipped through his mind: 'until we die how do we know that death is not the greatest joy of all?' As ever, George had been right. Death was nothing to fear when it was just round the corner. It was just a matter of floating away with his Spitfire into eternity.

Now he was never going to see Sue again, even though her letter about Watermill Cottage was still in his jacket pocket, probably beneath one of those holes with his blood soaking through it. Poor Sue! She was a fine girl and she'd have made him a good wife. Maybe she'd be somewhere on the farm, right now, where the first chills of autumn would be browning the stubble. Maybe she might even be writing to him at this very moment – as he was dying!

His eyelids began to droop. Thank God there was no fire! Thank God for that . . . and as for the DFC, his gong!, well . . . wasn't that a silly, bloody, joke . . . ? The ultimate reward for a fighter-pilot was death and it was just a matter of the luck of the draw whether it was a clean death or not. He'd been lucky!

Dominic Taylor was hit!

And with Jean-Michel Ferre still screaming over the R/T.

'You let Joe die, Taylor! You let him die! *Poltron! Meurtrier!*'

Taylor reached forward and turned his R/T switch to 'Send', cutting off the Frenchman's accusations, not caring whether the rest of the squadron heard or not. He knew it could only be a matter of seconds before he followed Joe Caton. What chance did he have in a dogfight when he couldn't see a damn thing and the pain in his head was driving him crazy?

He braced himself as cannon shells tore into his engine

from what he guessed must have been a near frontal attack. More shells crossed overhead and an aircraft flashed past to starboard.

Christ!

He shook his head in a vain attempt to clear some of his vision, hauling back on his stick and trying to boost the throttle; but there came no response from the Merlin. Yet, he managed to level in a heavy gliding motion with his airscrew windmilling in just the same manner as Caton's had done. It did cross his mind that, after what had happened to Caton, it might be better to let his Spitfire have its head, but he thrust the thought from him. He'd got a hell of a lot to straighten out before he took such an easy path. He'd be damned if he was going to die! The same kind of dominant self-preservation, which had pulled him through his crash in the Hampshire wood, took command and, with it, some of the pain lifted from his temples. He shifted his feet over the rudder bars and the positive feel of metal convinced him that the shrapnel could have done little more than graze his shins.

He began to shift his seat into the full 'up' position with all the time in the world at 20,000 feet where it was safer to stay with the aircraft than to risk a parachute drop through the middle of a dogfight. With his vision beginning to return he screwed up his eyes to focus on the altimeter. Then, when the needle had turned anti-clockwise to 9,000 feet, he went through his 'baling-out' drill, finally to roll the Spitfire on to its back and, when gravity took over, he dropped into space.

He counted slowly to five before he pulled the rip-cord and the white mushroom of his parachute billowed above him, checking his fall in a sudden jerk, whip-lashing his neck. But now his vision was fast becoming clear and he could see his Spitfire in its death dive, much lower and arcing towards the enemy lines. Then, from immediately above, there came the roar of another aircraft. His breathing quickened and he looked upwards, half-expecting tracer bullets to rake his body, but then he saw it was a Spitfire. Mike Norling! The bloody fool was banking above him in a wide protective circle –

sticking out his neck a mile!

But more movement in the sky to the west caught his eye and he saw that it had become crowded with aircraft; formations of bombers trundling north-east in the direction of the El Daba and Fuka Luftwaffe bases. Above them and on both flanks were hordes of Kittyhawks and Hurricane fighters, maybe a couple of dozen squadrons and more in the biggest circus he had ever seen. Thank God for that, anyway, he told himself. At least, whatever was left of Piper Squadron could make their way back to base safely, even though their ammunition must be gone and their fuel dangerously low.

High above Mike Norling a second Spitfire had appeared and Taylor recognised Chris Fenton's identification number, the boy evidently intent on giving Mike top-cover.

But, now, the ground was coming up to meet him fast, a flat stretch of stone-strewn sand across which a squadron of heavy tanks was moving in a deployed formation. Farther to the west, infantry was dug in facing the western edge of the Ridge which meant they must be British!

Then he noticed that Mike Norling was lowering his undercarriage and he lifted a fist to shake it at the boy, jabbing a forefinger upwards and to the east.

'Go back, you bloody fool!' He shouted impotently into the roar of Norling's Merlin. 'Go back!'

But Norling was too intent on his flying even to notice, watching the angle of drift of the parachute, then easing back the throttle, putting down the flaps.

The tank men watched, taking time off from the war, as Taylor crumpled to the ground. And, as he slipped the parachute harness from his shoulders, so Mike Norling taxied slowly towards him, his canopy fully open, his face showing white and tense. In one heave he lifted himself to perch on the rim of the cockpit.

'Climb in, sir!'

His tone of voice made it a command, hostile even, and it struck Taylor that either he had seen what had happened to Joe Caton, or that he was recriminating himself for letting his

CO get shot down.

Taylor picked his way unsteadily to the Spitfire, then shaking his head as a recurring bout of nausea hit him as he climbed on to the port wing.

He knew what Norling was suggesting. It had been done before, but it could be a hell of a dice with two men of their size and weight. Even so, he clambered into the cockpit and sank into the seat followed by Norling who jammed himself between Taylor and the control column, his head high above the windscreen as he squatted on Taylor's knees.

He smiled grimly as he turned into the wind.

'We'll keep the wheels down, just in case!' he said, and the tank men cheered as the Spitfire began to move forward.

Chapter Nine

During the flight from Kidney Ridge to the base airfield, Norling maintained an altitude of 2,000 feet with Chris Fenton up and behind. He had the advantage of flying into the sun but, even so, he had a man-sized responsibility for he was low on fuel and almost out of ammunition – he had fired the indicative concentration of tracer above the Ridge.

Yet, he enjoyed his brief spell flying his Spitfire as a taxi. He had heard of this being done successfully on other occasions by the US Squadron of 57th Fighter Group and, in a way, he was pleased for the opportunity to test his own flying skills with two men cramped in the cockpit. He also knew that he was unlikely to meet any enemy aircraft during the trip eastwards. If he did so, then he would have to risk a landing – the reason he had settled on 2,000 feet with Fenton on hand to create some kind of diversion until he got down. That was OK. But what still nagged him was the belief that, somehow, in the heat of the dogfight above Kidney Ridge he had let his CO down. No matter how deep his involvement, he should have been on Taylor's tail! In his usual, brusque, manner he condemned himself just as he would have condemned the next man.

Dominic Taylor sat uncomfortably beneath the weight of Norling, thinking that this was a hell of a way to make what was probably his last flight in a combat Spitfire. For, with the death of Joe Caton, it was already firmly established in his mind that he could not, knowingly, put more pilots at risk. Very soon, maybe within the next few hours, he would have to come to terms with himself and decide how he was to handle his future.

Above the airfield, Norling put down the flaps, throttled back and made a reasonable landing; then taxiing to Dispersal and, out of the corners of his eyes, spotting Penallan's Section grouped outside the tent and pointing.

He switched off the ignition and, somewhat laboriously, eased himself from Taylor's knees to push himself over the rim of the cockpit to stand on the port wing rubbing the circulation back into his limbs. He turned to grin ruefully at Taylor as he, too, climbed out.

'Wouldn't want too much of that!' he said and, as he spoke, the two of them turned to watch Chris Fenton make his landing and taxi to his dispersal point.

Norling jumped to the ground and when Taylor joined him he looked him in the eye.

'Sorry about what happened over the Ridge, sir!' he said harshly. 'I should have been behind you! Christ! My job is to make sure you don't get shot down, isn't it? But I got too involved with Chris. Anyway, there were too many of the bastards!'

Taylor took a deep breath.

'Forget it, Mike,' he said evenly. 'That was a hell of a dogfight. I doubt if there was anything you or anyone else could have done. But thanks for bringing me home. I'll see it doesn't go unnoticed at Gr . . .'

'No! Not that! Let's not get . . .'

Taylor interupted: 'There is something else, Mike.'

'Yes?'

'You know Joe bought it?'

'Yes!'

'Did you see it happen?'

Norling shook his head.

'No! I guess not! At the time I heard young Ferre bawling over the R/T, mostly in French. But what with that and so much static I couldn't tell a word he was saying. Then, when I looked down, I saw Joe spiralling.' He shook his head. 'That's going to be a hell of a blow to the squadron, isn't it? We'll miss Joe! He was a great guy.' Then he shrugged and pulled a face as he usually did when he had lost a close friend, covering his personal grief with the same impenetrable mask of indifference he had cultivated since he had become a fighter pilot. 'Let me buy you a drink, sir, before we wash up.'

But Taylor shook his head.

'Later, Mike!' he said. 'I'll see the rest of the lads come in and then I've got things to do.'

Taylor watched Norling join Chris Fenton and, as they neared the Dispersal 'Hut', Penallen's Section, still 'on-state,' ran to meet them and hoisted Norling up on to their shoulders.

Taylor turned from the commotion to the sound of aircraft approaching from the west as Jimmy Easton returned with the rest of the formation. He counted. Apart from Joe Caton they had all made it. It would have been fairer had the missing Spitfire been his own.

Ferre, Ordenneau, and Reed left the dispersal area together to go to the tent they shared. Ferre was silent and introspective, Reed and Ordenneau chatting noisily, screening the death of a friend behind a glaze of banal inconsequentialities. They would all miss Joe Caton, but he'd gone and the next sortie had to be faced – probably within the hour. Jimmy Easton would take over Yellow Section and would fly with three aircraft until a replacement pilot arrived. The war would go on. There was nothing to be gained by dwelling on sentimentality. Tomorrow, they too might no longer be around!

In the tent they took off their flying gear, Ordenneau and Reed now and then taking long glances at their friend. But it was Ferre, himself, who eventually raised the subject of Joe Caton's death and this he did guardedly.

'Did either of you see Joe go?' he asked, looking keenly at each in turn. 'Robert? Charlie?'

They shook their heads positively, but with worried frowns on their faces. Jean-Michel should have more sense than to hold such an inquest. Nothing anyone said would bring Joe back. It was better to have a couple of beers and forget.

But Ferre persisted.

'Did you hear me on the R/T?'

Ordenneau placed an arm around his friend's shoulders, shaking him as though attempting to jog the mood out of him.

'Of course we heard you, Jean-Michel!' he agreed brusquely. 'But we didn't listen. We were all too involved. Jimmy was in trouble and I'd no time for anything else.' His voice changed to a less serious note and he grinned into Ferre's face. 'But we must forget Joe! You and I have seen enough of this war to know that this is good advice.'

Charlie Reed wasted no time in driving the point home: 'Yeah! Yeah!' he broke in. 'I heard you chattering, too, but I couldn't understand a damn word you said. I expected the CO to bawl you out, but he didn't. Maybe he was also too busy for he bought it soon afterwards. But he's OK, isn't he? That's the luck of the draw. Come on, Jean-Michel! Snap out of it! Let's go get us a couple of John O'Keefe's!'

But Ferre shook his head.

'No! Not just now, Charlie.' he said not unkindly. 'You two go along and perhaps I'll join you later.'

After they had left, Ferre stretched himself out on his bunk and fixed his eyes on the apex of the tent, his mind once again running over those last, desperate, twenty seconds of Joe Caton's life. Once again he saw Dominic Taylor up and on Caton's starboard beam and blatantly ignoring his warning: even watching the two Bf 109s sandwich him. All Taylor had had to do was put down his nose and fire for he had been in a perfect position for a quarter-stern attack. Yet, he'd banked to port! He'd just turned away and let Joe get shot to pieces! Even now, Ferre found the facts difficult to believe.

As he lay there his resentment towards the Squadron Leader rekindled. It was Dominic Taylor who should have died. Not Joe! And unless he did something about it Taylor would get away with it and maybe, sometime later, some other luckless pilot would dive to his death with his body shredded by tracer bullets because the CO refused to commit himself.

He swung himself from his bunk and strode from the tent.

Taylor should know that his cowardice had not gone unnoticed. It was up to him to make sure of that.

Len Jupp, George Romain, Mike Norling and Chris Fenton were sitting at the customary NAAFI table when Ferre burst into the Officers' Mess. The welcoming smiles on their faces dissolved into frowns when they noticed the flush of anger on his face; the brittle brightness of his eyes; the hard line of his mouth.

Norling asked casually: 'What's upsetting you, mate?'

But Ferre thrust aside the question, swinging his eyes around the marquee, searching.

'Where's Taylor?'

Norling pulled a face as he shrugged.

'He says he's got things to do.'

'In his tent?'

'I guess so.'

At that moment, Len Jupp got to his feet and crossed quickly to Ferre's side, brow creased in consternation.

'What is it Jean-Michel?' he asked him quietly.

'I'm going to see Taylor!' Ferre replied and turned about to stride angrily from the marquee.

Jupp paused sufficiently long to shrug his incomprehension at his fellow officers before catching up with Ferre. He said: 'Don't you think you might have a word with me about it first, Jean-Michel?'

Ferre halted and as he looked at the middle-aged adjutant he recognised the patient understanding of the man who had befriended him since he and Ordenneau had first joined the squadron. Some of his anger left him.

'All right, Len!' he agreed. 'Why not?'

Jupp pointed across the sand square to the Orderly Room tent.

'We'll go in there, Jean-Michel,' he suggested. 'There'll be no one else around at this time of day.'

Ferre did not argue and a few moments later they were facing each other across one of the barrack-room tables which served as desks. Jupp nodded encouragingly, but Ferre hesitated, marshalling his thoughts and now showing a trace of diffidence as he faced the Adjutant.

'This is not easy for me to say to you . . .' he began, 'for you are not directly concerned. With Squadron Leader Taylor I am angry, but you are my friend.' A worried frown creased his forehead. Then he spoke out determinedly. 'This morning the CO let Joe Caton die, Len! When he could have saved him he turned the other way. I called him coward! *Poltron! Meurtrier!* I shouted the words over the R/T. Now it is for me to tell him again and this time face-to-face. He let my friend die and perhaps, at some future time, he could let others die in the same way!' He paused as though half-expecting Len Jupp to comment. And when the Adjutant said nothing his frown deepened. 'I think Taylor should know that he has not got away with it. That is why I came to the mess. I wanted everyone to know!'

Having made his point and still with no comment from Jupp he went on to describe more calmly his own involvement in the action which had caused him to leave Caton's tail to help Jimmy Easton who'd been in desperate trouble. But, even so, he'd still managed to keep an eye on Caton. That was when he'd shouted his warning to Dominic Taylor.

When he stopped speaking Jupp drew a deep breath, his eyes still on those of the Frenchman who shrugged and spread out the palms of his hands in a typically French manner and adding: 'As I said, Joe would be alive now if the CO had . . .'

But Jupp lifted a hand, interrupting him.

'What you have told me, Jean-Michel, is an account of your own personal involvement in the action. But you didn't at the same time suddenly develop some means of looking into the CO's mind! So far as he was concerned, you were no more than a spectator. Is that not true?'

Ferre scowled, a glint of his earlier anger in his eyes.

'I tell you he wouldn't fight!'

'Jean-Michel!' There came a suggestion of an edge to

Jupp's voice. 'You must listen to me! Please! There is something very important I must tell you, though I'm damned sure that the CO would have my hide if he were here right now!'

'But what can you say that will make any difference? I was there, Len!'

'Give me a chance to say my piece and then ask that question! All you've got to do is listen!'

And from that point Jupp went on to describe Taylor's pile-up in the Hampshire wood almost eighteen months earlier; his year in hospital and the strength and determination which had eventually brought him back to operational flying. Now he had got the whole of Ferre's attention and he began to talk of Taylor's recent bout of recurring nightmares; how he would awake screaming in the early morning with his face bloodless and the strength gone from his limbs.

'And that's not all!' exclaimed Jupp harshly as Ferre attempted in interupt. 'For the past week he's suffered blackouts during combat. They're something he can't control! Nausea. Impaired vision. Lack of co-ordination. Yet, he's not complained and continued to lead the squadron and he's got his share of kills. What's more, he doesn't even know that I know anything about it!' His eyes narrowed as they searched those of the French pilot who was little more than a boy. 'Just tell me, Jean-Michel, who was first into the dogfight this morning?'

'The CO . . .'

Jupp nodded and spread out his hands in very much the same way as Ferre had done a few moments earlier.

'Of course he was,' he said quietly. 'But just now you've branded him a coward. Believe me, Jean-Michel, Dominic Taylor is one of the bravest men it's been my privilege to serve with. He's already given his life to this war; even though he's still alive!'

After Ferre had gone Jupp waited a while, turning the gist of their conversation over in his mind and then hurried, not back to the mess, but to Taylor's tent where he found him sitting on his bunk with a blank combat report form on the chair beside him. He looked up wanly as the Adjutant entered.

'So what's worrying you now, Len?'

Jupp did not hesitate.

'You are!' he said, expecting to get the full broadside of Taylor's temper, but the CO only smiled tolerantly.

'Maybe you're right!' he said evenly and when Jupp offered no comment he went on: 'I lost one of my boys this morning, Len! But maybe you've heard? I could have saved him, but I didn't do a bloody thing about it!'

Jupp nodded. This was no time to pull punches.

'Yes! I heard, Dominic!' he said aggressively. 'Until I stopped him just now, young Ferre was on his way here lusting for your blood. He'd got you down as the biggest quitter who ever flew a plane!'

Taylor still remained calm. He nodded. 'Well, maybe the boy was right! I heard him say as much over the R/T and so did most of the other lads, but they won't admit it. Joe is dead, Len! It's as simple as that. Joe Caton! Joe with all that history behind him from Dunkirk to this bloody God-forsaken spot. And it had to be me who let him die!'

'I told Ferre the truth, Dominic!'

'What truth?'

'You ask me that? Your Adjutant may be getting on a bit in years but maybe not he's so dumb as you believe. I get around at Group HQ far more than you do, Dominic. I know all about your combat problems, about your battle nerves . . .'

For the first time Taylor's face mirrored his anger: 'And you told a sergeant pilot that? A bloody foreigner?'

'Someone had to tell him, Dominic! Some of us are proud of your reputation!'

He jerked a vicious laugh. 'But none of it makes any difference! I still let Joe Caton die! Can't you grasp that simple fact?'

'Bloody rubbish! For one thing you couldn't see either Caton or what else was happening around you! For another, you were in no way responsible for his death. You took no part, either way! Can't you accept that the situation developed around you – just as it would have developed if you'd not even been there? Ferre, himself, was Joe's wingman. Not you!'

Taylor shook his head.

'And then Mike Norling had to risk his life for me! For what? Are you suggesting I should go on commanding the squadron?'

'No, Dominic.' Jupp replied quietly and a little sadly, for it was now apparent that Taylor had already reached the same conclusions as himself. 'I'm not suggesting that. But what I do suggest is that I get the jeep and drive you over to Group. Alan Harcourt tells me he's had similar problems himself. You'll find he understands.'

Taylor frowned his disbelief at that.

'Like hell he does!'

But Jupp nodded emphatically.

'I think we should leave right now!' he said.

Jimmy Easton had seen nothing of Joe Caton's death-dive. In fact, he did not know he had gone until the squadron began to reform with the massive 'circus' coming over from the west and Mike Norling dropping out of the formation to chase after Dominic Taylor's plunging aircraft.

As Taylor spiralled, it struck Easton that probably, on seniority, he had become Piper Leader and the idea didn't please him at all.

Immediately after touchdown he hurried to the Dispersal 'Hut' shoving past the four members of Orange Section who were still clustered around Mike Norling and picking from alongside the telephone the letter which Caton had written to Sue before take-off.

It seemed incredible to Easton that not an hour had passed since Joe had sat there with a pen in his hand and a warm smile on his face as he had thought of his girl. Another instance of the utter finality of aerial combat. Joe, his friend and buddy for the past year, was gone forever. Months later some cross in some military cemetery near Cairo would mark the spot where his body lay rotting.

But thank God he'd got the letter! It was better that the poor kid who'd been planning a home for Joe in that never-never dream-time when the war was over – his studying, his degree, his veterinary practice and all of it so rich in her bright feminine mind – should believe he had not had a chance to read her letter. That way her heartache might not be so devastating.

But Joe hadn't really played the game with the girl, had he?

Easton wandered pensively across the loose sand to his tent with the letter in his hand and his brow creased. Joe could have gone to Stanmore three months back! There, he would have been close to Sue. He could have visited her most weekends and during the time they could have converted their dream cottage together. Joe need never have flown in combat again.

Yet, what had he done?

He'd insisted, Yes! insisted! on remaining with an operational squadron and risking his life half a dozen times a day!

Why?

Was this dedication? Partly, maybe. Joe had always been eager to emphasise his conviction that people had to fight if they wanted to win the war. But that didn't mean the same people had to do all the fighting all the time, did it?

Then what else had spurred Joe?

Vanity?

Joe had revelled in his role of Spitfire pilot for as long as Easton had known him and just couldn't bear to think himself as non-operational. He was also justly proud of his flying skills – as last week's Stuka party proved – despite his blasé way of refusing to tot up his kills!

He should have gone to Stanmore for the sake of Sue and his lonely, widower, father. As it was he'd caused a lot of sadness. Joe had been selfish that way!

He'd been a good and loyal pal but Joe, more than anyone, should have accepted that the squadron would live forever.

Only its pilots died!

AIR FORCE ONE

BY EDWIN CORLEY

AIR FORCE ONE: THE FAMOUS PLANE THAT CARRIES THE WORLD'S MOST POWERFUL MAN. SOMEONE WANTS TO TURN IT INTO AN AIRBORNE COFFIN . . .

A trip aboard AIR FORCE ONE amounts to the safest – and most exclusive – journey there is. Luxurious, closely guarded, superbly maintained, guided by a highly skilled and dedicated crew, she is the Free World's airborne nerve-centre, carrying the world's destiny as she flies.

Until one day, as she takes the President of the United States on a routine trip, that nerve-centre and the people aboard her have to face total terror. When a traitor strikes on board. And the radar screen shows a fully-armed World War II vintage fighter – HEADING STRAIGHT FOR AIR FORCE ONE . . .

'Topnotch thriller . . . an explosive climax'
PUBLISHERS WEEKLY

ADVENTURE THRILLER 0 7221 0496 0 £1.25

AN EXPOSITION

FREDK. A. TATFORD, Litt. D.

WITH A FOREWORD BY
W. E. VINE, M.A.

Pickering & Inglis
LONDON — GLASGOW

First published 1947
Paperback edition 1969
Reprinted 1970, 1971, 1974, 1978

ISBN 0 7208 0029 3
Cat. No. 01/1611

 Printed in Great Britain by Lowe & Brydone Printers Ltd, Thetford, Norfolk for Pickering & Inglis Ltd, 26 Bothwell Street, Glasgow G2 6PA.

Foreword

IN the production of this work, the Author has made a valuable contribution towards the exegesis of the Book of the Revelation, and I have much pleasure in recommending it to the careful perusal of readers.

As Mr. Tatford says, the primary design of the Apocalypse is the Revelation of the glories of Christ. The understanding of this is a key to the grasp of the contents of this closing Book of the Sacred Volume. That this is the great object of the Book can scarcely fail to arrest the attention of one who reads the first chapter. After the vision of His personal glory comes the unfolding of His thoughts, counsels and judgments concerning the ways and doings of those who form the churches. The instructions to the seven churches in Chapters II. and III. are evidently designed to guide them into a realization of their true relationship with Him. And what applies to the seven applies likewise to churches throughout the present period. The contents of these chapters are of essential importance for the warning, encouragement, and instruction of individual believers at all times. The Author rightly and helpfully shows how the seven messages, in their appointed order, have a correspondence to conditions in the successive stages of the history of the Church from Pentecost to the Rapture.

A fresh manifestation of Christ takes place in Chapters IV. and V., and this has a bearing upon the subsequent Chapters, VI. to XIX., in the last of which the Son of God is seen consummating the acts of divine judgment upon the nations of the world in His personal intervention in its affairs immediately prior to the setting up of His Kingdom of righteousness and peace, with the arch-enemy of God and man helplessly confined in the abyss for a thousand years.

So to the end of the Book. The redeemed are seen in company with Christ, sharing His regal authority. Again, it is before His tremendous Tribunal that the dead, small and great, stand to be judged. The succeeding vision of the new heavens and earth centres in Him. Of the glorious City-Bride of the Lamb He is Himself the *Phōstēr*, the Light-Giver, 21. 12 (the same word as in Phil. 2. 15). His is the voice of absolute authority that sounds at the end of the volume: "Behold, I come quickly: and My reward is with Me . . . I am the Alpha and the Omega, the First and the Last, the Beginning and the End." "I, Jesus, have sent My angel to testify." "I am the Root and the Offspring of David, the Bright, the Morning Star." "I testify to every man." "Yea, I come quickly." All this is a veritable climax of the shining forth of the glory and power of Christ throughout the whole Apocalypse, and a consummation of the Revelation of the Son of God, the great Creator, Lord and Saviour, Redeemer and Judge, throughout the entire Volume of Scripture.

The unfolding and interpretation of the contents of this closing Book have been undertaken by the Author with much careful thought, and as one who has manifested a competency to make a judicious discrimination in connection with the various lines of interpretation taken by those who have already handled the subject. It is a great satisfaction to the writer of this Foreword to observe how, in chapter VI. of his commentary, dealing with the opening of chapter IV. of the book, Mr. Tatford cogently sets forth reasons for the view that after chapter III. the churches are no longer seen on earth, the Lord having come to receive the Church to Himself. This view goes far to guide to an accurate interpretation of the remainder of the Apocalypse.

In chapter VII. he rightly avoids dogmatism respecting the First Seal. What he has set forth is helpful in exposing the weakness of certain interpretations. In later parts of this and subsequent chapters he shows how the historical interpretation may be partially true, but he does not accept the historical view in its entirety. He shows how details of past history are yet to be re-enacted. At the same time, upon occasion, he remarks upon the weakness of the historical interpretation, as, *e.g.* in chapter XII. This evidence of a careful handling of differing views adds no small value to his work.

An important point is the distinction made between the prophetic programme in the first eleven chapters, with the prophetic principles involved, and the remainder of the Book, which introduces special persons on the scenes, and marks the unseen conflict among the invisible and supernatural forces. The view that the Man-Child in chapter XII. is Christ is surely the right one.

It gives the writer pleasure to find the many important points of agreement between what he sought to set forth in his book, *The Roman Empire Revived*, and what is advocated by Mr. Tatford in this work, especially regarding the prophecies of Daniel and the seventy weeks, or hebdomads, and the fourteenth and seventeenth chapters of the Apocalypse.

In various parts the reader will find an example of the way in which the Author aptly refers to foundation doctrines of the Christian faith and to the character of true Christian conduct and walk. At the close of the exposition of the last chapter of the Book the Author utters a warning and expresses a desire, which we can heartily re-echo. The warning is against the usurpation of the place of Christ in the lives of believers by "the mundane pursuit, the materialistic ambition, and the temporal object." The desire is that God may reawaken the fervour of our first love for Christ and inspire us to cry, "Come, Lord Jesus."

May the labours of our brother in this excellent help towards an understanding of the Apocalypse be abundantly blessed of God.

W. E. VINE

Preface to the Paperback edition

AS indicated in the original preface, this book was originally written (in the form of articles in *The Harvester*) nearly 30 years ago and was subsequently issued in book form in 1947. It has been out of print for many years and so many friends have sought unsuccessfully to obtain copies that it as been reissued without revision. For this reason it has been impracticable to include references to more recent authorities or to give a fuller explanation of certain points regarding which some readers have sought elucidation.

Despite the lapse of time since the book's first appearance, the author would not wish, in general, to revise the news expressed therein, although there are inevitably a few revisions or corrections which could normally have been made, e.g. the reference on page 96 to a parenthesis between the sixth and seventh vials.

FREDK. A. TATFORD

Preface

EXPOSITIONS of the Revelation are so numerous that it may be questioned whether any justification exists for the production of yet another. It can only be pleaded in extenuation that so many friends have asked that the following chapters (most of which have appeared in *The Harvester*) should be published in the more permanent form of a book, that there seemed at least some small excuse for doing so.

The notes on which the book is based were made in an air-raid shelter, during nights of heavy raids when sleep was impossible, and the subsequent papers were penned at odd moments snatched from the hours of a busy life. The result may not, therefore, be as perfect in style and composition as the author would have desired, but in view of the many practical difficulties involved, the reader's sympathetic indulgence is craved if the blemishes and imperfections evidence themselves too forcibly.

It should perhaps be added that a slavish adherence to either the Authorised or the Revised Versions has been avoided, both in the Scriptural text at the head of each section and, to a lesser extent, in the quotations in the body of the book. Instead, a serious attempt has been made to arrive at the true meaning of the text.

No subject is so thrilling as that of eschatology, and if the following pages lead to a deeper study of the Prophetic Word, the effort put into their production will not have been completely wasted.

FREDK. A. TATFORD

Analysis of the Revelation

1 INTRODUCTION (chap. 1)

- (*a*) Prologue and Salutation 1. 1-11
- (*b*) Vision of the glorified Christ 1. 12-18
- (*c*) The Commission 1. 19-20

2 THE SEVEN CHURCHES (chaps. 2, 3)

- (*a*) Ephesus 2. 1-7
- (*b*) Smyrna 2. 8-11
- (*c*) Pergamos 2. 12-17
- (*d*) Thyatira 2. 18-29
- (*e*) Sardis 3. 1-6
- (*f*) Philadelphia 3. 7-13
- (*g*) Laodicea 3. 14-22

3 HEAVENLY SCENES (chaps. 4, 5)

- (*a*) The Throne 4. 1-11
- (*b*) The Book 5. 1-14

4 THE SEVEN SEALS (chap. 6. 1 to 8. 5)

- (*a*) First Seal 6. 1-2
- (*b*) Second Seal 6. 3-4
- (*c*) Third Seal 6. 5-6
- (*d*) Fourth Seal 6. 7-8
- (*e*) Fifth Seal 6. 9-11
- (*f*) Sixth Seal 6. 12-17
- (*g*) Parenthesis—the sealed Israelites and saved Gentiles 7. 1-17
- (*h*) Seventh Seal 8. 1-5

5 THE SEVEN TRUMPETS (chap. 8. 6 to 11. 18)

- (*a*) First Trumpet 8. 6-7
- (*b*) Second Trumpet 8. 8-9
- (*c*) Third Trumpet 8. 10-11
- (*d*) Fourth Trumpet 8. 12-13
- (*e*) Fifth Trumpet 9. 1-12
- (*f*) Sixth Trumpet 9. 13-21
- (*g*) Parentheses:
  - (i) The Mighty Angel 10. 1-11
  - (ii) The Two Witnesses 11. 1-14
- (*h*) Seventh Trumpet 11. 15-19

6 SATAN IN ACTION (chaps. 12 and 13)

- (*a*) The Woman and the Child 12. 1-17
- (*b*) The Beast out of the Sea 13. 1-10
- (*c*) The Beast out of the Earth 13. 11-18
- (*d*) Parenthesis—Grace and Judgment 14. 1-20

7 THE SEVEN VIALS (chaps. 15 and 16)

- (*a*) Preparation 15. 1-8
- (*b*) First Vial 16. 1-2
- (*c*) Second Vial 16. 3
- (*d*) Third Vial 16. 4-7
- (*e*) Fourth Vial 16. 8-9
- (*f*) Fifth Vial 16. 10-11
- (*g*) Sixth Vial 16. 12-16
- (*h*) Seventh Vial 16. 17-21

8 BABYLON THE HARLOT (chaps. 17 and 18)

- (*a*) The System 17. 1-18
- (*b*) The City 18. 1-24

9 MANIFESTATION AND MILLENNIUM (chap. 19. 1 to 20. 6)

- (*a*) The Marriage of the Lamb 19. 1-10
- (*b*) Christ's Return in Judgment 19. 11–20. 3
- (*c*) The Millennial Reign 20. 4-6

10 FINAL JUDGMENT (chap. 20. 7-15)

- (*a*) The Last Revolt 20. 7-9
- (*b*) Satan's Doom 20. 10
- (*c*) The Great White Throne 20. 11-15

11 THE ETERNAL STATE 21. 1-8

12 MILLENNIAL GLORY 21. 9–22. 5

13 EPILOGUE (chap. 22. 6-21)

- (*a*) The Imprimatur 22. 6-9
- (*b*) The Unsealed Book 22. 10-13
- (*c*) Final Messages 22. 14-21

Contents

Chapter I

Introduction

It has been said that it was largely the two factors of oppression and the Messianic hope which gave rise to Jewish apocalyptic literature. Under the inspiration of the Holy Spirit, the emotions of a persecuted people found expression in the prophetic writings of the Old Testament, and through the same medium was derived the assurance of ultimate deliverance at the advent of the Messiah.

Very similar conditions existed in the early days of the Church, and the current experiences of the period doubtless had their effect upon the mentality and outlook of God's people in that day. The Apocalypse of the New Testament, however, was not born merely of oppression and hope. As its title plainly indicates, it is primarily a revelation of the glory of Christ, and it is concerned only secondarily with the course and circumstances of human history.

The Apocalypse reveals the unseen Head of the Church in all His glory as Lord; it portrays the despised Carpenter of Nazareth as the object of heaven's worship; it shows the rejected King filling the throne of universal sovereignty; it depicts the Saviour of Calvary as the installed Judge. Prophecy and prediction may find their place herein, but the supreme subject of the Revelation is Christ. God is more concerned with the honour and glory of His Son than with the fate of empires, and His final vindication of His Beloved will bring heaven, earth and hell to bended knee and universal acclamation of the Supreme Lord.

It is fitting that this book should have been assigned the last place in the Bible. It fitly closes the inspired volume and concludes the whole story of God's purposes. In it is found the answer to the age-long problems of sin, sorrow and suffering. The 6,000 years' struggle between the forces of good and evil there reaches its climax in the victory of right and the defeat of wrong. Sin and Satan are for ever banished and an eternal state of righteousness ushered in. The mysteries of life then find their solution and the eternal plan is then laid bare. Fidelity in life reaps its reward in glory, and self-willed rebellion meets with its final retribution. The probation of earth is superseded by the finality of heaven, and the divine heart finds satisfaction in the fulfilment of the eternal will.

The Revelation is totally unlike any other of the inspired writings. Milton refers to it as "the majestic image of a high and stately tragedy, shutting up and intermingling her solemn scenes and acts with a sevenfold chorus of hallelujahs and harping symphonies." It is a book of visions and signs, of glorious heights and appalling depths, of marvellous scenes and terrifying pictures.

The abundance of symbols used in the book and the difficulty in understanding their meaning and implications have led to a considerable neglect of this part of Scripture and the absurd interpretations to which men have given way have only conduced to still greater neglect. Dean Farrar has truly said of this book that "intolerance, ignorance, sectarian fierceness, the sanguinary factiousness of an irreligious religionism, the eternal Pharisaism of the human heart, have made of it their favourite camping-ground. Men have wandered into the quagmire of private interpretations after the *ignis fatuus* of religious hatred. Its symbols have become plastic in the hot hands of party factiousness, but under such manipulations they have been rendered unintelligible to the eyes of truth and love." In consequence, the very book which, *par excellence*, should be the inspiration and joy of the Christian, is often completely ignored. Yet there is a special reward promised in connection with even its public reading.

Many of the Apocalyptic images are drawn from the Old Testament. There are actually 285 O.T. passages quoted or alluded to. The temple, the altar, the court and the ark find a special place. Indeed, many students have suggested that the temple forms the background of the Revelation and this receives some measure of support from passages such as 11. 19; 15. 5 to 16. 1, etc. In 6. 9 the altar is seen; in 11. 2 the outer court is in view; in 11. 19 the ark of the covenant is beheld.

The most casual reader will have observed the sevenfold structure of the Revelation. Seven series of sevens are detailed in the Scofield Reference Bible as follows: (1) seven churches (ch. 2. and 3); (2) seven seals (4. 1 to 8. 1); (3) seven trumpets (8. 2 to 11. 19); (4) seven personages (12. 1 to 14. 20); (5) seven vials (15. 1 to 16. 21); (6) seven dooms (17. 1 to 20. 15); and (7) seven new things (21. 1 to 22. 21). Five parentheses interrupt the course of the narrative as follows: (1) The Jewish remnant and the tribulation saints (7. 1-17); (2) the angel, the little book, the two witnesses (10. 1 to 11. 4); (3) the lamb, the remnant, and the everlasting gospel (14. 1-13); (4) the gathering of the kings at Armageddon (16. 13-16); and (5) the four alleluias in heaven (19. 1-6). These passages do not advance the prophetic narrative. Looking backward and forward, they sum up results accomplished, and speak of results yet to come as if they had already come.

Authorship

The author styles himself as John,[1] and it is fairly generally accepted that the reference was to John the apostle. As Fausset says, "None but he would thus sign himself nakedly without addition. As sole survivor and representative of the apostles, and eye-witness of the Lord, he needed no designation but his name, to be recognized by his readers."

The writer is described as he "who bore record of the Word (*Logos*) of God,"[2] a possible reference to the fourth Gospel, which may tend to confirm his identity.

Until the middle of the third century, it was commonly held that Zebedee's son was the author. Justin Martyr (140 A.D.), Melito (170 A.D.), and Theophilus (180 A.D.) attribute the book to the apostle. Irenæus (180 A.D.), who acquired his information from Polycarp, a disciple of John, confirms the tradition. Tertullian (200 A.D.), Clement of Alexandria (200 A.D.), Origen (233 A.D.), and Hippolytus (240 A.D.), all add their confirmation. Athanasius, Gregory of Nyasa, Ambrose, Augustine and indeed, "Fathers in all parts of the Church," says Alford, "held it in continuous succession."

Apart from an obscure Asiatic sect called the Alogi (180 A.D.), who denied the existence of spiritual gifts in the Church, the Johannine authorship was first questioned by Dionysius in the second half of the third century on the ground of the differences in style and grammar between the fourth Gospel and the Revelation. To satisfy his theory, Dionysius invented a new author, John the Presbyter of Ephesus, but of this worthy history knows nothing.

More recent research dismisses this theory and furnishes abundant confirmation of the traditional belief in the apostolic authorship. Wetstein and Lardner, for example, have found nearly 40 texts in Revelation which contain words, phrases and expressions that are almost identical with those used in the Gospel of John, while even modern critics like Bleek, Duesterdick and Ewald accept the apostolic authorship.

The admission of the Revelation into the canon of Scripture,

[1]Rev. 1. 1, 2, 4, 9; 22. 8. [2]Rev. 1. 2

Canonicity

says Westcott, "rests chiefly on the authority of the Western Churches." Syrian and Nestorian manuscripts of the *Peshito*, or Aramæan version (which is assigned to the most remote Christian antiquity) all omit the Apocalypse, but it has been adduced (and reasonably) from a quotation from the works of Ephraim Syrus of Edessa that it was originally included in the *Peshito*.

The *Vetus Latina*, or old Latin version, which was in use at the end of the second century, however, included the work. The anonymous work on the canon, known as the *Muratorian Fragment*, recognizes the Apocalypse as canonical.

It was omitted from the list of canonical books of the Council of Laodicea, but was admitted into the list of the Third Council of Carthage in 397 A.D.

In the Greek-speaking churches, "it never came into general ecclesiastical use" (Simcox), and it "was not translated till a comparatively late date into either of the vernacular dialects of Egypt."

There is considerable evidence from early Christian literature that the book was regarded as canonical and it is now fairly generally accorded a place in the canon.

Date

Although the date of the book has been the subject of much controversy, the arguments adduced for an early date in the reign of Nero are without much force.

Irenæus, the friend of John's disciple, Polycarp, states that the Revelation was written at the end of Domitian's reign in 96 A.D., and this is borne out by internal as well as historical evidence.

Chapter 1. 9 refers to a persecution which affected even the churches in Asia Minor. The first such persecution was in the reign of Domitian, that of Nero's day being confined to Rome.

John also refers to his exile in Patmos. History reveals that Domitian was the first emperor to adopt the punishment of banishment to the mines and quarries, so that the book could not have been written before his reign. In addition, Clement of Alexandria definitely intimates that it was during the reign of this emperor that John was banished to Patmos, and adds that he returned on the death of Domitian in 96 A.D.

The degeneration in the state of the churches, referred to in chapters 2 and 3, is, in itself, a strong argument for a fairly late date. It is most improbable that such a condition would have existed in the very earliest days of church history.

There is little question that the date may fairly confidently be placed about 96 A.D.

Plan of Book

"All sections of the Revelation are concurrent, contemporaneous and co-terminous," says Roadhouse, but this is controverted by even the first chapter. In verse 19, the apostle is commanded to "write therefore what thou hast seen, and the things that are, and the things that are about to be after these."

Three clear divisions are indicated in this verse, *viz.*:

(1) "What thou hast seen";
(2) "The things that are";
(3) "The things that are about to be after these."

In ch. 1. 11. the instruction was given to the seer: "*What thou seest*, write in a book." In verse 19 of the same chapter, he was directed to write: "*What thou hast seen.*" The plain inference is that the vision of the glorified Christ in the intervening verses, 12 to 18, forms the first section of the book.

In ch. 4. 1, the voice declares: "I will shew thee *the things which must take place after these things.*" To an unprejudiced mind it consequently seems evident that the third section of the book must commence at chapter 4.

The intervening two chapters are occupied with the letters to the seven churches and obviously constitute the second section, *i.e.*, "*the things that are.*" This is confirmed by the fact that the word "church" does not occur again after chapter 3. The history of the church on earth ends with that chapter, and the section may, therefore, reasonably be regarded as relative to the present dispensation.

Interpretation

Apart from those *eclectics* who, as Thompson says, "lay stress upon the spiritual elements of the book, and do not attempt to dogmatize upon the meanings of the details of the more mysterious visions," there are three main systems of interpretation.

(1) The *preterist* school maintains that the majority of the prophecies of the book have already been fulfilled and have, therefore, no significance for the present day, other than as moral lessons drawn from past history.

(2) The *historicist* declares that the book portrays a complete outline of human and ecclesiastical history and the story of the struggle between good and evil down to the end of time.

(3) The *futurist* regards the whole of the events described after ch. 3 as lying in the unfulfilled future.

There is undoubtedly a measure of truth in each of these views, and only foolish dogmatism would airily dismiss any of them as inconsequential and incorrect. There are spiritual lessons to be learnt from every part of the book and it is not essential that every detail should be understood in order that the underlying principles may be apprehended.

That the Apocalyptic prophecies find a partial and preliminary fulfilment in past and present history is also demonstrable, and it would be foolish to deny the fact.

On the other hand, the prophetic student discerns the essential differences between partial and complete fulfilments, and sees the Old Testament prophecies gathered up in a final revelation and still awaiting their complete realization at the coming of Christ.

Appendix to Chapter 1

Relation of Genesis to Revelation

The relation of the Book of Revelation to the Book of Genesis is most interesting. What *begins* in Genesis *ends* in Revelation. Dr. E. W. Bullinger has summarized the connection as under:

Genesis	Revelation
1 Genesis, the Book of the Beginning.	1 Revelation, the Book of the end.
2 The earth created (1. 1).	2 The earth passed away (21. 1).
3 Satan's first rebellion.	3 Satan's final rebellion (20. 3, 7-10).
4 Sun, moon, and stars for earth's government (1. 14-16).	4 Sun, moon, and stars connected with earth's judgment (6. 13; 8. 12; 16. 8).
5 Sun to govern the day (1. 16).	5 No need of the sun (21. 23).
6 Darkness called night (1. 5).	6 "No night there" (22. 5).
7 Waters called seas (1. 10).	7 "No more sea" (21. 1).
8 A river for earth's blessing (2. 10-14).	8 A river for the new earth (22. 1, 2).
9 Man in God's image (1. 26).	9 Man headed by one in Satan's image (13).
10 Entrance of sin (3).	10 Development and end of sin (21. 22).
11 Curse pronounced (3. 14, 17).	11 "No more curse" (22. 3).
12 Death entered (3. 19).	12 "No more death" (21. 4).
13 Cherubim, first mentioned in connection with man (3. 24).	13 Cherubim finally mentioned in connection with man (4. 6).
14 Man driven out from Eden (3. 24).	14 Man restored (22).
15 Tree of Life guarded (3. 24).	15 Right to the Tree of Life (22. 14).
16 Sorrow and suffering enter (3. 17).	16 No more sorrow (21. 4).
17 Man's religion, art and science resorted to for enjoyment apart from God (4).	17 Man's religion, luxury, art, and science in their full glory, judged and destroyed by God (18).
18 Nimrod, a great rebel and king and hidden anti-god, the founder of Babylon (10. 8, 9).	18 The beast, the great rebel, a king, and manifested anti-god, the reviver of Babylon (13-18).
19 A flood from God to destroy an evil generation (6. 9).	19 A flood from Satan to destroy an elect generation (12).
20 The bow, the token of God's covenant with the earth (9. 13).	20 The bow, betokening God's remembrance of His covenant with the earth (4. 3; 10. 1).
21 Sodom and Egypt, the place of corruption and temptation (13. 19).	21 Sodom and Egypt again: spiritually representing Jerusalem (11. 8).
22 A confederacy against Abraham's people overthrown (14).	22 A confederacy against Abraham's seed overthrown (12).
23 Marriage of first Adam (2. 18-23).	23 Marriage of last Adam (19).
24 A bride sought for Abraham's son (Isaac) and found (24).	24 A Bride made ready and brought to Abraham's Son (19. 9). See Matt. 1. 1.
25 Two angels acting for God on behalf of His people (19).	25 Two witnesses acting for God on behalf of His people (11).
26 A promised seed to possess the gates of his enemies (22. 17).	26 The promised Seed coming into possession (11. 18).
27 Man's dominion ceased and Satan's begun (3. 14).	27 Satan's dominion ended and man's restored (22).
28 The old serpent causing sin, suffering, and death (3. 1).	28 The old serpent bound for 1,000 years (20. 1-3).
29 The doom of the old serpent pronounced (3. 15).	29 The doom on the old serpent executed (20. 10).
30 Sun, moon, and stars associated with Israel (37. 9).	30 Sun, moon, and stars, associated again with Israel (12).

Chapter II

Revelation I

The Title

WHILE most copies bear the superscription, "Revelation of John the Theologue" (or "the divine"), it is obvious that this was not the original title of the book, since the first verse gives the inspired title, *viz.*, "The Revelation of Jesus Christ."

The book is pre-eminently the Revelation of Christ. He is central and upon His Person all the rays of glory converge. Philip Mauro says: "All things that are written therein are closely connected with Jesus Christ Himself as the Redeemer of man and as the duly invested Owner and Sovereign Lord of the Universe." Although it is concerned with future events, the Apocalypse is a revelation not so much of things to come as of the Lord Himself in relation to those events. Christ is both the Revelation and also the Revealer.

There is no other book in the Bible which so unveils His glory and, if for no other reason, it should therefore have attracted the attention and study of every believer.

It is perhaps not without significance that, at the outset, He is designated as "Jesus Christ"—the Saviour and Anointed One. His rightful title of Lord is omitted until His glory is revealed and the acknowledgment of His worth is unfeigned and unhesitating.

The Prologue

"The Revelation of Jesus Christ, which God gave Him to shew unto His bondservants the things which must shortly come to pass: and He sent and signified it by His angel unto His servant John; who bare witness of the Word of God, and of the testimony of Jesus Christ, even of all things that he saw. Blessed is he that readeth and they that hear the words of the prophecy, and keep the things which are written therein: for the time is at hand" (I. I-3).

The prologue states that the Revelation was given to Jesus Christ by God for the specific purpose of revealing to His bondservants what was about to happen. One of the primary objects is thus plainly indicated as the definite enlightenment of Christ's own people concerning the future. Nevertheless, the book is not merely a series of predictions, nor is it an outline of eschatological truth; it is rather an unfolding of the divine purposes as they affect the glory of God and the ultimate condition of man.

It is peculiarly the Revelation of Christ, since the divine purposes all revolve around Him. He is the Executor of divine judgments, the appointed Sovereign of the universe, the object of universal worship, the glorious Bridegroom of the Church, the hope of Israel, and the Deliverer of the world.

The Revelation was communicated to Christ by God, and transmitted by Christ through an angel to John, by whom it was penned for the benefit of the whole Church. Angelic ministry plays an important part in the Apocalypse and here, at the very outset, an angel is used as the medium of communication between our Lord and His apostle. The exact manner of the transmission is not plainly indicated, except that it is stated that the message was "signified" by the angel or, in other words, was made known by means of signs and symbols.

The human amanuensis, John, is described as the one who attested the Word (*Logos*) of God, a possible reference to the fourth Gospel (although this is disputed by Bengel and other commentators).

A benediction, such as appears in no other writing of the New Testament, is then pronounced upon the readers, hearers, and keepers of the words of the prophecy. The blessing upon those who keep the words of the prophecy is repeated again at the close of the book,[1] indicating the divine will that the Apocalypse should receive the special attention of God's people.

Public reading and exhortation were an integral and normal part of the usual synagogue service and also, to a great extent, in the gatherings of the early Church. Paul enjoined the young Timothy, for example, to "give attendance to (public) reading."[2] Verse 3 indicates that the public reading of the Revelation will meet with a special blessing from God. Dean Alford remarks that the words "form a solemn rebuke to the practice of the Church of England, which omits, with one or two exceptions, the whole of this book from her public reading." Unfortunately, the Anglican Church is not alone in her neglect of this book. Christians of all ecclesiastical views seem to have conspired together to avoid the teaching of the truths of the Revelation. Yet God has pronounced a blessing even upon its reading.

Those who listen intelligently to the reading and "keep," or apprehend, the truths and principles contained in the prophecy,

[1]Rev. 22. 7. [2]1 Tim. 4. 13

are also promised a blessing. As always in the New Testament, it is the "doer," and not the forgetful hearer, who receives the reward, but what is in view here is a more especial blessing than the normal recompence which is ever attendant upon the appreciation and assimilation of God's Word. It is the personal benediction of a Father who delights to see His people occupied with the unveiled glory of His beloved Son.

The reason for paying heed to the prophecy is then revealed: "the time is at hand." Fulfilment was imminent. In order that minds and hearts might be set free from disturbing care and rested in the eternal will of God, the revelation is given of the divine purposes. The knowledge of the certainty of those purposes reassures and establishes the soul, and dispels every doubt and fear. "The time is at hand."

Salutation and Response

"John to the seven churches that are in Asia: Grace to you and peace, from Him Who is and Who was and Who is to come; and from the seven Spirits who are before His throne; and from Jesus Christ, the faithful witness, the firstborn from the dead, and ruler of the kings of the earth. Unto Him that loveth us, and washed us from our sins in His blood; and He made us a kingdom, priests unto His God and Father; to Him be the glory and the dominion unto the ages of the ages. Amen" (I. 4-6).

The brief prologue is followed by an apostolic salutation, addressed not to the whole Church but to the seven churches of proconsular Asia (the reasons for this are referred to later).

From the Triune God issues a greeting of grace and peace—*grace*, the divine favour in which every blessing originates, and *peace*, the state of heart and soul resulting from the operations of grace.

God is presented here, not in the character and relationship in which He has made Himself known to the Church, but with titles and attributes which appear to pertain to the Old Testament rather than the New. This is patently deliberate and is in complete harmony with the governmental character of the book.

The Father is described as the One "Who is and Who was and Who is to come," *i.e.*, virtually the counterpart of the Old Testament name of Jehovah, and an ascription to God of eternal and underived being. In the temple of Athene at Sais was an inscription referring to the goddess in these words: "I am all that has come into being, and that which is, and that which shall be." The inscription was one of the familiar religious topics of that day, and it is extremely probable that there is a subtle reference to it in the divine name employed by the apostle. Whatever was claimed falsely for the idol was true only of the Eternal God.

The Holy Spirit again is described as "the seven Spirits who are before His throne."[1] It is clear that the reference is to the Holy Spirit. "The Spirit comes into consideration here," says Hengstenberg, "not according to His transcendence, but according to His immanence—not according to His internal relation to the Father and the Son, but according to His mission. This is indicated by the words *before the throne* here and in ch. 4. 5, and from ch. 5. 6, where mention is made of the seven Spirits of God that are sent forth over the whole earth." The reference to the Holy Spirit as the seven Spirits of God, is seen by Scott as an implication of "the plenitude of His power and diversified activity."

Christ receives a threefold description. He is first referred to as "the faithful witness." "Behold, I have given Him for a Witness to the people," declared God through the prophet Isaiah,[2] and our Lord Himself said: "For this cause came I into the world that I should bear witness unto the truth."[3] Many another witness has stood before God, but there has only been One Whose testimony was marked by undeviating fidelity and unswerving loyalty to God. He faithfully represented the Father and bore witness to Him in the midst of unfaithfulness and death.

He is also "the firstborn from the dead"—a title which had already been given to Him by the Apostle Paul.[4] Others had been raised from the dead prior to our Lord's resurrection, so that the title obviously has no allusion to chronological order. It denotes instead His pre-eminence even in resurrection. Of all those who rise from the dead, He is supreme in rank and dignity. He was "declared to be the Son of God with power . . . by the resurrection from the dead," declared the apostle.[5] Others have risen, but Christ alone rose *never to die again*.

The third title accorded to Him is "ruler of the kings of the earth." "I will make Him My Firstborn, higher than the kings of the earth," writes the inspired Psalmist.[6] When "the kings of the earth" break out in open rebellion against Jehovah and His Messiah, God plainly states: "Yet have I set My King upon My holy hill of Zion."[7] This mighty One, Whom he describes as His only begotten Son, shall assume universal sovereignty, shattering every opposing force and crushing every heathen power.

Immediately the dignities of Christ are brought into view, there results an unrestrained outburst of emotion from His own people.

[1]Rev. 4. 5 [2]Isa. 55. 4 [3]John 18. 37 [4]Col. 1. 18
[5]Rom. 1. 4 [6]Psa. 89. 27 [7]Psa. 2. 6

He is the One Who loved us unto death and Whose affection has surrounded us with mercy and grace all along our pilgrim path. His sacrifice has effected our redemption. His death has settled the question of sin and its penalty, and has freed us from the consequences of our guilt. He has "washed (or loosed) us from our sins in His blood." He has constituted us a kingdom of priests, setting royal dignity upon our brow and fitting us for sacerdotal ministry as kingly priests after His own pattern.[1]

It is little wonder that the response goes out to Him from those whom He has loaded with benefits: "To Him be the glory and the dominion unto the ages of the ages." Heartfelt worship and adoration flow out to Him in the unstinted homage and tribute of His own people. Their only desire is His exaltation and eternal glory.

The Coming One

"Behold, He cometh with the clouds; and every eye shall see Him, and they who pierced Him; and all the tribes of the earth shall mourn over Him. Even so, Amen. I am the Alpha and the Omega, saith the Lord God, Who is and Who was and Who is to come, the Almighty" (1. 7, 8).

As our Lord enlightened His disciples concerning the events connected with the Great Tribulation, He revealed that the period would conclude with His epiphany. "They shall see the Son of Man coming on the clouds of heaven with power and great glory.[2] Daniel, alluding to the same moment, says: "One like the Son of Man came with the clouds of heaven."[3] Similarly, the New Testament seer beholds Him coming with the clouds.

Trench points out that the clouds are "the symbols of wrath, fit accompaniments of judgment." The pavilion round about the Almighty is said to be "dark waters and thick clouds of the skies,"[4] while again it states that "clouds and darkness are round about Him,"[5] He "riseth upon a swift cloud,"[6] and "clouds are the dust of His feet."[7]

The dazzling epiphany of the Son of Man, as He descends in the transcendent and blazing light of the shekinah, and riding upon the clouds of heaven, will burst upon the eyes of the whole world. All mankind will behold that awful splendour, and terror will seize every heart. The sight of that glorious One, whom their fathers once crucified, will bow down the Jews in sorrowful mourning.[8] At that dreadful blaze of light, the rebellious nations whom He has come to judge will wail in fear and terror (cf. Matt. 24. 30). And in confirmation, it is added "Even so (Greek), Amen" (He-

[1]Zech. 6. 13 [2]Matt. 24. 30 [3]Dan. 7. 13 [4]Psa. 18. 11
[5]Psa. 97. 2 [6]Isa. 19. 1 [7]Nah. 1. 3 [8]Zech. 12. 10

brew), as though to indicate to both Jew and Gentile that His will is final and unalterable, and that His coming is a fact of absolute certitude.

Among the many titles assumed by our Lord in the Apocalypse, that in I. 8—"the Alpha and the Omega—" is perhaps one of the most remarkable. Alpha and Omega are, of course, the first and the last letters of the Greek alphabet respectively, so that the title is a tacit claim to the possession of every power, grace, virtue, and trait comprehended between the two extremes of human knowledge and understanding. All power and authority, all knowledge and sufficiency, all graces, virtues, and beauties, all dignity, majesty, honour, and right are held within those extremes and are, therefore, attributed in their entirety to Christ. He is, moreover, the summation of all thought, hope, and purpose. In fact, everything is comprehended in Him.

The significance is even more marked in Hebrew, however. Newell says: "The expression 'from *aleph* to *tau*' (the first and last letters of the Hebrew alphabet) was used by the Hebrew rabbis to signify *completely*, entirely." In Hebrew, moreover, every letter has a meaning and *aleph* stands for an ox, while *tau* signifies a cross. The ox is regarded as the figure of patient, unremitting service, whilst the cross is the potent reminder of the supreme sacrifice and devotion of Calvary.

Christ is the Alpha and Omega, the beginning and the ending, the One by Whom creation came into being and unto Whom it is all tending.

The title "Who is and Who was and Who is to come,"[1] is repeated, and the Speaker then claims to be "the Almighty." He identifies Himself with God the Father and virtually declares that He is the possessor of absolute power and infinite and inexhaustible resources: He is the Omnipotent.

Introduction to the Vision

"I, John, your brother and partaker with you in the tribulation and kingdom and patience of Jesus, was in the isle that is called Patmos, for the word of God, and the testimony of Jesus. I was in the Spirit on the Lord's day, and I heard behind me a great voice, as of a trumpet saying, What thou seest, write in a book, and send it to the seven churches; unto Ephesus, and unto Smyrna, and unto Pergamum, and unto Thyatira, and unto Sardis, and unto Philadelphia, and unto Laodicea" (I. 9-11).

Tribulation is the common heritage of the people of God, and the apostle enjoyed no immunity therefrom: he had passed through the same experiences as befell his fellow-believers. In the perse-

[1]Rev. I. 4

cution which broke out during the reign of Domitian, many Christians were banished to the mines and quarries, and Tacitus says that "the sea was thickly strewn with exiles, the crags were stained with the blood of victims." According to tradition, John's fidelity to his Master resulted in his being banished to Patmos and condemned to work in the marble quarries there.

The island was one of the Sporades, the south-eastern group of the islands of the Ægean, and it has been described as "a mere mass of barren rocks, dark in colour and cheerless in form. It lies out in the open sea. It has neither trees nor rivers, nor any land for cultivation, except some little nooks between the ledges of rocks. There is still a dingy grotto remaining, in which the aged apostle is said to have lived." It was in this dreary, inhospitable place that the Apocalyptic visions were seen.

There is no inconcinnity in the association of the three words "tribulation," "kingdom," and "patience" in verse 9. "Tribulation is the appointed path to the kingdom," writes Walter Scott, and only in the patience of Christ are the trials and suffering endured. Furthermore, "tribulation worketh patience."

"I was in the Spirit on the Lord's day," writes the exiled apostle. Considerable controversy has raged over this expression. Did John simply mean that he was under the control of the Holy Spirit on the first day of the week, or did he intend to imply that he had been conveyed in thought by the Holy Spirit to that awful time so frequently referred to in the Old Testament as "the day of the Lord"? It must be admitted that, if the intention was to indicate the date of the vision, the words "in the Spirit" have little significance. On the other hand, the greater part of the book is concerned with the events which will take place during "the day of the Lord," and if reference is to that period, the words "in the Spirit" emphasize at once the inspiration of the book.

The first day of the week is consistently termed "the first of the week" in the New Testament, and there is no evidence that it was ever called "the Lord's day" in the early Church. If it is argued that the expression differs in form from the Old Testament "the day of the Lord," it should be pointed out that "there is no adjective for 'Lord's' in Hebrew; and the only way of expressing 'the Lord's day' is by using the two nouns, 'the day of the Lord.' In Greek there are two ways of expressing this: either by saying literally, as in Hebrew, 'the day of the Lord,' or by using the adjective 'Lord's' instead. It comes to the same thing as to signification; the difference lies only in the emphasis" (Bullinger).

During Israel's journey through the wilderness, divine commands and instructions all reached the people through the media of two silver trumpets.[1] So, when Christ would impart the Revelation of Himself to the apostle, a great voice like the sound of a trumpet burst upon John's consciousness from behind. This was no matter of trivial significance, but a communication of the utmost importance to the people of God, and a full publicity was given to it by trumpet sound.

The phrase, "I am Alpha and Omega, the first and the last," which is here inserted by the A.V., is generally agreed to be an interpolation.

The seer was then directed to record in a book the visions which were about to burst upon his gaze and to send the book to the seven churches of Asia. The question naturally arises why these particular churches should have been singled out to be the recipients of this special revelation. With the possible exception of Laodicea, they were evidently neither large nor important ecclesiastically. Indeed, proconsular Asia itself was not very large, being composed merely of the western half of the peninsula of Asia Minor. Conquered by the Romans in the war against Antiochus the Great of Syria, it had been bestowed upon Eumenes, king of Pergamum, in 189 B.C., but 56 years later it was bequeathed by his nephew, Attalus III, to the Romans. A virtual bridge between the east and the west, its trade made it the wealthiest province of the Roman Empire, and even now, Crœsus, one of its kings, and Pactolus, one of its rivers, are proverbial for riches and prosperity.

The spiritual conditions of the seven Asian churches presented practically every problem and difficulty which have confronted the Church throughout her history, and it appears to have been for this reason that the communication was addressed to these particular gatherings. In addition, their peculiar circumstances and state combined to furnish a precise and detailed outline of the spiritual history of the Church from sub-apostolic days to the close of the present era.

Geographically the seven churches formed a rough circle, and the vision in the latter part of Rev. 1 portrays the Lord as standing in the midst of them, taking account of every happening.

The meaning of the names of the churches is extremely interesting. Asia itself means *slime* or *mire*—surely a type of the sinful world in which the Church is found. Ephesus means *desired* or

[1]Num. 10

desirable, a term applied by a lover to the maiden of his choice. Smyrna means *myrrh*, the symbol of sorrow and suffering. Pergamum means *marriage, elevation, or firm union*, a fitting name for the church in that city. The meaning of Thyatira is *incense*, but Sardis means *remnant* or *escaping ones*, whilst Philadelphia means *brotherly love*. Laodicea conveys the idea of *the people's right* or *the people's judgment*. An examination of the letters to these churches suggests very strongly that their names are by no means irrelevant, but are definitely indicative of their spiritual history or condition.

Little is now left of the churches. In fact, their present condition is a tragic commentary upon the transience of life.

Gibbon writes in *Decline and Fall* that "In the loss of Ephesus, the Christians deplored the fall of the first angel, the extinction of the first candlestick of the Revelation; the desolation is complete; and the temple of Diana or the church of Mary will equally elude the search of the curious traveller. The circus and three stately theatres of Laodicea are now peopled with wolves and foxes; Sardis is reduced to a miserable village; the God of Mahomet, without a rival or a son, is invoked in the mosques of Thyatira and Pergamos, and the populousness of Smyrna is supported by the foreign trade of the Franks and Armenians. Philadelphia alone has been saved by prophecy or courage. At a distance from the sea, forgotten by the emperors, encompassed on all sides by the Turks, her valiant citizens defended their religion and freedom above fourscore years, and at length capitulated with the proudest of the Ottomans. Among the Greek colonies and churches of Asia, Philadelphia is still erect—a column in a scene of ruins—a pleasing example that the paths of honour and safety may sometimes be the same."

The Vision of Christ

"And I turned to see the voice which spake with me. And having turned I saw seven golden lampstands; and in the midst of the lampstands One like unto the Son of Man, clothed with a garment down to the foot, and girt about at the breasts with a golden girdle. And His head and His hairs were white as white wool, white as snow; and His eyes were as a flame of fire; and His feet like unto burnished brass, as if it had been refined in a furnace; and His voice as the voice of many waters. And He had in His right hand seven stars: and out of His mouth proceeded a sharp two-edged sword: and His countenance was as the sun shineth in his strength" (I. 12-16).

Turning to see who spoke to him, John was confronted with a vision of Christ in His glory, standing in the centre of seven golden lampstands.

On the left side of the altar of incense in the Tabernacle stood a golden lampstand, consisting of a main shaft, out of which proceeded seven branches (one upright and three on either side). The branches were ornamented with calyces, knops, and flowers, and on their extremities were placed seven lamps containing pure olive oil. The lampstand furnished the only light in the sanctuary and was kept continually burning.[1]

In the Temple later erected by Solomon, ten golden lampstands, constructed on the same pattern, took the place of the one candelabrum of the Tabernacle.

In the Apocalyptic vision, however, the lampstands are seven in number and they all surround the Lord and throw their light upon His perfections. In verse 20, they are interpreted as a type of the seven churches. So that at least one of the responsibilities of the local church is to reveal, by its shining testimony to Him, the glories and beauties of the Lord.

Christ is here described as the Son of Man, a term used about a hundred times of Ezekiel, once of Daniel,[2] and some seventy times of Christ. It is a title expressive of His dominion as man (cf. Psa. 2. 4, 8; John 5. 27), and is, therefore, fittingly employed in relation to this glorified Personage Who is about to take His power and reign.

In the midst of the blaze of light, John beheld that majestic Figure, clothed, not, as in earthly days, in the short, seamless tunic and the flowing cloak of the peasant, but now in a garment down to the feet and encircled at the breast with a golden girdle. In the East the long robe or stole was always the garment of honour and dignity. The worker girded up his garments and girt them about his loins. His girdle would be fastened around the waist or loins (cf. Isa. 11. 5). But this One was robed to the feet and girt about the breasts. Here He was revealed in judicial glory and majesty. His affections were restrained and the sovereign cincture controlled His emotions. He stood as priest and as king.

The blinding whiteness, which John once saw on the Mount of Transfiguration[3] was seen once more. "His head and His hairs were white as white wool, as white as snow." White hairs are, of course, a sign of maturity. Christ's here were not the white hairs of senility or decay, but of the absolute holiness and wisdom of the Judge (cf. also the Ancient of days in Dan. 7. 9). The glittering splendour of His head indicated His dignity and majesty.

His eyes are likened to a flame of fire, penetrating everything in

[1]Exod. 25. 31-40 [2]Dan. 8. 17 [3]Mark 9. 3

their consuming and omniscient keenness. "His eyes behold, His eyelids try, the children of men," says the Psalmist.[1] Fire is a frequent symbol in Scripture for divine anger, and those burning eyes intelligently read the secret and hidden motives of the heart, and bring the hidden things to light.

His feet resembled burnished brass, refined in a furnace. The reference, however, is rather to the bronze used in military weapons and is indicative of the ruthless, unyielding character of the justice He was about to mete out. His foes will be utterly crushed and His enemies trampled in the dust.

His voice was "as the voice of many waters." Ezekiel uses a similar expression of the glory of the God of Israel, when he says: "His voice was like the noise of many waters"[2] and the Psalmist declares that "the Lord on high is mightier than the noise of many waters."[3] Above the roar of the mighty torrent and the ceaseless beating of the boisterous waves is the thunderous voice of the Son of God. "The grandeur, the majesty of His voice is beyond the ceaseless roar of many cataracts," says Scott, who aptly interprets the symbol as "the sign of His supreme sovereignty and majesty over all the waves of human passion, over the circumstances of a wrecked world and a ruined Church."

Like a wreath or galaxy around His right hand were seven stars, interpreted in verse 20 as the angels of the churches. "Stars," says Trench, "are symbols of lordship and authority, ecclesiastical or civil," and the right hand, of course, is indicative of power and authority. All ecclesiastical authority is vested in Christ. He appoints, maintains, upholds, and directs, and authority is derived from no other source but Him.

A sharp two-edged sword issued out of His mouth (cf. Isa. 49. 2), and this is identified as the Word of God.[4] It is not seen here, however, in its convicting and converting power, but rather in its judicial destructiveness. It discerns the thoughts and intents of the heart and divides soul and spirit. All that is contrary to the will of God is ruthlessly destroyed. Judgment is executed simply by the power of the Word.

"His countenance was as the sun shineth in his strength." Once that blessed face was marred and spat upon. Now it shone in the resplendent glory which earth had once seen on that Transfiguration Mount. The Eastern churches, to whom this message was sent, had formerly known the worship of the sun-god. To them the reference was plain. Here was One Whose radiant glory outshone

[1]Psa. 11. 4 [2]Ezek. 43. 2 [3]Psa. 93. 4 [4]Heb. 4. 12

the splendour of all the false gods of the East. Their brightness paled into nothing before His incomparable glory.

The wonderful description given of our Lord in verses 13-16 details all the essentials of His dignity, glory and character. When He later addressed the churches individually, He drew from this description certain especial characteristics which were applicable to the particular church. He presented Himself in a different aspect to each, and it needs the whole of the seven different aspects to make up the complete portrait in these verses, just as it similarly takes the conditions of the seven churches to make up the complete picture of the universal Church.

John's Commission

"And when I saw Him, I fell at His feet as one dead. And He laid His right hand on me, saying, Fear not; I am the first and the last, and the Living One; and I became dead, and behold, I am alive unto the ages of the ages, and I have the keys of death and of Hades. Write therefore the things which thou sawest, and the things which are, and the things which shall come to pass hereafter; the mystery of the seven stars which thou sawest in My right hand, and the seven golden lampstands. The seven stars are the angels of the seven churches: and the seven lampstands are seven churches" (1. 17-20).

The transcendent glory of the Almighty is such that even the seraphim veil their faces and dare not gaze thereon.[1] When Moses sought to behold that glory, Jehovah declared: "There shall no man see Me and live."[2] Isaiah could only acknowledge his sinfulness, whilst Daniel and Ezekiel could only fall upon their faces in fear before that blazing Presence.

So also, when John beheld the glorified Christ in the midst of the churches, he fell at His feet in a deathlike swoon. Worship and adoration might justly have bowed him to the ground, but the fear which filled his heart was a greater emotion still. But the touch of the One he had known as the companion of Galilee's lanes, and the voice of his Master dispelling his dread, brought him back to his senses once more.

"I am the first and the last," said that majestic Speaker, using an expression which He thrice applies to Himself in this book. The only other occurrences of this expression are in Isaiah's prophecy,[3] where it is employed three times as a title of Jehovah. It is clear in Isaiah that the title connotes all the fulness and attributes of the Godhead. Indeed, Jehovah declares: "I am the first, and I am the last; and beside Me there is no God."[4] So that the use of the title by our Lord is tantamount to a claim to identity with God in all His powers and attributes.

[1]Isa. 6. 2 [2]Exod. 33. 20 [3]Isa. 41. 4; 44. 6; 48. 12 [4]Isa. 44. 6

He is, in very fact, the first and the last. He is from eternity to eternity. "He is before all things, and in Him all things consist."[1] Everything originated in Him, and unto Him everything tends. He is the first in every realm and He reaches to every extreme as the last. All is comprehended in Him, and beyond Him there can be nothing.

Our Lord added further that He is the living One, Who became dead, but now lives for ever. He is the fountain and source of life, to Whom absolute being belongs by inherent right. He had an eternal subsistence with the Father. "In Him was life"[2] unoriginated, uncreated, and eternal. Yet that mighty self-existent One "became dead." Even in His incarnation, death could have no claim upon that sinless One, but He voluntarily bowed to the dust of death, "that through death He might bring to naught him that had the power of death, that is, the devil; and might deliver them who through fear of death were all their lifetime subject to bondage."[3]

Subjecting Himself to death, Christ entered Hades, the place of departed spirits; but neither death nor Hades could hold their prey. He broke their fetters, wrested from Satan the "keys" of death and Hades, and burst from the grave in triumphant resurrection, never again to taste of death but to live for evermore. The glorious Victor is Master of the devil and Lord over body, soul, and spirit.

The threefold division of the book indicated in verse 19 has already been commented upon. The mystery of the seven stars and the seven lampstands is then explained, the latter being interpreted as the churches and the former as their angels.

Controversy has long raged over these "angels." Scripture normally regards a star as the figure of authority or leadership. Faithful teachers, for example, are described as stars that shall shine for ever,[4] whilst false teachers are termed "wandering stars."[5] Were the "angels," then, the teachers of the churches?

Ebrard states that the churches had sent their messengers to John at Patmos and that they were therefore called the angels of the churches, but there is nothing to support this ingenious explanation. Many commentators suggest that the angel was either the presiding presbyter or the bishop of a diocese, but no episcopate was then in existence. Nor could the reference be to the pastor or minister in charge of the congregation, since a difference between clergy and laity was at that time practically unknown.

On the basis of Matt. 18. 10, Dean Alford assumes that literal

[1]Col. 1. 17 [2]John 1. 4 [3]Heb. 2. 14, 15 [4]Dan. 12. 3 [5]Jude 13

angels looked after the affairs of the churches. Anderson Scott goes even further by asserting that the angel of the church was "its heavenly counterpart and representative, the composite personality of the Church as seen by God. The angel is identified with his Church as partaker of its character and also of its destiny to a degree which could not be predicted of any human representative." But, as Trench says, "How could holy angels be charged with such delinquencies as are laid to the charge of some of the angels here?"[1]

The reference seems to be rather to the abstract spirit (or character) of the churches than to some spirit being. The words may have been applicable to some extent to some one person who was representative of the church and its character, but they could only apply strictly to the church as such and not to an individual therein. Godet is probably correct when he says that the angel is the "ideal embodiment of the Church . . . the spiritual personification of the Church."

The stars were held in Christ's right hand—the place of honour and authority. All ecclesiastical authority, whether in ministry or in spiritual rule, is vested in Christ. He appoints; He sustains; He empowers.

Unlike the seven-branched lampstand of the Tabernacle, the seven lampstands each stood upon its own base. In other words, each church had its individual responsibility to the Lord and was answerable alone to Him. He stood in the midst, sustaining and maintaining, reproving, correcting, and encouraging, and cognisant of every act.

The lighted lamps around Him all threw their beams of light upon the glorious central Person. The mission of the Church is to bear testimony to Christ. It is not creeds or dogma that the local Church is called upon to present to the world, but the matchless worth of her Lord and Master.

As lampstands of *gold*, the Churches (by divine grace) partake of the same nature as Christ. Divine righteousness has been imputed to them, and every member rejoices in the possession of a new life which originated above. The fact that there were seven indicates, of course, the moral completeness of the witness, as also of the picture which our Lord was about to paint.

[1]Rev. 2. 4; 3. 1, 15

Chapter III

The Seven Churches

Introductory

THE Lord's messages to the angels of the seven Churches of Asia form the contents of Chapters 2 and 3.

As suggested previously, these seven Churches were selected deliberately, and, in all probability, because their spiritual conditions, trials, and difficulties, as well as their character and failings, summarise broadly the condition and general state of the companies of God's people throughout the present dispensation. Whilst the letters had a local and direct application to the Churches to which they were addressed, they are also paradigmatic of the whole Church. Whatever the circumstances at any day or in any generation, there is a parallel in these two chapters.

The letters are of personal value to every believer, since they also portray the different types of Christian in existence at any and every period. The careful reader finds his own portrait there, and also discovers in the messages the Divine corrective or encouragement.

In addition, there is undoubtedly a prophetic outline of ecclesiastical history. The letters suggest seven distinct periods, each with its own peculiar characteristics, and it is significant to note that there have actually been seven such periods. (It is obvious, of course, that the periods overlap to some extent and that one does not necessarily cease before the next commences).

Scofield's note is very apt: "The messages to the seven Churches have a fourfold application: (1) *local*, to the Churches actually addressed; (2) *admonitory*, to all the Churches in all time as tests by which they may discern their true spiritual state in the sight of God; (3) *personal*, in the exhortations to him 'that hath an ear,' and in the promises 'to him that overcometh'; (4) *prophetic*, as disclosing seven phases of the spiritual history of the Church from, say, A.D. 96 to the end."

Wm. Hoste also traces "an analogy between the history of man, especially of Israel, and that of the Church. The history of the race begins with a fallen man, that of the Church with a fallen Ephesus. Man lost the tree of life; the overcomer here regains it. Smyrna, in the fires of persecution, may present an analogy with Israel in the brick-kilns of Egypt; Pergamos with Israel in the wilderness, fed with manna and opposed by Balaam; Thyatira, with Israel in the land, exposed to the wiles of Jezebel, the idolatress. The overcomer will reign. Sardis may correspond with Israel in Babylon. When tested, some of these could not find 'their names written.' In Philadelphia we have the return of the remnant. Laodicea has close analogies with the condition of the returned remnant in Malachi's day."

It is of interest to note the order of the promises to the overcomer in the letters to the seven Churches.

In *Ephesus*, he shall eat of the tree of life in the paradise of God, an undoubted reference to the tree of life in the earthly paradise in Genesis 1.

In *Smyrna*, he shall not be hurt of the second death, a reminder of the entry of the first death as a result of sin in Genesis 3.

In *Pergamos*, the hidden manna is to be his food, the unmistakable counterpart of the food of Israel's wilderness journey.

In *Thyatira*, he is to triumph over the nations, an unquestioned connection with the earthly reigns of David and Solomon.

In the last three epistles, however, the promises are all of a heavenly character.

In *Sardis*, he is to be confessed before the Father.

In *Philadelphia*, he is to enter the new Jerusalem as an avouched citizen.

In *Laodicea*, he is to reign with Christ.

EPHESUS

Once the chief harbour of Asia, the city of Ephesus was formerly situated on the coast, but it is now a practically unknown inland village with a few heaps of stones and mud, and some untenantable cottages. Owing largely to its position and to the silting up of the harbour, changes and vicissitudes characterised its history. As one writer says: "The land and the site of the city varied constantly. What was water became land; what was city ceased to be inhabited; what was bare hillside and cultivated lowland, became a great city, crowded with a teeming population." Mutability was in fact the law of its being.

These circumstances naturally had their effect upon the citizens, and even upon the Church, and the Apocalyptic message portrays an evanescent, changeable assembly, the members of which were unstable and uncertain.

The city was renowned for its huge temple of Artemis (or Diana), upon which untold riches had been spent, and which was one of the seven wonders of the world. The temple enshrined a tremendous image of the many-breasted goddess, which was reputed to have fallen from heaven. One of the principal Ephesian trades was the making of small silver shrines of Diana, for which a ready market was found all over Asia Minor.

Ephesus was also a centre for the study of the arts of magic, and was renowned all over the world for its talismans, incantations, and magical books and charms, for which the most fabulous sums were paid.

When the Apostle Paul preached in this city, he came with signs of just the nature that would appeal to such a people. Even handkerchiefs and aprons which had touched him had a miraculous healing power imparted to them,[1] and the Ephesians were arrested by these wonders. They acknowledged a supernatural power greater than their own magic, and those who accepted the Gospel burnt their books of magic in the marketplace.

At Paul's first brief visit, he found a ready ear in the synagogue from the Jews, who were subsequently instructed further by Apollos, Aquila, and Priscilla.[2] At a second visit, however, opposition drove him from the synagogue, and for two years he preached daily in the school of Tyrannus, with great blessing to Jews and Greeks,[3] ultimately leaving for Macedonia after the uproar caused by Demetrius, the silversmith, and other followers of Diana.

One of the most touching incidents in the life of the apostle was his farewell message to the Ephesian elders, who met him by appointment at Miletus, and their consequent sorrow as they realized that they would never see him again.[4]

From the Epistle to the Ephesians it appears that one of the chief characteristics of these young Christians was their love for Christ and for one another. Yet the picture portrayed in Rev. 2 is of a church in which love had waned and enthusiasm had disappeared.

The conditions of the local Church, however, were but a reflection of the general state of the whole Church at the close of the apostolic period, and there is little doubt that the Apocalyptic description has a much wider application than to a small Eastern assembly, and has reference to the period of ecclesiastical history immediately after the Apostles.

[1]Acts 19. 12 [2]Acts 18 [3]Acts 19 [4]Acts 20

THE LETTER TO EPHESUS

To the angel of the church in Ephesus write: These things saith He that holdeth the seven stars in His right hand, He that walketh in the midst of the seven golden lampstands: I know thy works, and thy labour and patience, and that thou canst not bear evil men, and didst try them, who call themselves apostles, and they are not, and didst find them false; and thou hast patience and didst bear for My name's sake, and hast not grown weary. But I have this against thee, that thou didst leave thy first love. Remember therefore from whence thou art fallen, and repent, and do the first works; or else I come to thee, and will move thy lampstand out of its place, except thou repent. But this thou hast, that thou hatest the works of the Nicolaitans, which I also hate. He that hath an ear, let him hear what the Spirit saith to the churches. To him that overcometh, to him will I give to eat of the tree of life, which is in the Paradise of God (2. 1-7).

In each of the seven letters, the communication is addressed to the angel of the Church, *i.e.* to the spiritual personification of the Church.

Further, in each of the seven epistles, Christ is presented in a different manner, but comparison indicates that, from the full description of His glory in Rev. 1, distinctive features are selected in each case, and that, in each instance, the particular characteristics selected are those which are either specially applicable, or else of peculiar significance to the particular Church addressed. This is obviously not accidental, but of deliberate design.

To Ephesus, Christ presents Himself as "He that holdeth the seven stars in His right hand, He that walketh in the midst of the seven golden lampstands." In Rev. 1. 20 it is explained that the stars are the angels of the Churches. In that chapter, they are seen on His right hand, but in the Ephesian letter, He *holds* them in His right hand. In this Divine security, there is confidence for the weak and assurance for the faithful. None can pluck them out of His hand. Nothing shall harm them there. Nor can His own with impunity neglect or despise Him: they cannot escape His hold.

He also walks in the midst of the lampstands. He takes cognisance of the testimony of the Churches and of their fidelity or failure in witness for Him. He supplies all needed power and grace, and is the sustainer of His people's testimony. As Dr. Plumptre has said, He trims the lamps in discipline and feeds them with the oil of grace. Never does He quench the smoking flax, although at times it may prove necessary to take away a lamp from its place, and to remove a local church from its earthly sphere of responsibility.

As in all the letters, He declares: "I know thy works." By His divine omniscience, everything is known and all things are apparent.

He perceives not merely the external act, but the inward motive that prompted it. In their weakness, His people may not be able to perform mighty exploits, but He is acquainted with their desires and intentions. He sees also below the veneer and outward show of the hypocrite, and reads the inward motives and character.

In addition to the general view of their works, He had appraised and approved the "labour and patience" of these Ephesian believers. He had seen their wholehearted toil in His name, and had regarded with satisfaction their faithful endurance.

It is not without significance that "work," "labour," and "patience" are joined together here. The same three things are connected in 1 Thess. 1. 3, but, in that passage, they are qualified by the cardinal virtues of Christianity, and the apostle writes of a "work of *faith*," a "labour of *love*," and a "patience of *hope*." The omission in Rev. 2 suggests that faith, love and hope had been lost to view, and that the work was a formality, the labour lifeless, and the patience uninspired.

Is not this the condition of many a church to-day? Christian work has become a form; the toil, which love should lighten and inspire, has become a burden; and the patient endurance, which should be brightened by glorious hope, has become a lifeless continuance. Meetings and services are still held, but inspiration has gone and enthusiasm has disappeared. Formal orthodoxy is the characteristic of the day. The Lord declares that He *knows*.

Despite their empty formality, however, the Ephesians were still unable to "bear evil men." In strict integrity of heart, they were intolerant of sin and evil men, and Christ singles out their fidelity to the truth as deserving of divine commendation. Their spiritual discernment detected the errors of the "false apostles" and heretical teachers who passed through the city on their way to Rome.

In that idolatrous city, the profession of Christianity was tantamount to an attack upon the principal trade—the manufacture of idols and shrines—and the Christian found his path to be no easy one. Suffering and persecution were the normal experience of those who acknowledged Christ. But the unfailing endurance of God's people was precious to the Lord, and met with His rich encomium: "Thou hast patience and didst bear for My name's sake and hast not grown weary."

In spite of all their fidelity and faithful endurance, however, Christ laments their desertion of their first love. Everything else paled into insignificance by the side of this. The first-named fruit of the Spirit is "love,"[1] and twenty references are found to this grace in Paul's Epistle to the Ephesians. Ephesus knew the meaning of love when *that* letter was penned, but there was apparently no evidence of love when the later message was sent to them. The fires of affection and devotion of early days had burned themselves out: they had left their first love.

The prophet Jeremiah paints vividly the warmth of first love: "I remember thee, the kindness of thy youth, the love of thine espousals, when thou wentest after Me in the wilderness, in a land that was not sown."[2] But now all the warmth had gone and their hearts were frozen.

Life holds few things more bitter than the tragedy of unrequited love. Throughout His earthly life our Lord cultivated the friendship and affection of His loved ones. He sought companionship wherever possible. Yet now He was robbed of the love of His own. Activity and service counted for nothing by the side of that.

Is not this true in some measure of the Church to-day? The intense devotion and wealth of love which were poured at the feet of the Lord Jesus Christ in earlier days are no longer in evidence. The stream of deep affection and heartfelt emotion, which flowed out to Him then, has now dried up. A formal relationship has superseded "the love of espousals," and the unsatisfied yearnings of the heart of Christ are ignored. The great need of the day is not so much a greater diligence in Christian service or a fuller sense of responsibility to the Church and the world, but rather a fresh realization of the love of Christ and the meaning of Calvary. In the responsive love of contrite spirits, affection might then well up to Him Who loved—and still loves—His people.

As a stimulus to a fresh outburst of affection, the Ephesians are exhorted to a remembrance of their former condition. By the reminder of the heights of their former joy and bliss, and of their one-time love for Himself, the Lord seeks to woo them back to Himself, to repentance and to a return to their previous frame of mind.

Unless there is repentance, He warns them: "I come to thee, and will move thy lampstand out of its place, except thou repent." The testimony of the church was valueless if true affection for Christ and His people no longer existed. There could be no power in their witness, nor any result from their service. So the removal —though not the extinction—of the lampstand is threatened.

In view of the natural conditions of Ephesus, our Lord's words

[1]Gal. 5. 22 [2]Jer. 2. 2

would appear specially apposite to the local Church. The city was constantly shifting; change was its characteristic, and the warning of possible removal was not only particularly applicable but readily understood. Indeed, it was not long before the words were literally fulfilled, and the lamp of testimony was actually removed. Elliott says: "The plough has passed over the site of Ephesus, and corn waves over the ruins. The candlestick of Ephesus has been removed."

In this respect history has not infrequently been repeated. More than one failing church, in which the real inspiration has been lost, has seen the removal of its testimony altogether, and the transfer of the lamp elsewhere. If love wanes until everything is an empty formality, the individual also may be removed from his sphere of service, and his witness and work transferred to another. Philip Mauro aptly remarks that "the maintenance of the testimony of the Church depends upon love for Christ, to Whom the Church belongs."

Despite their unsatisfactory heart condition, the Ephesians still retained a doctrinal faithfulness. They hated "the works of the Nicolaitans," which Christ also detested. Little is known of the Nicolaitans. It has been suggested by some commentators that the word is merely a symbolic name, derived from *nikao* (conquer) and *laos* (people) and indicative of the distinction which was drawn later between clerisy and laity.

On the other hand, the reference may be to the sect of the Nicolaitans, said by Irenæus to have been founded by Nicolas of Antioch, one of the deacons.[1] This sect apparently plunged into every kind of excess and licentiousness, professing Christianity but practising all the filthy impurities of the heathen around them. William Kelly says: "The essence of Nicolaitanism seems to have been the abuse of grace to the disregard of plain morality."

The Church of Ephesus took up an attitude of uncompromising disapproval of this extreme libertinism and the virtual vitiating of the doctrines of grace. It *hated* the loose living and shameless immorality of these men. Grace and freedom are not synonymous with indulgence and licence, and the carnality of Nicolaitanism is to be resolutely shunned by the child of God. Temptation was never greater than it is to-day, and ear and eye both require a constant guard set over them.

In the letters to the first three churches, the call to "hear what the Spirit saith," *precedes* the promise to the overcomer. In the last

[1]Acts 6. 5

four, it *follows*. In the first three messages, the repentance of the whole Church is viewed as a possibility. In spite of their failure, it was still possible for them all to overcome. But, in the last four only the few faithful ones in the Church are regarded as potential overcomers, and only to these overcomers is the word therefore addressed.

It is interesting to note also that, in each instance, the promise to the overcomer finds its basis in some symbol of the Old Testament. The Edenic tree of life[1] was removed from man's ken, with Adam's expulsion from the earthly Paradise. But the promise to the Ephesian overcomer is that he shall "eat of the tree of life, which is in the Paradise of God."

In each case the character of the promise contained in the peroration corresponds to the character of the faithfulness displayed. Those who had abstained from the idol meats and sinful dainties of the world, as offered by Nicolaitanism, are promised a corresponding reward or compensation. They shall eat of the tree of life. In Eden, "the life of innocence was dependent on obedience," says Walter Scott, but for the New Testament overcomer, "eternal life becomes an everlasting feast in the Paradise of God."

The Edenic tree was the symbol of life-giving power in a natural sense. The Apocalyptic tree is the type of eternal life that shall never fade. To the Asian Greek, to whom the promise was addressed, the tree was possessed of similar significance. Every man's life was commonly believed to be connected with some tree, into which it returned when he died (hence the planting of trees over graves). The tree was regarded as, in some mysterious sense, associated with divine life, and "to eat of the tree of life" would at once connote a partaking of the divine nature and power.

"We meet with echoes and reminiscences of this 'tree of life' in the mythologies of many nations," says Trench, "as in the Yggdrasil of our own northern mythology; and still more remarkable in the Persian Horn. This Horn is the king of trees, is called in the Zend-Avesta the Death-destroyer; it grows by the fountain of Arduisur, in other words, by the waters of life; while its sap drunken confers immortality."

The inspired writer thus carries back the gropings of paganism to the early Scriptural facts from which they sprang, and then gives their full and proper interpretation in the light of the fuller revelation of this later dispensation.

[1]Gen. 2. 9

SMYRNA

The city of Smyrna was situated some forty miles to the north of Ephesus, and was reputed to be one of the most magnificent cities of Ionia. During the reign of Tiberius it was almost destroyed by an earthquake, but it had risen phœnix-like from the ruins, and its splendid buildings around the hill of Pagos amply justified its reputation.

A wealthy commercial city, it had proved a faithful ally of Rome; indeed, this fidelity was the common boast of Smyrnean demagogues. This virtue of faithfulness, in which the people took such pride is, in fact, the keynote of the Apocalyptic epistle.

If, as is generally assumed, the reference of the Ephesian message is to the period immediately following apostolic days, the Smyrnean conditions obviously relate to the 250 years of the martyr period which culminated in the tenth and last persecution under Diocletian. Thousands of Christians died the death of martyrdom, flayed, burned alive, devoured by wild beasts, etc. The name of the city is closely connected with the aromatic myrrh and is, in itself, indicative of suffering and of the fragrance emanating from that which has been crushed and bruised.

The Letter to Smyrna

"And to the angel of the church in Smyrna write: These things saith the First and the Last, Who became dead and lived again: I know thy tribulation, and thy poverty (but thou art rich), and the blasphemy (or reviling) of them who say they are Jews, and they are not, but are a synagogue of Satan. Fear not the things which thou art about to suffer: behold, the devil is about to cast some of you into prison, that ye may be tried; and ye shall have tribulation ten days. Be thou faithful unto death, and I will give thee the crown of life. He that hath an ear, let him hear what the Spirit saith to the churches. He that overcometh shall not be hurt of the second death" (2. 8-11).

The character in which Christ presents Himself to this church is especially appropriate. These Christians had known the meaning of transience, of destruction, and (looking on to the more complete fulfilment in a later day) of persecution and danger. But Christ is essentially the permanent and abiding One. He is the end and the beginning. All things are summed up in Him and beyond Him there is nothing. All the storms beat in futility against this mighty rock.

In the character of the One "Who became dead and lived again," He presented a strong appeal to the Smyrneans. The patron deity of the city was Cybele, the nature-goddess, whose worship was based on her typical descent into death and resurrection in new life.

Taking up the very mythology of the people He addresses, our Lord indicates plainly that these are but the mists of human imagination, obscuring the glorious reality, and that He is the true life, which descended into death, and which, having burst forth again in resurrection power, still lives.

Not only was the appeal to religion, it was also to history. In 600 B.C., Smyrna was captured and destroyed by the Lydians, and Strabo states that for four centuries its name was obliterated from the roll of cities. But it was restored once more and again became an autonomous Greek city. It "*became dead and lived again.*"

It was practically wiped out by an earthquake, but again it revived. It "*became dead and lived again.*" These historical experiences were only shadows of something greater, and Christ assumes the place of the fulfilment of them all. "*I became dead and lived again.*"

The words carried their glorious message, moreover, to that enfeebled Church of a later day, suffering under the persecutions of pagan Rome. In effect, Christ declared that, even if their sufferings found their climax in physical death, yet from the dust of death would spring forth a far more glorious life, and they would still exist in the immortality of celestial realms of bliss. The One who Himself had died and Who now lived again was the personal pledge of His people's future life. No more appropriate message could there be for the period in question.

The tribulations and sufferings of God's people during the period of the Roman persecutions were at times almost unparalleled in history. But the Master declares, "I know thy tribulation." He took cognisance of every sorrow; His heart felt every pang; He counted every tear. The weight of oppression was fully known to Him, and the wealth of His divine sympathy went out to His people.

Still is that the experience of the Christian to-day. He knows our tribulation. Not a trial passes unnoticed, nor a difficulty unobserved. Our Great Shepherd knows every bruise sustained by His sheep, and every suffering experienced by them, and because He too has passed through suffering, He sympathises with His own.

Persecution was coupled, as ever in history, with spoliation of the victims' possessions. All property was confiscated by the imperial treasury, informers being paid a reward out of the estates of those whom they maliciously betrayed.

But the spoiling of their goods did not escape the eye of the Master, and He says that He knows their *poverty*, yet adds paradoxically that they are *rich*. Destitute and stripped of all their belongings, they were still rich in all the treasures of the eternal heights. The glorious inheritance of the saints in light was their possession.

The condition of Christians during the period of the Roman persecutions was simply deplorable. Stripped of everything, thrown out of employment, suffering physical hardships and tortures, even death at times proved a happy release.

We hardly realize the full weight of the Smyrnean difficulties. Plumptre says: "Persecution has its heroic and exciting side, and under its stimulus men do and dare much; but when, in addition to this, there is the daily pressure of ignoble cares, insufficient food, scanty, squalid clothing, the trial becomes more wearing, and calls for greater fortitude and faith."

The lot of these believers was worsened still further by the malignant opposition and calumniations of the Jews, many of whom acted as informers against them, and who are described enigmatically as "them who say they are Jews, and they are not, but are a synagogue of Satan."

The Apocalypse regards the Jewish antagonist as a sham and a hypocrite. He is not a true Jew, but inspired of the devil. His former nearness to God but emphasizes his present distance from Him. In his present state he is viewed as inspired of Satan.

"Fear not the things which thou art about to suffer," said our Lord. The storm was gathering. The savage cruelty of Rome was about to wreak its vengeance upon the inoffensive Christian, but the power of the devil who inspired it (and whose instruments the persecutors were) is limited and controlled. He cannot touch the feeblest saint without divine permission.

"Fear not." The Lord never conceals the cost of following Him, and never promises an easy path. Of Paul, for example, He says: "I will show him how great things he must suffer for My name's sake." But "Fear not." Even if the storm was about to break, neither dread nor despair need touch the child of God. The hour of trial would produce its own strength.

"The 'prison' into which the devil would cast some of the Smyrnean Christians," says Ramsay, "must be understood as a brief epitome of all the sufferings that lay before them; the first act, viz., their apprehension and imprisonment, is to be taken as implying all the usual course of trial and punishment through which the martyrs passed." Torture was the lot of many. Polycarp and others whose names still live were among those martyred at Smyrna.

Whilst enemies of flesh and blood were responsible for the physical sufferings, the divine Speaker traces the cause of all attacks to the sheer hatred of the devil toward divine things. But He assures the Church that the period of trial is limited to *ten days*, indicating that there is a limit beyond which the wrath of man and the bitterness of Satan are not permitted to go. We are never tried beyond the strength God gives us. The wind is tempered to the shorn lamb. The storm is limited in force to the individual's powers of resistance. But in all circumstances His grace is sufficient.

The "ten days" obviously refer to the ten persecutions through which the Church passed during her conflict with pagan Rome. The tenth, under Diocletian, lasted ten years, and the phrase may therefore have a dual significance.

Some, during the period, appalled by the dread of torture and death, denied their Lord. But He enjoins faithfulness unto death. The very words were a fresh reminder of the city's history. Smyrna had been the friend of Rome in times of adversity as well as in days of prosperity. On one occasion the citizens had even stripped themselves of their own garments to send them to the Roman soldiers who were suffering the hardships of a winter campaign against Mithridates. Cicero described the Smyrneans as "the most faithful of our allies." Faithfulness was the chief glory of the city. Ramsay says that the topic was "familiar to all inhabitants, and a commonplace in patriotic speeches."

As the citizens had been faithful, even unto death, for Rome, so Christ beseeches His people: "Be thou faithful unto death." He that persists to the end, he that is steadfast, shall triumph over death. Physical death may touch him, but he shall receive "the crown of life."

Just as the victor in the games received a crown or garland, so the faithful believer should be crowned. The figure goes further, however. Smyrna's patron goddess, Cybele, after typical resurrection, was crowned with a circlet of *battlements and towers*.* The Christian who passes through martyrdom should also be crowned. But the reference had an even fuller significance. The splendid buildings which encircled the rounded hill of Pagos, were commonly described as "the crown of Smyrna." The Smyrneans boasted of this "crown" to such an extent that Apollonius of

* Cybele wore a crown of towers because, as Ovid says, "she first created them in cities," by which fact she has been identified with Semiramis, the first queen of Babylon, who surrounded Babylon with a wall of brick and towers.

Tyana had advised them to be occupied rather with their own character than the glory of their city. "It is a greater charm," he said, "to wear a crown of men than a crown of porticos and pictures and gold." The *crown* was a common topic of the city.

Christ promises no fading laurel wreath, no earthly crown or glory, but the victor's crown of life.

"He that overcometh shall not be hurt of the second death." To be an overcomer in Smyrna meant a readiness for death and martyrdom. Reputation, possessions, and even life itself might be taken. Says Scott: "The overcomer may die under tortures prolonged and gloated over by the almost fiendish malice of men who delight in blood, but he is assured that he shall not be hurt of the second death." True life lay beyond. In no wise should he be touched by the second death and the very form of the expression but emphasizes the certainty of that truer and fuller life.

The name of the church (Smyrna) is a form of the word *myrrh* —an aromatic Arabian gum, used for embalming the dead. Death runs as a minor tone throughout the epistle, but there is a life beyond. The second death shall not lay hold upon the overcomer.

Chapter IV

The Seven Churches

(*Continued*)

PERGAMOS

PERGAMOS—or, more correctly, Pergamum—was the ancient capital of Asia. The Attalid kings all had their throne there, and when imperial Rome began to make her influence felt in the East, Eumenes II deemed it wise to ally himself with her, and in 133 B.C. Attalus III bequeathed the kingdom to Rome in his will. Pergamum then became the centre of Roman administration.

Little or no commerce was engaged in there. The city has been described by Dean Blakesley as a combination "of a pagan cathedral city, a university town, and a royal residence." It was renowned for its learning, refinement, and science. Scott says: "Its celebrated library, only second to that of Alexandria, with which it was ultimately incorporated, consisted of 200,000 books. It was here that the art of preparing skins of animals for writing upon was perfected, and from which our word *parchment* is derived."

Pergamum was also famed for its medical science, and among all its splendid temples for Zeus, Athene, Apollo, and other pagan deities, the most magnificent was that for Æsculapius, the god of medicine. Æsculapius was commonly termed the "Saviour" and "Preserver," and was frequently depicted in the form of a serpent. It is not surprising, therefore, to find the letter to Pergamum indirectly referring to the Pergamenian deity, when it speaks of "Satan's throne"* and "where Satan dwelleth."

Dispensationally, the period depicted in the epistle is that which followed upon the accession of Constantine. The night before the latter faced Maxentius in battle, he saw a vision of Christ with a cross, on which were the words, "*In hoc signo vinces*" ("In this sign thou shalt conquer"). Defeating Maxentius, he became

* In *Light from the Ancient East*, Adolf Deissman makes the suggestion that the huge altar of Zeus, which stood upon a base 100 feet square and was elevated 800 feet above the plain, is the object of the Seer's reference. "Actual inspection of the place," he says, "suggests that 'Satan's throne' can only have been the altar of Zeus; no other shrine of the hill-city was visible to such a great distance and could therefore rank so typically as the representative of Satanic heathendom."

emperor and, in A.D. 324, officially espoused Christianity and strove to force it upon the empire. Edicts of his predecessor relative to the persecution of Christians were repealed; Christians were honoured and pagans were banished from the court.

While still retaining his heathen high priestly title of *Pontifex Maximus*, Constantine assumed headship of the Church. Church and State were thus united and heathenism was gradually Christianised. Pagan temples became Christian churches; heathen festivals were converted into Christian ones; pagan priests slipped into office as Christian priests. In only too many respects the change was only one of nomenclature.

In the circumstances, the name of the city (which meant literally "twice married") seems singularly appropriate to the Church of Constantine's day. As Gaebelein pungently comments, it is "a typical name for the professing church which claims to be the bride of Christ, but is married to the world."

The Letter to Pergamum

"And to the angel of the Church in Pergamum write: These things saith He that hath the sharp two-edged sword: I know where thou dwellest, even where Satan's throne is: and thou holdest fast My Name, and didst not deny My faith, even in the days of Antipas My witness, My faithful one, who was killed among you, where Satan dwelleth. But I have a few things against thee, because thou hast there some that hold the teaching of Balaam, who taught Balak to cast a stumbling block before the children of Israel, to eat things sacrificed to idols, and to commit fornication. So hast thou also some that hold the teaching of the Nicolaitans in like manner. Repent therefore; or else I come to thee quickly, and I will make war against them with the sword of My mouth. He that hath an ear, let him hear what the Spirit saith to the Churches. To him that overcometh, to him will I give of the hidden manna, and I will give him a white stone, and upon the stone a new name written, which no one knoweth but he that receiveth it" (2. 12-17).

To the Church of Pergamum, the Lord appears as "He that hath the sharp two-edged sword." In the preceding chapter, the sword proceeds from His mouth, but here He holds it drawn and ready for use. The sword referred to is the sharp, pointed, two-edged military weapon and is figurative of the penetrative, searching power of the Word of God.

Prof. Ramsay writes: "In Roman estimation the sword was the symbol of the highest order of official authority, with which the Proconsul of Asia was invested. The 'right of the sword,' *jus gladii*, was roughly equivalent to the power of life and death; and governors of provinces were divided into a higher and a lower class, acccording as they were or were not invested with this power." Christ wears the symbol of absolute authority and, by it, tacitly claims to be invested with this power of life and death. It is in that character that He addresses the official capital of the province, the seat of authority in the ancient kingdom and also in the Roman administration. All authority is in His hands and everything is subject to Him.

"I know where thou dwellest, even where Satan's throne is," He declares. He is fully acquainted with the circumstances of His people and cognisant of all their peculiar difficulties and temptations. These Pergamenians dwelt in the centre of the serpent-worship, in the place where Satan was virtually enthroned. To remain faithful there would require more than normal strength and power.

The words have doubtless a subtle reference also to the conditions of that later day when Christianity came under imperial patronage, when paganism entered the Church, and pagan rites and ceremonies were assimilated by it. The Church of that period became so closely identified with the world-system of which Satan is the god, that Christians of that day could truly be said to dwell where Satan's throne was.

The bonds which exist to-day between many Christians and the world are a very real tragedy. So close is the alliance in some instances that it is well-nigh impossible to distinguish the child of God from the worldling. The separation, which should mark those who belong to Christ, is non-existent.

Despite the failure of so many and in spite of the constant difficulties around, loyalty to Christ was still in evidence and the fundamentals were firmly held. They had steadfastly held Christ's name and had not denied His faith. "Tried in the proconsular court and confronted with the alternative of conforming to the State religion or receiving immediate sentence of death," they had still remained faithful. Many suffered torture and martyrdom. One of their number, Antipas, was shut up in a brazen bull, which was then heated until it was red hot. The Lord always sets a high value upon fidelity to Him. The Pergamenians had not been ashamed to be known by His name and had remained loyal to Him, and He takes account of it with gladness.

In contrast there were some in Pergamum who held "the teaching of Balaam, who taught Balak to cast a stumbling-block before the children of Israel, to eat things sacrificed to idols, and to commit fornication." Bribed by Balak to curse the people of Israel, Balaam found his curses divinely transmuted to blessings on his very lips. So he then instigated the king to ensnare Israel (the word *stumbling-block* might as correctly be rendered a *trap* or *noose*, set in the path to entangle the unwary walker). Moabitish women prostituted themselves to the Israelites and then seduced them to idolatry, with the awful consequence of 24,000 deaths by the judgment of God.[1]

The implications of the Apocalyptic expressions are plain. Two sins were constantly before the Gentile believers in the early days of the Church: (1) the question of eating things sacrificed to idols, and (2) fornication.

Practically every beast slain was offered to some false god, part being taken by the priest and part remaining the possession of the worshipper. Most of the meat sold in the market would have been thus offered. Those who ate idol meat were regarded as identifying themselves with the particular idol, and the Council at Jerusalem accordingly forbade the Gentile Christians to eat thereof.[2] But a refusal to partake of idol meats meant abstinence from every festivity, and withdrawal from social life almost entirely, for sacrifice was bound up with almost every act of social life. When the problem arose at Corinth, Paul pointed out that the idol was nothing and the Christian a free man, but no one was to be stumbled.[3] The eating of idol meats was becoming a crucial test in the Gentile world, and it was essential for the Christian to separate himself from his fellows. Even to-day, the child of God finds the necessity at times to sacrifice legitimate pleasures in order to separate himself to Christ.

In the precincts of every temple, harlot priestesses offered themselves for prostitution. It was a part of the temple worship. The Lord holds against the Church of Pergamum that there were some there who tolerated these impure practices and suffered without protest (even if they did not actually encourage) the leading astray of His people. The illicit union of Church and world is again indicated in the picture drawn. Heart occupation with any other object than Christ is idolatry, and illicit intercourse with the world is spiritual fornication.[4] Our Lord claims absolute allegiance and loyalty. The Christian is sanctified unto Him.

The teaching of the Nicolaitans, which was in evidence in Ephesus[5] reappears in Pergamum. Dr. Ironside considers that "Nicolaitanism is really clerisy—the subjugation of those who were contemptuously styled 'the laity' by a hierarchical order who lorded it over them as their own possessions, forgetting that it is written, 'One is your Master, even Christ, and all ye are brethren.'"

The context, however, indicates a connection between Nicolaitanism and the teaching of Balaam. It has been stated by some

[1] Num. 24 and 25 [2] Acts 15. 20 [3] 1 Cor. 10. 25-27
[4] 2 Cor .6. 14-16 [5] Rev. 2. 6

that the Nicolaitans were an impure sect which indulged in extreme licentiousness, while still claiming to be children of God. A mixture of carnality and spirituality is always nauseating to God, and Christ plainly indicates His hatred of this evil teaching. It is still true for the present day that carnality and the indulgence of selfish desires are not for the true believer. His Lord demands sincere allegiance and a purity of heart and motive.

Christ is still the Head of His Church, and He warns the Pergamenians that unless they repent He will quickly exercise discipline therein "with the sword of His mouth." Evil will not continue unpunished.

To the overcomer in Pergamum was promised the gift of "the hidden manna"—an obvious reference to the golden pot of manna which was laid up in the ark as a memorial before the Lord.[1] Falling from heaven with the dew, manna became the food of Israel's wilderness journey. As the bread which came down from heaven it was a remarkable type of the Incarnation, whilst its description as small, round, and white beautifully suggested the lowliness, perfection, and purity of our Lord's earthly life.

No eye but Jehovah's rested upon the manna hidden within the ark, but for centuries it was the symbol to Him of that peerless life which should delight His heart in a then future day. The path of the overcomer was but a reflex of Christ's earthly life, and it is singularly appropriate that his reward should be the food of Christ's life. He had abstained from idol meats and should henceforth eat of the bread of God which came down from heaven.[2]

A white stone was also to be bestowed upon the overcomer, upon which was to be inscribed a new name, known only to the recipient. It was the practice to note days of festivity by a white stone, and days of calamity by a black stone. In the courts of justice also, when a vote was taken as to the guilt of an accused person, a white stone signified acquittal, and a black one condemnation. Many commentators see in the overcomer's white stone a reference to the *tessera*, or white stone, given to the victor at the games.

Ewald maintains, on the other hand, that it relates to the *tessera hospitalis*, which was bestowed upon close friends, on which the donor's name was inscribed, as an indication that the recipient could always claim a warm welcome and ready hospitality from him.

It is more probable, however, that what was intended was the *tessera*, or white stone, given to those who were invited to partake, within the precincts of the temple, of the sacred feast that naturally

[1]Exod. 16. 32-34 [2]John 6. 58

consisted only of meats offered to the idol. That stone bore the secret name of the deity represented by the idol and the name was known only to the recipient. Since the overcomer had refused fellowship with the idol and declined the idol stone, the Lord declared that He would bestow upon him a stone which would give him an entrée into the true temple, there to feast upon the bounties of heaven. There is always compensation in Him for every sacrifice made on earth.

"The name," says Ramsay, "acquired in popular belief a close connection with the personality, both of a human being and of a god. The true name of a god was kept secret in certain kinds of ancient religion, lest the foreigner and the enemy, by knowing the name, should be able to gain an influence over the god. The name guaranteed, and even gave, existence, reality, life; a new name implied the entrance on a new life . . . Knowledge of the compelling names of God, the names of God which influence nature and the mysterious forces of the universe, was one of the chief sources of the power which both the Mysteries and the magic ritual claimed to give their votaries. The person that had been initiated into the Mysteries learned not merely the landmarks to guide him along the road to the home of the blessed—he learned also the names of God which would open the gates and bars before him, and frighten away hostile spirits or transform them into friends . . . He who knows the right name of a demon or divine being can become lord over all the power that the demonic being possesses, just as he who knows the name of a man was considered to possess some power over the man, because the name partakes of reality and not merely marks a man's personality, but is almost identified with it."

What the Mysteries promised to give, Christ actually bestows. He gives His own new name—the source of power amd wisdom—to His own people. Those who are faithful to Him find all their desires satisfied in Him, whilst every sacrifice made in His name meets with a full and rich compensation.

THYATIRA

Now a wretched scene of poverty, with narrow, dirty streets and squalid houses—many made of mud—Thyatira was built by Seleucus I at the mouth of the long pass between the Hermus and Caicus valleys, and was originally a military city, garrisoned by Macedonian soldiers, set to guard the pass.

The city's tutelary deity was Tyrimnas, a sun-god, who was

generally depicted as a warrior riding forth to battle, armed with a double-edged battle-axe—the symbol of smashing military power. Such a deity might presumably be deemed most appropriate for a pagan military town.

It is, therefore, most significant that the character in which Christ is introduced to the Church of Thyatira is that of One with flaming eyes and feet of brass, whilst the promise to the overcomer is that he shall be rewarded with irresistible power among the nations—that smashing power which the city's own deity pretended to wield with his battle-axe.

From a prophetic standpoint, this epistle undoubtedly refers to the Popery of the Middle Ages, with all its corruptions, idolatries, and persecutions, practising its wickedness, Jezebel-like, under the cloak of religion. Early in the history of the Roman Church, her bishops claimed that Peter was primate among the apostles, and that his primacy was inherited by them. Their supremacy became generally recognized after the First Council of Nice, and from this sprang their claim to the right of government of the universal Church and the right of making all ecclesiastical appointments. The Bishop of Rome was declared to be vice-regent or vicar of Christ and the visible head of the Church, and was ultimately credited with infallibility on all doctrinal matters. He later became recognized as a temporal sovereign, and it soon became apparent that there were no limits to Papal ambition.

The Chaldee priest who interpreted the esoteric doctrine of the Babylonian mysteries was called Peter (*i.e.*, the interpreter), and it has been suggested that it is this Peter and not the Apostle, who is the origin of the Papal claim. Curiously enough, the two keys emblazoned on the Papal arms as insignia of spiritual authority closely resemble the two keys of Janus and Cybele, which the Chaldee priest wore.

It is interesting to note that one meaning of the name Thyatira is *continual sacrifice*, and that Roman Catholic priests state that, in the Mass, they offer a *continual sacrifice* for the sins of the living and the dead—a denial, of course, of Christ's finished work.

The Letter to Thyatira

"And to the angel of the church in Thyatira write: These things saith the Son of God, Who hath His eyes like a flame of fire, and His feet are like unto burnished brass: I know thy works, and thy love and faith and ministry and patience, and that thy last works are more than the first. But I have this against thee, that thou sufferest the woman Jezebel, who called herself a prophetess; and she teacheth and seduceth My servants to commit fornication, and to eat things sacrificed to idols. And I gave her time that she should repent; and she willeth not to repent of her fornication. Behold, I do cast her into a bed, and them that commit adultery with her into great tribulation, except they repent of her (their) works. And I will kill her children with death (or pestilence); and all the Churches shall know that I am He Who searcheth the reins and hearts; and I will give unto each one of you according to your works. But to you I say, to the rest that are in Thyatira, as many as have not this teaching, who know not the deep things of Satan, as they say; I cast upon you none other burden. Howbeit that which ye have, hold fast till I come. And he that overcometh, and he that keepeth My works unto the end, to him will I give authority over the nations: and he shall rule them with a rod of iron; as vessels of the potter, are they broken to shivers; as I also have received of My Father: and I will give him the morning star. He that hath an ear, let him hear what the Spirit saith to the Churches" (2. 18-29).

An essential part of the Papal claim to ecclesiastical supremacy is the pretence that Peter was the foundation and also the supreme administrator of the Church. The Epistle to Thyatira opens with the resounding words: "These things saith the Son of God," at once, by inference, nailing Rome's lie to the counter and recalling Peter's own confession immediately prior to our Lord's first reference to the founding of the Church.[1] It is the only instance in the seven epistles of Christ's introduction in the character of Son of God. In anticipation of Popery's claims, His words plainly refer to the immutable foundation upon which the Church is built. He (not Peter) is Founder and He (not Peter) is Administrator.

To this military city, with its sun-god deity, our Lord presents Himself in all the majesty and power of the Son of God, with flaming eyes and feet of military bronze. Those eyes of fire perceive in anger every trace of sin, searching it out from the hidden depths. Those feet of bronze trample down every opposing force and ruthlessly crush every evil thing. (The bronze was a very hard alloy used for weapons and was manufactured at Thyatira, so that the aptness of the figure is obvious.)

Here was One Whose face shone as the sun shining in its strength. The glory of the sun-god Tyrimnas paled into insignificance before His incomparable glory. Even the might of the cohorts of Rome, or the smashing, irresistible power of the Thyatiran deity dwindled to nothing before the supreme might and majesty of the Son of God.

The practical features of the Christian life—works, faith, ministry, and patience—were all to be seen in operation in the Church of Thyatira, together with the love which seemed so conspicuously absent in some of the other churches. The Christians in this Eastern town were particularly zealous in works: indeed, so diligent

[1]Matt. 16. 16-18

were they that their later works were greater than those of their earlier days. Even to-day, the devotion and practical piety of many Roman Catholics, for example, puts to shame many who are more enlightened and privileged.

Despite their virtues, the Thyatiran believers harboured evil of a nature abhorrent to God—an evil which is seen personified as a false prophetess named Jezebel. The historical Jezebel was a daughter of Eth-Baal, king of Sidon, who was a priest of Astarte and who murdered his predecessor, Pheles, in order to seize the throne. His daughter married Ahab, king of Israel, and proved herself a worthy descendant of her father. She not only tried to exterminate the prophets of Jehovah,[1] but strove hard to introduce the grossly impure Phœnician idolatries involved in the worship of Ashtaroth or Astarte. Her memory is stained with blood. She was a persecutor, murderess, thief, liar, and hypocrite. To acquire the vineyard of Naboth, for example, she lent herself to murder by treachery and false witness[2] whilst still professing piety and a hatred of blasphemy.

The metaphor is very apposite. All that was true literally of the Sidonian princess proved true spiritually of a later Jezebel—that persecuting, murdering, hypocritical system of Rome.

In the very midst of the Church, Jezebel propounded her false teaching with authority, although a woman is commanded not to teach.[3] It is a characteristic of Rome that she deprives the individual of his right to read the Bible for himself and declares that the Church alone is the teacher and interpreter.

The Council of Jerusalem directed Gentile converts to abstain from things sacrificed to idols and from fornication,[4] but Jezebel's teaching violated this fundamental rule. Her seductive power was used to lead the Thyatiran Christians into fornication and the eating of idol meats.

Rome's influence is exerted to the utmost to seduce God's servants to spiritual adultery and idolatry. The absorption of heathen practices and of the ceremonies, rites, titles, vestments, etc., of pagan religions has made this evil system a union of Church and paganism. Indeed, her celibate priests, nuns, and "spiritual brides" are not only reminiscent of the priesthood and vestal virgins of false religions, but also a reminder of the immorality of those pagan systems (an immorality which is unfortunately still paralleled in many Roman Catholic countries to this day).

Mariolatry, image and crucifix worship, veneration of the

[1] 1 Kings 18. 13 [2] 1 Kings 21 [3] 1 Tim. 2. 12 [4] Acts 15. 29

saints, and the adoration of the host are only idolatry masked by a Christian exterior. Purgatory, papal infallibility, transubstantiation, etc., are all part of Jezebel's false doctrines.

Opportunity had been afforded Jezebel to repent of her fornication, but no inclination to repent was evident. Divine forbearance was abused and she only hardened her heart. "The fact that punishment does not at once overtake sinners," says Trench, "is constantly misunderstood by them as evidence that it will never overtake them;[1] that God does not see or, seeing, does not care to avenge. The very time, during which ungodly men are heaping up for themselves greater wrath against the day of wrath, was a time lent them for repentance,[2] if only they would have understood the object and meaning of it."

Christ then threatens judgment upon Jezebel, upon those who commit adultery with her and upon her children.

Jezebel refuses to repent and she is therefore judged. The scene of her voluptuous pleasures is to become a bed of affliction. Her sins react upon her. The reference is undoubtedly to the future destruction of the great false ecclesiastical system by the political power which is so concisely described.[3]

Those who have intercourse with Jezebel are threatened with great tribulation unless they repent. Here were individuals who had been brought into the system or who had been attracted to it, and who were definitely in love with it. In all probability they were ignorant of the full significance of their associations and relationship. The Lord therefore makes provision for their possible repentance. If, however, they will not repent, judgment will fall upon them also. Many there are in the fold of Catholicism to-day who are perfectly sincere in their actions, even if misled, and divine grace provides for their turning to God if they will.

A third class, described as Jezebel's children, are to be slain by pestilence. Such owed their position, wealth, and influence to a system they knew to be corrupt and false. They were born of the system and clung to it for their own benefit. Whilst there is a special reference in Christ's words to the corrupt priesthood of the Middle Ages, they are still applicable in many respects to the present day.

The very act of judgment brings home to the Churches the fact that Christ is inquisitor of motives and affections. His careful and methodical investigation brings hidden evil to light. He searches the thoughts and reads the impulses and desires. He looks at the

[1]Eccles. 8. 11; Isa. 26. 10 [2]Rom. 2. 14; 2 Pet. 3. 9 [3]Rev. 17. 15-18

heart and discerns its intents, and not only systems but individuals are judged according to their works. He apportions praise or blame on a perfectly equitable and just basis.

In Jeremiah, Jehovah is described as the searcher of heart and reins.[1] Our Lord's statement in Rev. 2. 23, that He is the One Who searches reins and heart is therefore tantamount to a claim to be identified with Jehovah, and is a plain declaration of His own Deity.

Neither Roman Catholicism nor the mediæval Church to which Thyatira refers was wholly corrupt. There were (and are) some pious, misguided souls, who honestly believe that Roman Catholicism is a divine institution. They have never plumbed the depths of Satan, nor been personally acquainted with the evil practices of the system. Many are probably truly regenerate. Our Lord takes account of such. He will not burden them with commandments, or lay grievous weights upon them. Their knowledge may be little. Let them hold fast what they have until His return.

The mediæval Church sought to possess supreme authority over the nations. It was the goal of Papal ambition. But the overcomer, who remained loyal to Christ, is promised true authority over the nations, in contrast to the false power which had been arrogated by the Church. The sun-god Tyrimnas was usually pictured as riding forth with his terrible battle-axe to rule by force, but a far mightier power was to be committed to the overcomer.

At this date Rome was supreme over the nations of the civilized world and ruled them with a rod of iron, smashing them as potsherds. The overcomer was promised an even greater authority over the nations, with the power to rule them with a rod of iron and even to smash them to shivers like broken earthen vessels. His might was to be greater than the terrible force of Rome.

The power and authority bestowed upon the overcomer by the Lord are stated to have been the gift of the Father to His Son, and this is confirmed by the Psalmist[2] when the precise language is used in relation to God's King. It is His own authority over the nations that Christ shares with the overcomer.

A further reward promised to the overcomer is described as "the morning star." It is usually assumed that "the morning star"[3] is simply a synonym for Christ Himself, but this is open to question. Having regard to the prophetic setting, the primary reference is almost indubitably to the rising star of the Reformation, which immediately followed the period of ecclesiastical history

[1]Jer. 17. 10 [2]Psa. 2 [3]Rev. 22. 16

outlined in the Thyatiran epistle. Those who were faithful to their Master in the day of Rome's pretensions saw the rise of that star, with its promise of revival and reawakening.

In its full interpretation, however, "the morning star" probably anticipates the dawn of Christ's day and the ushering in of the millennial kingdom. The pledge of his participation in that day of joy and gladness is already in the possession of the overcomer: he has "the morning star."

It is noticeable that, in the first three letters, the call to hear *precedes* the promise to the overcomer, whereas, in the Thyatiran and the three following letters, it *follows*. In the first three epistles the Church is viewed as still capable of hearing and repenting, but in the last four it is contemplated that only a remnant—the overcomer—will hear.

SARDIS

Sardis was the ancient capital of Lydia, the kingdom of the wealthy Crœsus, and even at the time of the Apocalypse still retained something of its earlier dignity and splendour. Its decline, however, was fairly rapid, and at the present day it is little more than a heap of ruins.

Ramsay's description of the city is well deserving of quotation. "Looked at from a little distance to the north in the open plain," he says, "Sardis wore an imposing, commanding, impregnable aspect, as it dominated that magnificent broad valley of the Hermus from its robber stronghold on a steep spur that stands out boldly from the great mountains on the south. But, close at hand, the hill is seen to be but mud, slightly compacted, never trustworthy or lasting, crumbling under the influences of the weather, ready to yield even to the blow of a spade. It was an appearance without reality, promise without performance, outward show of strength betrayed by want of watchfulness and careless confidence."

The physical condition and nature of the city were reflected in the character of its inhabitants. They put their confidence in an external appearance of reliability, despite its unsoundness. They carelessly trusted in the strength of their rocky fortress, although the enemy had repeatedly found a means of entry through some point where the soft rock had crumbled away.

The character of the city was also the character of the local church. It is depicted as a church of false pretension and unfulfilled promises, dead in spirit while alive in name.

It is usually claimed that the Church era described in the Sardian letter is that of the Reformation. The Papal authority depicted in the Church of Thyatira had been crippled, and light and liberty had again burst forth. But Protestantism, with all its schisms, sectarianism and lifeless formalism, fell far short of the ideal. Its early promises never came to fruition; its appearance of spiritual power masked a spiritual weakness; it professed to have life but was spiritually dead.

The Letter to Sardis

"And to the angel of the Church in Sardis write: These things saith He that hath the seven Spirits of God, and the seven stars: I know thy works, that thou hast a name that thou livest, and thou art dead. Be thou watchful, and stablish the things that remain, which were ready to die; for I have not found thy works fulfilled before My God. Remember therefore how thou hast received and didst hear; and keep it and repent. If therefore thou shalt not watch, I will come as a thief, and thou shalt not know what hour I will come upon thee. But thou hast a few names in Sardis which did not defile their garments: and they shall walk with Me in white; for they are worthy. He that overcometh shall thus be arrayed in white garments; and I will in no wise blot his name out of the book of life, and I will confess his name before My Father, and before His angels. He that hath an ear let him hear what the Spirit saith to the Churches" (3. 1-6).

The Lord presents Himself to Sardis as the One who has the seven Spirits of God and the seven stars. As indicated previously, there is no justification for deducing from the expression used that there is more than one divine Spirit. The picture is rather of the sevenfold energy and activities of the Holy Spirit. The Lamb is seen as "having seven horns, and seven eyes, which are the seven Spirits of God, sent forth into all the earth,"[1] and Isaiah refers to Messiah's seven spiritual gifts, each described as attributes of the one Spirit.[2] In the exordium of the Sardian letter, the Holy Spirit is presented in the plenitude of His power and governmental action.

Sardis was sunk in spiritual torpor. Christ alone could recover the believers there from their spiritual death and revive them once more; and only by the sevenfold operations of the Holy Spirit could that result be achieved.

The seven stars are associated with the seven Spirits, since it is through the fulness of spiritual ministry that the Church is reached and reawakened. All spiritual ministry is derived from Christ through the Holy Spirit, and the guise in which He presents Himself to Sardis emphasizes His authority as Head of the Church and Director of all its activities.

Sardis is but typical of many a church of the present day—spiritually asleep and blind to the need of the world or of the Christian.

[1]Rev. 5. 6 [2]Isa. 11. 2

From that state of pitiful dormancy, only one power can arouse the sluggish soul. Only the mighty energy of the Spirit of God can revive and reinspire.

Pathetic is our Lord's complaint regarding Sardis: "Thou hast a name that thou livest, and thou art dead." The condition of the city amply justified the charge. Its past history was one of glory; it had been a mighty stronghold, and great kings had ruled over it. Yet its record was marred by repeated failures, and its character marked by unreliability and untrustworthiness. It always failed in the hour of testing and never seemed capable of fulfilling its promises.

The degeneration of the city was reflected in the instability of the Church of Sardis. It was a church of unjustified pretensions and unfulfilled promises. It had a name to live, yet was dead.

The Reformation—so plainly delineated in many respects in this epistle—early lost its power and vitality, and lapsed into an orthodox formality. Spiritual energy gradually disappeared, and denominationalism took the place of a living organism. The clanking of ecclesiastical machinery soon superseded the virile spontaneity of the first reawakening.

An omniscient eye saw the show of godliness without its power and records the deadness of the empty form.

Relying upon the supposed impregnability of their rocky fortress, the soldiers set to guard the stronghold had often betrayed their trust by falling asleep. On more than one occasion their failure had resulted in a successful assault upon the citadel by the enemy, and their carelessness ultimately brought about the fall of the Lydian Empire altogether.

"Be thou watchful," says Christ. All was not yet lost, and vigilance might even yet save what little was left. What remained to the church might seem weak and insignificant, but He adjured them to strengthen what remained, even if it seemed ready to perish. Deterioration had set in to such an extent that there was a risk of every trace of Christianity being blotted out. He therefore urged them to build up what was left despite its frailty. The reference may be, as some commentators suggest, to the few believers who remained faithful but who were spiritually dying. Before hope had entirely disappeared, they were to be strengthened and established by those who had been reawakened by Christ.

The most serious indictment, however, comes in our Lord's statement that no Sardian work for God was ever satisfactorily completed. Whatever laudable efforts might have been made at the commencement were outweighed by the imperfections at the end. Their work was never well-finished. All God's people, as one writer says, "constantly require the advice to be watchful, and to carry through to completion what they once enter upon, for all men tend more or less to slacken in their exertions and to leave half-finished ends of work. In all men there is observable a discrepancy between promise and performance; the first show is almost always superior to the final result."

The words are markedly applicable to the period of the Reformation. The Reformers concentrated primarily upon the truth of justification by faith and ignored many equally vital doctrines. Admirable although their efforts were, their defective teaching could never produce a balanced result. Their work was not perfectly finished in the sight of God.

Is it not true of many an individual Christian to-day that his labours have slackened and his zeal has waned? The meticulous care with which every detail was once executed, the scrupulous observance of the Scripture's requirements, and the complete and unfeigned subjection to the Spirit's will, which were once evidenced, are not now so prominently in view. In only too many cases an easy-going tolerance, a spiritual sloth and a compromising spirit have combined to lower the standard of the work performed. "I have not found thy works completed (or fulfilled) before My God," says the Master.

Their past love, joy and enthusiasm are used as incentives to awaken the Sardians to a fresh response to God's will. With the recollection of their first reception of the Gospel and the gladness with which they heard it, Christ demands a radical change in their present attitude. "Remember . . . and repent." They were not to give way to fruitless mourning, but rather to lay themselves open to the impulses of higher desires and principles. They may have failed, but the memory of their former joy should inspire them to renewed effort.

Upon the non-vigilant the Lord declares that He will descend as a thief, at an hour when He is not expected. This is not, of course, a reference to the Second Advent, but a warning concerning the stealthiness and certainty of discipline. The figure is drawn from the military practice of the day. The sentry had fallen asleep at his post. The officer, on his tour of inspection, stealthily approached like a thief and, drawing his short sword, cut off a piece of the sleeper's garment, which he produced next morning to the discomfiture of the sentry. On waking, the man discovered, to his consternation, what had happened, and realized at once that his failure and neglect of duty had been discovered and would be punished.

Similarly, the Christian who betrays his trust and neglects his responsibilities, is sooner or later called to account by his Lord. His lack of vigilance may cause the spiritual ruin of many, and the One who is cognisant of every detail may deem it essential to exercise discipline among His followers.

Among the general degradation and impurity of Sardis, there were some who had kept themselves unspotted from the world and who had maintained their integrity and moral rectitude. They "did not defile their garments." What the garments are to the body, so are habits to the real self. By our ways are we known. Unclean habits betray a corrupt character; kindness, gentleness, tenderness and purity reveal a nature of the same mould.

In recognition of their worthiness, those who had kept themselves pure are promised that they shall walk with Christ in white. The reference is to the day of a Roman triumph. All work was put aside, and all true Roman citizens donned the pure white toga. The specially privileged few—civic authorities or possibly relatives or friends of the honoured general—had a part in the triumphal procession. Clad in white, these Sardian believers were also to walk in triumph with Christ.

Moreover, the overcomer, who had lived and fought for his Master, should be clothed in white raiment in a coming day. The words used convey the sense of shining in intense whiteness, in a dazzling heavenly glory. A vesture of light should enrobe him and the glory should be his garb. Coming into the banquet after the triumphal procession, he should be clad in the brilliant festal robe.

In no wise, declares the Lord, shall the name of such be blotted out of the book of life. Is it to be deduced, then, that a believer's name can be deleted from the book of life? Moses certainly prayed, "Blot me, I pray Thee, out of Thy book"[1] but that prayer was never answered. The Psalmist says of the wicked, "Let them be blotted out of the book of the living and not be written with the righteous,"[2] but he does not suggest that the names of God's people may thus be obliterated.

Practically every city of that day kept a roll or register of its citizens. In that record was entered the name of every child born in the city. If one of the citizens proved guilty of treachery or

[1]Exod. 32. 32 [2]Psa. 69. 28

disloyalty, public dishonour was heaped upon him by the expunging of his name from the register. On the other hand, one who had performed some great exploit deserving of especial distinction, was honoured by having his name inscribed in golden letters in the citizens' roll. Our Lord's emphatic statement, therefore, implies not merely that the name of the overcomer shall not be expunged, but *per contra* that it shall be inscribed in golden letters in the heavenly roll.

Further, the one who did not shrink from confessing Christ during His earthly life, is to be acknowledged by Him before His Father and His angels. It is the same figure sustained throughout. The faithful, in the white toga of the freeborn son, should walk in the triumphal procession with the Victor; they should be brought into the banquet and clad in the shining festal robe; their names should be honoured in the civic register; and finally they should be confessed before the Sovereign. In the presence of the Emperor and his courtiers the victorious captain would relate the deeds of his mighty men and acknowledge their worth before the august court.

The one who follows Christ in the life on earth will follow Him in the path of glory in heaven. Sacrifice and loss may be our experience here, but abundant compensation is found in the glory above.

CHAPTER V

The Seven Churches

(Continued)

PHILADELPHIA

PHILADELPHIA was founded by Attalus, king of Pergamum, and acquired its name from his cognomen, Philadelphus, which he won by his loyalty to his brother, Eumenes.

The town was situated at the mouth of a long narrow pass on the main road from the coast to Phrygia, and was really the gateway to the high central plateau of Asia Minor. "The intention of its founder," says Ramsay, "was to make it a centre of Græco-Asiatic civilization, and a means of spreading the Greek language and manners in the eastern parts of Lydia and Phrygia. It was a missionary city, founded to promote a unity of spirit, customs, and loyalty within the realm, the apostle of Hellenism in an Oriental land. It was a successful teacher. Before A.D. 19, the Lydian tongue had ceased to be spoken in Lydia, and Greek was the only language of the country."

The church described in the epistle is one with little strength but of missionary spirit, brotherly love, and devotion to the Word of God. The dispensational period represented thereby has been variously interpreted as the Puritan and Quaker movements, the Methodist revival, the Brethren awakening, etc. All these and other evangelical movements are probably included in the picture, for the early nineteenth century saw a fairly widespread revival of Christian love and unity, of Bible study and missionary enthusiasm, even though spiritual strength and power were limited.

Gaebelein says: "It is a complete return to the first principles. Philadelphia repudiates all that dishonours Christ and owns alone that worthy Name. All human pretensions are rejected. The truth of the unity of all believers is owned and manifested in brotherly love towards all saints. They walk in the path of separation, in self-judgment, in lowliness of mind; they have a little strength, which means weakness; they are a feeble few."

The Letter to Philadelphia

"And to the angel of the Church in Philadelphia write: These things saith He that is holy, He that is true, He that hath the key of David, He that openeth, and none shall shut, and that shutteth, and none openeth: I know thy works (behold, I have set before thee an opened door, which none can shut), that thou hast a little power, and didst keep My word, and didst not deny My name. Behold, I give of the synagogue of Satan, of them who say they are Jews, and they are not, but do lie; behold I will make them to come and worship before thy feet, and to know that I have loved thee. Because thou didst keep the word of My patience, I also will keep thee from the hour of trial, that hour which is to come upon the whole world, to try them that dwell upon the earth. I come quickly: hold fast that which thou hast, that no one take thy crown. He that overcometh, I will make him a pillar in the temple of My God, and he shall go out thence no more: and I will write upon him the name of My God, and the name of the city of My God, the new Jerusalem, which cometh down out of heaven from My God, and Mine own new name. He that hath an ear, let him hear what the Spirit saith to the Churches" (3. 7-13).

The epistle to Philadelphia suggests a church which is feeble but intent upon truth and reality. The character in which Christ presented Himself to the Church was that most calculated to make an appeal to such a gathering. He declares Himself as the Holy and True. Here were the traits most greatly valued by Philadelphia. These, moreover, were just the attributes which appealed also to the evangelical movements of the last century. Revolting from empty, orthodox piety and the unreality and falseness of the great ecclesiastical systems, many a Christian of that day discovered the truth and reality for which he yearned, in the Person of Christ.

"Holy" was the name by which Jehovah made Himself known in a bygone day, and the Lord's assumption of the title is a tacit claim to identity with God. Absolute holiness is to be found in Christ alone, and it is only by His sanctifying power that His people partake of the same character.

The gods of the heathen are false idols, but He is essentially the *true* God. Not merely does His absolute veracity render it impossible for Him to lie, but He is the One in Whom the *truth* inherently resides.

The Lord also declares that He has the key of David and, with it, the supreme authority of opening and shutting. When David's treasurer, Shebna, was deposed and superseded by Eliakim, God said of the latter: "The key of the house of David will I lay upon his shoulder; so he shall open, and none shall shut; and he shall shut, and none shall open."[1] The very words used of Eliakim are quoted by Christ in reference to Himself, indicating that all

[1] Isa. 22. 22

faithless and unworthy stewards of God will ultimately be superseded by Himself as the only faithful and true Steward.

Possession of the key naturally invests the holder with the right of opening and closing. Christ has the key and is therefore invested with full administrative authority. He opens or shuts as it pleases Him.

There may be an oblique reference in the words to the ancient god, Janus, "the god of doors and hinges," who was sometimes called Patulcius and Clusius, "the opener and shutter." Janus held a key as a sign that he had the power to open the doors of heaven or to open or shut the gates of peace and war upon earth. This power was assumed by the Pope, and his privy councillors became known as cardinals (derived from *cardo*, a hinge), since they shared the right of turning the *hinge*.

The words had a particular significance for Philadelphia. It was a stage on the main line of imperial communication from the sea, and its natural position was such that it really held the key to Phrygia, and the road to the central plateau of Asia Minor was virtually open or closed by its attitude.

It is a far greater power that Christ claims, however. He has the supreme key and is Guardian of the road of life. His hand unlocks the door to all the treasures of spiritual wealth and bliss; He opens the path to service and honour; His key is the *open sesame* to the riches of wisdom and knowledge.

In the Pauline epistles, the apostle frequently uses the phrase "an open door" as the equivalent of an opportunity for service and missionary work (cf. 1 Cor. 16. 9; 2 Cor. 2. 12; Col. 4. 3). "I have set before thee an open door," says Christ to this Eastern church. By its history and position, Philadelphia had become a missionary city in secular things. It lay at the extremity of a long valley which opened back from the sea, and through it the Greek language and customs had been transmitted to the territories of Lydia and Phrygia beyond.

Just as the city had been a secular missionary—an apostle of Hellenism—so the Church had become a missionary company. An open door had been set before them and they had carried the Gospel to the cities and towns of Asia Minor.

The words are notably descriptive of the movements of the last century. A wave of missionary enthusiasm swept over the people of God. The responsibility of proclaiming the glad news was realized more than had been the case for centuries, and with the door of opportunity wide open, the messengers of the Gospel carried the evangel all over the world. To some extent, the Master's words are a challenge to the Christian of to-day. Opportunities still abound; the door is still flung open. Have we entered in?

The Philadelphian Christians were apparently but few in numbers and of small account in men's eyes, but they were faithful to their Master even in their weakness. Very little power was theirs and they had little of which to boast, but they had kept His Word and had not denied His Name, and the Lord treasured their fidelity to Him.

The companies of believers, who seek to hold to the Scriptures and to remain faithful to their Lord, may be small and insignificant. Their efforts may be weak and faltering, but if their motives are sincere, Christ reads the heart and treasures their loyalty. He places a far higher estimate upon such fidelity than upon the ostentatious labours of the unconsecrated life and heart.

As in the case of Smyrna, the Philadelphians found themselves opposed by Jewish leaders, who strove to undermine the teaching of the Gospel and to destroy those who propagated it. Boasting of their national privileges and assuming the position of the sole people of God, these are written off as hypocrites and liars, whose conduct reveals their association not with the synagogues of Israel but with that of Satan. Such would be made conscious of Christ's love for His people as He caused the Philadelphian church to glory over their enemies.

In the Smyrnean letter, that church was promised that the Jewish enemies should not prevail against her. The Philadelphian epistle, however, goes further and promises definite triumph over these foes. The false Jew should pay homage to the Christian believer and be brought to realize that divine affection now rested, not upon Israel but upon the Church. Ignatius—with a small measure of justification—refers this to the repentance of a number of these Judaizers, who turned to Christ, acknowledging the error of their ways, and identified themselves with the very folk whom they had scorned and despised.

Because they had kept the word of His patience, the Lord promises to keep His people from the dreaded hour of trial which is to come upon the whole world. These believers had not merely been patient, but *had kept the word of His patience*. They had held tenaciously the truth of His Second Advent and of His patient waiting.

It is not without significance that one of the principal truths recovered by the evangelical movements of the nineteenth century was that of the Lord's return for His Church. During the years which have since elapsed, many a faithful heart has learnt by the Spirit to keep the word of Christ's patience and to appreciate what that joyfully-anticipated hour will mean to Him.

Philadelphia was a city of earthquakes, and this natural danger had often been the cause of tribulation and trial. The Divine Speaker declares that a greater tribulation is coming, but that the Church shall be kept out of it. He does not promise that Christians will not experience trials in general, but He does indicate that He will take them out of this one. They will not pass through it, but will be completely exempted from it. The idea that the Church will pass through the Great Tribulation is without Scriptural support.

The Lord immediately associates His promise with the fact of His own speedy return, an evident intimation that the Christian's removal from the trial will take place at His coming. "I come quickly," He says, "hold fast that which thou hast, that no one take thy crown." Some were becoming weary of the long, trying contest, but here was the word of encouragement and inspiration: His coming will not be delayed. "*I come quickly.*"

Is not this the present inspiration of life? Earthly foundations are crumbling, everything around is transient, and the soul longs for the substantial and real. The battle grows wearisome and the race seems long. The burdens weigh heavier and the road becomes rougher. But He is coming quickly! Soon faith will give place to sight; the weariness, the toil, and the struggle will then be over and we shall be with Him whom our souls adore.

Until that blest moment, He exhorts His people to "hold fast." No distinguished achievement or notable action is demanded. The command is simply to hold on in faithfulness. They were to hold fast also, in order to avoid being deprived by another of the reward reserved for them. There is no hidden threat of the possibility of supersession, but rather a warning against the efforts of the adversary to rob the Christian of the reward which is his due by tripping him up or leading him astray. It is a very similar expression to that of the Apostle Paul: "Let no man beguile you of your reward."[1]

There is a constant necessity for the injunction. It is so easy to let things slip and the devil is ever waiting to ensnare the careless and unwatchful. "Hold fast," says the Lord, "that no one take thy crown."

In the porch of Solomon's temple there stood two mighty

[1]Col. 2. 18

pillars[1] which were called Jachin (*i.e.*, establish) and Boaz (*i.e.*, strength), and there is a patent allusion to these in the promise to the Philadelphian overcomer. There is probably also a reference to a pillar of one of the temples of Philadelphia, which still stands to-day.

The church had little strength, but the overcomer was to be established in strength as a pillar in the temple of God. No earthquake or natural disaster would shake that pillar of strength in the day of trial. Despite all the seismic disturbances, there still stands a pillar of great antiquity among the ruins of the city, a reminder of the greater spiritual promise of our Lord's words. We may be weak and feeble, but God takes account, not of our weakness or strength, but of our fidelity to Him and, in a coming day, He will establish His own in strength.

Philadelphia was subject to frequent earthquakes and, after every such occurrence, large numbers of the people camped outside the city. In the temple of God, however, Christ declared that no trial or seismal tremor should affect the overcomer. "He shall go out thence no more." Never should he camp outside in fear and trembling: the temple should be his shelter and safe refuge.

Just as the priests of the false idols bore the name of their god upon their brow, so upon the brow of the overcomer should be written the name of the true God. He should be manifestly marked as one who belonged to God (cf. Rev. 7. 3; 9. 4; 14. 1; 22. 4). Upon the mitre of Israel's high priest was a golden plate, upon which were engraved the words: "Holiness unto Jehovah."[2] So also the overcomer should be sanctified unto his God.

The name of the city, the heavenly Jerusalem, should also be inscribed upon the forehead of such an one. The name of the city is stated to be "Jehovah is there."[3] "He that has the name of this city written upon him is hereby declared free of it," says Trench. On earth, "his citizenship was latent; but now he is openly avouched and has a right to enter in by the gates into the city." Heaven is the Christian's city and his home, and he is the recipient of the freedom of that city.

Not only the name of God and that of the new Jerusalem, but also the new name of our Lord Himself shall be borne upon the brow of the overcomer. It is clear that this name is not one of the titles by which our Lord is now known to His people, for the seer later says that "He hath a name written which no one knoweth but He Himself."[4] This mysterious, uncommunicated name will be imparted to the citizens of the new Jerusalem.

[1] 1 Kings 7. 21 [2] Exod. 28. 36-38 [3] Ezek. 48. 35 [4] Rev. 19. 12

We do not know Christ in His fulness yet. Further revelations and a fuller knowledge still await us in a coming land. But in that day, all the mysteries of His Person will be unveiled to His loved ones, and He will communicate Himself to us in a way such as He has never before done.

LAODICEA

An extremely strong fortress, Laodicea occupied a position right on the line of the great road from the coast. The city derived its name from Laodice, the wife of its rebuilder, Antiochus II. Trench says that "the city suffered grievously in the Mithridatic War, but presently recovered again; it was overthrown by an earthquake in the reign of Nero (A.D. 61); but restored by the efforts of its own citizens, without any help sought from the Roman Senate (Tacitus, *Annal*. XIV, 27)." At the time of the Apocalypse, however, it was a prosperous, commercial city, renowned particularly for the quality of wool which it sold. It had also an important school of medicine, and its physicians were specially known for the ointments they produced and, in particular, a certain form of eye-salve.

This wealthy city might perhaps have been expected to produce a flourishing church, but the Apocalyptic description portrays an irresolute, half-hearted body, whose main interest was temporal prosperity rather than spiritual good. Enthusiasm and zeal were absent and the assembly was merely lukewarm. Not a word of praise is uttered regarding this church, and the Lord almost turns in nausea from her.

The description has reasonably been interpreted as a picture of present-day Christianity—the last phase of Church history prior to our Lord's return.

The Letter to Laodicea

"And to the angel of the Church in Laodicea write: These things saith the Amen, the faithful and true witness, the beginning of the creation of God: I know thy works, that thou art neither cold nor hot; I would thou wert cold or hot. So because thou art lukewarm, and neither cold nor hot, I will spue thee out of My mouth. Because thou sayest, I am rich, and have gotten riches, and have need of nothing; and knowest not that thou art the wretched one and miserable and poor and blind and naked; I counsel thee to buy of Me gold refined by fire, that thou mayest become rich; and white garments, that thou mayest clothe thyself, and that the shame of thy nakedness be not made manifest; and eye-salve to anoint thine eyes that thou mayest see. As many as I love, I reprove and chasten; be zealous, therefore, and repent. Behold, I stand at the door and knock; if any man hear My voice and open the door, I will come in to him and will sup with him, and he with Me.

He that overcometh, I will give to him to sit down with Me in My throne, as I also overcame, and sat down with My Father in His throne. He that hath an ear, let him hear what the Spirit saith to the Churches" (3. 14-22).

The Church of Laodicea was unstable and unreliable, and our Lord appropriately presents Himself to it as "the Amen, the faithful and true witness." The second title, "the faithful and true witness," is really the Greek equivalent of the first, the Hebrew "Amen." Christ is the only One who can add "Amen" to every word He utters. With Him is finality and immutability. Where others are fickle and changeable, He is stable, true and unchangeable. Other witnesses have failed; all other testimony for God has been deficient; but He is the faithful and true Witness.

This character of consistency and fidelity was just that which Laodicea lacked. Given to compromise, dallying with temptation, attracted by the lure of earthly things, this self-complacent body was always changeable, unreliable, neutral. It was never definite, straight and true.

It would be impossible to find more fitting words to describe the professing Church of the present day. Marked by latitudinarianism, it is always willing to accommodate itself to any view and to receive whatever doctrine may be presented—truly a spiritual chameleon.

Christ also describes Himself as "the beginning of the creation of God," *i.e.*, not, of course, the first object of God's creatorial work, but rather the active source and author of creation, and the first-born of it all, the pre-eminent One. The expression is indicative primarily of rank and honour; He is supreme above the creation of God.

The divine estimate of the Laodicean character is then given—"thou art neither cold nor hot." Each of the other cities referred to in Rev. 2 and 3 left a mark of some kind on the pages of history, but the history of Laodicea was vague, indefinite, and undetermined. There was nothing clearly-defined or characteristic about it.

The same lack of definiteness was found in the church. It was neither cold nor hot. Neutral and lukewarm, it adapted itself to everyone and had no pronounced character or outlook of its own. There was a complete indifference to Christ and His claims.

Cold food is often enjoyable, and hot food is excellent, but lukewarm is only nauseating, and the Lord accordingly says that He will spue this loathsome mess out of His mouth. Jeremy Taylor writes: "In feasts or sacrifices the ancients did use *apponere frigidam* or *calidam*; sometimes they drank hot drink, sometimes they poured cold upon their grains or their wines; but no services of tables or altars were ever with lukewarm. God hates it worse than stark cold."

"I would thou wert cold or hot," goes on the Divine Speaker. This is not just the fretful impatience of one who cares little what attitude is adopted so long as there is some decisive view. It is rather the yearning for material upon which it is possible to operate. There is some hope that the cold, untouched by the warmth of grace and love, may be won to the truth, while, on the other hand, there is good prospect that the hot, enthusiastic spirit may have its powers and energies directed into devotion to Christ.

A nominal Christianity, with its casual indifference to the things that matter, is powerless for God and useless to men. God cannot permanently tolerate such conditions, and Laodicea is therefore threatened with judgment. Lukewarm water is an emetic and, employing that metaphor, the Lord declares that the repellent mess shall yet be rejected with nausea and disgust.

Laodicea was an exceedingly wealthy city, which had prospered without external help. Although hard hit by the Mithridatic War, it recovered without assistance from those reverses. Moreover, when the town later suffered the severities of an earthquake, it once more regained its position unaided and, indeed, declined the proffered help of the imperial government, boasting that it had need of nothing.

It is not surprising that the Church of Laodicea should have absorbed something of the same spirit. It too was wealthy and in need of nothing. It was rich in spiritual gift and evidently boasted of its knowledge and light. To this self-complacent body, Christ says: "Thou sayest, I am rich, and have gotten riches, and have need of nothing; and knowest not that thou art the wretched one and miserable and poor and blind and naked."

Gift alone is not sufficient to create spirituality. The Laodiceans boasted of their spiritual insight, but the Lord declared that they were blind. They vaunted the fact that they had been divinely blessed and were in need of nothing, but the Lord laid bare their poverty and nudity. They puffed up themselves by reason of their glorious position, but the Lord depicts them as wretched and miserable. There are far too many Christians to-day who still boast of their spiritual intelligence, their special knowledge, or their privileged position, and the scathing condemnation of Laodicea might equally be justified in this later age.

The city was given over to trading and our Lord therefore

addresses these merchants in their own language when He bids them trade with Him.

It was a city of extensive money transactions. Cicero, for example, mentions that he used to take up money there when journeying to or from his provinces. The Laodicean bankers and money-changers could never issue untarnished gold to their clients. Christ counsels them to buy of Him gold tried in the fire. No gold from the interior could ever attain the high standard of *this* refined metal. Instead of occupation with earthly wealth, there is presented to these ancient financiers the enjoyment of the riches of heaven.

The raven-coloured wool of Laodicea was famous throughout the world, but the Lord offered these Christians raiment of dazzling white if they would but receive it. Divine righteousness would clothe them as a robe and cover their spiritual nudity.

The Laodiceans boasted of their ointment and of their superlative eye-salve. Christ exhorts them to purchase eye-salve from Him and to anoint their eyes, that the illuminating grace of the Holy Spirit might remove their spiritual blindness.

The conditions existing in this church could not be tolerated indefinitely. Because He loved them, the Lord threatened to rebuke and chasten His people there, seeking to bring them to an acknowledgment of their faults by the rebuke and to lead them to repentance by His disciplinary chastening.

In long-suffering, He takes the place of the pleader. He is the door at which the penitent should stand, but He condescends to reverse the order and Himself graciously stands at their door. He will never force an entry, but patiently knocks and waits admission. Through sickness and sorrow, suffering and loss, through the Scriptures or through circumstances, those gentle taps make themselves heard on the door of life, and the Master stands and seeks to enter.

To the one who throws open the door in whole-hearted response, He promises full communion. "I will come in to him, and will sup with him, and he with Me." There is little doubt that the picture is taken from the Canticles. Slow to open the door, the bride discovered when she eventually unfastened the latch that her Beloved had gone. "It is the *voice* of my Beloved that *knocketh*," she cried, "saying, Open to Me, My sister."[1]

The mystical feast of communion finds its reflection in the same book. "I sat down under His shadow with great delight, and His fruit was sweet to My taste"[2] was the blissful story of the bride, and again she anticipated the happiness of His presence as she said:

[1]S. Sol. 5. 2 [2]S. Sol. 2. 3

"Let my Beloved come into His garden and eat His pleasant fruits."[1] When the Lord Jesus Christ finds an entry into heart and life, endless bliss and communion are the believer's joyful experience.

To the Laodicean overcomer, Christ promises that he shall share His throne. An eastern throne was much broader than the single-seated western throne and afforded room for several in addition to the central occupant. As a mark of special favour, one who was to be given a place of authority or who was deserving of special honour, was sometimes summoned to sit by the side of the sovereign on his throne. Similarly the one who has suffered for Christ will also reign with Him.[2]

Christ overcame[3] and sat down with His Father on His throne. The overcomer in this decadent age shall therefore sit with Christ on His throne. Those who follow Him in humiliation, rejection, and suffering will also follow Him in glory.

The throne of God and that of Christ are not identical. Mede, for example, says: "Here are two thrones mentioned. *My throne*, says Christ; this the condition of glorified saints who sit with Christ in His throne. But *My Father's* (*i.e.*, God's) *throne* is the power of divine majesty; herein none may sit but God, and the God-man, Jesus Christ. To be installed in God's throne, to sit at God's right hand, is to have a Godlike royalty, such as His Father has, a royalty altogether incommunicable, where no creature is capable."

[1]S. Sol. 4. 16 [2]2 Tim. 2. 12 [3]John 16. 33

Chapter VI

Heavenly Scenes

The Throne in Heaven

"After these things I saw and behold, a door opened in heaven, and the first voice which I heard, a voice as of a trumpet speaking with me, one saying, Come up hither, and I will shew thee the things which must come to pass hereafter (after these things). Straightway I was in the Spirit: and behold, there was a throne set in heaven, and One sitting upon the throne; and He that sat was to look upon like a jasper stone and a sardius: and there was a rainbow round about the throne, like an emerald to look upon" (4. 1-3).

IN the opening vision of the Apocalypse, the Seer had been commanded to write (1) the things he had seen, (2) those which are, and (3) those which should come to pass hereafter (or after those things) (see 1. 19). The first obviously referred to the vision of the glorified Christ described in chapter 1, whilst the second plainly related to the Church-age, as described in chapters 2 and 3. The third section, including the whole catena of judgments following, clearly opens at 4. 1, since John was told that he was now to be shown "the things which must come to pass hereafter" (or after these things).

A door was opened in heaven and the trumpet-like voice of Christ, which the apostle had heard at first,[1] summoned him to the heavens to see the unfolding of the future. Since the events which were about to be revealed to him were to happen after those of the previous vision, it is not an unreasonable interpretation which sees in the apostle's rapture to heaven a figure of the rapture of the Church.[2] After chapter 3, the Church is never again referred to as on earth, and it seems evident that the judgment of a guilty world is suspended until the Church has been removed from the scene. J. C. M. Dawson points out that "from Rev. 4 to the end of chapter 19, God is not once addressed as Father. He is called God, Lord, Almighty, names by which He was known in Old Testament days; but the name Father, by which He has been known to the Church, is entirely absent. Surely this indicates

[1]Rev. 1. 10 [2]1 Thess. 4. 16, 17

that the Church's presence here and witnessing for Christ are past, and the things that occur after the Church's removal are in progress." (The reference in Rev. 14. 1 is, of course, to God as the Father of Christ, not of believers.) Judgment is about to be meted out but, prior thereto, the Church is removed from the earth into the presence of her Lord.

Immediately after the summons of the trumpet-like voice (cf. 1 Thess. 4. 16; 1 Cor. 15. 52), the seer was in the Spirit. Either the Holy Spirit laid hold upon him and controlled him, or else he was in an ecstatic state in which the spirit was projected from the body. (To be consistent, the interpretation given to the identical expression in Rev. 1. 10 ought also to be given to it in Rev. 4. 2.)

John's eyes first fell upon a throne set in heaven. He gives no particulars of that indescribably glorious and majestic seat. It is as if mere human words could never adequately paint its magnificent grandeur and awesomeness. The ensuing verses make it clear that the throne was that of the Eternal God and that it was set for judicial action.

No description is given of the mighty Occupant of the Throne, save that, in some way, He bore a resemblance to jasper and sardius. In Rev. 21. 11, the light of the heavenly Jerusalem is said to be like a crystal-clear jasper, whilst, in verse 23 of that chapter, the glory of God is said to lighten the city. The jasper is, therefore, a figure of the glory of God. It was a very precious stone, crystalline and purple in colour.

The sardius (or carnelian) was a costly stone of a fiery red appearance and seems to be symbolical of divine anger and punitive righteousness. God's infinite glory and His judicial wrath are thus connected here as the throne of judgment was set up. It is very significant that, in the breastplate of Israel's high priest[1] the jasper bore the name of Reuben (lit., "behold a son") and the sardius that of Benjamin (lit., "son of my right hand"). The reign of God's beloved Son was about to commence, and judgment and destruction were about to be poured out.

Surrounding the throne was an emerald rainbow, the reminder, perhaps, of the perpetuity of the Noahic covenant, but also indicating unmistakably that, whilst vengeance must take its course, grace and mercy were still divine attributes which would be demonstrated after the outpouring of divine wrath. The light green emerald is ever regarded as suggestive of promise and hope, and even in wrath God remembers mercy.

[1]Exod. 28. 17-20

The Elders

"And round about the throne were four and twenty thrones: and upon the thrones I saw four and twenty elders sitting, arrayed in white garments; and on their heads crowns of gold. And out of the throne proceed lightnings and voices and thunders. And there were seven lamps of fire burning before the throne, which are the seven Spirits of God" (4. 4, 5).

Around the central throne were ranged twenty-four other thrones, which were occupied by twenty-four elders. There has been considerable speculation as to the identity of these elders, and some very fantastic theories have been propounded in connection with them.

The number of elders under the old dispensation seems to have been seventy,[1] but in this heavenly scene, it was twenty-four, *i.e.*, the same as the number of the courses of the priests[2] and of the prophets.[3] The elders are clearly to be distinguished from the living creatures and also the angels, since they were enthroned and crowned and also sang of redemption (an experience into which angelic beings cannot enter). They are not identical, moreover, with the 144,000 redeemed saints, since these sang before the elders.[4]

Dr. Ironside writes: "When the 24 elders met in the temple precincts in Jerusalem, the whole priestly house was represented. The elders in heaven represent the whole heavenly priesthood. In vision they were seen—not as a multitudinous host of millions of saved worshippers, but just 24 elders, symbolizing the entire company. The Church of the present age and Old Testament saints are alike included." Bossuet also refers the type to the whole of the redeemed, as represented by the twelve patriarchs (as a type of the Old Testament saints) and the twelve apostles (as representative of the New Testament saints), and there seems no reason to question this identification.

The elders wore dazzling white garments and crowns of gold. (The crowns are the victor's crown and not the ruler's diadem.) Their long pilgrimage and constant struggle were finished and they now sat resplendent in glory. The coronation of the saints occurs *after* Christ's return for His own people.[5] There can, therefore, be no crowned elders in heaven until after the rapture of the Church, so that the events described in the chapter must clearly be subsequent to that glorious happening.

At the promulgation of the Law at Sinai[6] lightning and thunder from the Mount filled the people with dread. The same premonitory intimations, together with the sound of voices, now issued

[1]Exod. 24. 1 [2]1 Chron. 24 [3]1 Chron. 25 [4]Rev. 14. 3
[5]2 Tim. 4. 8; Rev. 22. 12 [6]Exod. 19

tion of the throne. During the present dispensation, the throne of God is one of grace.[1] That it is shown as one of judgment[2] is a further indication that the Church period is viewed as then complete and that the Church will then be in heaven and not on earth. The lightnings, voices, and thunders are a warning to a guilty world of impending judgment—swift, decisive, and overwhelming.

Before the throne burned seven lamps of fire, the type, as the text plainly indicates, of the fulness of the searching and consuming power of the Holy Spirit. Vengeance was about to fall, but it was the devouring wrath of the Holy Spirit which will unerringly search out the guilty and bring them to judgment.

The Living Creatures

"And before the throne, as it were a glassy sea like unto crystal; and in the midst of the throne, and round about the throne, four living creatures full of eyes before and behind. And the first creature was like a lion, and the second creature like a calf, and the third creature had a face as a man, and the fourth creature was like a flying eagle. And the four living creatures, having each one of them six wings, are full of eyes round about and within: and they have no rest day and night, saying, Holy, holy, holy, is the Lord God, the Almighty, Who was and Who is, and Who is to come (or, Who cometh)" (4. 6-8).

The pavement before the throne is likened to a crystalline sea. The sea is usually the symbol of restlessness and unceasing motion, but no winds ruffle this sea or disturb its deep tranquillity. The "fickle, movable waters" of the ocean, says Tuck, "represent the unguided, unreasoning, and unprincipled thoughts of men. By analogy, the calm, glass-like sea represents those counsels of God, those purposes of righteousness and love, often fathomless, *like unto crystal*, resplendent and pellucid." In the East, it was not uncommon for the floor (or "pavement") of a house to be composed of some expensive material. The diaphanic pavement seen by John was possibly one vast transparent jewel.

The Apocalyptic sea has sometimes been connected with the sea which stood in front of Solomon's temple, but the connection is more apparent then real.

The throne rested upon four animated, rational creatures, who are described as teeming with eyes, denoting not merely their vigilance, but their almost limitless powers of perception and discernment. The multiplicity of eyes is but a method of conveying the extreme perfection of their vision.

The mysterious beings depicted were, of course, the cherubim. These are consistently represented in Scripture as associated with the judicial authority of God's throne, and their number (four)

[1]Heb. 4. 16. [2]Rev. 4. 5

is indicative of the universality of the divine government. Four is also commonly regarded as the number of material creation and particularly of the earth.

Each of the cherubim portrays one phase of the character of the judicial activity, providence, and government of God. The first resembled a lion, the king of beasts, and therefore symbolized the majesty and royal dignity of the Sovereign. The second was like a calf or ox, the most valuable of the domesticated animals, and the type of unwearying strength and patient endurance. The third had the face of a man, suggestive of sympathetic comprehension and intelligence. The fourth was like a flying eagle, the chief characteristics of which would be keenness of sight, penetrating vision and discernment, and rapidity of action. "These living bearers of the Almighty's throne," writes Moses Stuart, "serve Him with great power, with patient obedience, with quickness of intelligence and reason, and with rapidity and perspicacity. The ultimate meaning is that God is everywhere present, and executes His purposes by an agency, powerful, wise, unremitted, and speedy."

The living creatures had each of them six wings. The cherubim had only four wings.[1] The seraphim, however, had six wings, two to cover their faces, two to cover their feet, and two with which to fly.[2] The Apocalyptic description therefore incorporates features of the seraphim as well as of the cherubim.

For these marvellous beings, there was no respite day or night; they declared unceasingly the holiness of the eternal God. In their character of the upholders of the throne of righteousness and universal government they aptly declared the perfect rectitude and purity of the Supreme Ruler of the universe.

The Worship of the Universe

"And when the living creatures shall give glory and honour and thanks to Him that sitteth on the throne, to Him that liveth for ever and ever (or unto the ages of the ages), the four and twenty elders shall fall down before Him that sitteth on the throne, and shall worship Him that liveth for ever and ever (unto the ages of the ages) and shall cast their crowns before the throne, saying, Worthy art Thou, our Lord and our God, to receive the glory and the honour and the power; for Thou didst create all things, and because of Thy will they were, and were created" (4. 9-11).

The closing verses of the chapter give a brief picture of an adoring universe pouring out its worship to Almighty God. The cherubim paid their homage to the Occupant of the throne as they rendered glory, honour, and thanks to Him, acknowledging His eternal

[1]Ezek. 1 [2]Isa. 6

being and ageless days. This is not merely the worship of nature being paid to Him, since these mysterious beings take precedence of the elders. It is the acclamation of the bearers of the throne of God as they gaze upon the Infinite.

At the note of praise the twenty-four elders prostrated themselves in lowly adoration before the throne, again declaring God's timeless existence. Casting their crowns before the throne in token of homage and allegiance to Him, they acknowledged the matchless worth of their Lord and God, and ascribed glory, honour, and power to Him. The unreserved allegiance and whole-hearted tribute of the creature were laid at the feet of the Almighty.

The worship of the cherubim was connected with the holiness of God; that of the elders related to His creatorial work. The claim of the Almighty from an intelligent creation is a recognition of His power and glory as Creator. J. N. Darby says: "The living creatures only celebrate and declare; the elders worship with understanding. All through the Revelation, the elders give their reason for worshipping. There is spiritual intelligence in them."

The elders concluded by acknowledging God as the Source, the Creator, and the Sustainer of the universe. By the will of the Almighty alone did created things come into being, and the appreciation of God's creatorial work and glory bows down the elders in heartfelt worship.

Such were the scenes which opened up to the apostle's eye, and such were the chords which fell upon his ear as he first entered the celestial courts.

The Book

"And I saw in the right hand of Him that sat on the throne a book written within and on the back, close sealed with seven seals. And I saw a strong angel proclaiming with a great voice, Who is worthy to open the book, and to loose the seals thereof? And no one in the heaven, or on the earth, or under the earth, was able to open the book, or to look thereon. And I wept much, because no one was found worthy to open the book or to look thereon: and one of the elders saith unto me, Weep not: behold the Lion that is of the tribe of Judah, the Root of David, hath overcome, to open the book and the seven seals thereof. And I saw in the midst of the throne and of the four living creatures, and in the midst of the elders, a Lamb standing, as though it had been slain, having seven horns, and seven eyes, which are the seven Spirits of God, sent forth into all the earth. And He came, and He taketh it out of the right hand of Him that sat on the throne" (5. 1-7).

If chapter 4 is occupied with the honour of Almighty God, chapter 5 revolves around the glory of the Lamb of God.

As the Seer gazed upon the Occupant of the throne, he perceived in His right hand a "book" or parchment roll covered with writing on both sides. The ensuing chapters make it clear that the book contained the record of the divine counsels concerning the world, the principles of divine government, and the judicial decrees which were about to be put into execution.

The full unveiling of God's purposes for the world has not yet taken place, for the book was sealed with seven seals, each of which closed a section of the book. The contents of the roll were disclosed only gradually as the seals were broken one by one. Until that day, the judgments of the Almighty are kept in check and the counsels of eternity remain secret from the mind of man.

The whole universe of celestial, terrestrial, and infernal beings was then loudly challenged by a strong angel to produce one worthy to open the book and to loose its seals, but, to the grief of the apostle, the challenge met with no response. In the whole realm of existence none might claim the moral fitness or personal dignity to be recognized as the qualified executor of the designs of God. None was even meet to look upon that roll.

The seer had been raptured to heaven for the express purpose of receiving the revelation of God's will for the future—but the book remained closed! Summoned into the presence of the Eternal, to know His mind and ultimate intentions, John stood frustrated. Little wonder was it that the tears flooded his eyes and that he wept copiously. As he gave way to his grief, however, one of the elders comforted him with the words of consolation and hope: "Weep not: behold . . .!"

Standing between the throne and the cherubim was One Whom the elder described as the Lion of the tribe of Judah, the Root of David. The dying Jacob, in blessing his sons, referred to Judah as "a lion's whelp," who "couched as a lion, and as an old lion."[1] Here was the fulfilment of the old patriarch's prophetic word: the Lion of Judah's tribe, the great Messiah, stood in the courts of heaven before the apostle's eyes. This was the One before whom Israel had declared that his brethren should praise and bow down, whose victorious hand should be on the neck of his enemies, from whom regal and legislative power (the sceptre and the lawgiver) should never depart, and who should be the rallying point of the peoples. Here, too, was the Root (or sprout) of David—the glorious Branch.[2]

This majestic and all-glorious Being, declared the elder, had overcome, to open the book and its seven seals. As John wonderingly gazed, however, it was no richly-clad monarch upon whom his

[1]Gen. 49. 9 [2]Isa. 11. 1; Zech. 6. 12

eyes rested, but a little Lamb with the marks of sacrifice upon Him—"a Lamb as it had been slain." Here was the mighty Conqueror, the great Messiah, for whom he had waited—a little Lamb! A lion in the guise of a lamb is paradoxical; but it was through weakness and apparent defeat that He overcame. His victory over every spiritual power is the outcome of His death of humiliation and shame and the lowly Man of Calvary is the Victor of the universe. As though God's delight was to be found in that outstanding work, twenty-eight times is Christ described in the Revelation as the Lamb and only once as the Lion.

Christ's victory had established His unchallengeable right not only to disclose but also to implement the purposes of God. He had previously been sitting with His Father in His throne,[1] but He now stood before the throne to act as executor of the judgments of God. His was the title to open the book and to unloose its seals.

The Lamb is depicted as "having seven horns and seven eyes," which are interpreted as being "the seven Spirits of God, sent forth into all the earth." The horns are a symbol of might and power, whilst the eyes are indicative of perception and knowledge. The number (seven) is, of course, suggestive of the perfection of the might and the knowledge so typified. Perfect competency is His by reason of His omnipotence and omniscience. The Holy Spirit, in all the plenitude of His power and wisdom, is the Lamb's enduement.

With the marks of His Passion still in evidence, the Lamb approached the rainbow-girdled throne and took the book out of the hand of the Almighty Sovereign. Knowing the heart of God, and being in full sympathy with the divine purpose, none but He was fit to be entrusted with that book. Judgment was about to fall and Christ was thus empowered as the executor thereof.

Universal Worship

"And when He had taken the book, the four living creatures and the four and twenty elders fell down before the Lamb, having each one a harp, and golden bowls full of incense, which are the prayers of the saints. And they sing a new song, saying, Worthy art Thou to take the book, and to open the seals thereof: for Thou wast slain, and didst purchase unto God with Thy blood men of every tribe, and tongue, and people, and nation, and madest them to be unto our God a kingdom and priests; and they reign upon the earth. And I saw, and I heard a voice of many angels round about the throne and the living creatures and the elders; and the number of them was ten thousand times ten thousand, and thousands of thousands; saying with a great voice, Worthy is the Lamb that hath been slain to receive the power, and riches, and wisdom, and might, and honour, and glory, and blessing. And every created thing which is in the heaven, and on the earth, and under the earth, and on the sea, and all things that are in them heard I saying, Unto Him

[1]Rev. 3. 21

that sitteth on the throne, and unto the Lamb, be the blessing, and the honour, and the glory, and the dominion, for ever and ever (or unto the ages of the ages). And the four living creatures said, Amen, and the elders fell down and worshipped" (5. 8-14).

Immediately the Lamb had taken the book, He became the object of the homage of a whole creation. The living creatures and the elders prostrated themselves before Him as they sang His praises, myriads upon myriads of the angelic hosts shouted His worth, whilst every animate being in heaven, earth, and sea acclaimed Him as the all-glorious.

John notes, as the cherubim and elders bowed low in adoration, that the latter accompanied their song of joy with harps and that they also held golden bowls or censers full of incense, the prayers of the saints. As the glad note of the harp sounded forth their praise, the odour of heart-prayers of God's people rose up as a sweet perfume, and the representative priests presented both to the blessed Lamb.

The song into which they burst acknowledged the Cross as the basis of blessing and proclaimed that its redemptive work had resulted in the purchase by blood of members of every branch of the human family to be a kingdom of priests who should presently reign over the earth. It is clear from this song that the elders were redeemed and regenerate creatures, who had tasted the joy of forgiveness of sins and of deliverance from the devil's thraldom. The eternal purpose of God for His redeemed people is also indicated—the beggar is to sit among princes, and the once-unworthy is to reign over the earth.

The unnumbered hosts of heaven then broke out unrestrainedly into a sevenfold doxology which is unsurpassed in its adoration of Christ. Power, riches, wisdom, might, honour, glory, and blessing were ascribed to Him. Every sphere of life or experience was made to bring forth its tribute to Him. All was laid at His feet in token of His inestimable worth.

Simultaneously, the whole creation joined in the same glorious theme and, linking the Lamb with the Occupant of the throne, ascribed all dignity and authority to Him. Blessing, honour, glory, and dominion unto the ages of the ages became the tribute of animate nature; in other words, the absolute sovereignty of the Lamb was recognized in every sphere. At last, the Man of Calvary received His rightful meed of praise, and the cherubim marked their complete concurrence in His exultation in their loud "Amen," whilst the priestly elders again bowed low in adoring worship.

CHAPTER VII

The Seven Seals

CHAPTER 6 is the commencement of the prophetic section of the Revelation, and it is just at this point that the exegetes most greatly differ. It is contended by some interpreters that the whole of the events described in chapter 6 *et seq.*, relate to the future; others discover a complete fulfilment thereof in the history of the Roman Empire; whilst others again see the experiences and trials of the Church in every chapter.

Bacon once opined that prophecies "are not fulfilled punctually at once, but have springing and germinant accomplishments throughout many ages, though the height or fulness of them may refer to some one age." There is little doubt that there has already been a partial and inchoate fulfilment of a large part of the Apocalyptic prophecies, but the final and complete fulfilment still lies in the future. This is very clearly the case in regard to the happenings under the seals.

FIRST SEAL

"And I saw when the Lamb opened one of the seven seals, and I heard one of the four living creatures saying as with a voice of thunder, Come. And I saw, and behold, a white horse, and he that sat thereon had a bow; and there was given unto him a crown; and he came forth conquering and to conquer" (6. 1-2).

The Lamb had taken the book from the hand of the Almighty, and standing in the middle of the throne and the vast assembled company, He began to unloose the seals and to reveal the dreadful contents of the roll of God's purposes. Judgment was about to fall and, as each seal was opened, one phase or stage of God's judicial actions was disclosed. In the case of each of the first four seals, the instrument of judgment was depicted as a human agent, who issued forth at the command of one of the four living creatures. Divine vengeance must be meted out, but the human executors were unable to move until so directed by the supporters of the throne.

As the first seal was opened, one of the living creatures thundered forth a summons, "Come." In response to the call, a white horse issued forth, bearing a rider armed with a bow. To this martial equestrian was given a crown, and the seer records that "he came forth conquering and to conquer."

The interpretations given to this first judgment are extremely varied. It has been said, for example, that this mysterious rider is representative of Christ issuing forth in grace at His first advent, but the horses and riders which emerged under the next three seals are undoubtedly connected with judgment, and it is patently faulty exegesis which can refer one to grace and the others to judgment. Newton is not very far wrong when he says that "the Revelation must be interpreted in consistency with itself," and adds that this seal "is not intended to describe the patient ministrations of God in grace, but the enforcement of His will by power." The whole scene is clearly subsequent to the church age of chapters 2 and 3, whereas Christ's first advent was antecedent to that age. It is impossible, therefore, for the rider to have any connection with our Lord's first coming.

Nor can the happenings under the first seal be applied to Christ's coming forth in vengeance to set up His earthly kingdom,[1] since that is the last judicial act prior to the millennium, whereas this seal is opened at the commencement of the period of the outpouring of divine wrath.

The symbol has also been interpreted as indicative of the triumphs of the Gospel; but the Gospel, as now preached, will never be universally triumphant. Furthermore, Rev. 6 refers to an initial sending forth and is plainly prophetic. It cannot, therefore, relate to the Gospel which had been sent forth half a century before.

Baines says: "A white horse only symbolizes victorious power and, like other emblems, is used without regard to the moral character of those with whom it is connected." Horses are usually associated with warfare in Scripture, but a white horse would indicate an almost bloodless victory.

The bow, moreover, is not such a destructive symbol as the sword, for example, but whereas the latter suggests a close contact, the former is suggestive of distant warfare. There may also be some significance in the fact that the bow is not a Roman emblem, but is reputed to have been discovered by the Grecian god, Apollo, who instructed the Cretans in its use.

A crown (the laurel crown which was the distinctive badge of reigning emperors) was bestowed upon this victor before the commencement of his career, so that he actually commenced as

[1]Rev. 19. 11

a royal conqueror. The seer's words indicate that this mighty one will be sent forth with a mission of unchecked conquest, and it is apparent that he will sweep over the world, gaining "victory after victory by the prestige of his name and reputation. There is no intimation of slaughter here" (Kelly).

The brilliant career of this imperial rider on the white horse has been interpreted by the historicists as applying to the golden age of prosperity and good government that elapsed from the death of Domitian to the accession of Commodus. It is far more probable, however, that the reference is to the rise and career of a mighty imperial ruler after the rapture of the Church, who brings under his sway a vast territory in an endeavour to maintain peace, order, and prosperity.

Even this interpretation is not entirely satisfactory, for the riders pictured under the next three seals clearly symbolize principles or forces rather than persons, and it is inconceivable that the first seal should differ so fundamentally in its basic ideas. It is suggested by some expositors that the rider depicts, not an individual, but the spirit of conquest such as animated Alexander, Napoleon, etc. This could hardly be bloodless conquest, however, and we are in agreement with the view expressed by Robert Tuck, when he writes: "A peaceful conqueror, who covers distances with his bow, is clearly indicated; and the only such conqueror that can be conceived is commerce and colonisation. From one point of view this is a woe, for commerce has its side of financial calamities, and colonisation breaks up family life."

The first seal is admittedly the most difficult of interpretation, and dogmatism here would be decidedly out of place.

Second Seal

"And when He opened the second seal, I heard the second living creature saying, Come. And another horse came forth, a red horse; and to him that sat thereon it was given to take peace from the earth, and that they should slay one another: and there was given unto him a great sword" (6. 3-4).

As the second seal was opened, there issued a rider on a red horse, who was authorized to take away peace from the earth and to let loose the passions and terrors of war. As a sign of his mission a great sword was given to him.

Among the Romans, none but a soldier had the right to wear a sword; it was the badge of his profession. The great sword plainly depicts the destruction of peace and the plunging of the world into war. The red horse, by its very colour, is indicative of bloodshed and slaughter. So that the period represented is obviously one of tremendous and extensive carnage.

The authority given by Commodus to the Prætorian guards and their prefect resulted, after his death, in sheer military despotism. The ruthless soldiery assumed supreme control and plundered or murdered whom they chose, even going so far as to sell the empire itself to the highest bidder. During the 92 years from A.D. 192 to 284, Sismondi says: "32 emperors and 27 pretenders to the empire alternately, by incessant warfare, hurled each other from the throne."

But the picture presented is of some more awful day still in the future, when concord will give place to lawless passion, when national amity will be superseded by slaughter and butchery, and all tranquillity will be destroyed by cruelty, revenge, and murder. The rider on the red horse had a divine mandate to take away peace and to unleash the horrors of internecine strife. It is impossible to grasp fully the awful conditions indicated in the Apocalyptic picture or to appreciate the suffering which a righteous God will inflict upon the world which rejected His Son.

Third Seal

"And when He opened the third seal, I heard the third living creature saying, Come. And I saw, and behold, a black horse; and he that sat thereon had a balance in his hand. And I heard as it were a voice in the midst of the four living creatures saying, A chœnix of wheat for a denarius, and three chœnixes of barley for a denarius; and the oil wine hurt thou not" (6. 5-6).

The third seal was opened to reveal a black horse whose rider carried a balance in his hand. Black is, of course, the hue of mourning, but it is also figurative of dearth and famine. Jeremiah, for example, laments: "Our skin was black like an oven because of the terrible famine."[1]

The "balance" adds confirmation of the scarcity of food. If food is measured or weighed, it denotes a shortage.[2] It may also suggest a system of general rationing in view of limitation of supplies.

From the midst of the four living creatures a voice fixed the price at which the two principal cereals were to be sold—a chœnix of wheat for a denarius, and three chœnixes of barley for a denarius. A denarius was the daily wage of a labourer,[3] and would normally purchase eight chœnixes of wheat or twenty-four chœnixes of barley. The prices at which these staple foods were to be sold under this seal were, therefore, eight times the normal prices.

[1]Lam. 5. 10; Lam. 4. 4-8; Jer. 14. 1-2 [2]Lev. 26. 26; Ezek. 4. 16 [3]Matt. 20. 2, 9

A chœnix (roughly the equivalent of a quart) of wheat was reckoned to be the minimum for a day's food, so that, in the period described under the seal, a day's food would cost the whole of a day's pay and would permit of no provision for dependants. Barley—the food of slaves and horses—was also to be sold at the ruinous price of a day's wage for three quarts, and it is evident that both cereals would be extremely difficult of procurement. Actual want will be widely experienced in the future period indicated.

Abundance of wine has often in the past been a concomitant of extreme scarcity of wheat and it is interesting to note that oil and wine were exempted from the Apocalyptic judgment. These were considered the rich man's luxuries, so that, although the poor man's food was to be severely restricted, the luxuries of the wealthy were to remain untouched—exactly the kind of thing that fosters class hatred and gives rise to civil unrest.

The balance held by the rider was an official badge of Roman prætors and provincial governors who had the administration of justice in their hands. "Under the old republic," says Elliott, "they were wont to have a balance over the magisterial chair, or on coins struck in honour of their appointment to high office; and sometimes also an ear of corn, with a reference to their duty of collecting the corn produce."

Historicist interpreters usually refer the occurrences under the third seal to the oppressive burden of taxation on provincials of the Roman empire resulting from the edict of Caracalla in A.D. 215. Prior to this, the main provincial taxes were tributes of corn, oil, and wine. The application of the prophecy to this past period, however, is not very convincing, although the experiences of seventeen centuries ago may perhaps be regarded as a foreshadowing of a future period in which a more complete fulfilment will be evident.

From the passage it seems clear that, in the space of time subsequent to the removal of the Church, severe judgments will fall upon the working classes. Whilst the affluent will escape major hardship, the masses will suffer the distress of want. The whole of the poor man's income will be absorbed by the purchase of bare necessities of food, and there will evidently be no provision at all for the aged and incapacitated or for children. This finds confirmation in our Lord's own statement that there will be famines in the last days.[1]

The retributive dealings of God with this world in the day of

[1]Matt. 24. 7

His wrath will be untempered by mercy, but will be based upon exact and inflexible justice.

Fourth Seal

"And when He opened the fourth seal, I heard the voice of the fourth living creature saying, Come. And I saw, and behold, a pale horse; and he that sat upon him, his name was Death; and Hades followed with him. And there was given unto them, authority over the fourth part of the earth, to kill with sword and with famine, and with pestilence, and by the wild beasts of the earth" (6. 7-8).

As the fourth seal was opened, the summoning shout of "Come" was uttered by one of the living creatures for the fourth and last time. In each of the first four seals their authority was very clearly emphasized. In close association with the throne and in perfect accord with it, they assumed the responsibility of calling forth the agent of judgment.

On this occasion a horse of wan, exanimate hue issued forth, bearing the grisly rider Death, who was quickly followed by his fearful companion Hades.

Under the previous three seals, war and famine had raged over the earth, probably decimating its population. Now there was something infinitely worse, for authority over a quarter of the earth was given to these dreadful emissaries of divine justice in order that they might kill with sword, famine, pestilence and wild beasts.

God's "four sore judgments" are described as "the sword, and the famine, and the noisesome beast, and the pestilence,"[1] and history shows that, in the past, there has been a very close association between these four. When war sweeps over a land, it is common for agricultural pursuits to be almost entirely deserted, whilst all able-bodied men take up the sword. In consequence, food stores are reduced and, if the war is of long duration, the inevitable result is famine. A widespread scarcity of food and correlative malnutrition are, in their turn, productive of disease and plague. The depopulation caused by war, famine, and pestilence ultimately encourages the wild beasts to prey upon men.

The commission given to the judicial agents under the fourth seal might be said to have been executed with precision in the history of the Roman empire during the third century. Rev. 6. 8 refers to a fourth part of the earth and it is curious that, during the reign of Gallienus, the empire was divided into four parts.

The pale, cadaverous horse—the colour of putrefying flesh—has been used as a symbol of the approaching dissolution which

[1]Ezek. 14. 21

began with the reign of Philip in A.D. 248. Barbarous invaders decimated the population, and their terrible ravages were followed by a widespread famine. "Famine is almost always followed by epidemical diseases, the effect of scanty and unwholesome food," wrote Gibbon as he referred to the "furious plague which, from the year 250 to the year 265, raged without intermission." Five thousand persons died daily in Rome alone. This scourge was followed later by the attacks of ferocious beasts. Arnobius, for example, alludes to them as afflicting the land even as late as A.D. 296.

Despite the exactness with which the Apocalyptic conditions were realized in the third century, the complete fulfilment of the prophecy appears still to lie in the future. In those dreadful days of divine judgment God's "four sore judgments" will be unleashed upon the world, and His guilty creatures will be delivered over to Death and Hades, the former seizing the body and the latter laying claim to the soul. In the final judgment even this will prove to have been but temporary, for Death and Hades will then be compelled to yield up their prisoners, and themselves will be destroyed in the lake of fire.[1]

It seems probable that the imagery of the first four seals is not unconnected with the vision of Zechariah.[2] The Old Testament prophet saw chariots driven by red horses, black horses, white horses, and bay horses, and was informed by an angel that these were "the four spirits of the heavens which go forth from standing before the Lord of all the earth." The New Testament seer also saw coloured horses and he, too, apprehended them as the messengers of the Almighty riding forth at His behest.

The Fifth Seal

"And when He opened the fifth seal, I saw underneath the altar the souls of them that had been slain for the Word of God, and for the testimony which they held: and they cried with a great voice, saying, How long, O Master, the holy and true, dost Thou not judge and avenge our blood on them that dwell on the earth? And there was given them to each one a white robe; and it was said unto them, that they should rest yet for a little time, until their fellow-servants also and their brethren, who should be killed even as they were, should be fulfilled" (6. 9-11).

Each of the first four seals is connected with one of the living creatures. Unlike its predecessors, however, the fifth seal is marked by no summoning shout from the cherubim nor by any further equestrian.

Instead, John beheld an altar, under which (*i.e.*, presumably at the foot, and not actually underneath) were the souls of martyrs

[1]Rev. 20. 14 [2]Zech. 6. 1-8

who had been slain for their witness to God. Under the Mosaic economy the altar was, of course, the scene of sacrifice. Upon it the slain animal was consumed in the flames as a holocaust, whilst at its base the blood of the sacrifice was poured out.

The sacrificial figure is used of those believers who will be martyred in a coming day. They are viewed as having been sacrificed upon the altar of devotion to their God and their blood poured out at its foot. The malignant hatred and cruelty of the world-rulers of that day will find in the faithful followers of the Almighty an object on which to vent their malicious spite and it would appear that the pogroms of the past will be surpassed in horror and extent in the future.

Because these martyrs are described as speaking, it is commonly suggested that the picture is of the intermediate state, but Hengstenberg pertinently remarks that these "are not the souls in the intermediate state; the souls are meant of which it is said in the Old Testament that they are in the blood—the animal souls;[1] they are murdered souls; but the blood itself might as well have stood." Like the blood of the murdered Abel[2] their blood cries out for vengeance.

The cause of the death of these saints is stated to be their testimony and their adherence to the Word of God. The restraint of the Holy Spirit having been removed, open allegiance to the Almighty will court tribulation. The baleful attention of the latter-day tyrants will be attracted by the very witness of the saints to divine things. and malevolent hatred will snatch away their lives.

Historical interpreters see in the fifth seal a description of the period of Roman persecutions, when Christianity was proscribed as *religio illicita* and Christians were treated as the offscouring of the earth. The plain reference of the passage is not to the past, however, but to the pious Jews of post-rapture days. Those who turn to the Scriptures and testify to the coming Messiah will pass through the most sanguinary persecutions and will eventually pay with their lives for the faith they hold.

As the blood of Abel cried out for vengeance, so these souls called aloud to God to judge and avenge their blood upon those who dwell on the earth. Their invocation of judgment upon their enemies plainly indicates that the martyrs are not Christians, since Christianity teaches its followers to love their enemies and to pray for those who despitefully use them. The cry, "How long?" is the familiar Jewish cry during the day of future trouble and

[1]Gen. 9. 5 [2]Gen. 4. 10

anguish, and is found repeatedly in the imprecatory Psalms which refer to that period. It would be improper for the Christian to pray for retribution, but the persecuted Jew of that day will be able to do so with perfect propriety.

The name by which these murdered saints addressed God, *viz.*, "the holy and true Despot," occurs only once in the Revelation, and Bengel points out that it signifies a landlord or the head of a house. The martyrs esteem themselves among the chattels of their Master and regard God as their Lord and Head.

Until the persecution which had been unleashed had exacted its full toll of the lives of God's people, compliance with the plea of the righteous victims was postponed. Divine laws are inexorable, but the Almighty acts always at the appointed moment—neither before nor after.

Pending divine action, white robes were given to the martyred throng as a token of divine approbation and they were commanded to rest until injustice had wreaked its anger upon those others who were destined to fall under the oppressor's wrath. Justice would eventually deal with injustice, but the Almighty, in His omniscience, acted with unhurried and inflexible rightness.

The Sixth Seal

"And I saw when He opened the sixth seal, and there was a great earthquake; and the sun became black as sackcloth of hair, and the whole moon became as blood; and the stars of the heaven fell unto the earth as a fig tree cast with her unripe figs, when she is shaken of a great wind. And the heaven was removed as a scroll when it is rolled up; and every mountain and island were moved out of their places. And the kings of the earth, and the princes, and the chief captains, and the rich, and the strong, and every bondman and freeman, hid themselves in the caves and in the rocks of the mountains; and they say to the mountains and to the rocks, Fall on us, and hide us from the face of Him that sitteth on the throne, and from the wrath of the Lamb; for the great day of their wrath is come; and who is able to stand?" (6. 12-17).

The opening of the sixth seal was marked by a serious disturbance in the whole fabric of nature. A great earthquake occurred, the forerunner of the more terrible earthquake[1]—the "shaking" of all terrestrial things.[2] Seismic phenomena were always anciently regarded as an indication of divine wrath or displeasure, but the figure is here used in a typical sense. Scott says: "A great earthquake denotes a violent disruption of the organized state of things, a complete subversion of all existing authority."

The sun, the natural light of the earth, and the symbol of supreme authority in this scene, became black as hair sackcloth. Its light

[1]Rev. 16. 18 [2]Haggai 2. 6; Heb. 12. 26-28

was completely blotted out and the world left in darkness. The sun is used as a figure of our Lord Himself,[1] and there may be a suggestion in Rev. 6 of the total rejection of His authority. It is more probable, however, that it is general authority or government which is in view.

The moon, whose light is derived from the sun, became like blood, thus filling the night with terror equal to that of the day. The ensanguined moon suggests the overthrow of all derived authority and the bloody triumph of anarchy.

The stars also fell to the earth, like unripe figs falling from a heavily-laden tree. All minor powers and authorities and all ecclesiastical leaders will lose their influence and position in the day described by the seer. The rapidly growing apostasy of the present day will later become the cause of the downfall of the religious leaders.

It is difficult to appreciate the stark horror of the scene described by the apostle. The awful elemental convulsion, the blackened sun, the bloody moon, and the terrifying fall of the celestial bodies might well fill the mind with dread. The picture is not a new one, however, and the imagery is undoubtedly drawn very largely from the Old Testament prophets. The details are repeated more than once in earlier Scriptures. "I will show wonders in the heavens and in the earth, blood and fire, and pillars of smoke," declared Jehovah through the prophet Joel. "The sun shall be turned into darkness, and the moon into blood, before the great and terrible day of Jehovah come."[2] And again, "The sun and the moon shall be darkened and the stars shall withdraw their shining."[3]

It is not without significance that just before the writing of the Apocalypse, extraordinary natural calamities did occur. Renan says: "Never had the world been seized with such a trembling fit; the earth itself was a prey to the most terrible convulsions. . . . The Campagna was desolated by typhoons and cyclones; frightful tempests spread terror in all directions. But that which produced the greatest impression was the earthquakes. The globe was undergoing a convulsion analogous to that of the moral world."

Elliott sees in the picture the entire destruction of heathenism before the progress of Christianity, and says that during the reign of Theodocius, "the stars of pagan power were fallen. Its heaven, or political religious system, had vanished; and on the Roman earth, its institutions, laws, rules, and worship had been all but annihilated. Pagans were now obliged to seek for dens and caverns wherein to

[1]Mal. 4. 2 [2]Joel 2. 30, 31 [3]Joel 3. 15

hide their devotions." Gibbon also writes: "The ruin of the pagan religion is described by the sophists as a dreadful and amazing prodigy, which covered the earth with darkness, and restored the ancient dominion of chaos and of night."

The historical interpretation may be partially true, since history repeats itself, but our Lord made it perfectly clear that primarily the events described in this section relate to the period subsequent to the great tribulation, for He expressly said: "Immediately after the tribulation of those days shall the sun be darkened, and the moon shall not give her light, and the stars shall fall from heaven, and the powers of the heavens shall be shaken."[1] The will of God having been rejected, men will be left to their own devices and the ultimate result as depicted in the Apocalypse is the end of all rule and authority, and the existence of a state of complete anarchy.

The seer then saw the material heaven rolled up like a scroll, and every mountain and island removed out of its place. The figures used are, of course, symbolical and although verse 14 states that the mountains are removed, in the following verse they are sought as hiding-places from the wrath of God. "The image of the heaven rolled together," says Vitringa, "denotes the annihilation of the whole civil and ecclesiastical system. For, in the prophetic style, the whole body of the rulers of a people have the designation of heaven applied to it; but the people that are subject to the rulers are represented as the earth."

Not only are individual authorities overthrown, but the whole system of government collapses. Divine restraint no longer holds human passions in check. Age-long principles and traditions no longer have any weight. An insensate and unreasoning wave of anarchy sweeps away all stable, settled rule (the mountains), and also the whole commercial system (the islands). As one writer says, it is "a universal disruption of society." It is the picture of a world without God.

Terrified by the removal of all that was stable and secure, and mistakenly fearing that the great day of divine wrath had already come, and that the final judgment was therefore about to take place, the inhabitants of the earth hide in caves and rocks, seeking shelter from the face of the Almighty and from the wrath of the Lamb. "The kings of the earth, and the princes, and the chief captains, and the rich, and the strong, and every bondman and freeman" are alike in their terror. In their dread they even cry to the mountains and rocks to fall upon them and hide them from the face of the Judge.

[1]Matt. 24. 29

Isaiah paints the picture graphically: "They shall go into the holes of the rocks, and into the caves of the earth, for fear of the Lord, and for the glory of His majesty, when He ariseth to shake terribly the earth. In that day a man shall cast his idols of gold, which they made each one for himself to worship, to the moles and to the bats; to go into the clefts of the rocks, and into the tops of the ragged rocks, for fear of the Lord, and for the glory of His majesty, when He ariseth to shake terribly the earth."[1]

Icy dread fills every heart as they cry "the great day of their wrath is come; and who is able to stand?"

[1]Isa. 2. 19-21

Chapter VIII

The Tribulation Saved

The Sealing of Israel

"After this I saw four angels standing at the four corners of the earth, holding the four winds of the earth, that no wind should blow on the earth, or on the sea, or upon any tree. And I saw another angel ascend from the sunrising having the seal of the living God: and he cried with a great voice to the four angels, to whom it was given to hurt the earth and the sea, saying, Hurt not the earth, neither the sea, nor the trees, till we shall have sealed the servants of our God on their foreheads. And I heard the number of them who were sealed, a hundred and forty and four thousand, sealed out of every tribe of the children of Israel" (7. 1-4).

IT is interesting to note that there is a parenthesis between the sixth and seventh seals, another between the sixth and seventh trumpets, and again another between the sixth and seventh vials.

Before the seventh seal opened, God drew aside the veil to reveal the work of grace which was still continuing even in the day of judgment. John saw the earth as a four-cornered plain, at each corner of which stood an angel restraining a mighty force, the powers thus held in check by the four angels being described as "the four winds of the earth." That there were four is surely indicative of the universality of their potential scope and influence.

The wind is frequently the cause of natural calamity and it is here used as a symbol of the agent of calamity. One writer declares that the "winds of *heaven*" in Scripture are "the providential agencies employed by God to execute His purposes," and that "the winds of *earth*" are political and other troubles on earth.[1]

Until the safety of God's elect was assured, the winds were restrained from blowing upon the *earth*, which the same writer describes as "the scene of settled government,"[2] the *sea*, symbolical of "nations and peoples in anarchy and confusion,"[3] or any *tree*, "human might and pride on earth."[4]

Another angel descended from the east (or sunrising), who had the seal of the living God. The forces of evil were to be kept bridled until the servants of God were sealed in their foreheads,

[1]Dan. 7. 2; Job. 1. 19; Jer. 49. 36 [2]Rev. 10. 2; Psa. 46. 2
[3]Dan. 7. 2, 3; Isa. 57. 20 [4]Dan. 4. 10, 22; Ezek. 31. 3-18; Isa. 10. 18, 19

and the seer learned that 144,000 out of all the tribes of Israel were sealed. These were accorded immunity from the terrible winds of trouble that were about to be unleashed. They had acknowledged the name of God and He now protected them by His seal.

It was the practice among the Romans for soldiers to be marked in the hand, and for slaves to be branded in the forehead. According to Herodotus, in some instances the name of the god whom an individual worshipped was branded upon the worshipper. In similar fashion, the living God here publicly marked and acknowledged His own by branding their foreheads. Divine ownership of the Christian is indicated by the seal of the Holy Spirit.[1] God's ownership of His latter-day servants is denoted by His personal seal.

After the rapture of the Church, the Gospel of the Kingdom will be preached, particularly among the people of Israel. Many will be converted and these will be marked by God as His own possession with a view to bringing them into millennial blessing.

The number sealed, *viz.*, 144,000, is clearly not a precise figure—12,000 out of each tribe—but merely an indication that God has appropriated a certain number of Israel for Himself.

This 144,000 of Israel are, of course, entirely distinct from the the company of Gentiles referred to in the latter part of the chapter, and also from the 144,000 of *Judah* mentioned in chapter 14. The Seventh Day Adventists and Millennial Dawnists claim that this company will be composed only of the faithful of their respective persuasions, but the picture is quite plainly a Jewish one. Whatever the correct interpretation, the record is a stimulus to deeper confidence in the One Who, in providential care, marks out and preserves His own people.

From Each Tribe

"Of the tribe of Judah were sealed twelve thousand: of the tribe of Reuben twelve thousand: of the tribe of Gad twelve thousand: of the tribe of Asher twelve thousand: of the tribe of Naphtali twelve thousand: of the tribe of Manasseh twelve thousand: of the tribe of Simeon twelve thousand: of the tribe of Levi twelve thousand: of the tribe of Issachar twelve thousand: of the tribe of Zebulun twelve thousand: of the tribe of Joseph twelve thousand: of the tribe of Benjamin were sealed twelve thousand" (7. 5-8).

Counting Joseph's two sons as Jacob's children, Israel, or Jacob, had thirteen sons but, in every Scriptural list of the tribes, only twelve names are given. Levi's name is usually omitted. In this instance Dan and Ephraim are excluded, but Joseph (Ephraim's father) is present. Dan and Ephraim were the first of Israel's tribes

[1]Eph. 1. 13

to go into idolatry,[1] and it is sometimes suggested that a descendant of Dan will be the leader in the idolatrous worship of Antichrist. If that be so, it is not surprising that Dan's name is omitted.

In the millennial distribution of the land[2] both Dan and Ephraim will be restored, but it is not insignificant that the lot of Dan will be in the extreme north and farther away from the temple than any of the other tribes.

Ephraim and Dan are not named in Rev. 7. The pledge of security against trouble, virtually given in the seal, was not for these rebellious tribes. H. P. Barker, however, writes: "Ephraim also is omitted but is, of course, included in Joseph. *So is Manasseh.* (Refer to Num. 13. 11.) The mention of Manasseh in Rev. 7 is therefore a duplication and is probably due to a copyist writing Man instead of Dan. Names were often abbreviated thus, especially at the end of a line. The Greek capital D is in the shape of a triangle, and might easily be mistaken for M in a worn copy where the bottom line of the triangle was hardly visible and there happened to be a mark at the side. Then another copyist, reading Man would write Manasseh in full. As the writer referred to says, one acquainted with groupings of the tribes in O.T. lists would expect to find Dan named as a fourth with Gad, Asher and Naphtali. This makes it more likely that we should read Dan in Rev. 7. 6.· Four cursives omit Manasseh, and the Bohairic version gives Dan in its place." This explanation is not unreasonable, and does at least avoid all speculation regarding the identity of Antichrist, etc.

Seiss ingeniously links the names of the tribes as follows: "Judah means *confession* or *praise of God*; Reuben, *viewing the Son*; Gad, a *company*; Asher, *blessed*; Naphtali, a *wrestler*, or *striving with*; Manasseh, *forgetfulness*; Simeon, *hearing and obeying*; Levi, *joining* or *cleaving to*; Issachar, *reward*, or *what is given by way of reward*; Zebulun, a *home* or *dwelling-place*; Joseph, *added* or *an addition*; Benjamin, *a son of the right hand, a son of old age*. These 144,000 then, are Israelites, living in the period of judgment, who are only then brought to be *confessors* and *praisers of God*, whilst the most of their kindred continue in unbelief and rebellion. *Viewing the Son*, as their fathers never would view Him, they acknowledge Him as their Messiah and Judge. As Jews, they thus constitute a distinct *company* to themselves, and are *blessed*. As the result of their conversion, they are also very active in practical righteousness. They *strive and wrestle* against their own and their nation's long

[1] Judges 18. 2, 20, 31, etc. [2] Ezek. 48

forgetfulness to the truth as it is in Jesus, *hearing and obeying* now the voice of the Lord, *cleaving to the reward* and the heavenly *home* promised by the prophets. They are a *superaddition* to the Church. They are *sons of God* indeed, but sons begotten in the day of God's *right hand* in the period of power and judgment, in the last extremity of this age."

THE SAVED GENTILES

"After these things I saw, and behold, a great multitude, which no man could number, out of every nation, and of all tribes and peoples and tongues, standing before the throne and before the Lamb, arrayed in white robes, and palms in their hands; and they cry with a great voice, saying, Salvation unto our God who sitteth on the throne, and unto the Lamb. And all the angels were standing round about the throne, and about the elders and the four living creatures; and they fell before the throne on their faces, and worshipped God, saying, Amen: Blessing, and glory, and wisdom, and thanksgiving, and honour, and power, and might, be unto our God for ever and ever. Amen. And one of the elders answered, saying unto me, These who are arrayed in the white robes, who are they, and whence came they? And I said unto him, My lord, thou knowest. And he said to me, These are they who come out of the great tribulation, and they washed their robes, and made them white in the blood of the Lamb. Therefore are they before the throne of God; and they serve Him day and night in His temple; and He that sitteth on the throne shall spread His tabernacle over them. They shall hunger no more, neither thirst any more; neither shall the sun strike upon them, nor any heat: for the Lamb who is in the midst of the throne shall be their shepherd, and shall guide them unto fountains of waters of life; and God shall wipe away every tear from their eyes" (7. 9-17).

Before the full force of the four winds was released, an elect remnant of Israel was sealed. Divine grace is not limited to the narrow borders of Judaism, however. The preaching of the Gospel of the Kingdom during the Great Tribulation will be used to the conversion of Gentiles as well as Jews, and the seer's eyes were opened to behold a vast concourse of every nationality and race, all of whom had found salvation through faith in the finished work of Christ.

It is sometimes suggested that this multitude is identical with the Church, but the latter is depicted as *enthroned*, whereas the former *stand* before the throne, clad in white robes of righteousness and carrying palm branches (the recognized symbol of victory and triumph). The picture is of the feast of tabernacles, when, the year's labour ended and the produce of the field gathered in, the people rejoiced before God. Booths constructed of "the boughs of leafy trees and willows of the brook"[1] became their temporary abode and, as they gathered before Jehovah with their psalms of happiness, they waved their triumphant palm branches. Their

[1]Lev. 23. 40

labour was ended, cares were past, and the winter period of rest was soon to commence. As Bahr says: "After having gathered in the produce of the field, the people found themselves at the end of their annual labours and occupations, were in possession of the promised and expected blessing, felt rewarded for all the trouble and the faith with which they had sown their seed in hope, and could now enjoy their rest. . . . With the feast of tabernacles, all field-labour ceased, and winter, their period of rest, began. Every-one saw himself recompensed for the labours of the year, his cares were gone, the whole fulness of divine blessing was in the hands of all. No time of the year was so appropriate for joy and rejoicing."

So with the vast company whom the apostle saw. The trials of the past were ended and they now rested from their labours. Their shout of triumph swelled up into a crescendo as they ascribed salvation to God and the Lamb. The Almighty was their Deliverer from earth's persecutions and heaven's judgments, and they gladly acknowledged His saving power.

The tribute of the great multitude provoked the whole of the heavenly host to worship. Angels, elders and living creatures—the whole of the spiritual realm—prostrated themselves in adoration before the throne and poured forth their sevenfold ascription of praise. "Blessing, and glory, and wisdom, and thanksgiving, and honour and power and might, be unto our God for ever and ever, Amen." The awe-inspiring spectacle of the mightiest spirits bent low in worship, the tremendous volume of their united symphony, the victorious shout of the redeemed and numberless Gentiles, are beyond human imagination. The details all merge into a faint impression of the presentation of the tribute to the Almighty Sovereign.

As John stood gazing in amazement at the scene, one of the elders explained that the redeemed multitude had come out of the Great Tribulation. Although sin was rampant and the Man of Sin had been revealed, they had found salvation through Calvary's work. They had "washed their robes, and made them white in the blood of the Lamb." The historicist interpreter sees in the picture an indication of the sufferings and tribulations of the Church during the persecutions of pagan Rome and suggests—as Tuck does—that these believers wear "white robes because they resisted sin and bore their earth-burdens and won the triumph of obedient submission as Christ did."

It seems evident, however, that the reference is to the period of trouble which still lies in the future. Although the Gospel of the grace of God, as proclaimed during the present age, will no longer be applicable, Jewish missionaries will carry far and wide the news of the coming King. Many will receive with gladness this Gospel of the Kingdom and will put their trust in Christ for salvation.

It is curious to note the difficulty felt by some commentators regarding the blood-washed robes of the multitude. The significance is, of course, merely that the triumphant host had availed themselves of the efficacy of Christ's atoning work. As one writer says: "Here are two things implied: the forgiveness of sins, indicated by their being *washed* in the blood; and the renewal of the character, indicated by their having their *robes washed*—robes being emblematical of character."

Whilst this Gentile company stood before the throne of God, the elder stated that they served Him day and night in His temple, *i.e.*, they exercised sacerdotal functions and stood there as priests. There will then be a temple on earth to which the elder presumably referred, so that the position of these Gentile converts appears to be an earthly one. Indeed, J. N. Darby declares: "They have a priest's place in the world's temple. The millennial multitudes are worshippers—these are priests."

During the wilderness journey Israel was under the shelter of a cloud which marked the presence of Jehovah. So, for these later saints, it is stated that "He that sitteth on the throne shall spread His tabernacle over them." A divine canopy will be spread over them.[1] They will be under the care and protection of the Almighty.

There will be a cessation from all earth's sufferings. Hunger and thirst will never again be their experience; they will be removed from want. Neither the burning sun nor heat shall touch their lives: the trials and privations of life will never again fall to their lot. The Lamb will shepherd them and guide them to fountains of waters of life. Under His guiding hand, the very sources of life and power will become available to His people.

Moreover, God Himself will dry their tears. These believers had known sorrow, sadness, and affliction, but all cause of such trials will be dispersed by the hand of the Almighty.

The promises made are all of a material and temporal character, confirming that the future and the position of the believers of that day will be earthly and not heavenly.

[1]Isa. 4. 5, 6

Chapter IX

The Seven Seals

(*Continued*)

The Seventh Seal

"And when He opened the seventh seal, there followed a silence in heaven about the space of half an hour. And I saw the seven angels who stand before God; and there were given unto them seven trumpets" (8. 1. 2).

UNDER the fifth seal John had heard the cry of the martyred saints for the avenging of their blood,[1] but before any response is made to their prayer a solemn pause intervenes. Immediately the seventh seal is opened, there is silence in heaven which lasts for the space of half an hour. Says Dr. Basil Atkinson: "It was a hushed and threatening stillness before the outbreak of a storm." It was no calm of placid repose and complacent quiet, but the oppressive and portentous hush that tells of looming trouble. Atkinson sees in the silence a description of conditions about A.D. 360, when the Roman world seemed obsessed by the feeling that something dreadful was about to happen—"a time when great barbarian armies were on the frontiers of the empire waiting for an opportunity to invade and ravage it." We prefer to think, however, that it relates to a calm preceding the storm of judgment which is yet to break upon the world during the period subsequent to the removal of the Church.

The last seal being broken, the whole scroll now lay open, disclosing in detail the whole of God's purposes for this earth. It may well be that so dreadful were the scenes of judgment thus revealed that an awestruck heaven was dumb at the sight. The awful silence endured for half an hour. Many attempts have been made to explain the length of this period, but none is very satisfactory, and it seems most logical to regard it as a brief respite of indefinite length.

As the seal was opened, the seer saw seven angels who stand before God—what one writer has described as "the glorious septemvirate of celestial arch-regents." It was popularly believed by the Jews that there were seven "presence angels," who were of the highest angelic order and comparable, for example, to the seven Persian princes referred to in Esther 1. 4, who "saw the king's face," and ranked next to the monarch in status and power. Indeed,

[1]Rev. 6. 9, 10

the Book of Enoch ventures to name six of them as follows (chap. 20): "These are the names of the angels who watch. Ariel, one of the holy angels, who presides over clamour and terror; Raphael, one of the holy angels, who presides over the spirits of men; Raguel, one of the holy angels, who inflicted punishment on the world and the luminaries; Michael, one of the holy angels, who, presiding over human virtue, commands the nations; Sarakiel, one of the holy angels, who presides over the spirits of the children of men that transgress; Gabriel, one of the holy angels, who presides over Ikesat, over paradise, and over the Cherubim."

It is clear from this and other passages that the heavenly state is not a democratic commonality but a sphere in which celestial orders tower one above another—"thrones, lordships, principalities, authorities"[1]—and in which the seven presence angels occupy a place of particular eminence and dignity. "These sublimest ministers of God," says Seiss, "are the prime executors of the on-coming administrations."

Unto the angels were given seven trumpets. The trumpet was, of course, closely connected with Israel and was the medium by which divine commands were issued to the people. The blast of the trumpet gathered them together, it directed their advance or retreat, it gave warning of the approach of the enemy, it heralded the year of jubilee, etc.[2] The trumpet is also connected with God's judgment,[3] and when the terrible judgments of the latter day are to be executed, the trumpet is again employed.

Another Angel

"And another angel came and stood at the altar, having a golden censer; and there was given unto him much incense, that he should add it unto the prayers of all the saints upon the golden altar which was before the throne. And the smoke of the incense, with the prayers of the saints, went up before God out of the angel's hand. And the angel taketh the censer; and he filled it with the fire of the altar, and cast it upon the earth: and there followed thunders, and voices, and lightnings, and an earthquake" (8. 3-5).

Before the trumpets sounded forth their message of impending wrath, there appeared at the altar another angel, who bore a golden censer. In the levitical economy the common priest used a silver censer; only the High Priest used a golden one and that for the purpose of carrying fire from the brazen altar to the golden altar of incense. The eighth angel, therefore, assumed the character of the High Priest.

This was further emphasized by the fact that much incense was given to him to add to the prayers of the saints upon the golden

[1] Col. 1. 16 [2] Num. 10, etc. [3] Exod. 19. 16; Joel 2. 1; Amos. 3. 6

altar. Only the High Priest had access to the golden altar in the earthly tabernacle, so that the mysterious angel clearly occupied the place of High Priest in the heavenly sphere. The reference, therefore, can only be to the Lord Jesus Christ, the great High Priest.

The golden altar stood in the holy place of the tabernacle and incense was burned upon it every morning and evening.[1] The incense was composed of myrrh, cinnamon, calamus, cassia and olive oil, and was beautifully figurative of the sweetness and fragrance of Christ's moral glories and perfections. To the prayers of the suffering saints of God, Christ added the incense of His own worth. "No mere creature could add efficacy to the prayers of the saints," says Walter Scott, "for that could only be effected by One having in Himself independent right and competency. Further, the action at the altar is of a mediatorial character."

It is only through the Lord Jesus Christ that the believer has access to the throne of God. All prayer to the Father is offered through the Son and derives its merit from the value of His intercessory work. Through the perfection of the Mediator, the prayers of His people find acceptance before God. In the Apocalyptic vision, the angel added the incense to the prayers upon the golden altar and the whole ascended as a sweet odour—a cloud of incense—before God "out of the angel's hand." The Lord personally presents the believer's petitions and secures their acceptance by virtue of His own worth.

Immediately after, the angel filled the now-empty censer with fresh fire from off the brazen altar and then cast it upon the earth. The prayers of the saints of that day will be for vengeance, and the answer is given without delay. Fire from the altar becomes the instrument of judgment. Scott writes: "As the altar was the expression of His holiness and righteousness in dealing with the sin of the people of old, so that same holiness and righteousness will search the earth and judge and punish it accordingly." The imprecatory prayers of that day are in perfect consonance with God's will for that period, and the action that ensues is in complete harmony with the divine purposes.

The fire from the brazen altar was emptied upon the earth and was at once followed by thunders, voices, lightning, and an earthquake, the expressive symptoms of coming catastrophe. All the terrors of nature are depicted in the fourfold reaction to the fire, culminating in convulsions and universal disorder. They are, however, only a foreshadowing and the sounding of the trumpets shows the development in detail of the terrible experiences they indicate.

[1]Exod. 30. 7, 8

Chapter X

The Seven Trumpets

The Seven Angels

"And the seven angels who had the seven trumpets prepared themselves to sound" (8. 6).

THE seven angels now stood prepared to sound out the blast of destruction. In each of the first four trumpets, judgment fell upon some particular portion of a third part of the prophetic earth. It is not without significance that, at the time at which the Revelation was given, the Roman Empire was actually divided into three sections, which Cumming lucidly details as follows: "To Constantine was assigned Gaul, Spain, Britain, Italy, Africa; to Licinius, the Illyrian Præfecture; to Maximin, the Asiatic provinces and Egypt."

Whilst the complete fulfilment of the trumpets lies in the future, there is also a clear historical reference to the four Gothic invasions of the western empire of Constantine—the third part which suffered so badly. The first trumpet is frequently applied to the invasions of Alaric and Rhadagasius, the second to the period of Genseric and the Vandals, the third to the scourge of Attila the Hun, and the fourth to the final subversion of the empire by Odoacer.

The First Trumpet

"And the first angel sounded, and there followed hail and fire, mingled with blood, and they were cast upon the earth; and the third part of the earth was burnt up, and the third part of the trees was burnt up, and all green grass was burnt up" (8. 7).

The seventh plague upon Egypt took the form of thunder, hail, and fire.[1] The sound of the first of the Apocalyptic trumpets resulted similarly in a judgment of hail and fire, mingled with blood, being inflicted upon the earth. Under the plague man and beast suffered, and every herb and tree was smitten. Under the trumpet, however, a third of the earth, the trees and the grass was burnt up.

Hail, as Jennings remarks, "is a striking figure of divine wrath. The genial warmth is no longer in the aqeuous vapour, causing it

[1]Exod. 9. 22-25

[illegible] distil upon the ground in soft showers of blessing. All *that* is withdrawn and, being withdrawn, the same vapour becomes hard and cold, ice. Cold is but heat withdrawn. Heat in its modified gentleness is a symbol of love and approval; its withdrawal, then, is a striking symbol of wrath and judgment." It is a type of merciless, devastating judgment.[1]

Fire, again, is the reminder of the fierce and consuming wrath of God.[2] He is a consuming fire and His vengeance is exhausted and His justice satisfied in the destruction of that which is evil.

Blood is patently indicative of death,[3] and when transferred to the spiritual realm, it must obviously imply cessation of spiritual life, or complete apostasy from God.

The divine wrath symbolized by the three expressions—hail, fire, and blood—fell upon a third of the earth. There can be little doubt that the historical reference is to the Gothic invasions of the Western Empire, but it is equally clear that complete fulfilment still lies in the future and is related to the Roman Empire in its final and revived condition.

In addition to the destruction of a third of the earth, a third of the trees and grass was burnt up. A *tree* is frequently used in the Bible as the figure of man or mankind,[4] principally in the strength, power, and exaltation of humanity. *Grass*, on the other hand, is figurative of man in his weakness and lowly estate. "All flesh is as grass," says Peter, "and all the glory of man as the flower of grass."[5] (It has been suggested by some expositors that grass is a type of the people of Israel, but this is hardly tenable.)

Taken in conjunction with each other, the trees and the grass portray the complete picture of humanity, from the highest to the lowest, from the most eminent to the most humble. Judgment paid no regard to status or attainments: one-third of human beings were destroyed as the blast of the trumpet sounded forth.

At the end of the fourth and the beginning of the fifth century, the Roman Empire suffered greatly under the invasions of Alaric and the Goths, who swept through Illyria and Greece, poured into Italy, captured and sacked the city of Rome, leaving carnage and destruction in their train. Rich and poor, high and low, suffered alike at the hands of the ruthless barbarians. It might be said with some justification that the trees and grass had been burnt up. No regard was paid to eminence or humility. All experienced the same tribulation and the same brutal treatment.

The Apostle John looked on to a far more distant day than that

[1]Isa. 28. 2; 30. 30 [2]Isa. 33. 14; Luke 16. 24 [3]Gen. 9. 5, 6
[4]Judges 9. 7-15, etc. [5]1 Pet. 1. 24; Isa. 40. 7

of the barbarian invasion of the Western Empire. From a prophetical viewpoint, the trumpet blast heralded a most devastating judgment which is yet to fall upon the revived Roman Empire, when those of every estate will suffer alike under the wrath of God. So extensive and indiscriminating will be the outpouring of divine vengeance on that day that a third of the whole race, from princes to paupers, will be stricken. Whether the fraction is intended to be taken literally or not, the widespread character of the judgment is patent.

The Second Trumpet

"And the second angel sounded, and as it were a great mountain burning with fire was cast into the sea; and the third part of the sea became blood; and there died the third part of the creatures who were in the sea, even they that had life, and the third part of the ships were destroyed" (8. 8, 9).

The first plague upon Pharaoh saw the waters of Egypt turned into blood. Under the second trumpet, a burning mountain was cast into the sea, and a third of the waters became blood, with the result that a third of the inhabitants of the ensanguined sea died and a third of the ships were destroyed.

In Scriptural typology, a *mountain* usually represents a kingdom or some established power.[1] The volcanic mountain seen by the seer, therefore, would appear to be a mighty power, degraded by punitive justice. A similar figure is painted where God declared that He would make of Babylon "a burnt mountain."[2]

The *sea* is an expressive symbol of the restless and uncontrolled nations of the world. "The wicked are like the troubled sea, when it cannot rest," says Isaiah.[3]

Ejected from its normal place, the burning mountain was cast into the restless sea of a turbulent world, with a calamitous effect upon commerce and with the result of an appalling loss of life. At the impact of the mountain, the waters became blood, and a third of the creatures in the incarnadined sea died and a third of the ships were destroyed.

So far as past history is concerned, it is usually considered that the second trumpet has reference to the ravages of Genseric and his Vandals, whose fleet swept the Mediterranean, plundering and destroying. "They plundered and pillaged," says Gibbon, "from the columns of Hercules to the mouth of the Nile." For seventy years the Vandals were the scourge of the Mediterranean. Italy, Spain, Carthage, etc., all suffered from their ravages, but it is difficult to see how the metaphor of a burning mountain can be regarded as applicable to them.

[1]Jer. 51. 25; Dan. 2. 35 [2]Jer. 51. 25 [3]Isa. 57. 20

It would, therefore, appear that there still remains a more complete fulfilment of the prophecy, when some mighty power, suffering judicially under the hand of God, will become the cause of untold suffering and destruction in this world, seriously affecting commerce and robbing of their lives and livelihood many thousands of the Roman Empire of that day. In a minor sense, nowadays, the downfall of an influential and unscrupulous financier often drags many down to poverty and misery. If, for example, the whole economic structure of a country was broken, or the financial system of some kingdom was destroyed, the effect upon the surrounding countries and peoples may well be imagined. It is probable that it is a catastrophe of this character that is depicted in the events following the blast of the second trumpet.

THE THIRD TRUMPET

"And the third angel sounded, and there fell from heaven a great star, burning as a torch, and it fell upon the third part of the rivers, and upon the fountains of the waters; and the name of the star is called Wormwood; and the third part of the waters became wormwood; and many men died of the waters, because they were made bitter" (8. 10, 11).

As the third angel sounded his trumpet, a great burning star, named Wormwood (or Absinth) fell from heaven upon a third of the rivers and fountains, communicating the poisonous bitterness of absinth to the waters upon which it fell.

This star should not be confounded with that in Rev. 9. 1. The two have different effects and are evidently not identical with each other. A star is usually regarded as representative of some powerful ruler or dignitary. This star, however, was burning like a torch, so that the potentate represented was apparently suffering under the consuming anger of God. Either by reason of deliberate apostasy or as a direct result of divine chastisement, the mighty "star" was ejected from his place of power and authority in the heavens in a manner reminiscent of Satan's earlier fall.[1]

Falling upon the rivers and fountains of waters, the star imparted its own bitterness to the waters. Hengstenberg sees in the rivers "an image of affluence, prosperity, and success," and in the fountain of the waters "the sources of prosperity," but the interpretation which refers *rivers* to the ordinary life of nations, and *fountains* to the sources and influences which act upon that life, is probably more nearly accurate. The falling star corrupts the waters of life, and the very springs of life, and its guiding principles are affected by its baneful influence. Centuries before, God had threatened

[1]Isa. 14. 12; Luke 10. 18

that He would feed Israel "with wormwood, and give them water of gall to drink,"[1] and this bitter luminary will one day implement the threat.

Historically, the star Wormwood is usually assumed to have reference to Attila, "the scourge of God," whose hordes of Huns swept over Europe, depopulating and devastating the banks of the *rivers* Danube and Rhine until, to quote Cumming, "after having thus burned up the rivers, he pushed his victorious forces towards the *fountains* contiguous to the Alps. Pavia, Verona, Mantua, Milan, successively were embittered with *wormwood*, and were made to drink waters of gall, and were scorched and destroyed by the heat of this 'great star burning as a lamp.'"

The events of the past are evidently to find a repetition in the future when the blast of the third trumpet actually does sound forth. Like the fallen Wormwood, some apostate leader of a later day will become an instrument of wrath in the hands of the Almighty. His evil influence or corrupting teaching will poison morals, principles, and motives over a very wide sphere, and the spiritual death of countless numbers will plainly ensue from the infection.

The precise details of the period have not been furnished by the Holy Spirit. Only such an adumbration as is necessary for a grasp of the heavenly plan and principles is ours to-day: doubtless God's people in a future day will be in a position to discern more plainly the events now foretold only in shadow and outline.

THE FOURTH TRUMPET

"And the fourth angel sounded, and the third part of the sun was smitten, and the third part of the moon, and the third part of the stars; that the third part of them should be darkened, and the day should not shine for the third part of it, and the night in like manner" (8. 12).

The ninth of the plagues upon Egypt and—from one point of view—the most awful of them was the infliction of three days of darkness upon the land.[2] At the sound of the fourth trumpet, a third of the sun, moon, and stars were robbed of their light and in consequence, the earth lost a third of its daylight and a third of its moonlight at night.

To be plunged suddenly into darkness or to be deprived of even a part of the light normally enjoyed is a trial which cannot fully be measured by those who have never experienced such a deprivation.

[1]Jer. 9. 15 [2]Exod. 10. 21-23

Whatever the significance of the Apocalyptic symbol, it obviously indicates a burden grievous to be borne.

The *sun* is clearly figurative of the supreme authority and the *moon* and *stars* of derived and lesser authority. When they first shone forth, it is recorded that "God set them in the expanse of the heavens . . . to rule during the day and during the night."[1] Jennings suggests that the judgment under the fourth trumpet indicates "a mighty political convulsion, in which all authority is subverted, from the monarch of the empire to the petty magistrate of the town. It is the success of atheistic, anarchical communism." In the past, Communism has aimed at the abolition of authority and the destruction of all law and order, and the events following the fourth trumpet show how successful such attempts will be in a future day. (A study of *The Conflict of the Ages*, by Dr. A. C. Gaebelein, provides considerable enlightenment upon the teachings and objects of Communism.)

The historicist interpreter sees the fulfilment of the Apocalyptic picture in the past history of Rome. Although the Roman Empire had been reduced in power and bereft of many possessions, it still retained its nominal sovereignty until the time of Odoacer, one of Attila's chiefs. Odoacer, who was chief of the Heruli, marched into Italy, abolished the title and throne of Emperor of the West, and transferred the imperial insignia to Constantinople. The western third of the Empire thus lost its glory and honour, and its light was obliterated.

It seems clear that, in similar fashion, in the future, great powers and authorities will be brought down and their light extinguished. Communism will have its way and, within the limits set by God, will destroy rule, order, and authority. The effect upon a world already sorely stricken can scarcely be imagined.

The Eagle

"And I saw, and I heard an eagle, flying in mid-heaven, saying with a great voice, Woe, woe, woe, for them that dwell on the earth, by reason of the other voices of the trumpet of the three angels, who are yet to sound" (8. 13).

There was no anticipatory proclamation in connection with the first four trumpets, but the last three were heralded beforehand by an eagle with a threefold cry of woe.

The eagle feeds upon carrion and was consequently prohibited as food for Israel.[2] It was also frequently used in the Old Testament as a type of swift and relentless oppression.[3]

[1]Gen. 1. 18 [2]Lev. 11. 13, 14 [3]Deut. 28. 49; Hos. 8. 1; Hab. 1. 8

As a harbinger of vengeance, an eagle flew through the mid-heaven, conveying in a loud voice a threefold message of woe to those dwelling on the earth. Judgments had already been poured out upon the earth, but the terrors still to come demanded prior warning: perchance even yet there was time for the truly penitent to seek God's face.

Elliott ingeniously interprets the premonitory cry of the eagle as the warning voiced by Pope Gregory of the imminence of the end of the world in view of the conditions then prevailing. This may have been a partial fulfilment but it is certainly not a complete fulfilment. As the vengeance of God slowly reaches its climax, He will permit a prior announcement of doom before the most awful judgments fall. It is interesting to note that it is the earth-dwellers (those whose mind is earth-bound) who are marked out as those presently to suffer.

The Fifth Trumpet

"And the fifth angel sounded, and I saw a star from heaven fallen unto the earth: and there was given to him the key of the pit of the abyss. And he opened the pit of the abyss, and there went up a smoke out of the pit, as the smoke of a great furnace; and the sun and the air were darkened by reason of the smoke of the pit. And out of the smoke came forth locusts upon the earth; and power was given them, as the scorpions of the earth have power. And it was said unto them that they should not hurt the grass of the earth, neither any green thing, neither any tree, but only such men as have not the seal of God on their foreheads. And it was given them that they should not kill them, but that they should be tormented five months: and their torment was as the torment of a scorpion, when it striketh a man. And in these days men shall seek death, and shall in no wise find it, and they shall desire to die, and death fleeth from them. And the shapes of the locusts were like unto horses prepared for war; and upon their heads as it were crowns like unto gold, and their faces were as men's faces. And they had hair as the hair of women, and their teeth were as the teeth of lions. And they had breastplates, as it were breastplates of iron; and the sound of their wings was as the sound of chariots, of many horses rushing to war. And they have tails like unto scorpions, and stings; and in their tails is their power to hurt men five months. They have over them as king the angel of the abyss: his name in Hebrew is Abaddon, and in the Greek tongue he hath the name Apollyon" (9. 1-11).

At the sound of the fifth trumpet, another great star was seen falling from heaven to earth. There is nothing to connect this fallen dignitary with the one in Rev. 8. 10, 11. Indeed, their operations and scope appear to be entirely different from each other. It may well be that the event described is that referred to when Satan is finally cast out of heaven.[1]

The fallen star was given the key of the pit of the abyss—the

[1]Rev. 12. 9

"deep" of Luke 8. 31 and the temporary prison of Satan.[1] Using the power thus acquired, he immediately unlocked the pit, which at once emitted a cloud of noxious smoke. Like the smoke of a great furnace, the cloud rose, blotting out the sun and darkening the air, and pouring forth swarms of terrible creatures like locusts.

The eighth plague upon Egypt took the form of a swarm of locusts, which devoured every green thing and so completely covered the ground as to darken the land.[2] Here, however, the locusts filled the air and darkened the heavens.

Historical interpreters refer the star to Mahomet, to whom, the Koran claims, was committed the key to the gates of heaven. Prophetic students, however, see in the key a symbol of the devilish power of the false prophet, and liken the smoke belched forth from the pit to the awful cloud of sensualism, fanaticism, and violence which were so characteristic of Mahommedanism. Even the "locusts" are regarded as a type of the warriors of Islam.

As previously suggested, the *sun* is representative of the supreme governmental authority, whilst the air probably refers to the spiritual atmosphere and environment. The smoke of the pit blotted out the sun and beclouded the air. Here was obviously some darkening influence or delusion of the evil one. Malignant and soul-perverting influences, which have been controlled or repressed for centuries, will, in a coming day, be allowed liberty to bewilder and blind the unenlightened.

The smoke of the abyss also generated swarms of locusts. The locust usually destroys every green thing, but these were strictly forbidden to hurt grass or tree or any green thing. Scorpion-like power was given them to torment—but not to kill—for five months (the length of life of the natural locust) those men who had not the seal of God in their foreheads. The torment of their scorpion sting was so intense that their victims longed for death and vainly sought it.

Many centuries earlier, the prophet Joel depicted the emissaries of divine judgment in the guise of the locust, etc., and the Apocalypse took up the same type in relation to a still future period.

A band of locusts will normally strip everything. Here, however, the effect of their depredations is strictly limited. Their attack was upon the unsealed of Israel—they were the scourge of God upon His earthly people. (Since the sealed were from the tribes of Israel,[3] it is justifiable to assume that the primary effect of this judgment will be felt by Israel.)

[1]Rev. 20. 3; Isa. 24. 21, 22 [2]Exod. 10. 12-20 [3]Rev. 7

The destruction of the mass of mankind (the *grass*) or the natural leaders or outstanding individuals (the *trees*) was not in view, but rather a specific judgment upon Israel. If the locust is a most destructive agent, the scorpion, as Seiss says, is "the most irascible and malignant insect that lives." The combination of locust and scorpion suggests a scourge which is destructive of happiness, ease and comfort. The tormented anguish of the unfortunate victims of the locusts' attack was unrelieved by death, since the locusts were not permitted to kill them but only to torment them for five months.

Some partial fulfilment of the prophecy may have been seen in the sufferings inflicted by Mahomet and his followers, but it seems clear that a more complete fulfilment is yet to be realized in a latter day. The irruption from the pit may have in view the release of hosts of evil spirits from their prison. The awful dangers attendant upon spiritism are not fully appreciated, and the power of man's invisible foes cannot possibly be measured. If ever the restrained forces of evil break loose, the consequences for mankind cannot even be imagined. Whatever is intended to be conveyed by the images employed, it is clear that intense spiritual suffering awaits the people of Israel ere their final deliverance comes.

The locusts had tails like scorpions and their stings were in their tails. It is not without significance that our Lord connected *scorpions* with Satan,[1] and that Isaiah declared that "the prophet that teacheth lies, he is the *tail*."[2] The assault of the amphisbæna-like locusts upon the unsealed thus probably indicates the dominance of some terrible heresy or error which brings agony of soul and torment of conscience, and from which there is no relief. The oblivion of death would be welcome to the tortured soul, but even that merciful release will be denied to the sufferers.

In appearance, the locusts resembled battle-horses prepared for the fray, whilst their heads were adorned with golden crowns. Their faces were like those of men but they wore long hair like that of women, whilst their teeth were like those of lions. Breastplates like iron shielded them, and the sound of their wings was comparable with the noise of chariots and of an army of horses rushing into battle. The picture is one of a fearsome and dreadful host of monstrosities, but the language is obviously figurative, and the details not intended to be taken literally.

The historical interpreter usually claims that there is a distinct reference to Mahomet and the Saracen invasion, and there is certainly some support for the claim. Elliott says that the symbol

[1]Luke 10. 18, 19 [2]Isa. 9. 15

of the locust "is wholly Arabic. It was the 'east wind which brought the locusts' on Egypt[1]—pointing to Arabia, east of Egypt. The terms *Arab* and *locust* are in Hebrew almost the same. The symbol is used in 'They (the Midianite Arabs) came as grasshoppers,' meaning locusts."[2] The horse, of course, was peculiarly Arabian and has been regarded as signifying here hordes of cavalry.

The *man's face* of the locust has been referred to the Arab beard and moustache; the *women's hair* to the uncut long hair of the Arab; the *golden crown* to the Arab turban (which was often adorned with gold); the *iron breastplates* to the renowned Saracen coats of mail, etc.; and the *lionlike teeth* to the characteristic Arab ferocity. The resemblance to *horses* is again regarded as particularly relative to the Saracens, who were principally horsemen. There is unquestionably a reference to the Saracen invasion but, as in many prophecies, history holds, more than one foreshadowing of the final and complete fulfilment of the prophecy.

William Kelly sees a picture of a warrior army in the description. He writes: "The resemblance to horses prepared for battle is the expression of their aggressive attitude, and the crowns like gold seem to intimate their vaunted confidence in a divinely-righteous mission of victory. Their faces as of men, but with the hair of women, may denote that, with all their claim to act authoritatively in the name of God, they were nevertheless subject to the merest human authority, and not to God after all. The iron breastplates, the lion-like teeth, the sounding wings, are the figure of the unflinching courage of fanaticism, and the ferocious depredations that accompanied that wonderfully rapid warfare."

The origin of these fearsome creatures in the pit of the abyss, their emergence as a cloud to fill the air and darken the sun, their spiritual head, and various other features suggest a spiritual host rather than a material army, and the only satisfactory interpretation appears to be that the reference is to a latter-day outbreak of spiritism in a particularly virulent form. Spirit beings, who are at present under restraint, will apparently be liberated for a short period and allowed to have their way with the unhappy descendants of Jacob.

"The locusts have no king," declared Agur,[3] but those of Rev. 9 have as sovereign "the angel of the abyss," Abaddon or Apollyon, *i.e.*, the Destroyer. There can surely be no doubt as to the identity of this dark personage. The leader of these hordes in their foul work can only be Satan himself, and this tends to confirm the view

[1]Exod. 10. 13 [2]Judges 6. 5 [3]Prov. 30. 27

that "the first woe" is a spiritual one rather than a material—and therefore all the more fearful for those who must pass through the experiences of that period.

The Sixth Trumpet

"The first woe is past: behold, there come yet two woes hereafter. And the sixth angel sounded, and I heard a voice from the horns of the golden altar which is before God, one saying to the sixth angel, who had the trumpet, Loose the four angels who are bound at the great river Euphrates. And the four angels were loosed, who had been prepared for the hour and day and month and year, that they should kill the third part of men. And the number of the armies of the horsemen was twice ten thousand times ten thousand: I heard the number of them. And thus I saw the horses in the vision, and them that sat on them, having breastplates as of fire and of hyacinth and of brimstone; and the heads of the horses are as the heads of lions; and out of their mouths proceeded fire and smoke and brimstone. By these three plagues was the third part of men killed, by the fire and the smoke and the brimstone, which proceeded out of their mouths. For the power of the horses is in their mouth, and in their tails; for their tails are like unto serpents, and have heads and with them they do hurt. And the rest of mankind, who were not killed with these plagues, repented not of the works of their hands, that they should not worship demons, and the idols of gold, and of silver, and of brass, and of stone, and of wood; which can neither see, nor hear, nor walk; and they repented not of their murders, nor of their sorceries, nor of their fornication, nor of their thefts" (9. 12-21).

As the sixth angel sounded, a voice was heard from the horns of the golden altar (*i.e.*, the altar of incense) which was before God.

In an earlier scene[1] the prayers of God's suffering saints and their cries for vengeance were offered upon the golden altar with the incense given to the angel who stood there—obviously the High Priest (*i.e.*, our Lord Jesus Christ), since the High Priest alone had access to that altar. In reply to those petitions, a voice was now heard from the altar, to which the cries had been directed. The voice came from the four horns of the altar. Four is, of course, the figure of universality, and a horn of power. So that, as Scott says, "the whole strength and power of the altar of intercession is put forth in the divine answer to the mingled prayers and incense which gathered round it."

The voice commanded the sixth angel to loose the four angels who were bound at the great river Euphrates, who had been prepared to commence at a specific moment the slaughter of a third of mankind.

On the year-day basis, historical interpreters have ingeniously interpreted the denominations of time in verse 15 ("the hour and day and month and year") as 396 years and 106 days, and referred it to the holy war of the Turks upon Greek Christendom. The

[1]Rev. 8. 3

Turks left Baghdad to attack Constantinople on the 18th of January, 1057. Constantinople fell on the 29th of May, 1453, so that the total time taken was 396 years and 106 days. Despite this coincidence, it seems clear that the meaning of the verse is only that the angels were set apart by God for action at a particular moment and that, at the precise moment when the hour struck, they would enter upon their appointed mission.

Action came from the Euphrates. Hengstenberg writes: "The Euphrates is mentioned as the river, from the regions on the further side of which, during the times of the Old Testament, and through the course of centuries, the scourge of God came forth upon the nearer districts of Asia."[1]

When divine restraint was removed, the four powers who had been bound at Euphrates at once inspired mighty forces to invade and destroy the territories of the West. Horsemen numbering 200 million formed the vast invading armies, mechanized forces apparently giving place to cavalry since the Arab is far more at home on horseback. This is probably symbolic, however, since the horses are themselves described as active agents.

The horsemen had breastplates as of fire, hyacinth and brimstone. The fire and brimstone at once connect with hell and eternal torment and the breastplates have been termed "the defensive armour of hell." Here is the unleashing of terrible judgment by the permission of God and under the direction of Satan.

The heads of the horses are said to have been like those of lions, indicative of their might and majestic power. Out of their mouths proceeded fire, smoke and brimstone, which are described as three plagues by which the third part of men were killed. Tormenting delusions and spiritual darkness sapped and destroyed life. The horses were active agents in the work of destruction. The plagues issued from their mouths, and it is stated that the power of the horses was in their mouth (singular) and in their tails (plural), which resembled serpents and had heads by which they hurt, suggesting, as Scott says, that "all are animated by *one* spirit, but that the teachings and lies of Satan are multifarious. There is not only the *open* power of Satan but, in addition, his *secret* malignant and soul-destroying influence. Both are contemplated here." "The serpent is synonymous with craft, deceit, guile, subtlety. The 'tail' of the serpent is the expression of malignant influence, falsehood, mischief.[2] Further, the tails have 'heads,' intimating that the mischievous influence is intelligently directed. The

[1]Cf. Isa. 7 .20 Jer. 46. 10 [2]Isa. 9. 15; Rev. 12. 4

purpose to injure is pursued with relentless and intelligent activity."

In the events of the sixth trumpet or second "woe," students of the historical school of interpretation see portrayed the holy war of the Turks on Greek Christendom. As soon as Togrul Bey became head of the Ottoman Empire, he declared war against Christendom. Immense masses of Turkish cavalry crossed the Euphrates and assaulted Constantinople, but the city was not captured, and Christendom was saved by the Crusades. At the end of the 14th century, however, myriads of Turkish horse crossed the Danube and fell on the city, ultimately reducing it to ruins.

It is possible that the Turkish military apparel of scarlet, blue and yellow may have been a reflection of the Apocalyptic breast-plates of fire, hyacinth and brimstone. It has been suggested that the fire, smoke and brimstone which issued out of the horses' mouths had reference to the gunpowder and cannon, which were first used in the siege of Constantinople.

The seer was informed that the power (or authority) of the horses was in their tails. A curious interpretation is frequently given to this. It is said that one of the Turkish standards having been lost in the battle, a commander cut off the tail of his horse and mounted that upon a pole as a rallying ensign. Ever since that time, the horse's tail has been a distinctive official badge of authority, and the relative dignity of a Turk is indicated by the number of tails he has.

Whilst some of the details may already have been satisfied in the past, it is clear that the future still holds a fuller and final fulfilment.

It is frequently suggested that there is a reference to the future terrible invasion of the west by the kings of the east. The Euphrates, as Newell points out, was "the place where human sin began and also Satan's empire over man; where the first murder was committed; where the first war confederacy was made;[1] where Nimrod began to be 'a mighty one in the earth'; and where the vast system of Babylonian idolatry originated." The river was the eastern boundary of the Roman Empire, and formed a natural barrier between the east and the west. The difficulty of its passage was an effectual safeguard against invasion from the east. In a coming day, however, this barrier is to be removed, and the river will be dried up, as indicated in Rev. 16. 12, to facilitate military movements.

The description given makes it clear, however, that what is in view is more than a military expedition. A spiritual onslaught is also involved and those who refused to hearken to the truth will

[1]Gen. 14

be tormented by lies and deception. One third of mankind were slain. One third of the race fell under the power of the awful influence which was at work.

Despite the horror with which they had been confronted, those who were left alive still showed no sign of repentance. Nothing touched the heart of the impenitent. They continued to worship demons, and blind, deaf, and immobile idols of gold, silver, brass, stone and wood (note the gradually descending value!), and still continued in their murders, sorceries, fornications and thefts.

In impenitent obduracy, they continued to worship evil spirits and lifeless idols. It is not only the pagan idolater who is depicted here. The Roman Catholic invocation of saints and of the Virgin Mary is not entirely irrelevant, and the doings of the Middle Ages undoubtedly find some place in the picture. The murders—not isolated acts of passion, but a habitual practice—conjure up the vision of the "liquidation" of medieval "heretics," such as the Waldenses. Monsters such as the Borgias ruthlessly swept away those who were opposed to them, and the poisoner's cup and the assassin's dagger made murder a common occurrence in the Papal court.

It seems clear that the history of the past is to be re-enacted. The Gentile idolatry denounced by the Apostle Paul[1] will be openly and universally practised once again. The hatred directed against dissenters will again lead to their merciless extermination, while the standards of righteousness having been discarded, human life will be lightly regarded, and murder (particularly political murder) will be a commonplace.

The witchcraft and sorcery, not only of ancient times, but also of mediæval days, is even now reappearing in the form of spiritism, astrology, etc., and an even fuller outburst is foretold in this passage. Communication with evil spirits is consistently condemned in the Scriptures, but the plain warnings of the Word of God on this subject are ignored to-day, and flagrant defiance will evidently characterize the period described.

The "fornication" of the Middle Ages is too well known to require emphasis. At the Council of Constance, Gerston publicly denounced the convents of that day as *prostibula meretricum*, and the compulsory celibacy of the priesthood and their resultant deplorable degeneracy were not unrelated to this. Indeed, the example of several of the "Vicars of Christ" gave the lead to it.

Conditions of the present day show clearly that the human heart

[1] 1 Cor. 10. 20, 21

is unchanged and that the description of the future character of the race as given in Rev. 9 is only too probably accurate. In Russia the marriage tie means little or nothing, since its dissolution can be effected without difficulty at the cost of a few roubles. In the U.S.A. it is estimated that a very large percentage of marriages end in the divorce court, whilst companionate marriage and free love are on the increase, and fifty per cent of high school students are said to have had experience of sexual relationship. Moral standards in England are not free from blame, and burning language has been used recently of certain "plague spots." In Germany, Nazism declared that matrimony was no longer regarded as a divine institution, but simply as a means of increasing the race. No normal civilized compunctions were to be allowed to interfere with this breeding programme. The *Schwarze Korps* urged that "artificial insemination should be called into play in marriages where no children were produced." The State provided special guardians for children born out of wedlock.

When divine restraint is withdrawn, human passions will break loose, and morality will be generally discarded in favour of a new liberty (or licence). The indulgence of unbridled lust will become a commonplace, and all the licentious practices of paganism will be adopted by so-called civilized countries.

"Thefts," too, find a place in the picture. Payments for masses for the dead, the sale of ecclesiastical dignities and of indulgences, etc., were nothing less than theft in the dark days of the Middle Ages. During the Pontificate of John XXII, for example, a book was issued, listing the prices to be paid for absolution of particular crimes, and no crime (however bad) was omitted. Forgiveness might be secured for anything on payment of the appropriate amount, and the Roman Catholic revenues were swollen by the amounts received from the "penitent."

Whilst it is improbable that the "thefts" of the future will take this precise form, the lack of principle will apparently remain unchanged. The Nazi sequestration of Jewish property and the wholesale and systematic plundering by the Germans of the occupied countries are illustrative of what the future may hold during the period described. If all restraint and fear of punishment were removed, literal theft would be an inevitable result. Business morality would disappear and all sense of *meum et tuum* would vanish. The possibilities of the days in question are almost too appalling to contemplate.

CHAPTER XI

The Open Book

THE STRONG ANGEL

"And I saw another strong angel coming down out of heaven, clothed with a cloud, and the rainbow upon His head, and His countenance was as the sun, and His feet as pillars of fire, and He had in His hand a little opened book. And He set His right foot on the sea, and the left upon the earth, and cried with a loud voice as a lion roars. And when He cried, the seven thunders uttered their own voices. And when the seven thunders spoke, I was about to write; and I heard a voice out of heaven saying, Seal up the things which the seven thunders have spoken, and write them not" (10. 1-4).

BEFORE the seventh seal was broken, there was a brief interlude, during which a vision was granted to the seer of the sealed of Israel and the saved of the Gentiles.[1] Likewise, before the seventh trumpet was sounded, there came a further interlude, with a vision of the Angel of the Covenant in all His power.

A mighty Angel descended from heaven. A cloud enrobed Him and a rainbow encircled His head. The cloud is ever the symbol of the presence of the Almighty, and the rainbow is the token of the divine remembrance of mercy even in judgment. There can be no doubt, therefore, as to the identity of the majestic One whom the apostle saw: it could be no other than the Angel of the Covenant Himself—our Lord Jesus Christ.

His countenance was radiant as the sun. The solar orb is the ruler of the heavens, and supreme power shone out in the face of this glorious Being. That face, once marred and spat upon, was now resplendent in its dazzling glory.

His feet also resembled pillars of fire. The massive and unyielding character of a crushing judgment is seen in the pillars, whilst the fire indicates what Hengstenberg calls "the consuming character of God's punitive righteousness." His right foot was planted on the sea and the left on the earth, in token of His determination now to take possession of His own property and to resist all assaults by His enemies. The turbulent sea of the nations was subdued by the strength of His foot; the weary earth of Israel was

[1]Rev. 7

trodden down by the One who was formerly spurned. The mighty Conqueror was now about to indicate His power and authority.

In His hand a little book lay open. Cumming sees in the vision the intervention of Christ at the Reformation. "Priests and people" he says, "were without light or life. Christendom groaned beneath a system that had in it all the corruption of the dead, and beneath a sacerdotal despotism that was instinct with all the wickedness of the damned. The crisis was come; Christ must interpose, either to crush or to convert. Mercy, not judgment, was vouchsafed—a Reformation came." Consistently with this—and in agreement with many other expositors—he interprets the little book held by the Angel as the Bible discovered by Martin Luther at the University of Erfurt. But this feeble interpretation does not suffice. This is not an intervention by Christ in mercy, but in judgment. With the title-deeds of the universe and the revelation of the divine purposes in His hand, He was about to declare His sole proprietorship and to eject every false claimant and usurper.

The mighty Angel cried with a loud voice like a lion's roar, and then seven thunders uttered their voices. Cumming says that the thunders issued from the Papal Olympus and were the voice of the Pope, commanding Luther to desist from his preaching, but that is almost too ludicrous to require comment.

Here was the mighty roar of the lion of the tribe of Judah. On several occasions has the voice of Jehovah been likened to a lion's roar (cf. Hosea 11. 10; Joel 3. 16; Amos 1. 2; 3. 8) and, in each instance, it is a prelude to judgment. Nor was this occasion any exception to the general rule.

As if in answer to that awful roar, seven thunders *uttered their voices*, i.e., not in meaningless *claps*, but rather as the intelligent expression of thought in sound. Thunder is a frequent type of the voice of God in judgment,[1] and, in this case, the Almighty responded to the Angel's cry in a declaration of impending judgment. Beyond the fact that the seven thunders were clearly in harmony with the Angel's roar, nothing is indicated as to the actual substance of those fearsome peals, but it seems clear that the rolling thunder was confirmatory of the judgments announced in the Angel's cry.

Just as Paul was not allowed to utter the things heard in Paradise,[2] so John was forbidden to write what was uttered by the seven thunders. "Seal up the things which the seven thunders have

[1] 1 Sam. 7. 10 [2] 2 Cor. 12. 4

spoken, and write them not," commanded a voice out of heaven. Conjecture as to what was said is consequently vain since the definite disclosure has not been made.

An End to Delay

"And the Angel whom I saw stand on the sea and on the earth lifted up His right hand to heaven, and swore by Him that liveth for ever and ever, Who created the heaven and the things that are in it, and the earth and the things that are in it, and the sea and the things that are in it, that there should be no longer delay; but in the days of the voice of the seventh angel, when he is about to sound the trumpet, the mystery of God also shall be completed, and He hath made known the glad tidings in His own bondmen the prophets" (10. 5-7).

After the sound of the seven thunders, the mighty Angel lifted up His hand and swore by the Eternal Creator that there should be no longer delay. The cup of human iniquity was full. Divine patience was exhausted and the time had now arrived for the punitive vengeance of the Almighty to burst forth. The Angel was about to give effect to the divine sentence, and the rejected Nazarene was preparing to assume His rightful position.

In connection with the Abrahamic covenant, it is stated that God swore by a supreme oath when He swore by Himself,[1] and by that confirmatory oath, the covenant became final and irrevocable. In the scene enacted before the apostle in Patmos, however, the Lord Jesus Christ swore by the One who eternally lives and by whom all things were created—an oath incapable of being retracted and which was assured by the Eternal God.

The age was finished and a new era was to be ushered in. As foretold by the prophets, a glorious millennial day was about to dawn, when all the visions and glad tidings of the past would be fulfilled, and God's King would take His power and reign. As soon as the seventh angel began to sound his trumpet, the mystery of God would be completed.

God has borne patiently with human rebellion and sin, but when the hour strikes His wrath will be poured out in unmitigated fury. Commentators differ considerably in their interpretation of "the mystery of God." It has been variously suggested that the completion of the mystery relates to the completion of the Church of God, to the end of the age, to the closing of the hidden workings of grace, to the end of the veiling of God's glory in Christ, etc. It is more probable, however, that the reference is to the mystery of the silent heavens. For centuries God has remained silent and there have been very few indications of divine intervention in

[1]Heb. 6. 13

terrestrial affairs. Sin has walked unashamed, and iniquity has gone unrebuked, but soon the hand of God will be laid upon the world and His righteousness will be revealed in judgment, and then in the revelation of His appointed King.

The Little Book

"And the voice which I heard from heaven was again speaking with me, and saying, Go, take the little book which is opened in the hand of the Angel who standeth on the sea and on the earth. And I went to the Angel, saying to Him that He should give me the little book. And He saith to me, Take it, and eat it up; and it shall make thy belly bitter, but in thy mouth it shall be sweet as honey. And I took the little book out of the Angel's hand, and ate it up; and it was in my mouth sweet as honey: and when I had eaten it, my belly was made bitter. And they say unto me, Thou must prophesy again concerning peoples and nations and tongues and many kings" (10. 8-11).

The heavenly voice which John had heard before then commanded him to go and take the little book which lay open in the hand of the Angel. The revelation of the divine purposes was now to be made to the seer and, as he obediently approached the Angel with the request, he was instructed to take and eat it. He was to digest the message of God and to assimilate it into his very being so that it became part of himself. "This represents the most complete spiritual assimilation," says Godet. "This nourishment is to strengthen him for taking up again the great prophecy relating to 'peoples and nations and tongues and kings.'"

A similar experience was granted to Ezekiel many centuries earlier. In a roll of a book spread before the young prophet were written "lamentations and mourning and woe," and after he had eaten, he was commanded to convey God's message to His earthly people.[1]

Like Ezekiel, John took the little book and ate it, finding it as sweet as honey to the taste but bitter on digestion. Immediately he had eaten, the seer was informed that he must prophesy again "concerning peoples and nations and tongues and many kings." It is clear in both instances that the book is the revelation of the divine purposes for earth. Any divine communication must be sweet to the taste, "but as the revelations are weighed, the judgments they announce considered, the next effect is to cause bitterness and sorrow." The seer had so fully assimilated the message that the divine sorrow expressed itself in his own feelings. Says Tuck: "The first effect of being admitted to share in the divine counsels is delightful, but when those counsels are known and realized, they

[1]Ezek. 2. 9—3. 4

may cause grave distress and anxiety: the Christlike sorrow for those against whom God's wrath is revealed, who 'knew not the time of their visitation.'"

After eating, John was told that he must prophesy again. Girdlestone ingeniously suggests that "that command really implied his giving forth prophetic truth a second time concerning the whole of the same period. The *first* part of his prophetic message (chapters 6 to 10) dealt with matters largely in connection with catastrophic disturbances of the earth, sun, moon and stars and elements generally, and their terrible effect upon mankind. The *second* part of his prophecy, though not excluding such events, deals with matters chiefly from a national point of view during the same period, and soon introduces us to the great world-ruler." The Apocalypse is not, of course, arranged as one consecutive narrative, nor are all the events detailed necessarily in chronological order. The Holy Spirit occasionally retraces His steps to describe one incident in more detail or in a different manner, but we do not believe that that is the meaning of verse 11. The obvious meaning is simply that the apostle had further prophecies to communicate.

Chapter XII

The Two Prophets

The Temple Measured

"And there was given me a reed like a rod; and one said, Rise, and measure the temple of God, and the altar, and them that worship therein. And the court which is without the temple leave (or cast) without, and measure it not; for it hath been given up to the nations; and the holy city shall they tread under foot forty and two months" (11. 1, 2).

THE millennial temple seen by Ezekiel was measured by a reed,[1] and the holy city, Jerusalem, by a golden reed.[2] So here, John was given a reed like a rod and bidden to measure the temple, the altar and the worshippers. The court of the temple was not to be measured, since it was given over to the nations, by whom the holy city was to be trodden under foot for 42 months.

The determination of dimensions or boundaries by measurement is a common indication of an intention to appropriate or take possession. On the other hand, it is sometimes employed to intimate a separation for destruction. Both ideas may be embodied in the measuring reed given to the Apostle since it was a reed resembling a rod—"a measuring implement having the prevailing aspect of an instrument of chastisement."

When the Jews return to their own land in unbelief, it appears from many references that the temple will be rebuilt and the Levitical ceremonies and worship restored. Although at first unacknowledged by God, the temple will later receive some recognition—it will be measured for Him—and the true worshippers will come under His protection. Scott writes: "The 'temple' would express the *worship*, and the 'altar' the *acceptance* of the godly remnant of Israel." Wherever there are true believers, God will acknowledge them as His and even bestow His name upon the temple wherein they worship. Seiss declares that "the measurement of the temple, its altar, and its worshippers is the receiving again of the Jew, his regrafting upon the old theocratic root and native olive-tree, and his re-establishment as the chosen of God among the nations of the earth," but this carries the impli-

[1]Ezek. 40 [2]Rev. 21. 15

cations of the measurement too far. It is clear, however, that the Almighty takes account of even a nominal acknowledgment of His name, and that the penitence of the believing remnant of Israel is dear to His heart.

The court of the temple was not measured, but was rejected because it was given up to the nations. "The unmeasured and rejected court given over to the Gentiles," says Scott, "signifies the apostate part of the people, the mass in outward religious profession abandoned by God to the nations, who will wreak their vengeance on the guilty people, in spite of the promised assistance of the Beast."[1] Religious persecution will again have sway, even if only for a short time, and nominal Jewish professors will pay the penalty for the emptiness of their profession.

It is stated that the holy city (*i.e.*, Jerusalem) will be trodden under foot by the nations for 42 months. Isaiah declares that the Assyrian will take the spoil, seize the prey and "tread them down like the mire of the streets."[2] For three and a half years, the city of Jerusalem will know the meaning of ruthless oppression and merciless brutality. It will be the "time of Jacob's trouble," the "great tribulation."

A limit is set to the period, however. It will last only 42 months. This period is, of course, identical with the 1,260 days of verse 3, and the "time, times and half a time" of Rev. 12. 14, and is synchronous with the last half week of Dan. 9. 24-27, concerning which further comment will be made later.

The Two Witnesses

"And I will give unto my two witnesses, and they shall prophesy a thousand two hundred and sixty days, clothed in sackcloth. These are the two olive trees and the two lamps, standing before the Lord of the earth. And if any man desireth to hurt them, fire proceedeth out of their mouth, and devoureth their enemies: and if any man shall desire to hurt them, in this manner must he be killed. These have power to shut the heaven, that it rain not during the days of their prophecy; and they have power over the waters to turn them into blood, and to smite the earth with every plague, as often as they shall desire. And when they have completed their testimony, the beast that cometh up out of the abyss shall make war with them, and shall overcome them, and kill them. And their dead body shall lie in the street of the great city, which spiritually is called Sodom and Egypt, where also their Lord was crucified. And from among the peoples and tribes and tongues and nations do men look upon their dead body three days and a half, and suffer not their dead body to be laid in a tomb. And they that dwell upon the earth rejoice over them, and make merry; and they shall send gifts one to another; because these two prophets tormented them that dwell on the earth" (11. 3-10)

[1]Isa. 28. 17-22 [2]Isa. 10. 6

Two individuals next appeared upon the scene, whom God described as His "witnesses," and who are later referred to as "two prophets" (verse 10). The witnesses were clothed in sackcloth and prophesied for a period of 1,260 days (the same period as that described in verse 2 as 42 months).

There has been much speculation regarding the identity of these two witnesses. The later description of them as prophets has led to the suggestion that Moses and Elijah will return to earth again to prophesy against the unrepentant mass of sinners. Cumming sees in them the successive witnesses against the Papacy for 1,260 years until their extermination at the beginning of the sixteenth century—the Eastern line through the Paulicians, etc.; the Western through Augustine, Vigilantus, Claude of Turin, Agobard and Peter Waldo, both lines meeting in the Waldenses. It is more likely, however, that the number is simply indicative of an adequate testimony,[1] and that the actual number of those bearing a faithful witness to God in the period in question will be considerable.

The witnesses were clothed in sackcloth as an indication of their sorrowful repentance and afflicted condition.[2] They identified themselves with their nation and, by their condition, acknowledged penitently the sinful state of their people. It might well be asked whether the hearts of God's people to-day are as exercised regarding the condition of their neighbours as will be those of these latter-day Jews.

The witnesses are further described in verse 3 as "the two olive trees and the two lamps (or lampstands), standing before the Lord of the earth." Both expressions relate to the matter of testimony. Centuries earlier, Zechariah had seen a vision of a golden lampstand, on either side of which was an olive tree, from which golden pipes supplied the lampstand with oil. It is by no means a coincidence that the "olive branches" of Zechariah's vision were described as "the two anointed ones that stand by the Lord of the whole earth."[3] The olive is a consistent type of testimony,[4] and the lampstand is also figurative of witness. The witnesses of the Apocalypse are clearly identical with those seen by Zechariah. Under the inspiration of the Holy Spirit, these individuals bore witness to the power of God and to the state of moral and spiritual degradation surrounding them.

Their witness was not to Christ as Saviour nor to Jehovah as the God of Israel. They stood before the Lord of the earth. The burden of their message was no longer the salvation available

[1]Deut. 17. 6; 19. 15; Matt. 18. 19 [2]Joel 1. 13; 1 Kings 20. 31; Jer. 4. 8
[3]Zech. 4. 14 [4]Rom. 11

through Cavalry's work, but rather the authority of the Creator and the inevitable judgment which must fall upon the unrepentant guilty.

Supernatural power was given to them. At any attempt to attack them, fire proceeded out of their mouths and destroyed their antagonists—a reminder of the signal judgment inflicted by Elijah upon the messengers sent to him by Ahaziah.[1]

As Elijah did,[2] they had also the power to shut up the heaven, that rain might be stopped. Following the example of Moses,[3] they had the power to turn water into blood and to smite the earth with plagues. The repetition of the miracles of the ancient lawgiver and of the prophet of fire would accredit their mission to Israel, whilst their invulnerability and their avenging actions would constitute adequate signs to the Gentiles.

To the people of Israel, it will appear that all the prophetic power of the past centuries has been reincarnated. The actions and characteristics of the two men who stood out most prominently in their past history will be reproduced afresh in these latter-day prophets, and the effect of such a startling testimony will obviously be very great.

Until their work was done, the two witnesses had immortal lives. None might attack them with impunity; death met every aggressor. But when their mission was ended, the mysterious power referred to in chapter 13—the Beast who comes up out of the abyss—made war upon them and defeated and slew them.

From a historical point of view, it may perhaps be said that the war of extermination waged against the Waldenses is a fulfilment of this prophecy, but the details are by no means satisfied in the events of the past. It could hardly be claimed that the Waldenses exercised the power of turning the waters into blood, or of inflicting plagues upon the earth. The future yet holds a more precise fulfilment of the events,[4] and it seems clear that this martyred remnant are the Jewish witnesses of the day of judgment, who eventually find their doom at the hands of the political power of the Western Empire.

For three and a half days their carcass (singular) will lie in the street, to be seen of everyone, and people of all nations will gaze upon their carcass. It is possible that there is a reference here to the broadcasting of the scene by television, so that, during the period of three and a half days, it will be before the gaze of the whole world. Burial will be refused to the dead bodies, but all the "earth-

[1] 2 Kings 1 [2] 1 Kings 17 and 18 [3] Exod. 7 20 [4] Rev. 11

dwellers" (who are said to have been tormented by these prophets) will rejoice and make merry over their death, even making it an occasion for sending gifts to one another. Their consistent witness and condemnatory prophecies will so rouse the ire of their hearers that a definite onslaught will be made upon them and they will be massacred *en masse*. Tortured consciences will find relief in the death of the accusers, and so great will be that relief that the murder will be heralded as an occasion for supreme rejoicing.

Herod and Pilate became reconciled to each other in the murder of the Lord Jesus Christ, God's perfect Servant.[1] So here, people of all types will join in rejoicing over the death of God's servants. As Scott points out, "the sending of presents or gifts on occasions of public joy is an old and universal custom,"[2] and the joyful crowds will demonstrate their relief in the exchange of gifts and presents.

For three and a half days the bodies lie in the street of "the great city, which spiritually is called Sodom and Egypt, where also their Lord was crucified." There can be no doubt as to the meaning of these words: the reference is plainly to Jerusalem, where the Lord Jesus Christ was slain. "This is the abode of wickedness and defiant pride," says Jennings. "God thus expresses, in the name He gives this city, its moral conditions of 'corruption,' in Sodom, and of 'violence,' in Egypt. To meet the corruption the witnesses have brought fire, as in the case of Sodom, to meet the violence, the water has been turned into blood, as in Egypt."

Resurrection of the Witnesses

"And after the three days and a half the breath of life from God entered into them, and they stood upon their feet; and great fear fell upon them who beheld them. And they heard a great voice from heaven saying unto them, Come up hither. And they went up to heaven in the cloud; and their enemies beheld them. And in that hour there was a great earthquake, and the tenth part of the city fell; and there were killed in the earthquake seven thousand persons: and the rest were affrighted, and gave glory to the God of heaven. The second woe is past: behold the third woe cometh quickly" (11. 11-14).

At the end of the three and a half days, the two witnesses were miraculously resuscitated. The "breath of life from God entered into them and they stood upon their feet." The Almighty breathed again into the bodies of His faithful servants and raised them from their mortal sleep, their amazing resurrection striking dread into the hearts of all beholders. Then, at the summons of a great voice from heaven, these risen saints were raptured to heaven in the cloud in the presence of all their enemies.

[1]Luke 23. 12 [2]Prov. 19. 6; Esther 2. 18; 9. 22

Unlike the rapture of the Church, this resurrection and rapture were public and, therefore, all the more awe-inspiring and fear-instilling. The cloud of the divine presence enwrapped them and snatched them away. A brilliant effulgence of light—the Shekinah itself—burst upon the scene and, in that wonderful blaze, these living ones were translated from the scene of their suffering to the glory of the celestial heights.

The weakness of historical interpretation becomes very evident in this particular instance. Cumming, for example, maintains that the period of three and a half days of verse 11 relates to the three and a half years from the 5th May, 1514, when the Council of Lateran proclaimed that heresy was extinguished, to the 31st October, 1517, when Luther initiated the re-enunciation of the truths of the Gospel by posting his theses upon the gates of the church of Wittemberg. In the resurrection and ascension of the prophets, he sees the raising of the Protestants from the depth of depression to a position of power by the peace of Passau in 1552, which not only confirmed the toleration of Protestants, but also admitted them to civil power and invested them with normal political privileges.

There is no evident reason for assuming the three and a half days to be anything other than three and a half days. The martyred band of Jewish missionaries, who have witnessed for God in days of apostasy and evil, will be literally raised from the dead and divinely carried away to a scene of glory and blessing. God never deserts His own people and divine intervention on behalf of His own is inevitable sooner or later. He abides faithful.

Scarcely had the witnesses been raptured away than an earthquake suddenly shook the city and a tenth part of the city was destroyed, seven thousand people being killed in the awful catastrophe. "The hour of triumph for the witnesses," says Scott, "was the hour of retributive justice on the city wherein they had testified and in which their blood had been wantonly shed."

Seismic disturbances have been experienced in Jerusalem before and will be again. The earthquake is a figure of judgment, and Jerusalem has been threatened with future 'quakes.[1] It is possible that a literal earthquake is indicated here and that the judgment of God on the guilty city will take the form of such physical vengeance. A tenth of the city will come under the hand of the Almighty, and death will lay toll upon seven thousand lives. Whether or not the numbers are intended to be figurative, it is

[1]Zech. 14; Matt. 28. 2

clear that full retribution will be exacted for the people's opposition to God's witnesses.

Stricken with terror, the survivors gave glory to the God of heaven, obviously not in true penitence or contrition, but simply in sheer dread of the exhibition of judicial power.

The two witnesses had evidently testified of "*the Lord of the earth*" (verse 4), but these affrighted souls humbled themselves to "*the God of heaven*" (verse 13). They completely ignored the divine claim upon *earth* and vainly strove to avert any intervention from *heaven*. They were clearly motivated by the idea of keeping God at a distance—remote in the heavens—and securing themselves from any interference on earth

Thus ended the second woe.

Chapter XIII

The Seventh Trumpet

The Gathering Storm

"And the seventh angel sounded: and there followed great voices in heaven, and they said, The kingdom of the world is become the kingdom of our Lord, and of His Christ: and He shall reign for ever and ever. And the four and twenty elders, who sit before God on their thrones, fell upon their faces, and worshipped God, saying, We give Thee thanks, O Lord God, the Almighty, Who art and Who wast; because Thou hast taken Thy great power, and didst reign. And the nations were wroth and Thy wrath came, and the time of the dead to be judged, and the time to give their reward to Thy servants the prophets, and to the saints, and to them that fear Thy name, the small and the great; and to destroy them that destroy the earth. And there was opened the temple of God that is in heaven; and there was seen in His temple the ark of His covenant (or testament); and there followed lightnings and voices, and thunders, and an earthquake and great hail" (11. 15-19).

As the last of the seven trumpets sounded, there was immediately rejoicing in heaven as there came into view the establishment of the millennial kingdom, the judgment of the dead, and the eternal state. Although these things were still future, they were regarded as having already taken place. Great voices in heaven declared that the kingdom of the world was to become the kingdom of our Lord and of His Christ and that His reign should be eternal.

On more than one occasion, the Apocalyptic seer is carried in thought and vision to the closing scenes, only to revert soon afterwards to events which must necessarily precede them. So here, the judgment upon Jerusalem is followed immediately by the glad picture of the millennium and even the eternal state, although the Book later goes back once more to the events which will occur prior to the millennium.

At present the cosmic system is controlled by the age-long adversary of God and man, but a glorious day is coming when the world-kingdom which is the rightful possession of Christ shall acknowledge His sway. The usurper banished, the lawful heir will appropriate His own property and exercise universal rule.

As the thunderous voices of the heavens proclaimed the news, the 24 elders fell down and worshipped God, giving thanks that the Almighty had assumed His great power and sovereignty.

Heaven was united in recognition of His title, but the elders pay tribute to the eternally-existent and Almighty One who was about to take His power and reign over the eternal kingdom (not merely the earthly one of the millennium).

Upon the wrathful nations the wrath of God descended. Judgment must be poured out before the earthly reign of Christ could commence. So the seer declared that the time had come for the judgment of the dead and the reward of the faithful. This obviously looks on to the last great assize of Rev. 20. 12, but probably also has in view that at the ushering in of the millennium. Just as the judgment of the dead will have relation (at least partially) to the acts of the life, so also will the rewards to the faithful. Their recompense will be proportioned to, and be based upon the fidelity, loyalty, and service of God's people during the period of their earthly probation. Those who have suffered and endured will find a full compensation in Him.

The character of the Christian's walk on earth *does* matter. The short span of earthly life is a period of testing, during which the character of that other life is gradually formed, and what the believer does and is on earth will determine his character for eternity. The rewards bestowed by Christ at the judgment-seat will have a direct relevance to earthly conduct and manner of life.

Rewards were given to (1) God's servants, the prophets, *i.e.*, those to whom a special revelation was made at some time and who were the medium by which the communication of the divine will was made; (2) the saints, a title used of God's people in every age; and (3) those that feared His name, both small and great, a reference probably to those who were faithful to Him in days of tribulation and trial. It is sometimes suggested that the second class refers to saved Israelites and the third to converted Gentiles, but it is difficult to find Scriptural support for this theory.

The nations were filled with anger as the divine wrath descended upon them. War and destruction filled the earth, but the Eternal God destroyed those who sought to destroy the earth.

Verse 18 thus closes the main section of the Book. The final assize is the last action before the eternal state, which is also referred to in the passage. Chapters 1 to 11 describe the prophetic programme from the apostolic period of the Church down to the close of the millennium and deal with the general *principles* involved. The remainder of the Book introduces the *persons* on the scenes.

Verse 19 sees the temple of God opened in heaven. However, it is made clear that there will be no temple in the holy Jerusalem.[1]

[1]Rev. 21. 22

It therefore appears that Israel's affairs on earth will have become the subject of divine interest in heaven. The temple is symbolic and a reminder of Jehovah's relationship to Israel. There is no obvious reason to assume a literal temple in that heavenly scene.

As the temple (*i.e.*, the *inner* temple) was opened, the ark of the covenant was seen therein, "the token," as another says, "of Jehovah's presence with, and His unchanging faithfulness to, His earthly people." The ark was housed in the holy of holies of the earthly temple and it was, therefore, the inner shrine which was laid open to view. It was upon the ark of the covenant that the shekinah cloud—the outward manifestation of the presence of Jehovah—formerly rested, and at which God met with the representative of His earthly people. The fresh appearance of the ark accordingly intimated plainly that God was still with His people in all their changing circumstances and that He was about to manifest Himself on their behalf.

The storm was about to break. Immediately there followed lightnings, voices, thunderings, an earthquake and great hail. All the voices of nature awoke to threaten the earth, and natural disturbances filled the soul with dread. The sky was rent by the dazzling and fearsome lightning; the roar of thunder broke upon the fearful ear; heavy hail broke down resistance, and the trembling earth shivered in the throes of an earthquake. Well might men's hearts be filled with terror at the impending judgment.

CHAPTER XIV

Satan Unveiled

THE BIRTH OF THE MAN-CHILD

"And a great sign was seen in heaven; a woman arrayed with the sun, and the moon under her feet, and upon her head a crown of twelve stars; and she was with child; and she crieth out, travailing in birth, and in pain to be delivered. And there was seen another sign in heaven; and behold, a great red dragon having seven heads and ten horns, and upon his head seven diadems. And his tail draweth the third part of the stars of heaven, and did cast them to the earth: and the dragon stood before the woman who was about to be delivered, that when she was delivered he might devour her child. And she was delivered of a son, a man-child, who is to rule all the nations with a rod of iron: and her child was caught up unto God, and unto His throne. And the woman fled into the wilderness, where she hath a place prepared of God, that there they may nourish her a thousand two hundred and threescore days" (12. 1-6).

CHAPTER 12 marks the commencement of a new section of the Revelation and makes plain not the external facts and events which are to occur, but rather the unseen conflict between invisible and supernatural forces. "Hitherto," says Bishop Boyd Carpenter, "we have seen the more outward aspects of the great war. Now we are to see its secret, hidden and spiritual aspects, that we may understand what immeasurably divergent and antagonistic principles are in conflict under various and specious aspects in the history of the world."

A great sign was seen in heaven. A woman appeared, who was garbed with the sun, who had the moon beneath her feet, and who was crowned with twelve stars. It was a very impressive vision. Gen. 1. 14-18 indicates that the luminaries in the expanse of heaven were set in their place as rulers over the day and night. The sun, moon and stars were all associated with the woman and suggest that she was invested with full earthly authority and governmental rule. "All authority," says one writer, "supreme as the sun, derived and subordinate as the moon, and lesser lights for rulers as the star, centre in the woman. She has royal dignity, as the crown on her head signifies."

In Joseph's second dream,[1] the sun, the moon, and the eleven

[1]Gen. 37. 9

stars made obeisance to him—a vision which his father Jacob interpreted as signifying that his father, mother, and brethren should one day bow down before him. The description of the woman bears so many marks of similarity as to suggest that it is not entirely unrelated, thus discounting at least some of the many interpretations given of the chapter.

The woman is depicted as suffering in childbirth and being eventually delivered of a son—the symbol, according to many expositors—of the work of the Church in bringing forth Christ to men! Other teachers have suggested that the woman was the Virgin Mary and the man-child Christ; others again have propounded the theory that the Kingdom of Heaven is symbolized here; or again that the woman represents the Church and the man-child the 144,000 sealed Christians. Jer. 4. 31, Micah 5. 2, 3, etc., however, indicate that the mother is a type of Israel and that the man-child is the Messiah, and the remainder of the passage appears to confirm this. "It may be difficult to reconcile the material anguish as applicable to Israel with the facts of the case when Christ was born, for when was the crying, the travail and pain when the Messiah came into the world? The solution is contained in: '*Before* she travailed, she brought forth; *before* her pain came she was delivered of a man-child.'[1] The travailing and pain refer to Israel's coming hour of trial, the Great Tribulation. But *before* that great event the Messiah, the Man-child, is born. The prophet Micah confirms this in a clear and unmistakable passage. After referring to the birth of Messiah,[2] he adds 'Therefore will He give them up, until the time that she who travaileth hath brought forth; then the remnant shall return unto the children of Israel.'[3] The travail of the woman is at least 2,000 years subsequent to the birth of the Messiah, and refers to her sorrow in the coming Tribulation. Why, then, is the travail of the woman put in juxtaposition to the birth of the Messiah? First, notice that the present lengthened period of Israel's rejection, coming in as it does between the birth and the travail, is passed over in silence; it is a parenthesis, the history of which is not given in prophecy. Second, it shows the deep interest which the Messiah takes in His people. He thought of the Tribulation, and made certain provisions so as to lighten it many centuries ago.[4] Third, at the time at which our chapter has its place, the nation is about to pass into its awful sorrow, and the object of going back in the history to the birth of Christ is to connect Him with them in it" (Scott). It may be claimed that this explana-

[1]Isa. 66. 7 [2]Micah 5, 2 [3]Micah 5. 3 [4]Matt. 24. 15-28

tion is ingenious and slightly far-fetched, but no other interpretation satisfies the remainder of the chapter than that the woman is Israel and that the Man-child is the Messiah.

The seer then beheld a second great sign in heaven. A great red dragon was seen, whose identity is explicitly stated in verse 9 to be the devil or Satan. The semi-mythical monster of fable and story is an apt type of the great adversary of mankind. Typho, the cruel and voracious crocodile or dragon god of Egypt, was regarded as the origin and author of all evil. The powerful and subtle antagonist of good; the insatiable and bloodthirsty cruelty of this terrible foe is indicated in the sanguinary colour of the dragon. Hislop suggests that the red dragon was properly a *fiery serpent*, the embodiment of the fire worship and serpent worship which characterized the primeval apostasy of Nimrod.

The dragon had seven heads and ten horns, and wore seven diadems upon his head. As the following chapter of the book reveals, the Roman Empire is yet to be revived in the form of a confederacy of ten powers (*or horns*). The supreme power, which will evidently be one of the ten, will displace three of them,[1] so that the actual number of rulers (*or heads*) will be only seven. Rev. 12. 3, therefore, identifies the dragon with the empire. The real, though unseen, ruler of the empire will be Satan himself. Hence he is shown as wearing the golden fillets of royalty upon his heads.

It is clear from this passage that the devil is a person and not merely an evil influence. The extent of his power, the ubiquity of his malignant agents, and his consuming hatred of everything pertaining to God, are insufficiently realized, even by God's people. Satan is a terrible adversary, whose might and subtlety might well fill the soul with dread, but the power of the Holy Spirit is ever present to protect and preserve the trusting believer.

The dragon's tail drew along a third part of the stars of heaven and cast them to the earth. As in other passages, the tail is indicative of evil teaching and false doctrine.[2] Jennings suggests that the stars must be Jews in view of Dan. 8. 10, and that the third part who were destroyed were "the apostate mass of the Jews, induced by Satanic influence (the tail) to enter into an allegiance with the apostate Gentile power, the revived Roman Empire—in a covenant with death, an agreement with hell.[3] On the other hand, the angelic hierarchy are referred to as "the morning stars,"[4] and Satan himself is described as Lucifer (or "day-star").[5] With

[1]Dan. 7. 8 [2]Isa. 9. 15, etc. [3]Isa. 28. 15 [4]Job. 38. [5]Isa. 14. 12

some measure of justification, therefore, Vitringa declares that the "stars of heaven" are the angels who were infected by the impious presumption of Satan and who were dragged down to destruction in his headlong fall. It is clear that "the stars of heaven" are not the "stars" or coronal gems of verse 1, and it seems extremely probable that the reference is to the angels who fell with Satan when he conspired against the Most High.

The dragon stood before the woman, waiting to devour the Man-child as soon as he was born. Hislop sees in this a reference to Nimrod (whom he identifies with Moloch), "as the representative of the devouring fire to which children were offered in sacrifice," and for which reason he was regarded as the great child-devourer; but this is rather far-fetched, and it seems clear that it is the child Christ who is in view. It was at the instigation of Satan that Herod sought to destroy the infant Christ, when he slew all the male children of Bethlehem who were under two years of age.[1] The devil had undoubtedly noted the details of Messianic prophecy and realized that fulfilment was at hand, and he accordingly determined upon the destruction of the Man-child.

All his machinations and schemings were fruitless, for the child was born and preserved from his murderous hatred. The travailing woman brought forth a Son who was to rule all nations with a rod of iron. The Messianic reference is very plain. The Psalmist states that Jehovah's Son will "break them with a rod of iron."[2] Yet Elliott claims that the pregnancy and travailing in birth-throes relate to "the mind's full possession by any momentous truth or object of desire and earnest longing to be delivered of it; whether in the announcement of that truth, or accomplishment of that object." Others again see in the woman the visible Church, agonizing to bring forth the genuine children of God or the invisible Church. The inflexible rule of the iron sceptre is then interpreted as the inflexible and irrefragable dominion of the members of the Church as kings. But the picture is so plainly one of Christ as to make the emptiness of such vapourings very evident.

The Man-child was then caught up to God and His throne. The details of Christ's life—an unmentioned parenthesis of 33 years—are omitted, since the object of the Apocalypse is "first, to connect the Messiah with Israel about to enter her appointed hour of sorrow, Jacob's trouble;[3] second, to connect the Child with His marvellous destiny, the rule of all nations. Both these are dependent on His birth, not on His life here" (Scott). Coming

[1]Matt. 2. 16 [2]Psa. 2. 9 [3]Jer. 30. 7

of the seed of Israel, the Messiah was born in humiliation, His very existence threatened by Satan, but was finally raptured away to God and His throne.[1] Seiss maintains that it is the rapture of the Church[2] that is in view here, but the following verses militate against that view.

The Child was in heaven, but His mother was left on earth to face the continued persecution of the dragon. There is again an unnoticed parenthetical period—this time of over 19 centuries. Subsequent to the ascension of her Son, the woman fled into the wilderness, and the reason for her flight is revealed in verses 13 and 14 (which refer to the same flight) as the expulsion of Satan from heaven. Our Lord's ascension took place 1900 years ago, but the devil's expulsion and the woman's flight have not yet taken place. The intervening period is completely ignored and the seer looks on to the time of "Jacob's trouble" after the present age has closed. The devil's expulsion from heaven will mark the commencement of the Great Tribulation, during which, as the later part of the chapter makes clear, Satan will endeavour to blot out the godly remnant of Israel, who will flee from his persecution.

The woman fled into the wilderness, to a place prepared by God, carried there on "the two wings of the great eagle" (v. 14). Our Lord warned the godly in Judæa, when the day of trouble was about to break, to "flee into the mountains,"[3] and when persecution again threatens the inhabitants of Jerusalem, those who are faithful will take their flight from the idolatrous and blasphemous power in Judæa.

The statement that the woman's hiding-place had been prepared by God is most significant. In the midst of Mount Seir, situated in a hollow, 2,000 feet above the Arabah, stands the city of Petra, the ancient capital of Edom, which is completely uninhabited and is hidden in the mountains. The only way of approach is a very long and narrow ravine through which the river flows. In *New Bible Evidence*, Sir Charles Marston identifies Petra with Pella, to which the early Christians fled for refuge when Titus besieged Jerusalem in A.D. 70. In this remote spot, protected by all manner of rock shelters, caves, and subterranean passages, they were saved from the slaughter which attended the destruction of Jerusalem.

The narrow cleft in the rock which provides an entrance to the city gives no indication of being more than a gash in the mountains. The whole of the city—houses, temple, and theatre—is carved out

[1]Luke 24. 51; Acts 1. 9 [2]1 Thess. 4. 16, 17 [3]Matt. 24. 16

of the red sandstone rock. The great open theatre would accommodate 50,000 people, and the empty dwellings would need little preparation to make them fit for habitation. Moreover, the city has a copious water supply, and the district was once very fertile. Obad. 3; Jer. 49. 15, 16 (the rock Petra), etc., indicate the natural strength and security of the city.

There are not wanting indications that this is the place prepared by God for His faithful remnant. Isaiah, for example, says: "Send ye the lamb to the ruler of the land from Sela (Petra) *in the wilderness* unto the mount of the daughter of Zion . . . *hide the outcasts;* betray not him that wandereth. *Let Mine outcasts dwell with thee, Moab;* be thou a covert to them from the face of the spoiler."[1]

It would appear that, as soon as warning has been given of the impending persecution, the wealthier Jews will charter a fleet of aeroplanes (v. 14) and many of the faithful remnant left in Palestine will fly to the refuge in the mountains. They will flee, says Faussett, "into a prepared place, believed to be Edom's old dwelling to the south-east of the Dead Sea, the rock-hewn caverns affording a place of secure refuge for a large multitude and easily defended at a narrow defile, through which the river flows."

In that secure hiding-place, the woman was nourished for 1,260 days—the same period as that referred to in verse 14 as "a time, and times, and half a time," *i.e.*, 3½ years, and the second half of the seventieth "week."[2]

War in the Heavens

"And there was war in heaven: Michael and his angels going forth to war with the dragon; and the dragon warred and his angels; and they prevailed not, neither was their place found any more in heaven. And the great dragon was cast down, the old serpent, he that is called the Devil and Satan, the deceiver of the whole world; he was cast down to the earth, and his angels were cast down with him. And I heard a great voice in heaven, saying, Now is the salvation, and the power, and the kingdom, become our God's, and the authority is become His Christ's; for the accuser of our brethren is cast down, who accuseth them before our God day and night. And they overcame him because of the blood of the Lamb, and because of the word of their testimony; and they loved not their life even unto death. Therefore rejoice, O heavens, and ye that dwell in them. Woe for the earth and for the sea because the devil is gone down unto you, having great wrath, knowing that he hath but a short time" (12. 7-12).

The heavens at present are peopled with spirit beings. In addition to the angels who are commissioned by God to act as ministers to the needs of His people,[3] there are the fallen angels

[1]Isa. 16. 1-4; Psa. 60. [2]Dan. 9. 27 [3]Heb. 1. 14

"who kept not their own principality" (some of whom are, of course, kept enthralled),[1] and also the lowest class of spirit-beings, the demons. The angels of God own allegiance to the Almighty alone and, in His name, they continually cope with their fallen fellows on behalf of Christians on earth. The other two classes are subject to Satan himself; he is their Lord and prince and, under his orders, they wage war on mankind, sometimes openly as evil ones, at other times in the guise of "angels of light." Dan. 10. 13 and Eph. 6. 12 throw some light upon this spiritual warfare, whilst many instances are given in the Scriptures of the working of demons.

Although degraded from his original position of "anointed covering cherub" on his act of presumptuous sin,[2] Satan is still allowed a place in the heavenlies and, indeed, is called in Scripture "the prince of the power of the air."[3] He stands before God, accusing day and night those who are striving to live godly lives.[4] But there is coming a day when he will be ejected from the heavens and cast down to the earth.

It is this which is portrayed in this section of the chapter. Open war broke out in the heavens. Govett suggests that the devil desired to bar the Man-child's entrance into His heritage and therefore rushed upon His angelic defenders. Other writers have propounded the theory that the scene refers to an attempt to stop our Lord's return to heaven at His ascension. It seems clear that verses 7 to 12 are parenthetic and that they explain the reason for the woman's flight, mentioned in verses 6 and 14 which, however, is still future and therefore removed by at least nineteen centuries from the Ascension. It is conceivable that, in his character of "accuser of the brethren," the devil will be present at the judgment-seat of Christ[5] to discredit the believer and to emphasize his failings, and that, when the process of examination has been completed, he will no longer be permitted a place in heaven and will accordingly be ejected.

The Apocalypse depicts the forces of good arrayed against the forces of evil, Michael and the hosts of heaven issuing forth to thrust back Satan and his minions.

Michael is described as "the archangel,"[6] and as "the first of the chief princes."[7] He is clearly the head of the angelic hierarchy, but stands in peculiar relationship to Israel. The five Biblical references to him all associate him with Jewish interests, and he seems to be the patron or guardian spirit of God's earthly people. (Daniel suggests that every nation has its angelic protector.)[8] His

[1]Jude 6 [2]Ezek. 28. 15-17; Isa. 14. 12-15 [3]Eph. 2. 2 [4]Job 1 and 2
[5]2 Cor. 5. 10 [6]Jude 9 [7]Dan. 10. 13 [8]Dan. 10. 13, 21

name ("who is like God?") has led to the conjecture that Michael is identical with the Lord Jesus Christ, but this is by no means clear.

The mighty forces under the leadership of Michael fought against the evil angels of Lucifer, and that terrible adversary of God's people, together with all his hosts, was thrust for ever out of the heavens and cast down to the earth. Satan's ignominious expulsion was accompanied by a declaration of his true character. (Hislop sees in this the defeat of Nimrod and his sun-worshippers by Shem and the faithful of that day.) He was described as the "dragon" the personification of relentless cruelty; the "serpent," the subtle author of sin; the "devil," the consummate traducer; and "Satan," the constant adversary of all God's people. The access to God's presence, which has been permitted to the devil for so many centuries, will finally be denied to him, and his activities henceforth limited strictly to earth. Tuck sees in the combat waged in heaven a battle between the representative of monotheism (Michael) and the seducer of men (Satan) and claims that it "represents the final conflict between monotheism and paganism. Satan loses his place in the celestial sphere, from whence he had been ruling over men's hearts and making himself worshipped as God. He is cast down to earth; that is to say, his reign in the sphere of religion comes to an end. The diabolical superstitions of paganism disappear from human society. But a certain degree of power is still left to this enemy in the terrestrial sphere." As the following chapter plainly indicates, however, the devil's fall by no means connotes the immediate end of idolatry.

At Satan's expulsion, a victorious shout arose in heaven, glorying anticipatively in this initial step towards the crushing of evil and the establishment of the kingdom of God. Heaven viewed the work as potentially complete and rejoiced in the fact that the salvation of a shackled and groaning creation was now in the hands of God with irresistible power; the kingdom was potentially His and the authority that of His Christ. All other rule and authority would be crushed and He would reign supreme.

While heaven exulted over the downfall of the relentless accuser of the brethren, there was apparently some reflex upon earth, for martyrs, who had "loved not their life even unto death," are stated to have "overcome him by the blood of the Lamb and the word of their testimony." Their victory resulted from no personal merit or might but was on the basis of "the blood of the Lamb." Despite every attack upon them they had maintained the truth committed to them and had overcome by reason of "the word of their testimony." The blood of Calvary spells out the message that Satan is a defeated foe, and he who identifies himself with the Christ of Calvary experiences glorious victory over the devil through the blood of the Lamb. The life of Christ within expresses itself in Christian energy and witness and equips the believer with the power to live the life of an overcomer. The work of Christ has made victory over Satan experimentally possible for every child of God.

If heaven rejoiced, earth might well fear. A woe was pronounced upon earth and sea by reason of Satan's fall. Scott states that it is "a prophetic announcement of coming judgment on the *earth*, *i.e.*, on all settled and stable governments and peoples; also on the *sea*, *i.e.*, the restless or revolutionary part of the world." Far from being dispirited by his defeat, Satan's wrath consumed him. With his close acquaintance with prophecy, he was aware that the manifestation of Christ would not be long delayed and that his own time was short. Exasperated and enraged, he turned to furious activity against the peoples of earth, determined to work the utmost havoc in the limited time left to him.

Lucifer once stood in the closest proximity to the throne of God and occupied a place of glory and splendour. Sin alone robbed him of heaven's honour but, impenitent and rebellious, that mighty spirit will defy the Almighty to the very end.

The Serpent's War on the Woman

"And when the dragon saw that he was cast down to the earth, he persecuted the woman who brought forth the man child. And there were given to the woman the two wings of the great eagle, that she might fly into the wilderness unto her place, where she is nourished for a time, and times, and half a time, from the face of the serpent. And the serpent cast out of his mouth after the woman water as a river, that he might cause her to be carried away by the stream. And the earth helped the woman, and the earth opened her mouth, and swallowed up the river which the dragon cast out of his mouth. And the dragon waxed wroth with the woman, and went away to make war with the rest of her seed, who keep the commandments of God, and hold the testimony of Jesus" (12. 13-17).

The cause of the woman's flight having been revealed in the glimpse given in verses 7-12 of the conflict in the heavenlies, the record reverts to the flight and to the active hostility of the dragon. Immediately the dragon was dispossessed of his access to heaven and cast down to earth, he commenced to persecute the woman. Knowing his time to be short, Satan will, at the period in question, attempt to wreak his vengeance on the little band of faithful Israelites then in Palestine.

The exact form of the persecution is not indicated, at least so far as the initial stages are concerned, but it is evident that its duration is 3½ years ("a time and times and half a time")—the period of the woman's exile—and that the period doubtless synchronizes with that of Dan. 7. 25 and with the second half of Daniel's seventieth "week."[1] As previously suggested, the chapter is an exposure of the unseen conflict between invisible and supernatural forces. It, therefore, covers periods both preceding and succeeding the chapters in which it finds its context.

To the persecuted woman were given the two wings of a great eagle to facilitate her flight into the wilderness. After Israel's exodus from Egypt, Jehovah declared that He had borne them on eagles' wings,[2] and when a second hurried journey becomes necessary in a future day, He will again bear them on eagles' wings. The expression may be only a metaphor for the divine protection afforded to God's people in the day of stress and trouble or—as many suggest—there may also be more than an oblique reference to an escape by air. It is extremely probable that the persecuted Jews will flee from Palestine to the place prepared for them by means of aeroplane and that the Apocalypse hints at such a mode of travel.

In the prepared shelter referred to in verse 6, the woman was preserved from the devil's attacks for 3½ years. With serpentine cunning, Satan attempted to sweep her away by means of a flood of water emitted from his mouth, but the earth opened and swallowed up the river. There is a curious conflict of opinion regarding the significance of this river. Bishop Boyd Carpenter for example, sees in it "all great popular movements against Christianity: they diffuse themselves for a time, but mother earth absorbs them all. The eternal laws of truth and right are ultimately found stronger than all the half-truths, whole falsehoods, and selfishness, which give force to such movements." Others regard the river as representative of "the ordinary life of a nation characterized by certain principles," the devil using powers, which are under his influence, to accomplish the destruction of the Jewish nation. The flood pours forth from the serpent's mouth, however, and can, with some measure of justification, be viewed as symbolic of the false teachings which issue from the devil and which are directed to the spiritual corruption of the people of God.

The earth miraculously opened its mouth and swallowed up the flood. Viewing the earth as other powers, Scott says that "the settled governments of that day befriend the Jew, and providentially

[1] Dan. 9. 27 [2] Exod. 19. 4; Deut. 32. 11, 12

frustrate the efforts of the serpent. The means employed by Satan are rendered abortive, not by war, but in neutralizing and circumventing Satan's plans to destroy the people." If the interpretation of the flood as false doctrines be adopted, the expositor is in difficulties in explaining their absorption by the earth, and we prefer the more obvious interpretation of the river as a power (or powers) under Satanic influence, whose inspired efforts to destroy the Jews are defeated by the attitude taken by the other nations. The world will not allow the extermination of the Jews which will be attempted.

Roused to anger by the failure of his plan, the dragon made war upon the remainder of the woman's seed, who adhered to the Word of God and bore faithful witness to His Son. The remnant who did not flee to the mountains with the bulk of the refugees will be the subject of bitter and malicious attack for their relationship to the woman and their fidelity to God.

It may be gathered, then, that there will be an attack upon the main body of the Jews and also upon the remnant who were left behind by those who fled, but that, in neither case, will the Almighty suffer His people to be wiped out.

CHAPTER XV

The Two Beasts

THE BEAST OUT OF THE SEA

"And he stood upon the sand of the sea. And I saw a beast coming up out of the sea, having ten horns and seven heads, and on his horns ten diadems, and upon his heads names of blasphemy. And the beast which I saw was like unto a leopard, and his feet were as the feet of a bear, and his mouth as the mouth of a lion: and the dragon gave him his power, and his throne, and great authority. And I saw one of his heads as though it had been smitten unto death; and his death-stroke was healed: and the whole earth wondered after the beast; and they worshipped the dragon, because he gave his authority unto the beast; and they worshipped the beast, saying, Who is like unto the beast? and who is able to war with him? and there was given to him a mouth speaking great things and blasphemies; and there was given to him authority to continue forty and two months. And he opened his mouth for blasphemies against God, to blaspheme His name, and His tabernacle, even them that dwell in the heaven. And it was given unto him to make war with the saints, and to overcome them; and there was given to him authority over every tribe and people and tongue and nation. And all that dwell on the earth shall worship him, every one whose name hath not been written from the foundation of the world in the book of life of the Lamb. If any man hath an ear, let him hear. If any man leadeth into captivity, into captivity he goeth; if any man shall kill with the sword, with the sword must he be killed. Here is the patience and the faith of the saints" (13. 1-10).

THE sounding of the seventh trumpet at the end of chapter 11 denoted the end of the age and the judgment of the dead. In the following chapter the prophecy reverted to God's relations with Israel, both in the past and in the future. In chapter 13, the revelation is made of the form and activities of the principal agents of Satan in the day of apostasy. Chapter 12 relates to the "counsels of God as opposed by Satan"; chapter 13 describes "the plan and instruments by which Satan gives battle to those divine counsels" (Kelly).

The dragon stood upon the sand of the sea. The sand is an expressive type of the countless multitudes of mankind, and the sea of the restless nations, tossed and driven by wild, uncontrolled forces. The dragon stood, as if to exorcise some supernatural spirit out of the restless sea, and the seer saw an awesome beast emerge from the waters. The predominant form of the beast was that of a leopard, with all its grace, stealthiness, and swiftness;

but its feet were as those of a bear—a ponderous, crushing weight; whilst its mouth was like that of a lion—regal, dignified, and yet ferocious.

It needs little knowledge of Dan. 7 to realize that the characteristics of three of the great empires referred to therein are combined in this picture. The features of the lion of Babylon, the bear of Persia, and the leopard of Greece were all assimilated by this later beast. Newton points out that, whilst the principal form of the beast is that of the Grecian leopard, with its obvious reference to the refinements, beauty, and culture of civilization, yet "as the lion of Babylon, he has the majesty and dignity of Oriental power; like the bear of Russia he will be marked by the fierce savageness of conquest; his sway, as regards both its iron strength and its geographical extent, will resemble Rome." Clearly what is portrayed is the culmination of Gentile dominion.

The beast had ten horns, each of which was crowned by a diadem, and also had seven heads on which were names of blasphemy. Comparison with Dan. 7 leads inevitably to the conclusion that it is the fourth (or Roman) empire which is here in view. The ten horns are stated to be ten kings,[1] so that the Apocalyptic vision is of a Rome which dominates ten contemporaneous kingdoms. For fourteen centuries the Roman empire has been out of existence, but it is evident from this passage that her history has not yet been concluded, and that she will again be revived in a future day.

When the great empire disintegrated, many petty states and kingdoms sprang into being from the fragments, but the diademed horns of the beast of Rev. 13 plainly reveal that, in a future day, ten kingdoms will be bound together in one cohesive whole to form an empire of a different character from anything in the past.

The beast had seven heads, doubtless symbolic of successive forms of government,[2] and on the heads were seen names of blasphemy. There may be a reference here to the former practice (evidently to be revived, as the passage suggests) of the deification of the Roman emperors, or the purport may simply be that each successive form of government was characterized by apostasy and infidelity. A lawless and impious contempt of God will be an outstanding feature of the imperial government.

The beast derived his might from the dragon who inspired him; the dragon bestowed upon him his power, throne, and great authority. "Not only is the Beast the inheritor of the world-wide dominion directly bestowed upon Nebuchadnezzar," says Scott,

[1]Dan. 7. 24 [2]Rev. 17. 10

"but he also represents the dragon in cruelty and brute force in the world." The world-authority, which Satan offered to Christ on the mountain of temptation,[1] will be his gift to his imperial agent in a later day.

When this revived imperial power rises out of the turmoil and confusion of a troubled world, men will probably be longing for strong and settled rule and stable government. The Roman empire will provide the answer to their yearnings, and they will voluntarily and gladly yield their allegiance to its iron strength.

A curious feature was then observed by the seer. One of the Beast's seven heads bore the evidence of being mortally wounded: it was "smitten unto death." To the amazement of the whole world, however, the death-stroke was healed. Some have seen in this the death of Nero and the fulfilment of a popular notion of the day that he would reappear. Godet, on the other hand, says: "We see here one of the earlier forms of anti-divine power on the earth, which, after having been put down by an act of the divine power, reappears suddenly in the person of the Antichrist himself, in such a manner that the kingdom of the latter seems to be only the restoration of that ancient power." It seems, clear, however, that the beast's heads represent consecutive forms of government. At the time when the Revelation was written, the Roman empire had known five different forms of government and a sixth was then in being. The seventh was (and is) still future. "The empire ceased to exist A.D. 476. The world-wide dominion of the Cæsars has lain in the iron grip of political death from that time until now." Not until seven heads had appeared was one smitten. We, therefore deduce that it will be the final or seventh form which will be smitten. The power and authority of the empire will be broken—apparently irrevocably and irretrievably. (What is in view is not the death of an individual but the destruction of the power of the empire.)

The smiting of the head was an event of which the whole world was cognisant. By the devil's power the head was healed. In other words, there was a miraculous resuscitation of power, which proved a source of amazement to the whole world. As Jennings says: "there had been such a political convulsion, such an upheaval of the under-strata of the social fabric, as had overturned all authorities beyond the possibility of recovery, apart from the supernatural intervention. The devil picked up the fallen prince from this dust of death, this political hopelessness, infused a new spirit—his own spirit—into him." An eighth form of government, deriving from one of the previous seven was the result.

[1]Luke 4. 5-8

The whole world wondered after the Beast. The revival of an extinct power in such a marvellous fashion filled mankind with awe, and they worshipped the Beast as they beheld his power and warlike prowess. Universal admiration was won, and homage was paid to the imperial power. In worshipping the Beast, the apostate mass unconsciously worshipped the devil who bestowed authority upon him, and a new and unrealized idolatry swept over the earth. The bodily resurrection of Christ, although one of the best attested facts of history, is still called in question, but the diabolical travesty of the last days will attract the admiration of the whole of Christendom.

The title of the Beast is used in some instances for the great empire, and in other cases is limited to the imperial head himself.

The influence of oratory cannot fully be measured; the tongue can sway the emotions and excite the passions; its eloquence can be a power for good or a force for evil. To the Beast was given "a mouth speaking great things and blasphemies," and, in boastful arrogance he railed against God, against the Divine Name, and dwelling-place, and against the occupants of heaven. "Blasphemy against God," says Bengel, "is committed in three different ways: when anything is attributed to Him which is contrary to His holiness; when anything is disowned that rightfully belongs to Him; and when anything is ascribed to the creature which belongs to Him alone." All three are probably included in the calumnies uttered by the Beast. His mockery of the Almighty, his assumption of personal superiority over every god, and his misrepresentation of spiritual matters constitute a studied blasphemy of all things sacred and holy. In swelling pride, he spoke "great things."

Authority to act was given to him for a period of forty-two months (*i.e.*, 3½ years), during which he made war upon the saints and overcame them. The persecution of Antiochus Epiphanes lasted 3½ years, and that of Nero was of the same duration. For this reason, some expositors have stated that the prophecy was fulfilled in the days of Nero, but the ensuing verses show plainly that this could not be so.

Satan had persecuted the Woman and her Child. His diabolically-inspired instrument continued with the devil's plans and succeeded in overcoming the godly Jewish remnant—"the saints." Probably many suffered torture, imprisonment, and martyrdom. For forty-two months they endured unremitting persecution.

Dan. 9. 27 reveals that the Roman empire will enter into a covenant with the Jews for one "week" (or seven years), but that the treaty will be broken after 3½ years and idolatry forced upon God's earthly people. For the remaining 3½ years, therefore, Israel will pass through trouble and tribulation. Rev. 12. 13-17 portrays a similar picture: the dragon persecutes the woman for a period of the same length ("a time and times and half a time"). In Rev. 13. 5, the period allowed to the Beast, during which he persecuted the Jewish remnant, is stated to be forty-two months. The references would, therefore, all appear to be to the same period of time.

In Daniel, the prophet describes an imperial ruler, who became the most prominent among ten horns of a fearsome beast, who possessed "a mouth speaking great things,"[1] who wore out the saints of God and whose power lasted 3½ years ("a time and times and the dividing of time"—verse 25). The "little horn" of Dan. 7 is obviously identical with the Beast out of the sea of Rev. 13.

It may consequently be deduced that Satan's expulsion from heaven will take place at the date of the breaking of the Roman treaty with the Jews, and that, for 3½ years, unparalleled persecution will be meted out to that unfortunate people at the hands of the Roman empire and its atheistic head. It will be truly "the time of Jacob's trouble."

Authority was given to the Beast over every tribe and people and tongue and nation. Universal dominion was his. "Whatever may be the territorial extent of the empire, the authority of the Beast seems unlimited in its range and extent," writes Scott. "Countries and peoples outside the Roman empire will yet be found under its powerful influence and authority." The travesty of the rule of Christ is obvious from a comparison with Rev. 7. 14. Universal sovereignty has been the dream of more than one man. It was actually bestowed upon Nebuchadnezzar,[2] although he never appropriated what was potentially his. It was offered to Christ by Satan,[3] and will ultimately be the devil's gift to his own chosen instrument.

The earth-dwellers paid their homage to this supreme monarch. The phrase "all that dwell on the earth" occurs frequently in the Revelation. Those so described as Dr. Burton says, "are not merely the inhabitants of the earth as such, but a special class morally distinguished from the 'kindreds and tongues and nations.'" It aptly describes those who have had the advantage of Christian testimony but have refused it. Heaven had been offered to them but they chose the earth. They are satisfied with earth and will have nothing to do with the pilgrim character of the Church.

[1]Dan. 7. 8 [2]Dan. 2. 38 [3]Luke 4. 6

The homage paid to the Beast was more than civil reverence: it was religious adoration. This new Cæsar demanded divine worship as did the deified emperors of a past age. Says Govett. "First comes the burst of astonishment consequent on his resurrection. Multitudes bow, in voluntary, inward veneration of soul, to him as their god. Then follow his acts and deeds of power; and that which was voluntary at first is at length enacted by law and made compulsory on all." Everyone whose name is not written in the Lamb's book of life was found among his worshippers. Only those chosen of God from the foundation of the world will decline to yield to this new idolatry.

A sudden note of admonition breaks into the record. "If any man hath an ear, let him hear." It is an implicit warning to the earth-dweller and an appeal to the souls of all, directing attention to the sovereign grace of God and the possibility of life through the work of the Lamb.

At the same time, God announced the immutable law of retribution. The one who gathered others into captivity should himself become a captive, and the one who slew others with the sword should himself perish by the sword. For forty-two months, evil might ride victoriously, and good might seem enslaved. But God is not deaf to the cries of His people, nor is He unmindful of the right, and the oppressor must inevitably suffer in the end. In this assurance were the saints to possess themselves in patience, their faith rising undoubting to the faithful God.

The Beast out of the Earth

"And I saw another beast coming up out of the earth; and he had two horns like unto a lamb, and he spake as a dragon. And he exerciseth all the authority of the first beast in his sight. And he maketh the earth and them that dwell therein to worship the first beast, whose death-stroke was healed. And he doeth great signs, that he should even make fire to come down out of heaven upon the earth in the sight of men. And he deceiveth them that dwell on the earth by reason of the signs which it was given him to do in the sight of the beast; saying to them that dwell on the earth, that they should make an image to the beast, who hath the stroke of the sword, and lived. And it was given unto him to give breath to it, even to the image of the beast, that the image of the beast should both speak and cause that as many as should not worship the image of the beast should be killed. And he causeth all, the small and the great, and the rich and the poor, and the free and the bond, that there be given them a mark on their right hand, or upon their forehead; and that no man should be able to buy or to sell, save he that hath the mark, even the name of the beast or the number of his name. Here is wisdom. He that hath understanding, let him count the number of the beast; for it is the number of a man; and his number is six hundred and sixty and six" (13. 11-18).

The first beast seen by the seer rose up out of the *sea*, or the troubled and restless nations. But a second beast was then seen rising up out of the *earth*, *i.e.*, probably the land of Israel, indicating that the individual so described was a Jew. Superficially the two beasts were dissimilar in features and characteristics, but essentially their natures were very much alike.

The second beast bore horns like a lamb but spoke like a dragon. The gentleness of the lamb was combined with the cunning and ferocity of the devil. His lamb-like appearance was obviously imitative of the Lord Jesus Christ, the Lamb of God, and he was thereby marked out clearly as a false Christ or Antichrist.

A horn is always a symbol of authority, and the beast had therefore a double realm of authority—both secular and religious. His horns bore no diadems and were like those of a gentle, domestic animal. Seiss says, "Political sovereignty, war, conquest and the strength of military rule are therefore out of the question here. This beast is a *prophet*, a spiritual teacher, and not a king or a warrior. His power has a certain softness and domesticity about it, which is sharply distinguished from the great regal horns of the first beast." We are not sure that Seiss' deduction is sound. Our Lord will be acknowledged in a later day both as sovereign and as religious leader—as king and priest[1]—and this apostate Jew will apparently counterfeit the true king-priest.

The second beast was a coadjutor of the first beast and exercised all his authority before him, but the power delegated to him was used primarily for the glorification of his master. Even his ecclesiastical influence was apparently directed to the same end. He spoke with a draconic voice, with all the subtlety and cunning of the devil who inspired him.

It is maintained by some expositors that this individual (who is later termed "the false prophet") is of Jewish descent and is to reign as king at Jerusalem. It is claimed that the description of the king in Dan. 11. 36-39 goes beyond Antiochus Epiphanes and relates to the individual described by the Apocalypse as the beast out of the earth. The picture in Dan. 11 is of a man of insolent countenance, in league with the powers of darkness and understanding the occult. Disregarding the religion of his fathers, that evil king will exalt himself against the Almighty, and impiously direct worship to the first beast. His personal influence being limited to Palestine, he will evidently throw in his lot with the emperor of the western empire and will use the full force of his delegated authority to force idolatry upon the nations of the world. Against the force of the cold, calculating western blasphemer, with his colossal

[1]Zech. 6. 13

federation of ten kingdoms, few will be able to stand and the devil will have his way with mankind.

When the Levitical priests were first consecrated, fire came down from heaven and consumed the sacrifices. Again, when Elijah pleaded the cause of Jehovah against Baal, the fire of heaven fell to consume the offerings presented by the prophet. In similar fashion, the false prophet caused fire to descend from heaven in the sight of men. This was just the type of miracle to accredit him and to authenticate his claims.

His miracles deceived those who dwelt on earth and they obeyed his behests to make an image of the beast, to be the object of worship. "The true Christ," says Jennings, "directed worship to the Father,[1] while still accepting it Himself.[2] The false Christ puts the first Beast in the place of God,[3] directing worship to him. His god is not in Palestine, so he makes an image of him, puts it in the holy place, and directs worship thereto; yet does he, as imitating the mystery of the Divine Trinity, equally controlled by the spirit of the wicked one, identify himself with his god; and sitting himself in the temple, present himself to the apostate mass of Christendom and Israel as God, even taking to himself the highest place. It is easily credible that, while the Jew would desire a spiritual supremacy of this character and assume it, the mighty Gentile monarch would care comparatively little for such matters; he would be satisfied with the actual power, and leave all these 'religious' affairs to his dependent priest-king. Antichrist cannot be the first Beast. First, we should have the anomaly of a Gentile taking the place of a false Messiah. The elect[4] would be little affected by a Gentile claiming to be Messiah. Second, the Antichrist would then no longer be a *religious* impostor, a false prophet, as 1 John 2. 22 and 2 John clearly define, but simply a civil governor. Nor does the first Beast *exalt himself* as an object of worship at all, as does the Man of Sin,[5] for this is the work of the second Beast for him."

So great was his occult power that the prophet imparted breath to the image of the emperor and enabled it to speak. We do not think, as some suggest, that the simple explanation of this is ventriloquism. Rather does it appear another evidence of the diabolical power which will be unleashed in those days. All who refused to worship the image were slain.

The false prophet also compelled everyone to be branded on their right hand or upon their forehead with a mark (*charagma*, a brand) which consisted of the name or number of the Beast.

[1]John 4 [2]John 9. 38 [3]Dan. 11. 38 [4]Matt. 24. 24 [5]2 Thess. 2

None were exempt. From the noble to the lowest estate, from millionaire to pauper, freeman and slave, all were compelled to receive this mark. Without the possession of the mark, a man could not buy or sell. Trade was entirely dependent upon allegiance and fealty to the emperor.

The derivation of the idea is, of course, the *charagma*, or brand, of earlier days, which the papyri always connect with the Emperor and which often contained not only the Emperor's name but also his effigy and the year of his reign. The *charagma* was necessary for buying and selling, and it was required to be affixed to all kinds of documents to attest their validity, after the fashion of an official seal.

There may also be in the brand the tacit implication of the deification of the Emperor. The Brahmans, for example, wear a distinguishing mark upon their foreheads in honour of their god, and it may that the mark in Rev. 13 signified the subservience not only of subjects but of worshippers.

Even to-day cattle and sheep are branded with the name or mark of their owner and, in earlier days, slaves were similarly branded. Rather than face the alternative of starvation and unemployment, the subjects of the latter-day emperor will voluntarily submit to the brand.

There is, of course, no need to assume an actual mark. As Hengstenberg says, the mark "belongs only to the vision, in which everything must become visible and possess form. Substantially, it means confession." What is portrayed is a tremendous union in which capital and labour are both subject to the control and direction of one man. Anyone who is outside that vast combination will be ruthlessly boycotted: no one will work for him or employ him; no one will purchase his produce or sell goods to him; trade and commerce will close their doors to him. Bankruptcy and starvation face such a man. Fascism has already shown the possibilities of such a procedure. In the Fascist State, the individual exists for the good of the State. "Industrial production is presided over by trades councils, and all individual action which might be prejudicial to the State, such as strikes and lockouts, is forbidden. Trade unions are encouraged so long as their influence is constructive, but all disputes between employers and employed are subject to compulsory arbitration." It is clear that, in the period referred to by the Apocalypic seer, trade unionism, business federations, and commercial combines will all be bound together and made subject to the domination of a single head.

The mark of the Beast was borne in hand or in forehead, suggesting that both manual and intellectual workers were alike subject to this autocratic control. The mark might be either the name or the number of the name of the western emperor, and the number is stated to be 666.

This number is probably the gematria of some name, and countless attempts have been made by isopsephia to arrive at an understanding of the name. The number has been treated by many Christians almost as a conundrum, for the solution of which there is no limit upon speculation. One writer says that "by the employment of the Greek, Hebrew and Latin alphabets the most diverse names have been arrived at as thus divinely indicated. This number has been taken to mean Nero, Domitian, various Popes, Luther, Calvin, the Jesuits, Napoleon, Balaam, Cæsar, Rome, the Roman Empire, and even the founder of Mormonism, Joseph Smith."

Six is, in a peculiar sense, the number of man. For example, Adam was created on the *sixth* day and man labours for *six* days a week. It falls short of the perfect numeral *seven* and is usually considered by numerologists to signify human imperfection and toil. Bullinger says: "Goliath was *six* cubits in height, his spear's head weighed *six* shekels, and he had *six* pieces of armour. Nebuchadnezzar's image was *sixty* cubits in height, and *six* cubits wide; and *six* instruments of music summoned its worshippers. The number 666 is marked by the triple concentration of 6, being the *sum* of all the numbers which make up the *square of six*. But the greatest significance of this number is seen when we remember that the secret symbol of the great ancient pagan mysteries was SSS or 666."

In the Old Testament, the number 666 occurs only once, and then in connection with a name—"The sons of Adonikam, six hundred sixty and six."[1] From this, Hengstenberg deduces that "the name Adonikam must be the name of the beast. It means *the Lord arises*, and is in excellent agreement with the watchword of the worshippers of the beast: Who is like the beast, or who is able to make war with him?' It combines all that in the preceding description had been said to characterize the beast."

The very appearance of the number was awful, says Farrar. "The first letter was the initial letter of the name of Christ. The last letter was the first double-letter (*st*) of the Cross (*stauros*). Between the two, the serpent stood confessed with its writhing sign and hissing sound."

Whatever the interpretation of the symbol, identification of the individual referred to will doubtless be impossible until the particular period in which he lives. But the clue given by the Apocalypse will probably then be adequate for the godly of that day to realize the identity of their foe and to act accordingly.

[1]Ezra 2. 13

Chapter XVI

Prelude to Judgment

The Redeemed on Mount Zion

"And I saw, and behold, the Lamb standing on the Mount Zion, and with Him a hundred and forty and four thousand, having His name, and the name of His Father, written on their foreheads. And I heard a voice from heaven, as the voice of many waters, and as the voice of a great thunder: and the voice which I heard was as the voice of harpers harping with their harps; and they sing as it were a new song before the throne, and before the four living creatures and the elders; and no man could learn the song save the hundred and forty and four thousand, even they that had been purchased out of the earth. These are they who were not defiled with women; for they are virgins. These are they who follow the Lamb whithersoever He goeth. These were purchased from among men, to be the firstfruits unto God and unto the Lamb. And in their mouth was found no lie: they are without blemish" (14. 1-5).

BEFORE divine judgment broke upon the two Beasts, and their followers, a parenthesis intervened, and John beheld the Lamb standing on Mount Zion in the midst of a redeemed company of 144,000. This is the only mention of Zion in the Revelation. It was the city of David,[1] the prototype of the victorious Messiah, "the city of the great King,"[2] and the future seat of Messiah's government.[3]

In anticipation of the Lamb's millennial reign, He was seen already standing on the mount of regal power, whilst around Him stood a rejoicing company, who had been purchased out of the earth. "The 144,000 here witnessed are of *Judah*," says Walter Scott; "a similarly numbered company of all *Israel*[4] forms a separate vision," but the support for this differentiation is not very obvious. 144,000 of Israel's tribes were sealed in chapter 7, and 144,000 were seen on Zion as purchased out of the earth. Gaebelein's remark is probably more apposite: "The 144,000 are the same company which was sealed in chapter 7, but they also include the distinctly Jewish remnant which suffered more specifically in Palestine. The number 144,000 being symbolical and not actual, permits such an interpretation. They represent the "all Israel" saved by the coming of the Deliverer out of Zion.[5] They have passed

[1] 2 Sam. 5. 7 [2] Psa. 48. 2 [3] Isa. 2. 3 [4] Rev. 7. 4 [5] Rom. 11. 26

through the great tribulation and are seen as redeemed from the earth."

Openly in their foreheads the redeemed company bore the names of the Lamb and of His Father. The character of God was impressed upon them and they were marked out as His. The followers of the Beast bore his name on their hands or forehead, these on Zion bore the name of their God.

From the heavens, the seer heard a volume of sound like the thunder of many waters—a noise which was presently distinguished as the voices of singers mingled with the strains of harps, and choristers and harpists burst forth into a glad new song before the throne of God and the living creatures and elders who surrounded it. The song of the martyred ones in heaven rang in the ears too of the preserved on Zion, who alone were capable of learning that song. Those who had suffered death during the great tribulation and those who had passed through alive were conjoined in that glad hymn of praise.

The 144,000 are described as virgins who had not defiled themselves with women. A literal interpretation of this would imply that the company was composed solely of males. It is obvious that the reference is not to literal celibacy but to a retention of purity in the midst of a corrupt world. "Marriage is honourable in all, and the bed undefiled,"[1] and whilst the apostle Paul declares that "it is good for a man not to touch a woman," he gives explicit instructions regarding the marital relationship.[2] At the same time, there is an undoubted blessing for those who deliberately separate themselves for the service of God.[3] The saints in Rev. 14, however, are apparently a group who walked undefiled and free from contamination in an abandoned world. The blandishments of worldly systems of religion (and such false systems are not infrequently depicted in Revelation in the guise of a *woman*) and a meretricious connection with what was opposed to Christ were abhorred by these faithful ones. They followed the Lamb wherever He went. Theirs was a true discipleship based on a full and unqualified allegiance to their Lord.

James describes God's people of the present age as a "firstfruits of His creatures,"[4] and the redeemed on Mount Zion are also stated to be "purchased from among men, to be the firstfruits unto God and unto the Lamb." The millennium still lay ahead when the whole earth would acknowledge the rule of the Lamb, but these had already bowed to His sway and were the earnest of His coming inheritance.

[1]Heb. 13. 4 [2]1 Cor. 7. 1-9 [3]1 Cor. 7. 27 [4]Jas. 1. 18

The age in which these saints lived was peculiarly one when falsehood reigned. The Man of Sin will come "with all power and signs and lying wonders" (Greek, *pseudos*), deceiving the masses, who, under a divinely-permitted delusion, will "believe *the lie*" (Greek, *to pseudei*). Counterfeits of God and His Christ will be the object of universal worship: falsehood will prevail. In the midst of such conditions, in the mouth of the 144,000 was found "no lie" (Greek, *pseudo*). During the millennium, Zephaniah declares that "The remnant of Israel shall not do iniquity, nor speak lies, neither shall a deceitful tongue be found in their mouth."[1] Already the character of that day was evidenced in the Tribulation saints: "in their mouth was found no lie."

They were indeed "without blemish." It is not that they were sinless, but that they had refused to listen to the blasphemous seductions of the evil dupes of Satan or to conform to the will of the Beast or of the False Prophet. As regards the worship of the Beast, they were faultless.

Well might the Christian of the present day find a pattern in these saints of another age. The world is still inimical to spirituality and to God; evil is at liberty and falsehood prevails. The true disciple of Christ will turn with loathing from the boasting and blasphemous pretensions with which he is so often confronted, refusing to sacrifice principle for advantage or comfort; and determining to follow none but the One who is the Truth as well as the Life and the Way.

The Everlasting Gospel

"And I saw another angel flying in mid-heaven, having the everlasting gospel to announce to those settled upon the earth, and to every nation and tribe and tongue and people; and he saith with a great voice, Fear God and give Him glory; for the hour of His judgment is come; and worship Him that made the heaven and the earth and sea and fountains of waters" (14. 6, 7).

The vision of Mount Zion faded away to give place to a further series of visions revealing the stages preceding it. First of all, the seer saw an angel flying in mid-heaven, having the everlasting Gospel.

During the present dispensation, the Gospel preached is the grace of God in Christ—His death to put away sin and His resurrection to justify the believer. This aspect of the Gospel, however, is strictly limited to the present period. During our Lord's lifetime, the good news preached was the Gospel of the Kingdom and of

[1]Zeph. 3. 13

the coming King. The message carried by the angel seen by John, on the other hand, was "the everlasting Gospel." The fact that it is termed "everlasting" infers that the message is essentially that which has consistently been proclaimed from the commencement of God's dealings with man. "It is the good news of all the ages," says Dr. Ironside, "that God is sovereign, and that man's happiness consists in recognizing His authority." The Gospel has various phases and during the Great Tribulation the characteristic note will evidently be the claims of the Creator upon His creature. This is singularly appropriate since the Beast will seek complete sway over the spirits as well as the lives of men, and the Gospel preached will be diametrically opposed to the claims of the devil's tool.

Whilst the Gospel was borne by the flying angel, its actual proclamation will be in the hands of Israelites.

The essence of the Gospel borne by the angel is the Creator's claims upon man, coupled with a warning of impending judgment. When our Lord read in the synagogue of Nazareth the opening verses of Isaiah 61, He stopped in the middle of the second verse. The message declared by the evangelists of the Tribulation period will take up the words at that point—"to proclaim . . . the day of vengeance of our God."

The message was announced to the earth-dwellers and to every class of mankind, so that not a soul was left with excuse.

Babylon's Fall Announced

"And another, a second angel, followed, saying, Fallen, fallen is Babylon the great, who has made all the nations to drink of the wine of the fury of her fornication" (14. 8).

Babylon is here mentioned for the first time in the Revelation. The city originated in the desire of Nimrod (whose name means "rebel") to found a World-Empire. He commenced by building Babel (literally *confusion*) or Babylon.[1] Instead of scattering to replenish the earth after the Flood, the people gathered together in Shinar and built a mighty tower at Babel, only to be dispersed by the hand of God.[2] The city was always a centre of idolatry and of oppression.

It is, however, a religious system rather than the city which is viewed in Rev. 14. The destruction of the system is described later in chapters 17 and 18, but the seer already heard the declaration of that impending event. A second angel followed the first, announcing that Babylon the Great had fallen. The harlot church

[1]Gen. 10. 10 [2]Gen. 11. 7-9

had sought to ally herself with the temporal powers and to enslave the people of God. She "made all the nations to drink of the wine of the fury of her fornication," declared the angel. There is more than a reflection of the prophet Jeremiah's words: "Babylon has been a golden cup in the Lord's hand, that made all the earth drunken; the nations have drunken of her wine, therefore the nations are mad."[1] She "had, by her seductions, unholy allurements and incitements to evil, enthralled the nations," says one writer. "Their passions had been fearfully aroused. In the height of the ungodliness and folly of the unholy union between the corrupt church and the equally corrupt nations, the welcome message falls upon our ears, 'Babylon has fallen.'" In 1 Pet. 5. 13, the apostle refers to Rome under the name of Babylon, and there seems no question that the Apocalyptic seer follows the same course here.

The Doom of the Beast-Worshippers

"And another angel, a third, followed them, saying with a loud voice, If any man worships the Beast and his image, and receives a mark on his forehead, or on his hand, he also shall drink of the wine of the fury of God, which is prepared unmixed in the cup of His wrath; and he shall be tormented with fire and brimstone in the presence of the holy angels, and in the presence of the Lamb: and the smoke of their torment ascends for ever and ever; and they have no rest day and night, who worship the Beast and his image, and whosoever receives the mark of his name. Here is the endurance of the saints, who keep the commandments of God and the faith of Jesus" (14. 9-12).

A third angel crossed the seer's vision, giving a further warning with a loud voice. Not only was judgment declared upon Babylon but also upon the worshippers of the Beast. Rev. 13 indicates that all will be compelled to worship the Beast or his image under pain of death, and that no trading will be possible without the mark of the Beast. For all such, mercy will be withdrawn. They "treasure up for themselves wrath in the day of wrath."

Whosoever worshipped the Beast and his image or received his mark should suffer, declared the angel, at the hand of God. He should drink of the undiluted fury of God, prepared in the cup of God's wrath. Those who refused to worship the image of the Beast were martyred.[2] In just retribution, vengeance fell upon their murderers. Wine is normally used in the Scriptures as a symbol of joy and pleasure but here it becomes a type almost of intoxicating fury. The undiluted fury of the Almighty became the compulsory draught of the idolatrous apostates. No mercy

[1]Jer. 51. 7 [2]Rev. 13. 15

will be evidenced in that day, and yet the unparalleled severity of the judgment was entirely justifiable. Those who had previously drunk gladly of the wine of Babylon's fury[1] were now compelled to drink of the wine of God's fury.

Moreover, eternal torment was meted out to each individual. "He shall be tormented with fire and brimstone." The touch of brimstone is agony; combined with fire, it spells unutterable torture.[2] This vengeance was suffered in the presence of the angelic beings and of the Lamb Himself. This, says Brodie, "seems to contain the pungency of the curse, in the same way as is expressed in chapter 6. 16, which expresses the horror felt by the wicked at seeing 'the face of Him that sitteth on the throne.'" The angels are frequently employed in the execution of God's decreed judgments and they identify themselves as faithful servants with His will. Just as they observed deliberate refusal of God's grace and open revolt against Him, they now beheld the full recompense to each rebel. And the Lamb Himself, whose blood was shed for guilty men and Whose love was wantonly spurned and rejected, beheld, with solemn and awful approval, the judgment of those who had been willing adherents and abettors of the Beast. The very presence of the holy angels and of the Lamb Whose love was once proffered them could only add immeasurably to the mental suffering and remorse of the now disillusioned idolaters. How terrible their reactions can scarcely be comprehended.

The torment of these creatures was not only unalleviated but unceasing. "The smoke of their torment ascends for ever and ever; and they have no rest day and night." They had allied themselves to the Beast and accepted his complete sovereignty; he was their god and absolute lord. For all eternity the wrath of the God they had thus despised rested upon them. The references to fire, brimstone and smoke are undoubtedly figurative and not intended to be taken literally, but if the expressions are only symbolic, the reality itself must be dreadful. The picture drawn is of unremitting misery under the unalterable displeasure of Almighty God.

The conscious and awful punishment of the wicked, although clearly stated in the Scriptures, is often questioned. If there is a divine law at all, there must of necessity be a penalty for transgression of the law. Wrongdoing cannot go unpunished or the authority of the law is destroyed. Punishment is essential to the idea of a law.

The penalty imposed for the breaking of a law or command

[1]Rev. 14. 8 [2]Gen. 19. 24

must be "some suffering, inflicted by an external cause and directed by an intelligent agent possessed of legal authority, under the express idea of retribution or some kind of compensation for moral wrong done, and so painful as to bear, in rational estimation, a proportion to the magnitude of that wrong, both in the impression which it will make upon the delinquent, and in its public operation as an example for the deterring of others" (Dr. J. Pye Smith in *First Lines of Christian Theology*). The very consciousness of criminality must, in itself, result in mental suffering, and conviction of sin by God, with the full revelation of all that it means, must inevitably be productive of remorse, self-reproach and mental anguish. When this is coupled with the *penal* suffering which justice *must* inflict, the picture painted in Rev. 14 cannot be regarded as too lurid.

Whilst eternal suffering awaited the Beast-worshippers, there were saints of God on earth who were even then passing through tribulation. With no means of defence, they endured the onslaughts of their foes, directed against them because they kept "the commandments of God and the faith of Jesus." They might go through the furnace of affliction, but the Lord treasured their patient endurance and their consistent fidelity to things divine. These were not, of course, the Church, but the elect remnant of Israel, who obeyed the law and adhered to the earthly confession of Jesus.

The Blessed Dead

"And I heard a voice fom heaven saying, Write, Blessed are the dead who die in the Lord from henceforth. Yea, saith the Spirit, that they may rest from their labours, for their works follow with them" (14. 13).

The words of verse 13 are often used at the death of God's people in this age. In some measure, they are, of course, applicable, for death is but the gateway into the presence of the Lord, and it is very far better to be with Him than in this scene of sin and misery. There is no hopeless sorrow at the deathbed of the Christian.

But the words from heaven to which the apostle John listened related, not to believers of this dispensation, but rather to those martyred during the reign of the Beast. "Blessed are the dead who die in the Lord from henceforth," declared the heavenly voice. These Jewish martyrs, as one expositor says, had not only lost their part in the rapture of the Church, but also in the glory of the Kingdom. They had lived too late for the one and had died too soon for the other. Was there nothing for them? Blessed are they, came the assurance. In the midst of earth's diabolical persecution, there was no rest for them, but death ushered them into a rest from their labours. Toil and suffering were for ever ended. Moreover, their works accompanied them, to receive their proper appraisal of God and to earn for them a more blessed and privileged position in the presence of God.

A definite time-mark was intimated. It was *from henceforth* (*aparti*, denoting a change of conditions or circumstances), and John was accordingly instructed to write the words, presumably that the special emphasis might be recognized by these latter-day saints as peculiarly their own.

Chapter XVII

Harvest and Vintage

The Reaper

"And I saw, and behold, a white cloud, and upon the cloud One sitting like the Son of Man, having on His head a golden crown, and in His hand a sharp sickle. And another angel came out of the temple, crying with a loud voice to Him that sat on the cloud, Thrust in Thy sickle and reap, for the harvest of the earth is over-ripe. And He that sat on the cloud put forth His sickle upon the earth, and the earth was reaped" (14. 14-16).

ANOTHER class of judgments was now unfolded. John beheld a white cloud, upon which sat One like the Son of Man. In His Olivet discourse to His disciples, our Lord declared that, after the tribulation, the Son of Man should be seen coming on the clouds of heaven.[1] Here, He sat on the cloud in mid-heaven, executing judgment over the widest possible scene. In the final judgment, a great white *Throne* fills the gaze, but in this case, it was a white *cloud*. Both were indicative of the absolute righteousness of the One who sat as Judge. Unbiased and unprejudiced, untouched by wrong motive, and unaffected by imperfect knowledge, the Judge meted out justice on an unquestionably holy and righteous basis.

It is worthy of note that the One by whom the earth was reaped was termed the Son of Man. Says T. B. Baines: "This is the title in which Christ takes the kingdom from God's hand,[2] intervenes for the deliverance of His chosen people,[3] and has all things put under His feet."[4] The way was being prepared for His advent to take up His kingdom as the universal Sovereign and all judgment was entrusted to Him. In token of His sovereignty, a golden crown adorned His head.

In the hand of that mighty One was a sharp sickle with which to reap the earth, and an angel emerged from the temple, bidding Him thrust in the sickle and reap the over-ripe harvest of the earth.

In Rev. 11, the temple was seen opened in heaven, and the vision which now filled the seer's eyes was again associated with the temple, the emissary of justice actually issuing therefrom. The

[1] Matt. 24. 30 [2] Dan. 7. 13, 14 [3] Psa. 80. 17, 18; Luke 21. 27, 28
[4] Psa. 8 4-6; Heb. 2. 5, 8

reference clearly links the event with Israel, but expositors part company regarding the precise interpretation to be placed upon the passage. It is maintained by some that retribution upon the apostate mass for their persecution of the godly remnant is what is in view. Others suggest that the object of the reaping is the punishment of the Gentile oppressors of Israel. In support of the latter, Joel plainly refers to the gathering of the Gentiles in the valley of Jehoshaphat and the reaping by sickle of the already ripened harvest.[1]

The reaping in question is not of the wheat prior to the destruction of the tares, as in Matt. 13, for the harvest is stated to have been over-ripe, *i.e.*, not rich with the full ear of wheat, but withered and dried up. For such, the only possibility is destruction. We have little sympathy with the view that regards the reaping as preparatory and the vintage (which follows) as the actual judgment. Both are clearly part of the same action and do not differ greatly in import, although dissimilar in nature.

It is evident, even in this day, that the earth is rapidly becoming more and more corrupt and that, sooner or later, its rottenness must render it objectionable and repellent to the God who created it. When that day arrives, the only course left open is the removal of the corruption by a direct judicial act, and it is that which is portrayed in the passage. The Son of Man put forth His sickle and the earth was reaped.

The Vintage

"And another angel came out from the temple which is in heaven, having himself also a sharp sickle. And another angel came out from the altar, having authority over fire; and he called with a loud voice to him that had the sharp sickle, saying, Put forth thy sharp sickle, and gather the clusters of the vine of the earth; for her grapes are fully ripe. And the angel thrust his sickle into the earth, and gathered the vine of the earth, and cast it into the great winepress of the wrath of God. And the winepress was trodden without the city, and there came out blood from the winepress, even unto the bridles of the horses, for a thousand and six hundred furlongs" (14. 17-20).

Another angel with a sickle emerged from the temple, but on this occasion, it is stated to be the temple which is in heaven. The earthly tabernacle and temple were fashioned after "the patterns of things in the heavens." It is thence that Christ the great High Priest has gone and from thence that He will come again.

A second angel came out from the altar—obviously the golden altar of incense,[2] the fire from which was cast upon the earth. Authority over fire—the altar fire of divine justice—was attributed to this messenger of God. At the bidding of this angel, the first

[1]Joel 3. 12, 13 [2]Rev. 8

thrust his sickle into the earth and gathered "the clusters of the vine of the earth."

With reference to Israel, the psalmist declared that God had "brought a vine out of Egypt," prepared room for it and planted a vineyard by His right hand.[1] The choice vine which He planted and from which He anticipated a rich fruitage, "brought forth wild grapes."[2] All Jehovah's efforts on behalf of Israel were wasted; the only result from His care was wild grapes. Hence the prophet foretold that He would take away the hedge and break down the wall of the vineyard and lay it waste. Rev. 14 is the fulfilment of the prophecy. The clusters of wickedness were fully ripe. Evil was consummated in earth's vintage, and the judgment of God must now fall upon the matured fruit of apostasy.

Cut down by the sickle, the vine was gathered and cast into "the great winepress of the wrath of God" outside the city, there to be crushed and trodden down. The words: "I have trodden the winepress alone; . . . I will tread them in Mine anger, and trample them in My fury; and their blood shall be sprinkled upon My garments, and I will stain My raiment,"[3] are vividly descriptive of the scene.

Joel indicates that the nations will also share in this suffering of the winepress and that the scene will be in the valley of Jehoshaphat,[4] just outside Jerusalem, whilst Isaiah identifies the site as Bozrah. The Revelation merely states that it is without the city (evidently Jerusalem). "The march of the terrific indignation of God on this occasion would, therefore, seem to be from the Sinaitic hills, crashing through Idumea, thundering by the walls of the holy city, and thence on to the great field of Esdraelon, where the chief stress of the awful pressure falls. Along this line will the main bodies of these assembled nations lie, eager, determined and confident in the schemes that occupy them, not knowing that they are already in the great winepress of the wrath of God. 'Multitudes, multitudes,' armies on armies, hosts on hosts, are there. The Beast is there; the False Prophet is there; and the kings, captains, mighty men, and drilled legions of all the nations in league with Antichrist are there; all gathered into one pen of slaughter" (Seiss). The awful occasion is undoubtedly that where again it is stated that Christ will tread "the winepress of the fierceness and wrath of Almighty God."[5] As the forces of men were gathered together, consummate, exterminating vengeance fell upon them.

As the winepress was trodden down, rivers of blood streamed out which reached to the bridles of the horses for a distance of 1,600

[1] Psa. 80. 8 [2] Isa. 5. 2 [3] Isa. 63. 3 [4] Joel 3. 12 [5] Rev. 19. 15

furlongs—4 ft. of human blood for 200 miles. It may be maintained that the expression is simply prophetic hyperbole, but it is at least clear that the judgment of that day will be appalling in its horror and extent.

When Titus took Jerusalem, Josephus says that the Roman soldiers "obstructed the very lanes with dead bodies; and made the whole city run down with blood, to such a degree indeed that the fire of many of the houses was quenched with these men's blood." Plutarch relates that when Sylla took Athens, the blood shed in the market-place covered all the ceramicus as far as Dipylus. The terrible fury of God cannot be grasped by human intelligence.

The present day is one of grace and mercy, but there yet remains a day when the Eternal God will deal with His rebellious creatures in unsparing and unmitigated wrath.

A Great Sign

"And I saw another sign in heaven, great and wonderful, seven angels having the seven last plagues, for in them is completed (or filled up) the wrath of God" (15. 1).

The order of the Revelation is sometimes a little confusing to the superficial reader. The book is cast in the form of sections, which frequently overlap one another. It is not a consecutive narrative. From time to time in the book, God reverts to some particular point which requires emphasis or amplification. An outline may be given and, when completed, a part may receive separate mention and further details added regarding it. For instance, as Dr. A. H. Burton points out, "Chapter 11. 18 carries us in a general way right down to the end of God's judicial dealings with earth—His wrath come upon the living nations, His judgment of the dead, and the time of reward to His servants during the millennium. Then in chapters 12, 13, and 14, we get a separate section, going back to give fuller details, especially connected with the Jewish people, and linked on the one hand with His grace to them through the victorious Christ, the Man-Child caught up to God's throne, and on the other with Satan, the inveterate enemy of Christ and His people, whether earthly or heavenly."

Chapter 14 gives an outline of events from the sealing of the Jewish remnant to the vintage judgment. Chapter 15 opens the subject of the seven vials of wrath. It is clear, however, that the chapter does not follow immediately upon the one which precedes it, since the fall of Babylon occurs early in the outline in chapter 14, whereas it is the last event connected with the vials. It may, therefore, he concluded that the vials are poured out during the actual period of the preaching of the Everlasting Gospel, when divine grace will still be active, but whilst concurrently therewith blasphemous rebellion against God will be rapidly developing. Even during this period of the Great Tribulation, divine mercy will not be entirely withdrawn.

In chapter 12, John told of the signs of the sun-clad woman and of the great dragon. Here he saw another sign, which he describes as great and wonderful. The sign was of the seven angels with the seven last plagues. His amazement was evidently connected with the extent and the unparalleled character of the judgments about to be poured out. The judgments under the seals were largely providential and were, in fact, preliminary. Those under the vials were directly due to divine wrath and were conclusive in their nature. Emphasis is laid upon their finality. In them was completed, or filled up, the wrath of God.

The angels with the vials of wrath have sometimes been likened to the priests who poured out the libations, or drink offerings, in the temple service—an offering of wine upon the body of the sacrifice before it was consumed to ashes. The world was now devoted to wrath and before the fury of the Almighty broke out upon it, the libation was poured out upon the sacrifice.

The Overcomers

"And I saw as it were a sea of glass mingled with fire, and the overcomers of the Beast, and of his image, and of the number of his name, standing upon the sea of glass, having harps of God. And they sing the song of Moses, the servant of God, and the song of the Lamb, saying, Great and wonderful are Thy works, Lord God Almighty; righteous and true are Thy ways, Thou King of nations, Who shall not fear Thee, O Lord, and glorify Thy name? For Thou only art holy; for all the nations shall come and worship before Thee; for Thy righteousness (or righteous acts) have been made manifest" (15. 2-4).

Before particulars of the seven vials (or bowls) were given, another vision was interjected. The seer beheld a sea of glass mingled with fire. In chapter 4, a crystal sea extended before the throne as a pavement, but in this later scene, the sea was strangely commingled with fire, and resembled rather "a mighty reservoir of just judgments about to be precipitated upon the world below."

Upon the sea stood a company, who had overcome the Beast and gained the victory over his image and the number of his name. From this it is evident that these saints were contemporaneous with the Western Emperor and had lived during the Great Tribulation. They had probably been slain during the persecutions of that awful period, but God described them as overcomers. Refusing to bow to the Beast or his image, denying his blasphemous assumptions and declining to accept his mark, these martyrs had suffered the bitterness and pain of earthly conflict—*but they had overcome*. The tyrannical despot seemed almost omnipotent, but they still retained their loyalty to their God, and they overcame.

Is there not a message here for the believer to-day? The scales may be weighted against him, but the Almighty is on his side. Temptation may assault, the hostility of the world may be aroused against him, persecution, tribulation and sacrifice may be his portion, but by the power of God he overcomes. Compromise with evil there cannot be, payment of homage to another god he dare not give. Even of our Lord it could be said:

> "By weakness and defeat
> He won the meed and crown;
> Trod all our foes beneath His feet
> By being trodden down."

The overcomer may lose everything: he still has Christ.

With the harps of God, the overcomers take up the song of Moses, the servant of God, and the song of the Lamb. They are thus identified with the harpers of the previous chapter.

As the Israelites stood on the shores of the Red Sea and watched the discomfiture of their enemies by the intervention of Jehovah, they took up the song of Moses: "I will sing unto the Lord, for He hath triumphed gloriously; the horse and his rider hath He thrown into the sea. Who is like unto Thee, O Lord, . . . glorious in holiness, fearful in praises, doing wonders?"[1] Likewise, these victors of a later day voiced their song of praise and thanksgiving; "Great and wonderful are Thy works, Lord God Almighty."

They had proved His power and they extolled His ways. Evil might predominate, but they confidently acclaimed Him as the King of the nations and looked forward anticipatively to the day when all nations should acknowledge His sway and adore Him for His righteous acts.

J. N. Darby says: "Their song is very peculiar. The song of Moses is triumph over the power of evil by God's judgments. The song of the Lamb is the exaltation of the rejected Messiah, of the suffering One, and like Whom they had suffered; for it is the slain remnant amidst unfaithful and apostate Israel whom we find here." The song of Moses celebrated the glorious victory of Jehovah, His deliverance of His people, and His wondrous acts on

[1]Exod. 15. 1-11

their behalf. The song of the Lamb tells of redemption and of coming exaltation. Material and spiritual salvation are combined in this dual song.

The Seven Angels

"And after that, I looked and behold, the temple of the tabernacle of witness in the heaven was opened: and the seven angels who had the seven plagues came out of the temple, clothed in pure white linen, and girded about the breasts with golden girdles. And one of the four living creatures gave to the seven angels seven golden bowls, full of the fury of God, Who liveth for ever and ever. And the temple was filled with smoke from the glory of God and from His power; and no one was able to enter into the temple until the seven plagues of the seven angels were completed" (15. 5-8).

As John listened to the song of the overcomers, there was opened "the *temple* of the tabernacle of witness in the heaven." The expression is curious and apparently self-contradictory, but a more appropriate rendering would probably be "the *holiest* of the tabernacle." As in chapter 11. 19, the holy of holies was thrown open to provide egress for the emissaries of final fury. In the earthly tabernacle, the *sanctum sanctorum* was concealed from the eye of all but the high priest, but now "the mystery of God is finished" and the holiest was thrown wide open.

It is significant that it was the tabernacle and not the temple which was beheld. Govett remarks: "As the tent of the desert disappeared in the temple of the city, so does this tabernacle vanish in the temple of 'the city of God.' Its contents pass away with the passing of the millennial dispensation. The tabernacle lasts during the millennium. But as, after David's day, the tent became the temple, so, when the peaceful reign of God is fully established, the tent ceases."

Seven angels issued from the inner shrine. They were clothed in the pure white linen of the priest and their breasts were girded with golden girdles—again after the sacerdotal pattern. "They appear as priests," says one commentator, "because they come for the sacrificing of a great sacrifice to the offended holiness and justice of God. The girdle of the Jewish high priest was a mixture of blue and purple and scarlet and fine twined linen, along with the gold;[1] the girdles here are pure gold; for the temple is higher, and the administration holier, and the officiators belong to heaven, not earth." The garb of the heavenly High Priest in Rev. 1 was similar in character—a long garment to the feet and a golden girdle encircling His breasts.

[1]Exod. 28. 8

The angel-priests are stated to be the bearers of the seven plagues. The judgments no longer originated in the throne of justice but now in the ark of holiness.

To the seven angels one of the living creatures gave seven golden bowls (or vials), full of the fury of the eternal God. "The vessels intended," says Govett, "were broad and flat like a saucer to which a handle was attached, able to contain liquids and designed to pour them out at once. They are called 'basins' or 'bowls' in the Old Testament. They belonged to the altar; and all vessels belonging to the copper altar were of copper.[1] These are of gold. Out of the bowls oil was poured over the accepted meat-offering, wine over the victim slain.[2] This is the sevenfold cup of God's fury, given to the living offenders to drink, a *measured* vengeance." Some expositors suggest that the bowls referred to the golden censers in which the priest carried the incense, but Govett's interpretation seems nearer the mark. Just as the drink offering was poured out over the body of the burnt offering which was wholly consecrated to God and wholly consumed in the fires of the altar, so the contents of the bowls of wrath were to be poured out upon a world which was devoted to destruction in the fires of divine wrath.

The holy of holies was the shrine in which God's presence was indicated in the cloud of the Shekinah. Before that blazing glory, the cloud of incense rose from the high priest's censer and, sheltered in the fragrant cloud, the intercessor represented his people before Jehovah.

No intercession was possible in the holiest seen by the Apostle. A cloud of smoke filled the "temple" so that none could enter. "Thou hast covered Thyself with a cloud," said Jeremiah, "that our prayer should not pass through."[3] The scene of worship and mediation was now one of consuming wrath. God was hidden in the thick cloud of His glory and power; grace was withdrawn and prayer unanswered. The Almighty would listen to no cry and would allow no plea to arrest the breaking of the storm of judgment. His power and glory were now moved to action, and the glorious Shekinah became a devouring fire. None might enter the holiest until the angel-priests had completed their allotted work. "The mount was fenced about till the burst of displeasure was over."

[1]Exod. 27. 3; Num. 4. 14; Zech. 14. 20 [2]Lev. 23. 13 [3]Lam. 3. 44

Chapter XVIII

The Seven Vials

"And I heard a great voice out of the temple, saying to the seven angels, Go and pour out the seven bowls of the wrath of God upon the earth" (16. 1).

THE longsuffering of God spells out mercy to the transgressor until the moment arrives when judgment can no longer be delayed. In love, the Almighty seems to linger before refusing an ear to intercession, but finally His glory must break out to vindicate His name and character in a scene of corruption. Not only had there been rejection of His Son but of God Himself, for the followers of the Beast now paid their adulatory homage and worship to him and even to his image.

From out of the smoke-filled shrine there came a great voice, commanding the seven angels to pour out upon the earth the seven golden bowls of the wrath of God which had been placed in their hands by the living creature. "Seven seals," says Govett, "have unfolded the mystery of God. Seven trumpets have opened the war of Satan and of his Christ against the Most High. Now seven bowls from the temple prepare the sacrifice for slaughter." Israel prayed that God would render unto their neighbours "sevenfold into their bosom their reproach, wherewith they have reproached Thee, O Lord,"[1] and full response will be given to that petition.

It is interesting to note the similarity between the Apocalyptic vials of wrath and the plagues of Egypt. The first bowl corresponds with the sixth plague, the second and third with the first plague, the fifth with the ninth, the sixth with the second, and the seventh with the seventh, and in many respects the resemblance is more than superficial.

That there has been at least a partial fulfilment of the vials already in history cannot be doubted. As Scott remarks: "The precursory fulfilment of these seven vials on the year-day historical scale by way of rehearsal is held by numerous expositors to have been the sanguinary French Revolution of 1790 to 1806, as regards the first

[1]Psa. 79. 12

three vials; the fourth bowl, the tyranny and military oppression of Napoleon I; the fifth bowl, the calamities which befell the city of Rome and the Pope in consequence of the French Revolution, or the humiliation of France from 1815 to 1818; the sixth bowl, the wars of the Turkish power, the return of the Jews to Palestine, and the subtle influences of infidelity, revolutionary democracy, Popery, and Mahommedanism; and the seventh, the Great Tribulation of three and a half years." It is possible that later interpreters may see a further partial fulfilment in Adolf Hitler and his machinations. For most prophecies there is more than one rehearsal, but the final and complete fulfilment will be unmistakable.

The First Vial

And the first went and poured out his bowl upon the earth; and there came an evil and grievous sore upon the men that had the mark of the beast and those who worshipped his image" (16. 2).

In many instances in the past, divine punishment has been by an infliction of boils. Israel were threatened with such a plague if they broke the law.[1] It was the sixth plague upon Egypt.[2] Job, of course, suffered from this malady.[3] The Philistines were supernaturally stricken with the same disorder.[4]

The first angel went forth and poured out his bowl upon the earth, and upon those who had the mark of the Beast or worshipped his image were inflicted malignant ulcers or boils. Those who had voluntarily received the mark of Satan were now impressed with the mark of divine wrath—the loathsome external sign of the inward corruption. Miraculous healing of diseases came by the true Messiah; miraculous diseases fell upon the disciples of the false Messiah.

Whilst this judgment probably depicts moral suffering resultant upon moral degradation, it is not unlikely that there is a reference to physical malady. History reveals that an inevitable accompaniment of idolatry is immorality: moral standards are adjusted to a different level, the unlawful becomes lawful, and the sinful becomes an act of worship. Without the deterring influences of the Holy Spirit and the Scriptures, men will give rein to their lusts and indulge their desires to the full, the very licence and promiscuity of their sin, as a result, reacting upon their bodies in physical disorders.

The historical interpreter maintains that the contents of the first vial were poured out at the French Revolution. Elliott writes:

[1]Deut. 28. 27, 35 [2]Exod. 9. 8-12 [3]Job 2. 7 [4]1 Sam. 5. 6

"The sore indicates the outbreak of some corruption which had been festering within, and which, breaking out, would spread its infection and produce great distress. A tremendous outbreak of social and moral evil, democratic and popular fury, atheism and vice, characterized the French Revolution. From France, as a centre, the plague rapidly spread through its affiliated countries; and the whole of Papal Christendom soon imbibed the poison and shared the punishment."

The scepticism and infidelity of Voltaire, D'Alembert, Diderot, and many another writer of that day, combined with the prevailing immorality and loose-living of the French clergy, indeed constituted an ulcerous growth. In his *Life of Napoleon Bonaparte*, Sir Walter Scott wrote: "The licentiousness, which walked abroad in such disgusting and undisguised nakedness, was marked by open infamy, deep enough to have called down, in the age of miracles, an immediate judgment from heaven; and crimes, which the worst of the Roman Emperors would at least have hidden in his solitary isle of Caprea, were acted as publicly as if men had no eyes and God no thunderbolts."

The "evil and grievous sore" finally discharged its offensive humours in the most dreadful manner. In his *French Revolution*, Alison has graphically described the "reign of terror," with the unparalleled horrors of Carrier's massacres and atrocities and the lascivious abominations perpetrated by Chaumette. Churches were stripped of their treasures and consecrated vessels and furniture were treated with the utmost contumely. A prostitute was elevated on the high altar of the Cathedral of Notre Dame in substitution for the Deity, and every kind of obscenity was allowed full sway both here and elsewhere. The baleful contagion infected neighbouring countries also, and Isaiah might well have said that "the whole head is sick and the whole heart faint. From the sole of the foot even unto the head there is no soundness in him: wounds, and wheals, and open sores."[1]

However apt the description may be of the French Revolution of 1789, it is fairly clear that the pouring out of the first vial has not yet taken place and that the curses of Deut. 28. 27, 35, will yet be fulfilled in the experience of the worshippers of the Beast. Their internal moral condition will be exposed and the hidden putrescence brought to the surface.

The Second Vial

And the second angel poured out his bowl on the sea; and it became blood, as of a dead man; and every living soul died in the sea" (16. 3).

[1]Isa. 1. 5, 6

When the second trumpet was sounded, a third of the sea became like blood, a third of the creatures therein died, and a third of the ships were destroyed. When the second bowl of fury was poured out, the whole of the sea became as blood and all the living creatures therein perished. Moreover, the sea was not merely changed in colour but also in essence; it became like the blood of a dead man. Nothing could live in that: every living thing died.

Cumming and others see in this vial the destruction of the maritime power of the great Roman Catholic countries between 1793 and 1815. It is claimed that England, as the bulwark of Protestantism, was divinely selected to pour out the vial upon the maritime forces, colonies, and dependencies of the Papal empire. The British fleets annihilated those of the Continental nations and completely paralysed their naval power.

We prefer, however, to believe that the reference is to a day still future. The sea is normally the figure of the restless nations. The masses make no profession of Christianity but, on the contrary, deliberately reject the Lord of life. In their surrender of every vestige of religious profession, their alienation from God will be complete. They will be viewed by God as dead. As judgment falls upon them, their spiritual death will be plainly revealed. The sea will become like the blood of a dead man.

The Third Vial

And the third angel poured out his bowl on the rivers, and on the fountains of waters; and they became like blood. And I heard the angel of the waters saying, Thou art righteous, Who art and was, the Holy One; that Thou hast judged so; for they have shed the blood of the saints and prophets, and Thou hast given them blood to drink; they are worthy. And I heard the altar saying, Yea, Lord God Almighty, true and righteous are Thy judgments" (16. 4-7).

When the third trumpet sounded, a burning star fell upon the third part of the rivers and the fountains, turning them into the bitterness of wormwood.[1] When the third angel poured out his bowl, it was upon the rivers and the fountains of waters, which at once became like blood. Whereas under the trumpet the judgment was restricted to a third part, the whole of the rivers and springs suffered under the vial.

Scott sees in the *rivers* the ordinary life of a nation, characterized by known and accepted principles of government—social and political—and, in the *fountains of waters* the sources of prosperity and well-being. Whether red dust or red animalculæ coloured the waters or whether they were literally turned into blood matters little.

[1]Rev. 8. 10, 11

Figuratively, the streams of life and the sources of well-being were destroyed.

The normal streams of pleasure and happiness were polluted and the springs of natural joy corrupted and baneful.

From a historical point of view, as Elliott points out, there is depicted the invasion of Germany, Sardinia, Austria, Italy, etc., by the French revolutionary power. The cities and countries on the banks of the rivers Danube, Po, and Rhine and their various tributaries were deluged with blood. From the declaration of war by the French National Assembly against Germany in 1792, the rivers seemed to be turned into blood. Worms, Mentz, and Spires, on the banks of the Meuse, Savoy, and Piedmont and the middle Rhine, the Alpine rivers on which Sardinia and Austria bordered, Bormida, Tanaro, Adda, Marengo, Hohenlinden, all became fields of sanguinary battles. "Never, in the history of Europe," says Cumming, "were there more sanguinary scenes in the valleys of the Rhine, the Danube, and the Po, than at this memorable era. There was not an acre on the banks of those rivers that was not furrowed with a soldier's grave—scarcely a river or tributary stream that rolled to the main that was not tinged with a soldier's blood—nor was there a forest, nor a wood, nor a capital, nor scarcely a cottage that was not ploughed by the wheels and torn by the shot of artillery." Had Cumming lived until the recent war, it is probable that he would have revised his opinion as he saw the Russian armies fighting from river to river and stream to stream, and waters all over the world literally stained by the blood of the slain. But prophecy has normally more than one foreshadowing before the final fulfilment, and all these partial fulfilments give some faint picture of the horrors of the future.

As the judgment was poured out upon the waters, John heard the angel acclaim the righteousness of the Eternal God who had so judged. He acknowledged the appropriate character of God's retributive act. The victims had shed the blood of saints and prophets, and now had been forced to drink blood themselves. Just as Athens gave its condemned criminals hemlock to drink, so these viler criminals could slake their thirst in blood alone. When the head of Cyrus was brought to Thomyris, the Scythian queen, she immersed it in a bowl of blood with the pertinent gibe, "Cyrus, thy thirst was blood. Now drink thy fill."

If God was absolutely just in His rewarding of the martyred saints,[1] He was equally righteous in meting out wrath upon their

[1] Rev. 15. 2-5

persecutors. It was a just requital. They had shed the blood of saints and prophets: now they should drink blood. "They are worthy" cried the angel. The avenging hand of the Almighty meted out retribution on a perfectly just basis.

In view of the remarkable way in which suffering came upon Piedmont and Savoy (by whom the Vaudois had been so cruelly treated), upon Austria (the author of the barbarity experienced by the Hussites and Lutherans), and later upon France (under whom the Waldenses and Huguenots had suffered), Alison was prompted to comment that "the impartial justice of Providence made that terrific period the means of punishing the national sins of the contending parties." And who shall not say that the blood of murdered Jews and Christians has not so recently been required of German hands?

The blood of the martyrs had cried unto God from the altar and now, from the altar, came acquiescence in and approval of the the judgment of the brutal persecutors. "True and righteous are Thy judgments," declared the voice from the altar.

The Fourth Vial

"And the fourth angel poured out his bowl on the sun; and power was given to it to burn men with fire. And the men were burnt with great heat, and blasphemed the name of God, Who had authority over these plagues, and did not repent to give Him glory" (16. 8-9).

When the fourth trumpet was sounded, the light of the sun, moon, and stars was diminished by a third. When the fourth angel poured out his bowl of wrath, it was upon the sun, with the result that the solar heat was increased to an unbearable extent. Men were scorched by the intolerable heat and, in their anguish, blasphemed the name of the God Who permitted these plagues. In reference to the same period, Isaiah depicted Jacob as set on fire and burnt,[1] and Malachi declared that the day would come, "burning as a furnace," when the proud and the wicked should be burnt up.[2] In his last words to Israel, Moses foretold that they should be "consumed with hunger and devoured with burning heat."[3]

The supreme governing authority became, under the hand of God, the source of bitter suffering to men. Elliott again sees a literal fulfilment of this in the history of Napoleon Bonaparte. Connecting it with the events of the fourth trumpet, he says: "Most of the independent sovereigns of Europe were revolutionized and their light eclipsed in the political heaven. Bonaparte exer-

[1]Isa. 42. 25 [2]Mal. 4. 1 [3]Deut. 32. 24

cised his assumed office of king-maker to the no small distress of nations." Quoting from official reports, Cuninghame says: "The distress and destruction which marked the countries through which the French Army fled from the bloody field of Leipsic were altogether indescribable. Dead bodies covered the roads, while districts were depopulated by disease. For a month after the retreat, no human being, no domestic animal, no poultry, not even a sparrow was to be met with, only ravens feeding on corpses." The insatiable ambition of the little Corsican scorched men with fire and inflicted intense suffering on the greater part of Europe.

If, however, historical fulfilments are sought, many a later interpreter will probably see a further partial fulfilment in the cruelty and unbridled terrorism of Nazism. The thousands of Belgians, Dutch, French, Czechs, Poles, Danes, and Norwegians, dragged from their homes to form members of Hitler's slave gangs, the terrible massacres of Warsaw's ghettos, the atrocities perpetrated by the Gestapo throughout the whole of the enslaved lands of Europe, the deliberate attempts to exterminate the whole of the Jewish race, the indiscriminate bombing of civilians, might well find their description in the effect of the fourth vial.

The powers of rulers have often in the past, been used in oppression and despotic tyranny, and it seems clear from this chapter that the world is destined to pass through similar experiences again in the future. The Beast, or Western Emperor, with his satellite rulers, will probably seek to curtail individual liberty and to impose intolerable restrictions upon all who come under his sway.

In impotent rage men will be goaded into blasphemy of God. Instead of turning in repentance to the only One capable of relieving their awful state, they will but cry out against Him. They "did not repent to give Him glory."

The sufferers viewed the Almighty as the cause of their sufferings and, incorrigibly evil, their hatred boiled up into cursing and blaspheming. There was no confession of the sin which had rightly drawn upon them divine judgment. There was a recognition that the plagues falling upon them had been directed by some intelligence, and their rage overflowed against the Author of their woes.

As the first angel flew through mid-heaven, he cried: "Fear God and give Him glory, for the hour of His judgment has come."[1] These men deliberately decide upon their attitude and refuse "to give Him glory." As their sufferings increased, so also did their

[1]Rev. 14. 7

sin and, impenitently, they heaped up wrath for themselves in the day of wrath. They refused to learn the lessons which God had set and chose rather to ally themselves with the forces of evil. Although conscious that the punishment inflicted upon them came through the medium of the Beast, they apparently resigned themselves to his rule and thereby invoked the utmost severity of heaven.

The Fifth Vial

And the fifth angel poured out his bowl upon the throne of the Beast; and his kingdom became darkened; and they gnawed their tongues with distress, and blasphemed the God of heaven for their distresses and their sores, and repented not of their works" (16. 10, 11).

Divine judgment now drew nearer to the Beast, although he personally still escaped. The fifth angel poured out his bowl of wrath upon the throne of the Beast, with the result that darkness fell upon his kingdom, and his subjects gnawed their tongues with distress. When Moses stretched forth his hand towards heaven, a thick darkness covered the land of Egypt for three days—a darkness that could be felt.[1] So, in that plague of a later day, a moral cloud descended upon the empire of the Beast.

The judgment was directed against the central executive of the Western Empire—it was poured upon the throne of the imperial ruler. The waves of divine fury not merely lapped the steps of the throne but overwhelmed it in a flood of wrath.

As Cumming points out, the throne of the Beast is "the metropolitical spot on which this head of the apostacy sits and reigns. In short, it is at Rome." Like many of the same prophetic school, he identifies the effects of the fifth vial with the troubles experienced by the Papal power when Napoleon issued the decrees from Schœnbrunn which abolished the temporal power of the Pope, and resulted in the confiscation of church lands, the destruction of churches and monasteries, the abolition of tithes, etc. "In 1809," says Elliott, "Napoleon declared the Pope's temporal dominion at an end. The estates of the Church were annexed to France and Rome was degraded to be the second city of the French Empire. Subsequently the Pope was brought prisoner to France; and then, as a pensioner, he received a stated salary. He afterwards gained back the privilege of fixing his seat at Rome." The nations which had previously been crushed by the Pope felt the judgments but gave no sign of repentance: they relapsed into their former ways and revolted against God.

[1]Exod. 10. 21-23

Both Cumming and Elliott were too near the period of the French Revolution to be able to gauge its importance correctly, or to see its correct position in history, and they laid far too much stress upon details which, in the light of later happenings, are seen to have been of relatively little importance.

The Beast of whom the Apocalypse speaks is a personality not yet seen upon the public stage—the great Western Emperor who will be opposed to all things sacred and holy. Judgment will be meted out upon that mighty power at the epiphany of the Son of Man,[1] but, prior to that, the nations of Europe will turn in flattery and adulation to the powerful dictator who has his seat at Rome. As another says, however, those who "bow at his feet, will find his kingdom one of darkness instead of light, of confusion instead of prosperity, of pain instead of pleasure. It will be an atheistical government—a land where no mention of God will be allowed except in blasphemy." The darkness of error and falsehood will descend upon the willing subjects of the Beast, and the glory of his rule will be obscured by the mist of a moral darkness.

So terrible was the darkness to those described by the seer that they gnawed their tongues in anguish. "This is the only expression of the kind that we have in all the Word of God," writes Ramsay, "and it indicates the most intense and excruciating agony." Men reaped the harvest of the seeds of infidelity they sowed.

Forced to acknowledge the existence of a God in heaven, the victims only blasphemed Him for the distresses and the ulcerous sores inflicted upon them. No trace was there of repentance. Their hearts were only hardened by their trials and, in helpless rage, they cried out against the Author of their troubles.

It is impossible not to be impressed by the fact that the world is already tending to assume the character portrayed in the Revelation. Although many have turned to Christ for salvation in recent years, the general mass of mankind seems more estranged from God than ever. Atheism and free-thinking are spreading rapidly, and religion is regarded as obsolete and pertaining to earlier tribal days. The inflictions may not be so very remote.

The Sixth Vial

"And the sixth angel poured out his bowl upon the great river Euphrates; and its water was dried up, that the way of the kings from the east (or 'the rising of the sun') might be prepared. And I saw three unclean spirits like frogs come out of the mouth of the dragon, and out of the mouth of the Beast, and out of the mouth of the false prophet. For they are the spirits of demons, working miracles (or 'signs'); which go forth unto the kings of the whole habitable world, to gather

[1]Rev. 19.

them together to the battle of that great day of God Almighty—Behold, I come as a thief. Blessed is he that watches and keeps his garments that he may not walk naked and they see his shame. And He gathered them together to the place called in Hebrew, Armageddon" (16. 12-16).

When the sixth trumpet was sounded, four angels who were held in bondage at the great river Euphrates were liberated and allowed to go forth to destroy a third of mankind. When the sixth bowl was poured out, it was upon the Euphrates, with the result that the water was dried up that the way of the kings from the east might be prepared.

The eastern boundary of the Roman Empire, the river Euphrates, was an insurmountable obstacle to any threatened invasion from the east. The drying up of its waters left the way wide open to the invader, and the eastern powers swept over the dry bed of the river to make Judæa a battlefield between east and west. If the scene is that already described in chapter 9, it means that vast hordes of the eastern races, to the extent of 200 millions,[1] will pour into Palestine like the hordes of Ghengis Khan. The population of China and Japan is estimated to be about 567 millions, and that of India 330 millions, so that an enormous army of the size indicated by the seer is by no means an impossibility.

The majority of historical interpreters regard the Euphrates as typical of the Turkish Empire, and refer the drying up of the river to the decline of that Empire, commencing with the revolt of Ali Pacha in 1820 and the general insurrection of the Greek provinces in 1822, until Russia finally crippled the Ottoman power. The way was thus prepared for the return of the Jews (who were of eastern origin) to their own land.

Such an interpretation needs no comment. We prefer the obvious conclusion that the barrier to eastern invasion is one day to be removed and that God will gather the nations together in Palestine for destruction.

The Apostle saw three unclean spirits like frogs issue out of the mouths of the dragon, the Beast and the false prophet. Power was given to these demon spirits to perform miracles or signs, and they went forth into the whole habitable world to gather together the nations to battle.

Elliott interprets the spirits as earthquake, pestilence, and famine, whilst Cumming insists that they represent infidelity, Popery, and Tractarianism. Whatever they signify, the Revelation depicts them as loathsome and repulsive—"like frogs." In the plague on Egypt, frogs came up out of the river to enter into every house and

[1]Rev. 9. 16

defile every room. The emergence of these frog like spirits coincided with the drying up of the river. They issued from the mouths of the trinity of evil.

These filthy spirits had the power to give miraculous signs to aid them in luring on the peoples to their ultimate destruction. The natural barrier to an open revolt against God had been removed; the forces of evil were in collusion to spread their corrupting influence; miraculous signs were given for the deception of the world; and then, at the summons of the demons, the whole world seems to have been gathered together for the battle. All were united in a common bond against the Almighty.

Suddenly the narrative was broken by the cry of the Lord Jesus Christ: "Behold, I come as a thief. Blessed is he that watches and keeps his garments, that he may not walk naked, and they see his shame." The picture is of the officer who, coming in the night as a thief, finds the sentry asleep at his post, his garments carelessly laid aside, and who removes the soldier's robe, leaving him unclothed, to his shame and to the contempt and ridicule of his fellows at daybreak. Christ had already warned the Sardians that, if they did not watch, He would come upon them as a thief,[1] and He now gave similar admonishment to the saints of the tribulation days. When everything around seemed dark and faith might despair, He was about to return. There was universal laxity: let the one who was waiting for Him be watching for that Advent that his habits be undefiled.

After this parenthesis, it is revealed that the mission of the three spirits had been successful. From all parts of the world, kings and armies assembled. The prophecy states, however, that "He" (*i.e.*, God, and not merely the unclean spirits) gathered them together. The demon emissaries were but the involuntary messengers of the Almighty. "My determination," He said centuries before, "is to assemble the nations, that I may gather the kingdoms together, to pour upon them Mine indignation—all My fierce anger: for all the earth shall be devoured with the fire of My jealousy."[2] Again, Joel's prophecy declares: "I will also gather all the nations, and will bring them down into the valley of Jehoshaphat, and I will enter into judgment with them there."[3]

The assembly-point is stated to be Armageddon, or the hill of Megiddo, a district frequently mentioned in the Old Testament. Megiddo was the broad valley of Jezreel, where Barak defeated Sisera,[4] and where Josiah slew Pharaoh-nechoh.[5] "There the

[1]Rev. 3. 3 [2]Zeph. 3. 8 [3]Joel 3. 2 [4]Judges 5. 19 [5]2 Kings 23. 29

Canaanitish kings gave battle to Israel," says Scott, "but Jehovah fought with and for His people. Now the one great object which the assembled nations have before them is to crush and overthrow Israel,[1] but God intervenes and effectually destroys them and delivers His own. The early victory is here alluded to as a pledge and earnest of the latter. It is not that the actual hill of Megiddo or its valley is to be the gathering centre of the nations; its circumscribed area must forbid any such notion. But the simple meaning is that God will have gathered by Satanic agency many of the nations of the earth to Palestine, their object being to overthrow and crush Israel, and fling themselves in their combined might against Jehovah. But, alas for them, they do so only to their own destruction. God pours upon the assembled nations His fury."

The Seventh Vial

"And the seventh angel poured out his bowl upon the air; and there came a great voice out of the temple of heaven from the throne, saying, It is done. And there were lightnings, and voices, and thunders; and there was a great earthquake, such as was not since men were upon the earth, such an earthquake, so great. And the great city was divided into three parts; and the cities of the nations fell: and great Babylon was remembered before God to give her the cup of the wine of the fury of His wrath. And every island fled, and mountains were not found; and a great hail, as of a talent weight, came down out of heaven upon men; and men blasphemed God because of the plague of hail; for the plague of it was exceeding great" (16. 17-21).

At the close of the series of judgments under the seven seals, there came an indirect reference to the temple, an angel coming forth to stand at the golden incense altar to fill his censer with fire from the altar.[2] When the seventh trumpet had been sounded, the heavenly temple was opened and the ark of the covenant revealed.[3] Now, the seventh angel poured out his bowl of wrath upon the air, and again the temple came into view. A great voice out of the temple of heaven from the throne (as though the throne occupied the central place of the holy of holies) cried: "It is done." "The action of the *throne* of God ceases," says Govett; "that of *Christ* begins. This is the last stroke, ere the Saviour descends to the battle (19. 11). The smoke now clears away from the temple and leaves the priests at liberty to enter it. Hence we next see the great company of the victors and the saved before the throne at the beginning of chapter 19."

The bowl was emptied upon the air—the realm of Satan.[4] Dr. A. H. Burton, who is normally a fairly reasonable expositor, takes the view here that the prophecy may envisage the destruction

[1]Psa. 83. 3-5 [2]Rev. 8. 3-5 [3]Rev. 11. 19 [4]Eph. 2. 2

of a vast population by poison gas emanating from bombs dropped from the air. That which follows indicates the irrelevance of this suggestion.

The previous bowls were more or less localized in their effect, but since the seventh affected the air—which is, of course, universal —its action was presumably universal. As one writer says: "We may expect that, during the action of this vial, the mountaineer amid his fastnesses, the miner in his subterranean caves, the voyager upon the ocean's bosom, the Arab in his desert, the Moslem in his mosque, the Cossack on his steppes, the king upon his throne, the mother in her household, the babe in the cradle, all will feel its vibrations, receive the taint of its influence, and respond in a thousand echoes to the voice from above, 'It is done.'" That the physical atmosphere is indicated, however, is extremely doubtful although many interpreters of the historical school insist that the air simply stands for the atmospheric vehicle by which disease—blight, influenza, cholera, etc.—was conveyed after the French Revolution. Others, regarding the air merely as symbolic of the moral, social, and political atmosphere, see in the prophecy the disorganization of great political parties and the confusion in ecclesiastical and social circles in the early nineteenth century.

There is no event in past history which adequately corresponds with the passage, and there can be little doubt that what is depicted is a future and universal judgment upon everything related to man's social and moral well-being.

As a result of the outpouring of the bowl, there were lightnings, voices, and thunders, and an earthquake unprecedented for its greatness. The flashing lightning, the pealing thunder, and the mysterious voices tell of the complete convulsion of the air. But the earth, too, was shaken as never before. To quote Scott, there is "a violent disruption of all government, the total collapse of authority from the highest down to the lowest. Under it, thrones totter and fall, crowns are broken, sceptres are shivered." A literal interpretation of the earthquake is rendered impossible by what follows: it is a symbolic disturbance of widespread effect.

The terrible upheaval resulted in the division of "the great city" into three parts, and in the fall of "the cities of the nations." The contrast between the *great city* and the *cities of the nations* has led some to the conclusion that the city must be that of Jerusalem, but the Jewish metropolis is not otherwise referred to under such a title, and it is considered indubitable that the reference is to Rome, the great centre of the future revived Western Empire. The calamity which falls upon the empire results in its dismemberment: the city is rent into fractions and left completely disorganized, although not entirely destroyed.

The cities of the nations were not even partially spared, but suffered total destruction. The civic organization of nations other than those federated with Rome was completely disintegrated.

Babylon the Great came next under review for judgment. She was "remembered before God to give her the cup of the wine of the fury of His wrath." The following chapter reveals that Babylon is the devil's counterfeit of the Church of God. For her was reserved the bitterest draught of all since she was the most deeply dyed in guilt. The precise nature of the cup given her to drink is reserved for the following section; the mere fact of the judgment is mentioned here.

Moreover, every island fled. They were not destroyed, but there was a sudden recession from their normal positions. As islands are detached from the mainland, so there are isolated centres of organization and government. Even these were displaced in this overwhelming catastrophe.

In addition, the mountains were not found. "The foundations also of the mountains moved and were shaken, because He was wroth," said the Psalmist.[1] "I beheld the mountains, and lo! they trembled," declared Jeremiah, because of "His fierce anger."[2] The "seats of authority and stability, as mountains, are dissolved."

Not only were systems judged, but a great hail fell from heaven upon men. Under the first trumpet, hail, mixed with fire, and blood, fell upon grass and trees; here it fell upon men. Each hailstone weighed a talent (about 125 lbs.). Jennings remarks that "a talent is the measure of human responsibility.[3] The weight of the wrath of God is in exact proportion to the measure of responsibility; *i.e.*, to the love rejected, the blessing contemned, the privileges despised." Whilst very true, it is hardly likely that this play upon two different measures was in the mind of the Apostle as he penned the words. Hail has frequently, in the past, been one of God's "engines of war." The enormous weight of this hail, if taken literally, would be sufficient to exterminate everything. That it is symbolic is evident from the fact that the sufferers under this dreadful artillery of heaven, entrenched in their obstinacy of sin, only blasphemed God for the terrible plague. Unsoftened and impenitent, they only cried out in bitterness against the Judge.

[1]Psa. 18. 7 [2]Jer. 4. 24-26 [3]Matt. 25. 15-29

Chapter XIX

Babylon

IN the story of human declension, there is no more outstanding example than the city of Babylon. Originating as Bab-el (*the gate of God*), a centre of true worship, its degeneration was swift, and it is best known as the source of all idolatry.

Early in the world's history, a mighty hunter named Nimrod (literally *a rebel*) arose, who determined to found a world empire, and Gen. 10. 10 states that "the beginning of his kingdom was Babel . . . in the land of Shinar." The son of Cush, Nimrod has been identified by archæologists with Bar-Chus (*i.e.*, *son of Cush*), or Bacchus, "who figures among the Greek and Roman gods as the great overflowing, enlivening, healing and directing power," and also with Tammuz (or Adonis), for whom the women of Israel wept.[1] Cush himself was the son of Ham and has been identified with Hermes (the Egyptian synonym for *son of Ham*), or Mercury.

Nimrod, who was also known as Ninus, was married to Semiramis, who was probably identical with the nature goddess Rhea, or Cybele, and also with Aphrodite of Greece and Venus of Rome. The fame of Semiramis' beauty still lives in ancient history and there is little doubt that she was, as one writer declares, "the historical original of that goddess that by the ancient world was regarded as the very embodiment of everything attractive in female form, and the perfection of female beauty."

Nimrod, or Bacchus, was the first leader of human apostasy from God. All pagan mythologies and systems of idolatry show an underlying unity of character, which indicates their common origin and all may, in fact, be traced back to the Babylonian system and to the schemes of its first ruler. In Assyria, Egypt, Greece, and many widely-separated countries, this remarkable individual, under varying names, was an object of worship. "The amazing extent of the worship of this man," says Hislop, "indicates something very extraordinary in his character. Though by setting up as a king, he invaded the patriarchal system, and abridged the liberties of mankind, yet he was held by many to have conferred benefits upon

[1]Ezek. 8. 14

them that amply indemnified them for the loss of their liberties, and covered him with glory and renown. By the time he appeared, the wild beasts of the forest, multiplying more rapidly than the human race, must have committed great depredations on the scattered and straggling populations of the earth, and must have inspired terror in the minds of men. The exploits of Nimrod, therefore, in hunting down the wild beasts of the field and ridding the world of monsters, must have gained for him the character of a pre-eminent benefactor of his race. As the first great city-builder after the Flood, by gathering men together in masses, and surrounding them with walls, he enabled them to pass their days in security, free from the alarms to which they had been exposed in their scattered life. Within the battlements of a fortified city, no danger from savage animals was to be dreaded. No wonder, therefore, that the name of the 'mighty hunter,' who was at the same time the prototype of the 'god of fortifications,' should have become a name of renown."

He continued further with his work of liberation, however, and proceeded to emancipate men from the fear of God and the old patriarchal faith. The Flood left the people with a sense of awe and dread of the Almighty and His judgments, but the Nimrodic apostasy delivered them from this fear and gained for their leader the title of "Deliverer." No longer was spiritual regeneration considered essential for man; any necessary change could be effected by external means. The Bacchanalian orgies, which commemorated his history, make it "evident that he led mankind to seek their chief good in sensual enjoyment, and showed them how they might enjoy the pleasures of sin, without any fear of the wrath of a holy God. In his various expeditions, he was always accompanied by troops of women; and by music and song, and games and revelries, and everything that could please the natural heart; he commended himself to the good graces of mankind."

The great rebel was apparently cut off suddenly. Tradition has it that he was either put to death with judicial rigour for apostasy or was torn to pieces in the chase. The sudden death of the mighty hero was a catastrophic blow to the devotees of pleasure, and lamentations arose on every side.

Persian records reveal that, after his death, Nimrod was deified under the name of Orion and placed among the stars. The bruising of the serpent's head by a mighty deliverer is found in the mythology of practically all races, and the ancient world was acquainted with the Edenic promise and rightly concluded that the bruising of the heel of the woman's seed implied the death of the Deliverer. In brazen blasphemy, Semiramis proclaimed that her husband was the woman's promised seed (*Zero-ashta*—later corrupted to *Zoroaster*), whose death in pursuit of the wild beasts had really been a voluntary sacrifice for the benefit of his partisans.

The daring design so fully accorded with the inclinations of the apostate followers of the dead hunter that it was gladly accepted and worship was paid to the deified king.

At that time, the whole race (probably then about 500 families) had but one language. Breaking up their encampments and moving eastward along the Euphrates valley, they came to a fertile plain in the land of Shinar. Here they conspired to build a city and also a great tower. The A.V. suggests that the intention was to build a tower reaching to heaven, and this is usually claimed to be the origin of the heathen fable of the giants' attempt to climb the heavens, but there is some doubt as to whether there is really any connection between the historical event and the story of the Titans' war with heaven and their resultant discomfiture.

Josephus states that, quite early in human history, man arranged the astronomical signs of the Zodiac, which are to be found in precisely the same arrangement in practically every nation and country. These Zodiacal signs clearly depict the great story of redemption and re-emphasize the fact that the ancient world was fully cognisant of God's wondrous plan of salvation as foretold in Gen. 3. In order that these records of the heavens might be preserved, the ancient race constructed pillars of brick and stone, on which were inscribed the signs and predictions of the stars. The Ziggerats, or towers in which the Babylonian astrologers later made their stellar observations and prophetic deductions, are probably not unconnected with these pillars or towers. When the tower of Babel was constructed, it was not with the idea of reaching to the heavens, since the phrase is literally "a tower whose top with the heavens." As Wilson Heath writes: "It is no question of height, but of the ornamentations of the top of the tower with the Zodiac signs. Such towers, with pictures of the stars around their tops, are found in Dendera and Esneh in Egypt. The so-called 'Tower of Babel' was thus built and embellished to preserve after the Flood the revelations given before the Flood." This seems highly commendable until it is appreciated that the real purpose was to perpetuate, not the story of the coming Christ, but the false story of the deified Nimrod, who had been blasphemously substituted for the true Deliverer.

The Almighty consequently intervened, confounding the project by imposing diversity of languages upon the builders, and Babel, whose meaning was formerly "the gate of God," came to be known as the place of confusion.

The worship of Nimrod (under various names) was for long practised only in secret and herein originated the ancient "mysteries." In *Eleusinian Mysteries*, Ouvaroff has proved conclusively that Egypt, Greece, and Phœnicia all derived their religious systems and secret rites from the Babylonians. The object of these Chaldean mysteries has been clearly summed up by Hislop as the attempt "to bind all mankind in blind and absolute submission to a hierarchy entirely dependent on the sovereigns of Babylon. In the carrying out of this scheme, all knowledge, sacred and profane, came to be monopolized by the priesthood . . . The priests were the only depositories of religious knowledge." "The secret system of the Mysteries gave vast facilities for imposing on the senses of the initiated by means of the various tricks and artifices of magic," says Hislop. "Everything was so contrived as to wind up the minds of the novices to the highest pitch of excitement, that, after having surrendered themselves implicitly to the priests, they might be prepared to receive anything. After the candidates for initiation had passed through the confessional and sworn the required oaths, strange and amazing objects presented themselves."

Gradually, by the machinations of his depraved widow, Nimrod was coupled in worship with his spouse, Semiramis, and their images were set up everywhere. Nimrod's negro countenance causing offence, this difficulty was soon obviated. Since the Chaldeans believed in the transmigration of souls, it was taught that he had reappeared as a fair-complexioned, posthumous son, supernaturally born by his wife. Thus arose the worship of the mother and the child, which rapidly spread throughout the world, the cult being accompanied by corrupt and immoral practices. "The image of the queen of heaven with the babe in her arms was seen everywhere," says Ironside, "though the names might differ as the languages differed. It became the mystery-religion of Phœnicia, and by the Phœnicians was carried to the ends of the earth. Ashtaroth and Tammuz became Isis and Horus in Egypt, Aphrodite and Eros in Greece, Venus and Cupid in Italy." When the Gospel came to Egypt, the Babylonian goddess and her son were simply converted into the Virgin Mary and her Son.

The worship of Baal, introduced by Queen Jezebel, was identical with the Babylonian system.

Idolatry thus originated with Babylon, and throughout Scripture the city stands as the figure of false worship and idolatry. Upon it, God's sternest judgment must fall. It was a city of glory and splendour. "Is not this great Babylon that I have built?" asked Nebuchadnezzar.[1] Yet it was reduced to nothing. Its desolate condition is referred to in Jer. 51, and again in Isa. 13. 19, 20; 21. 9, 10; 47. 7, 8, etc. The prophecy of Jer. 51 was fulfilled in detail, and the closing verse of the chapter declares: "Thus shall Babylon sink, and shall not rise from the evil that I will bring upon her." Never again should that proud city raise her head; never again should the banks of the Euphrates know her glory.

Yet, when the Revelation is opened, Babylon reappears upon the scene. In chapter 14, an angel foretells her fall and in chapter 16. 19 declares that God will bring her into remembrance for judgment. What Babylon is this, then? The O.T. prophecies leave no future for the city, but here is an idolatrous system of the same ilk as Babylon of old represented in chapter 17 again as a woman and in chapter 18 as a city.

A comparison with the last six chapters of the Apocalypse shows that this idolatrous power is set in antithesis to another type. The great harlot of Rev. 17 is in contrast to the spotless Bride of Rev. 19, and the idolatrous city of chapter 18 is in contrast with the holy city of chapter 21. Since the Bride of the Lamb is not an actual woman and the new Jerusalem not an actual city, there is no ground for assuming that Babylon is anything but symbolical.

The Apocalyptic Babylon is an apostate religious system, which is clearly identifiable with Papal Rome, although possibly covering far more than Rome. Sargent writes: "The 'mystery' of Romanism, branded as 'Babylon,' is the same old evil of idolatry which came forth from Nimrod and Babylon. After the destruction of ancient Babylon, the source of corruption moved, and in the days of the Apostles the seat of its power was at Pergamos, the capital of the Roman government in Asia. It was there that heathenism reigned supreme. To the Church, located at Pergamos, the Lord said: 'Even where Satan's seat is.' Finally, the fundamental doctrines of this system became centred in Rome, and here it is that we find a great ecclesiastical system, known as the Papal Church, holding by the mystery of her performances the superstitious in idolatry." When the Babylonian initiates migrated from Pergamos to Italy, they settled in the Etruscan plain, from whence they propagated the Etruscan Mysteries, which were

[1]Dan. 4. 30

precisely the same as those of the old cult. When the chief priest was established in Rome, he assumed the title of Pontifex Maximus. When Julius Cæsar became "head of the State, he was elected Pontifex Maximus, and this title was held henceforth by all the Roman emperors down to Constantine the Great, who was, at one and the same time, head of the Church and high priest of the heathen!" In A.D. 378, Damasus, the then bishop of Rome, a thoroughly unprincipled individual, was appointed Pontifex Maximus and thus became the legitimate successor of the old Babylonian pontiffs, with his pontificate extending over the pagans. The College of Cardinals, with the Pope at its head, is really the counterpart of the pagan college of Pontiffs, with its Pontifex Maximus (or sovereign Pontiff) deriving from the original Council of Pontiffs at Babylon.

The worship of the queen of heaven and her son, purgatorial purification after death, holy water, priestly absolution, dedicated virgins, reservation of all knowledge to the priests, unification of political and religious control, and many another feature of the ancient Babylonian system have been taken over *en bloc* and absorbed by Papal Rome. Other systems may have a part in the Apocalyptic picture, but whatever else is portrayed, Roman Catholicism has by no means a minor part.

Chapter XX

The False Church

The Great Harlot

"And one of the seven angels, who had the seven bowls, came and spoke with me, saying, Come hither; I will show thee the judgment of the great harlot who sits upon many waters; with whom the kings of the earth have committed fornication; and the inhabitants of the earth have been made drunk with the wine of her fornication. So he carried me away in spirit to a desert; and I saw a woman sitting upon a scarlet beast, full of names of blasphemy, having seven heads and ten horns. And the woman was clothed in purple and scarlet, and had ornaments of gold and precious stones and pearls, having a golden cup in her hand full of abominations and filthiness of her fornication; and upon her forehead was a name written, Mystery, Babylon the Great, the mother of harlots and of the abominations of the earth. And I saw the woman drunken with the blood of the saints, and with the blood of the martyrs of Jesus; and when I saw her, I wondered with great wonder" (17. 1-6).

THE fall of Babylon is referred to in Rev. 14. 7 and 16. 19, but, as happens more than once in the book, the narrative is interrupted in order to revert to an incident or fact previously recorded and to reveal fresh details regarding it. So here, the judgment already mentioned is described in greater detail in chapters 17 and 18.

The seer was summoned by one of the angels of the bowls of wrath to behold the judgment of the great harlot who sat upon many waters. As the ancient Babylon found a place on the banks of the Euphrates, so this great harlot sat upon (or beside) many waters, which are interpreted in verse 15 as "peoples and multitudes and nations and tongues." She thus dominated the masses of human beings and, as the context shows, in an ecclesiastical rule. Of only one system could the description be appropriate, that is, Roman Catholicism, under the cloak of which other systems had also found a refuge.

The designation of "great harlot," with its obvious reference to spiritual adultery, at once labels the woman as an apostate system, unfaithful to the Lord Himself. With this foul system, the Beings of the earth had formed a guilty intrigue: the political leaders "committed fornication" with her. In the full consciousness of what they did, they had commerce with the Papal power and willingly gave themselves over to Rome influence and control.

Furthermore, all the earth-dwellers were "made drunk with the wine of her fornication." Jeremiah declared of the literal Babylon long before: "Babylon hath been a golden cup in the Lord's hand, that made all the earth drunken: the nations have drunk of her wine; therefore the nations are mad."[1] Those who sought initiation in the ancient Chaldean mysteries were forced to drink of an intoxicating cup, and the Apostle probably had this in mind as he referred to the mystery of the last days. The deception of false doctrines, combined with Rome's meretricious display, were the cause of a general turning from God by the major part of Christendom.

Carried away in the Spirit to a desert, the seer now beheld the one of whom the angel spoke. The literal city of Babylon is described as "the desert of the sea."[2] In Revelation, the spiritual Babylon appropriately found its congenial home in the desert—a dry and thirsty land, devoid of water. She was out of touch with the fountain of life and was spiritually dead. Sargent sees in the desert "the desolate Campagna of Rome, which for generations was one of the few uncultivated pieces of land in Europe. This condition was brought about by the raids upon imperial Rome in the fifth and sixth centuries." In confirmation, Gibbon says that "the Campagna of Rome was speedily reduced to the state of a dreary wilderness." While there may be an indirect reference to this geographical feature, the direct reference is clearly to a *spiritual* wilderness.[3] The whore was carried by a scarlet beast, which had seven heads and ten horns; and which was "full of names of blasphemy." From the description given later in the chapter, there can be no question that the beast was the revived Western Empire mentioned in Rev. 13. Riding upon the beast, the woman dominated the great apostate empire, and was supported by its military and political might. No external sign of godliness was evident in the beast. It was characterized by blatant and unashamed blasphemy. It was deliberately and unreservedly opposed to divine things.

Arrayed in purple and scarlet and decked with gold and jewels, the great harlot held in her hand a golden cup full of her adulterous abominations and filthiness. Purple and scarlet were the apparel of the Roman emperors and senators: they are also the garments of Popes and cardinals, and the identity of the woman is slowly but

[1]Jer. 51. 7 [2]Isa. 21. 1 [3]Rev. 17

surely made plain by the seer. Her ornaments were a flaunted symbol of Papal wealth, grandeur, and glory. It is not without significance that all the ornaments came out of the earth or the sea and that silver (the type of redemption) was not named among them. Here was a proud, imperious creature, glorying in her wealth; and denying the faith of Christ by life and character. In her hand was a cup of filth, and it is not irrelevant to note that Venus (whose prototype Semiramis was connected with the literal Babylon) was originally represented as bearing a cup of temptation.

As 2 Kings 23. 13, Isa. 44. 19, Ezek. 16. 36, and other Scriptures indicate, abominations, such as those which filled the harlot's golden cup, were simply a symbol of idolatry. Rome's idolatry has always been productive of immorality, and the filth which filled the cup was comprised of all her encouragements to sin, indulgences, enforced celibacy, auricular confession, conventual life, etc.

As the common prostitute wore her name upon her brow, so a name was impressed upon the forehead of the great whore: "Mystery, Babylon the Great, the mother of harlots and of the abominations of the earth." There seems a clear reference here to the ancient Chaldean mysteries, first introduced by Semiramis and impressed with "the image of her own depraved and polluted mind" (Hislop). These mysteries formed an essential part of the ancient Babylonian system of idolatry and, in more than one detail, they have been taken over and incorporated in the Papal system. The Apocalypse brands Catholicism with the marks of its Chaldean predecessor and traces its idolatry back to its source.

The appellation marked the character of the woman as the virtual parent of every idolatrous system. When the true Church has been raptured from earth, Rome will probably gather into her fold many of the so-called schismatic bodies. Reunion with the Anglican Church will then be possible, and reconciliation may even be effected with the Greek Church. Whether other religious systems will ally themselves with this great ecclesiastical power is a matter for speculation, but her title of *mother of harlots* suggests that other systems will link themselves with her.

The striking likeness of Rome is again emphasized by the fact that the woman was intoxicated with the blood of the saints and martyrs. She revelled in the murder of God's people. All the past cruelties of Rome, as well as those which still lie in the future, are compressed in the concise and graphic sketch which the Holy Spirit gives. Well might the seer be filled with awe and wonder as he gazed upon the nauseating sight.

The Mystery Explained

"And the angel said unto me, Why didst thou wonder? I will tell thee the mystery of the woman, and of the beast which carries her, which has the seven heads and the ten horns. The beast which thou sawest was, and is not, and is about to come up out of the abyss and go into destruction: and they who dwell on the earth, whose names are not written from the foundation of the world in the book of life, shall wonder, when they behold the beast that was, and is not, and shall come. Here is the mind that has wisdom: The seven heads are seven mountains, whereupon the woman sits. And there are seven kings: five have fallen, one is, and the other has not yet come; and when he comes, he must continue a little while. And the beast that was, and is not, he also is an eighth, and is of the seven, and goes into destruction. And the ten horns which thou sawest are ten kings, who have not yet received a kingdom, but receive authority as kings one hour with the beast. These have one mind and give their power and authority to the beast. These shall make war with the Lamb, and the Lamb shall overcome them; for He is Lord of lords and King of kings: and they who are with Him are called, and chosen, and faithful" (17. 7-14).

As the seer stood marvelling at the sight he beheld, an angelic being intervened to interpret the scene for him.

Long before John's vision, it was revealed to Nebuchadnezzar,[1] and to Daniel himself,[2] that the sword of world government should pass through the hands of four great empires, the Babylonian, the Medo-Persian, the Grecian, and the Roman. The latter condition of the last of these, as described in the prophecy, is one, however, in which the Roman Empire has never yet existed. The empire is to assume the form of a league of ten kingdoms, ruled over by a mighty emperor, who so completely impresses his character upon the empire that Scripture often treats the one as synonymous with the other and the ruler as the personification of the empire. This latter-day Cæsar will commence with the subjugation of three countries, after which seven others will give their power into his hands.[3]

Not only in form but also in nature will the empire be essentially different in its last stages. Daniel graphically describes the difference as a mingling of iron and miry clay, so that the empire is partly strong and partly fragile.[4] The coalition of rulers and lower classes has as its result lack of cohesion and ultimate dissolution.

It is upon this great empire that Babylon was seen sitting. As Scott says, "The woman is in the zenith of her prosperity, proud, seductive and murderous. She is on the highest pinnacle of pride and power just previous to her downfall." John reveals quite clearly the chequered history of the western empire. It "was and is not and is about to come." The Roman Empire came into being

[1]Dan. 2 [2]Dan. 7 [3]Dan. 7. 8, 24 [4]Dan. 2. 41-43

in 753 B.C. and it continued in its imperial form even in the seer's day, being ultimately destroyed in A.D. 476. Standing prophetically in a later period, the Apocalypse declares that the empire (still then in existence) had finished its first history. It *was and is not.* For fifteen centuries it has ceased to exist as a political force. It is yet to be revived out of the abyss. Satanic agency will bring it once more into being—to the amazement and wonder of all who behold the sight.

The identity of Babylon is plainly indicated, when it is stated that the seven heads of the beast represent seven mountains whereon she sits. Propertius, for example, speaks of Rome as "the lofty city on seven hills, which govern the whole world." Virgil says: "Rome has both become the most beautiful city in the world, and alone has surrounded for herself seven heights with a wall." It was commonly called the seven-hilled city. Since Babylon's authority was centred herein, it seems fairly clear that what is in view is the power and sway of the Papacy.

The seven heads are a dual figure. Not only do they represent the seven hills of Rome but also seven kinds or forms of government. Five forms had passed away, one was in existence at the time of the vision, and one still lay in the future. When John wrote there had already been five forms of government—kings, consuls, dictators, decemvirs, and military tribunes—each of which had been superseded in turn. One—the imperial introduced by Julius Cæsar—was actually in being at the date of the Apocalypse; this has also since disappeared. There remains only the final form of a federal head of a great confederacy, and the Revelation indicates that this form will continue for only a short time. The final state is to be similar in some respects to at least one of the preceding forms, but is yet to be distinct from it.

The ten horns upon the beast are undoubtedly identical with those of Dan. 7 and with the ten toes of Dan. 2. They represent ten kings and their kingdoms, which, as one writer puts it, "will be *contemporaneous* in contradistinction to the seven heads which were *successive.*" With the revival of the empire these powers voluntarily handed over their authority to the beast. Historical interpreters refer the whole passage to the Germanic tribes, but speculation as to the identity of the ten kingdoms appears quite unprofitable. Some have suggested that a reappearance is indicated of the cluster of petty contemporary kingdoms which replaced the Roman Empire on its disintegration; others insist that all countries within the limits of the old Roman Empire must be excluded; the only fact which is plain is that the ten kings, as Auberlin and Black state, are to co-ordinate in dignity and time. The "little horn" of Dan. 7 arose *among* the other horns and not *after* them. The Apocalypse also declares that these kings receive their authority as kings one hour with the Beast. Their period of rule is strictly limited by the reign of the mighty sovereign to whom they pay allegiance.

Under the sway of the great dictator, these sycophantic tributaries combined to make war upon the Lamb, only to be completely overthrown. The details of the conflict are not given until chapter 19, but the victory of the One who is Lord of lords and King of kings is announced immediately reference is made to the future battle, and the character of His followers is stated to be "called and chosen and faithful." In other words, His elect—those redeemed by His blood—who have walked in fidelity to Him on earth, form His victorious host in the day of martial triumph.

The Harlot's Destruction

"And he saith to me, The waters which thou sawest, where the harlot sits, are peoples and multitudes and nations and tongues. And the ten horns which thou sawest, and the beast, these shall hate the harlot, and shall make her desolate and naked and shall eat her flesh, and shall burn her with fire; for God has put in their hearts to do His mind, and to act with one mind, and to give their kingdom to the beast, until the words of God shall be fulfilled. And the woman which thou sawest is the great city, which has kingship over the kings of the earth" (17. 15-18).

The angel now gave the seer the last details of the interpretation. The waters beside which the mystic Babylon sat were the masses of mankind—the four principal divisions of the human race being particularized.

The rulers of the Western Empire made use of the religious system, portrayed in the harlot, for the unification of the empire, but on the achievement of that desired end, the practical value of the system had disappeared. The beast and his satellite powers became restive under her intolerant sway and, coveting her wealth, turned upon her to "glut their vengeance on the guilty system that had so long enslaved them." Just as Henry VIII plundered the English churches and monasteries, so will this later church suffer spoliation and destruction at the hands of the political power. "There seems a gradation in the punishment meted out to the harlot," says Walter Scott. "First, *hated;* this refers to the loathing and disgust with which her late confederates and supporters regard her. Second, made *desolate;* despoiled of her wealth and utterly wasted.[1] Third, *naked;* stripped of her purple and scarlet robes,

[1]Rev. 18. 19

she appears before all in her true character as a shameless and abandoned woman,[1] her moral nakedness and shame apparent to all. Fourth, '*eat her flesh*'; there is significance in the fact that 'flesh' is in the plural; the abundance of the wealth and all she gloried in is devoured by her late admirers, now her bitterest enemies (*cf.* James 5. 3; Psa. 27. 2; Micah 3. 2, 3). Fifth, '*burn her with fire*'; utter social and political ruin is here indicated. The main element in the destruction of the literal Babylon was water.[2] The mystical city of that name 'shall be utterly burned with fire'."[3] The end of the great Roman Catholic system is to be destroyed by the very powers which allowed her to exercise despotic control over the lives of their subjects.

The Holy Spirit makes it clear that the action of the western kings was not by their own initiative. Their minds were directly influenced by God and He inspired them to act as His unconscious instruments. He put into their hearts unitedly to fulfil His will in their complete subjugation to the Beast until the divine purposes were accomplished. They had been subject to the ecclesiastical authority; they now willingly gave their allegiance to the civil power.

The angel again confirmed the identity of the harlot. It was "the great city, which has kingship over the kings of the earth." Sargent sees in this the possibility of a somewhat wider interpretation than merely Rome, and he points out that, "by the edict of Caracalla, the city was decreed to be considered co-extensive with the empire." But the reference to the Catholic system is too patent for any doubt to arise. Roman Catholicism finds its centre in Rome and is almost always associated with the city. Moreover, in greater or less degree all countries are affected by the power of this vast system. Even nowadays, nations which are nominally Protestant take note of the view of the Papacy, accredit representatives to the Vatican, and give at least outward recognition of many of the Papal claims. Babylon is a fitting type for this far-reaching system.

[1]Ezek. 23. 29; Rev. 3. 18 [2]Jer. 51 [3]Rev. 18. 8

Chapter XXI

Babylon the City

Babylon's Fall

"And after these things I saw another angel descending out of heaven, having great authority: and the earth was lightened with his glory. And he cried with a strong voice, Fallen, fallen, is Babylon the great, and has become the habitation of demons, and a hold of every unclean spirit, and a hold of every unclean and hateful bird; for all nations have drunk of the wine of the fury of her fornication, and the kings of the earth have committed fornication with her, and the merchants of the earth have been enriched through the abundance of her luxuries" (18. 1-3).

In chapter 17 the destruction of Babylon, the great whore, is attributed to the kings of the Western Empire, but in chapter 18 Babylon is again seen—this time under the judgment of God. The majority of commentators insist that the two chapters relate to the same event, the earlier passage referring to the denudation and burning inflicted by human agency, and the latter to the devastating judgment poured out by the Almighty. Ironside suggests that Babylon will continue to the very end of the tribulation period, its destruction by the Beast and his confederates being a last frantic effort to rid themselves of this dreadful incubus just before they are destroyed by the appearing of the Lord in glory. It is clear,[1] however, that the deification of the Beast and the direction of worship to him (which could scarcely run concurrently with another recognized system of religion) will conclude with the second advent of Christ, and the destruction of the religious Babylon will therefore presumably take place prior to the entry of the Emperor into the temple.

The contents of chapter 18 suggest that it is not a religious system which is in view, but rather a social and commercial one. It is a political and economic Babylon, not an ecclesiastical one. As Bruce Corbin says, "The final Babylon will be that city which holds complete dominion and control over the governments and financial and commercial affairs of the nations." The historical interpreter sees in the picture the downfall of a pagan Rome, but the prophecy goes much further than that.

[1] 2 Thess. 2

In an earlier scene, an angel had emerged from heaven with a declaration that Babylon, who had made all the nations drink of the wine of her fornication, had fallen.[1] Almost identical phraseology was now repeated. John saw a mighty angel, possessed of great authority, descending from heaven with the triumphant announcement of the city's fall. The outshining glory of this radiant being lightened the earth (an expression used of Jehovah in Ezek. 18. 2), and a comparison with chapter 10. 1 (cf. also Psa. 72. 19; Isa. 6. 3; etc.) indicates that the angel is none other than our Lord Himself. As one writer says: "He by Whose glory the whole earth was illuminated can be no other than the Lord of the earth."

His cry was repetitive: "Fallen, fallen, is Babylon the Great," implying a dual fall—first of the religious system and then of the political and commercial economy. The first was the great counterfeit of the true Church, for whom He shed His precious blood, and the measure of His love for His blood-bought Bride is the measure of His hatred of that false system which assumes her place and title. He therefore issued forth in all the glory of His might to proclaim the fall of the harlot and also the end of the godless economy of the latter days.

"Babylon, the glory of the kingdoms, the beauty of the Chaldeans' pride, shall be as when God overthrew Sodom and Gomorrah," declared Isaiah of the ancient city.[2]

The Apocalyptic announcement reiterated the message. The prophet foretold that the city should be the habitation of owls, ostriches, jackals, and dogs, while demons danced there. The Revelation paints the picture as a habitation of demons and a hold of impure spirits and of hateful and unclean birds. Ruins and desolate places are frequently regarded in Scripture as the home of evil spirits.[3] Bengel maintains that the impure spirits of whom the angel spoke were the spirits of human beings who, during their lifetime, had hardened themselves in impurity, but we see nothing to support this view, since the term "demons" is clearly interchangeable with "unclean spirits" in more than one passage.

Evil forces hold this Babylon in their grasp. As Corbin says, "Satan's political and economic system is in the control of demon-possessed men. It is filled with foul-spirited men, who conduct governmental and business affairs like greedy vultures. What a picture of the wind-up of present forms of materialistic commercialism and soulless finance." The commercial realm is not merely

[1]Rev. 14. 8 [2]Isa. 13. 19 [3]Isa. 34. 14; Matt. 12. 43

godless: it is controlled by evil forces and, when every spiritual restraint is withdrawn, those influences will be exerted to the full. Behind the foul traffickers in women's bodies are impure spirits. At the back of frenzied finance and ruthless, dishonest commerce are spiritual forces. In many countries the political world is full of nepotism, jobbery, and graft, and behind it all are unseen, demoniacal powers. The whole cosmic system—essentially opposed to God as it is—is controlled by the devil himself.

Even if the chapter be referred to the ecclesiastical system of Babylon, the same conditions are discoverable. Beneath the external decadence and the teachings which so readily open the door to sin are evil forces and, as Jennings remarks, "It is not popes or councils, but demons that have promulgated the doctrines of celibacy, abstinence from meats,[1] and all the distinctive dogmas of what claims to be the Church."

The unclean birds alluded to by the angels are also of the same character, as the parable of the mustard tree[2] indicates. As the evil birds took shelter in the branches of Christendom's tree, so did the unclean fowls find refuge in the ruins of Babylon's city.

All nations had drunk of the wine of the fury of Babylon's fornication, declared the angel. "As wine makes the drinkers helpless, so does her wrath the nations," says Hengstenberg. "The making of the nations drunk with wine is a very common image in the Old Testament. The point of comparison is always the impotence, helplessness, misery, degradation, shamefulness of the condition."[3] It is more than adultery. It is rather the deception of the dupe for the gratification of lust—the insinuation into the affections of the nations for the purpose of ensnaring and destroying them (*e.g.*, the fornication of Nahum 3. 4 is described as deceit in verse 1).

The kings of the earth were also named as having committed fornication with great Babylon. These can hardly be the kings of the Western Empire by whom the harlot was destroyed, since in this chapter they bewailed the fall of Babylon. They had been seduced, consciously or unconsciously, by a system which destroyed all sense of rightness and morality and had given their power to evil forces.

Babylon had been a source of enrichment to the merchants of the earth and they also bewailed her fall. "She, who drugged the nations with her intoxicating draughts, who flaunted as the paramour of earthly sovereigns, whose luxury and splendour enriched

[1] 1 Tim. 4. 3 [2] Matt. 13. 32 [3] Hab. 2. 15, 16; Psa. 60. 3; Nahum 3. 11; Obad. 16

the merchants of the world, was now left empty and desolate, like a ruined city in whose tenantless abodes all unclean creatures make their dwelling-place" (Baines).

The Call to Separation

"And I heard another voice from heaven, saying, Come out of her, My people, that ye have not fellowship in her sins, and that ye do not receive of her plagues; for her sins have been heaped on one another up to heaven, and God has remembered her iniquities" (18. 4, 5).

Another voice (not another *angel*) was heard from heaven, calling the people of God to separation from the evil Babylonian system. The voice was clearly divine, since it addressed the saints as "My people." Those addressed could scarcely be Christians and could only be the Jewish saints of that latter day, but the words might well be applied to God's people in every age.

Even now from an ecclesiastical point of view, the summons has had a constant application. The Reformation itself was a revolt from the sinful condition of Papal Rome and, at many periods of history, there has been an outgathering of a faithful remnant to God. When the condition of an apostate body is irremediable, there is only one course open to the loyal few. The divine voice called to those of Babylon's day: "Come out of her, My people, that ye have not fellowship in her sins, and that ye do not receive of her plagues."

"Flee out of the midst of Babylon, and save every man his life; be ye not cut off in her iniquity," cried the prophet Jeremiah[1] in an earlier day. Utter and complete destruction was about to fall upon the guilty system and the Lord would, if possible, deliver His own.

As in that day, so in this, many have become enmeshed in the toils of Babylon. Greed of gold, the lust for power, the grasp for worthless baubles and empty honours characterize not only the world at large but many a professing Christian too. Principles seem to count for nothing where personal aggrandisement is at stake, and spiritual testimony is only too frequently sacrificed for temporary benefit. "Come out of her," is the cry of the Lord. The Christian should be of another ilk, and fellowship with the world cannot be consonant with communion with Christ.

As the stones of the first tower of Babel were heaped together in that lofty pile, so the sins of the last Babylon were heaped upon one another until they reached up to heaven.[2] So great had become

[1]Jer. 51. 6 [2]Jer. 51. 9

her guilt that God could no longer overlook it and the divine voice recorded that He had remembered her iniquities.

The Recompense of Sin

"Recompense her even as she has recompensed; and double to her double according to her works. In the cup which she has mixed, mix to her double. So much as she has glorified herself and lived luxuriously, so much torment and sorrow give her. Because she says in her heart, I sit a queen and am no widow; and I shall in no wise see sorrow. Therefore shall her plagues come, death and sorrow and famine, and she shall be burnt with fire; for strong is the Lord God who has judged her" (18. 6-8).

"Recompense her according to her work," said Jeremiah of Babylon,[1] but the Apocalypse goes much further than this. "Recompense her even as she has recompensed," cried the voice from heaven, "and double to her double according to her works." Here was the cry of retribution—a cry which would be foreign to the child of God in this dispensation but which is absolutely appropriate to the faithful Jew in the last days. A full recompense for her persecution of God's people was to be meted out to her. The double (or the *counterpart*) should be given her for the double, according to her works. The judgment should be in direct proportion to the crime. The cup which she had mixed for others should find its counterpart in one mixed for her. The measure of her haughtiness and ostentatious pride, of her glory and luxury, should be the measure of her torment and sorrow.

If this is—as so many expositors suggest—a type of the false Church, the expressions used are very significant. Instead of clothing herself in widow's weeds in memory of her absent Lord, Babylon sat as a queen and no widow. Confident that sorrow would never be her portion, she received the full blast of divine wrath in the fourfold plague of death, sorrow, famine, and fire. Whether the words are taken literally or figuratively, the picture they present is that of a judgment which spells complete and final destruction, attended by suffering and torment.

The first Babylon commenced in rebellion against God and throughout history the apostate system has set itself against the Almighty. Heaven now gave the answer to the challenge of the centuries and the divine voice pronounced that "strong is the Lord God who has judged her." His might was now exerted to dash to pieces the rival claimant to His glory, and His strength was evidenced in her utter and complete destruction.

[1]Jer. 50. 29

The Mourning over Babylon's Fall

"And the kings of the earth who have committed fornication, and lived luxuriously with her, shall weep and wail over her, when they see the smoke of her burning. And they shall stand afar off, through fear of her torment, saying, Woe, woe, the great city, Babylon, the strong city. For in one hour is thy judgment come. And the merchants of the earth weep and mourn over her, because no one buys their merchandise any more; merchandise of gold, and silver, and precious stones, and pearls, and fine linen; and purple and silk, and scarlet, and all thyine-wood, and every article in ivory, and every article in most precious wood, and in brass, and in iron, and in marble, and cinnamon, and ammonum, and incense, and unguent, and frankincense, and wine and oil, and fine flour, and wheat, and cattle, and sheep, and of horses and of chariots, and of bodies, and souls of men. And the ripe fruits which were the lust of thy soul have departed from thee, and all fair and splendid things have perished from thee, and thou shalt no longer find such things. The merchants of such wares, who had been enriched by her, shall stand afar off for fear of her torment, weeping and mourning, saying, Woe, woe, the great city, which was clothed with fine linen and purple and scarlet, and had ornaments of gold and precious stones and pearls; for in one hour is so great wealth laid desolate. And every steersman, and everyone who sailed to any place, and sailors, and all who exercise their calling on the sea, stood afar off, and cried when they saw the smoke of her burning, saying, What city is like the great city? And cast dust upon their heads, and cried, weeping and mourning, saying, Woe, woe, the great city, by which all who had ships in the sea were enriched through her costliness; for in one hour she has been made desolate" (18. 9-19).

The fall of Babylon affected the whole world. The vast commercial and economic system, which had brought nations and kingdoms into its toils, suddenly collapsed without warning, and so complete was its destruction that the Apocalypse depicts it as a mighty conflagration, which struck fear into the hearts of the spectators. From every quarter rose the wails of those whose temporal prosperity had been destroyed. Kings, merchants, and mariners joined in the bitter lamentation, "Woe, woe, the great city," whose judgment had come "in one hour."

The details of the picture which the Revelation gives indicate clearly that Babylon was the personification of the commercial spirit. It is significant that Scripture gives no commendation of Solomon's commercial enterprises and that it makes no mention of commerce in the new earth. The spirit of commerce is opposed to the things of God. "As a nail sticketh fast between the joinings of stones," said the son of Sirach, "so doth sin stick close between buying and selling."[1] There may be no principle violated in buying and selling. Integrity may mark every deal, and yet selfishness, covetousness, and unscrupulousness do undoubtedly spring from the commercial source. "Exchange on just and right

[1]Ecclesiasticus 27. 2

principles may be a thing of beneficence and good, involving nothing against God or His truth," says one writer. "But the tendency is otherwise. The disposition is to concentration and consolidation on selfish principles for selfish ends. The struggle is continually more and more to monopolize, to crush out rivalry and competition, and to enter into world-wide combinations to seize first one interest and then another, till everything is finally swallowed up in one great centralized aristocracy of unbounded wealth, to which all the kings and governments on the earth must truckle." "How hardly shall they that have riches enter the Kingdom of God," said our Lord. "It is easier for a camel to go through the eye of a needle than for a rich man to enter the Kingdom of God."[1]

Combines to-day are slowly squeezing out the small business man. Trade federations are leading to the centralization of wealth and power. For many years, world-wide cartels have had but one thing in view, and arbitrarily and ruthlessly, that object has been pursued. Into the hands of the great Colossus of "big business" all control is rapidly being drawn, until one fears for the future of free enterprise and competition. Herein are really the formative principles of apostacy. As B. W. Newton asks contemptuously: "Have we heard nothing respecting the wondrous results expected from commerce in making nations happy, in bringing men together in ties of amity and brotherhood, in developing the resources of the earth, in making nations conscious of their mutual dependence on each other, and so effecting, by the suggestions of self-interest, a result which the Gospel (it is said) has failed to accomplish?"

It was just when human schemes were reaching fruition that Babylon fell. The kings of the earth, who had prostituted their honour and enjoyed illicit intercourse with the evil system, wept and wailed as they stood fearfully watching the smoke rising from the dreadful conflagration. They had been enamoured of her power and wealth, they had sold themselves to her desires, and had encouraged and supported her policies, but now, in an hour, she was completely ruined, and the mighty force upon which they had relied was stricken down. All the advantages and benefits they had received from their association with Babylon had now come to an end, and it was impossible to determine the ultimate effect of her mighty fall. Well might fear grip their hearts.

When the fulfilment of the prophecy actually does occur, the

[1]Mark 10. 23-25

devastation wrought by God's judgment of the corrupt commercial and economic system will be universal. Great mercantile powers will experience unprecedented difficulties. The whole structure will be shaken, as the Almighty demonstrates His opinion of the greed and unprincipled lust for gold.

Those principally affected by the catastrophe were, of course, the merchants. They had thrived whilst the demand for their wares continued. As the vast system grew and its power increased, so was their prosperity enhanced. The schemes of Babylon transmuted everything to gold, but now the very foundations of their economic existence were shaken. From factory, warehouse, store, and counting-house the merchants poured forth to weep over the burning of Babylon. They had filled her markets with every kind of merchandise and the Revelation details eight different classes:

(1) Precious metals and jewels (gold, silver, precious stones, and pearls).
(2) Costly clothing (fine linen—or byssus—purple, silk, and scarlet).
(3) Furniture materials (thyine-wood and ivory).
(4) Vessels (of wood, brass, iron, and marble).
(5) Perfumes (cinnamon, ammonum, unguent, and frankincense).
(6) Food (wine, oil, flour, wheat, cattle, and sheep).
(7) Conveyances (horses and chariots).
(8) Slaves (bodies and souls of men).

The merchants' distress was rooted in the fact that no one now would want their wares. Their prosperity had disappeared in one hour. So far as Babylon was concerned, the ripe fruits which delighted her and the dainty and precious things in which she took such pleasure were now for ever gone. The merchants stood and mourned over the great city which had been such a wonderful market and bewailed that in one hour so great wealth had been laid desolate.

Ship captains, travellers, and sailors also wept as they threw dust upon their heads. From all corners of the globe they had brought precious things, but their cargo would now no longer be wanted. Their livelihood had disappeared in one hour. Their grief was inconsolable as they realized the extent of the calamity. Babylon had fallen and, in her fall, she had dragged down all who had ministered to her needs and desires. The mariners, enriched by the demands of the great system, mourned over the burning city.

The whole commercial and economic structure had been broken up.

The irremediable catastrophe called forth universal lamentation. It is not difficult to visualize even now the widespread consternation and fear which would eventuate if the present economic systems of the world were irretrievably destroyed. But these systems are only moving towards the great culmination portrayed in the Apocalypse—great Babylon, in which will be concentrated the mercantile and economic power, and which will be the centre of utilitarian philosophy. The day may not be very far distant when the development may become more rapid and the vast Babylonian organization gradually come into full growth. When that day comes, the God, who prefers a vine and a fig tree for every man to the ruthless dictatorship of Babylon, will intervene in judgment upon that soulless system.

The End of the City

"Rejoice over her, thou heaven, and ye saints and apostles and prophets; for God has judged your judgment on her. And a strong angel took up a stone like a great millstone, and cast it into the sea, saying, Thus with violence shall Babylon the great city be cast down and shall be found no more at all. And the voice of harpists and musicians and flute-players and trumpeters shall be heard no more at all in thee: and no artificer of any art shall be found any more at all in thee; and the sound of millstone shall be heard no more at all in thee; and the light of a lamp shall shine no more at all in thee; and the voice of bridegroom and bride shall be heard no more at all in thee; for thy merchants were the great ones of the earth; for by thy sorcery have all the nations been deceived. And in her was found the blood of prophets and saints, and of all the slain upon the earth" (18. 20-24).

Three classes (kings, merchants, and mariners) mourned on earth at the judgment of Babylon, but three classes in heaven (saints, apostles, and prophets) were called upon to rejoice therein. Unrestrained jubilation broke forth as the people of God were at last vindicated and as retribution was meted out to the city which had persecuted and martyred them. God had finally avenged them upon their adversary.

The seer then beheld a strong angel hurl a great stone, like a millstone, into the sea as a symbol of the violent destruction of Babylon. Our Lord, when on earth, declared of the one who offended a believing child that it were better for him that a millstone were hung about his neck and that he were drowned in the depth of the sea. To the neck of the great godless power, a tremendous millstone is virtually hung that she might be hurled into the abyss of judgment. Thus with violence was the mighty city cast down, never again to be found.

"No more at all," should she be found; "no more at all," should songs fill her streets; "no more at all" should mechanic or artificer be found in her; "no more at all" should the women grind their corn in the city; "no more at all" should the light of lamp illumine the night; "no more at all" should the bridal procession enliven the stillness of evening with its joyous shouts; it was a picture of utter desolation. "The world's greatest power will be concentrated there, which all the kings of the earth delight to court and serve; but in one hour all her greatness, might, and majesty came to nought. She will be a mart for the nations, enriching multitudes, on land and sea, but in one day the harvest of her soul's desire is gone, and all her bright and dainty things perish, with no one left to buy or enjoy them any more. She had great riches, and was clothed in fine linen and purple and scarlet, and decked with gold and precious stone and pearl, but not a scrap or fragment of all her costliness and treasure is left. She was the paradise of musicians, harp-singers, flute-players, and trumpeters; for these are always a feature of a rich, gay, luxurious, and worldly city; but every note is silenced, and no voice of song or dance or opera is ever heard there again. The finest artists and artisans of the world had found there a very Golconda, but in one hour their glorious Elysium is gone. It was the centre of the grandest of bridals, and the sublime resort of grand bridal tours, but with one stroke of heaven's judgment, every sound of joy is hushed, and the voice of bridegroom and bride ceased to be heard there any more" (Seiss).

Three reasons were given for the guilty city's fall. First, her merchants were the great ones of the earth." Her vast transactions had so enriched the traders and merchants that they proudly exalted themselves as the great ones of the earth. The disciples of Christ are humble and lowly, and earthly greatness is not for them. "To become great on earth," says Govett, "discloses secret unbelief of the glories of heaven." Earth's greatness must end in destruction and the one who seeks position and glory here expresses his disbelief of the threatened judgment.

Secondly, by Babylon's sorcery, all nations had been deceived. Here was a potent ingredient in her cup of doom. Many commentators see actual spiritism and necromancy here, and the growth in the practice of intercourse with spirits lends colour to this view. Magicians were formerly State officials in Babylon. But Seiss is probably correct when he suggests that what is intended is "some bewitching attractiveness going along with a mercantile system, and drawing after it the admiration and sympathy of the world.

Meretricious allurement, gathering around it the homage of governments and kings, is the idea." It is the deception by philosopher and political economist—the glorification of human cupidity as a desirable end—the distortion of covetousness as benignity.

Thirdly, the blood of prophets and saints of all the slain upon earth was found in her. Wordsworth maintains that this clearly points to Rome. "She has erected the prisons, and prepared the rack, and lighted the fires of what she calls the holy office of the Inquisition in Italy, Spain, America, and India. She lauds one of the canonised popes, Pius V, in her breviary, as an inflexible Inquisitor. She has engraven the massacre of St. Bartholomew's Day on her papal coins and there represents it as a work done by an angel from heaven." There may be a reference to Rome here, but the primary reference is doubtless to the untold number of victims of the unscrupulous avarice of the servants of the Babylonian system. An irreconcilable antagonism was felt for those who were animated by the spirit of Christ, and their intolerable witness to Him cost them their lives. But God, in His turn, dealt with the guilty city and for ever removed her testimony from earth.

Chapter XXII

The Advent of the King

Rejoicing in Heaven

"After these things I heard as a loud voice of a great multitude in heaven, saying, Hallelujah: the salvation and the glory and the power of our God: for true and righteous are His judgments; for He has judged the great whore, who corrupted the earth with her fornication, and has avenged the blood of His servants out of her hand. And a second time they said, Hallelujah. And her smoke goes up for ever and ever. And the twenty-four elders and the four living creatures fell down and worshipped God Who sits upon the throne, saying, Amen, Hallelujah. And a voice came out of the throne, saying, Praise our God, all ye His servants, and ye that fear Him, small and great. And I heard as a voice of a great multitude, and as a voice of many waters, and as a voice of mighty thunders, saying, Hallelujah, for the Lord our God the Almighty has taken to Himself kingly power" (19. 1-6).

ON earth, the downfall of Babylon gave rise to mourning and lamentation, but in heaven the same event became the subject of rejoicing. Three different classes on earth voiced their dolorous plaint; the redeemed, the twenty-four elders, the four living creatures, and the throne all rejoiced together in heaven.

Chap. 18. 20 called upon saints, apostles, and prophets to join in the song of joy. In response thereto, the apostle heard the loud voice of a great multitude ascribing praise to God. Four times over, the shout of "Hallelujah" arose in triumphal celebration of the victory of God over the guilty Babylon. The word, "Hallelujah," as Hengstenberg points out, "is found in the whole of the New Testament only here, where it occurs four times in reference to the victory of God over the earth, the signature of which is four. It is borrowed from the Psalms, of which fifteen begin or end with Hallelujah." Its original mention is: "The sinners shall be consumed from the earth, and the wicked shall be no more. Praise the Lord, my soul, Hallelujah."[1] The circumstances outlined in the Psalm will be fulfilled—at least in part—in the day of Babylon's doom and, as the Psalm indicates, the destruction of the wicked will simply lead to the lauding of the God by whom destruction comes.

The great multitude burst forth into a doxology, ascribing

[1]Psa. 104. 35

salvation, glory, and power to the God of justice. (The similarity to Matt. 6. 13 is deserving of notice.) The truth and righteousness of His judgments formed the appropriate basis for the song of joy.

When the fifth seal was opened, the souls of the slain under the altar cried out for vengeance upon their murderers. "How long . . . dost Thou not judge and avenge our blood on them that dwell upon the earth?"[1] The answer was now given. God had judged the evil system which had corrupted the earth with her policy of religious fornication and had avenged the blood of His servants (*lit.* "bondmen") at her hand. The reference to 2 Kings 9. 7, where God declared that He would avenge the blood of all His servants *out of the hand of Jezebel*, is clear. "So long as the blood remained unavenged, she had it in her hand, under her power," says one writer. "By means of the revenge, it is withdrawn from her."

A second time the cry of "Hallelujah" burst forth, and it was added that the smoke of the guilty Babylon goes up for ever and ever. Of Edom, the prophet Isaiah declared that her land should be burning pitch, never extinguished by day or night, but that "its smoke shall go up for ever and ever." The permanence and finality of the judgment was an additional reason for the praise of God's people.

The twenty-four elders and the four living creatures prostrated themselves in worship before the Occupant of the Throne as they also voiced their "Hallelujah." This is the last mention of the elders, the Church appearing on the scene next as the Bride.

A voice from the Throne then called upon all the people of God to praise Him, and immediately like the voice of a great multitude or of many waters or of mighty thunders, came the response of the people of God, with a final cry of "Hallelujah." The song of praise swelled up to the full, not merely now because of Babylon's destruction, but also because the Almighty God had now entered upon His kingdom. "He now reigned as the Lord God Omnipotent," says J. N. Darby, "that character in which He dealt with the earth, whether as God, Creator, Promiser, and Shield of His people while strangers, or the everlasting Accomplisher of all He had promised, Jehovah, Elohim, Shaddai. All these He took now in power and reigned." The complete removal of sin had not yet taken place, but God had commenced to display His regal power and victory already attended His acts.

The historical interpreter maintains that the period described

[1] Rev. 6. 10

falls within the fourth and fifth centuries. Grotius refers the prophecy to the capture of Rome by Attila, but Bossuet sees in it the capture of the city by Alarich. Others declare that "what was historically realised in the course of centuries is in the prophecy compressed into one scene," but there seems no reason to interpret the passage on any other basis than the futurist.

The Marriage of the Lamb

"Let us rejoice and exult and give Him glory; for the marriage of the Lamb is come, and His wife has made herself ready. And it was given to her that she should be clothed in fine linen, bright and pure; for the fine linen is the righteousness of the saints. And he says to me, Write, Blessed are they who are called to the marriage supper of the Lamb. And he says to me, These words are true (they are the words) of God. And I fell before his feet to worship him. And he says to me, See thou do it not. I am thy fellow-servant and the fellow-servant of thy brethren who have the testimony of Jesus. Worship God. For the testimony of Jesus is the spirit of prophecy" (19. 7-10).

The triumphant Hallelujah of the exulting multitude swelled out in a song of rejoicing. The context makes it clear that the vast choir did not include the Bride of the Lamb, but it is probable that the whole of the redeemed otherwise were embraced. In their joy, they ascribed glory to God because the marriage of the Lamb was about to take place.

The normal order was reversed. On earth, it is customary to speak of the marriage of the bride; here, it was the marriage of the Bridegroom. Our Lord spoke of Himself as the Bridegroom,[1] and John the Baptist also referred to Him in that character.[2] Psalm 45 and many other Scriptures refer to the union of Christ with His Bride.

A certain measure of difficulty exists in regard to the Bride. In the Old Testament, Israel is described as the wife of Jehovah;[3] because of her sin, she was divorced by Jehovah,[4] but in a coming day, she will be reunited to Him.[5] She can hardly, however, be said to satisfy the type of the Bride of the Lamb. The Apostle Paul declares that he had espoused the Corinthian believers to one man, to present them as a chaste virgin to Christ.[6] He again refers to earthly marriage as typical of the relationship of Christ to His Church.[7] There can be little question that the Bride of the Lamb is the Church. The whole of the believers from Pentecost[8] to the Rapture[9] form part of that glorious company.

The Psalmist declares that the queen's "clothing is of wrought

[1]Matt. 9. 15 [2]John 3. 29 [3]Jer. 3. 14; Isa. 54. 5; Ezek. 16, etc. [4]Hos. 2. 2
[5]Hos. 2. 19, etc. [6]2 Cor. 11. 2 [7]Eph. 5. 23-32 [8]Acts 2 [9]1 Thess. 4

gold; she shall be brought unto the king in raiment of embroidery."[1]

The seer states that the bride had made herself ready and that she was "clothed in fine linen, bright and pure," the fine linen being interpreted as "the righteousness of the saints." During the believer's life on earth, he prepares himself for the coming day. His righteous actions become his garb in the day of nuptial bliss. Habits and actions are to the soul as the clothes are to the body, and the life in this temporal scene determines the clothing of the eternal day.

John the Baptist referred to himself as a friend of the Bridegroom and, in Psalm 45 once more, the king's bride is described as having virgin companions who follow her. So also in the Apocalypse, John was instructed to write, "Blessed are they who are called to the marriage supper of the Lamb." Whilst the privileged position of bride is reserved for the Church, the redeemed of other ages and dispensations found a place at the bridal banquet.

Precisely what is to be understood by the marriage is not plainly stated. Vaughan regards it as "the ideal concourse and combination of the blessed company of all faithful people on their entrance into rest." Dusterdieck sees in it "Christ's distribution of the eternal reward of grace to His faithful ones, who then enter with Him into the full glory of the heavenly life." Lange describes it as "the reciprocal operation of a spiritual fellowship of love" and says that it represents "the union of the whole body of the saints with a personally present Christ in glory and government—the establishment of the Kingdom." It is at least the union of Christ with His people and the formal acknowledgment of them as His co-partners in glory and power. The bridal supper is the place at which this full acknowledgment is made and at which the social joy of the guests is fully expressed.

The certainty of the facts was then emphasized by the angelic statement that the words were, as Alford puts it, "the very truth of God and shall veritably come to pass." In response, the Apostle fell down at the angel's feet to worship him, but was immediately checked. Worship is due to God alone, and the angel at once declared that he was a fellow-servant of John and of those who had the testimony of Jesus. Even the angelic hierarchy are only the servants of God and worship of these noble beings is idolatry. God alone is the true object of worship.

"The testimony of Jesus is the spirit of prophecy," said the angel. "The testimony of Jesus in the Apocalypse," says Scott, "is of

[1]Psa. 45. 13, 14

a prophetic character, referring to His public assumption of governmental power to be displayed in the Kingdom."

The Faithful and True

"And I saw the heaven opened, and behold, a white horse, and One sitting on it, called Faithful and True, and He judges and makes war in righteousness. And His eyes are a flame of fire, and on His head were many diadems, and He had a name written which no one knows but He Himself; and He is clothed with a garment dipped in blood; and His name is called the Word of God. And the armies which are in heaven followed Him upon white horses, clad in fine linen, white and pure. And out of His mouth goes a sharp two-edged sword, that with it He might smite the nations; and He shall rule them with an iron rod; and He treads the wine-press of the fury of the wrath of the Almighty God. And He has upon His garment and upon His thigh a name written, King of kings, and Lord of lords" (19. 11-16).

Following immediately upon the bliss and joy of the nuptial scene came the final scenes of judgment. Out of the opened heaven, John saw a mighty Conqueror ride forth, of whose identity there can be no doubt. He went forth on a white horse, emblematic of His judicial righteousness, for the purpose of judging and making war in righteousness. "The powers of judging and making war are often separated in earthly sovereignties, but it is only a conventional separation. They necessarily go together. Wherever there is war, there is first a judgment made or entertained against those upon whom it is made or in behalf of those whom it is to benefit. The general in the field is simply the sheriff and hangman of the court" (Seiss).

The name of the Rider is stated to be Faithful and True, and also the Word of God, thus making it perfectly evident that it was Christ alone who was in view. "Against Him, whose name is the Word of God, all His enemies are but as stubble to the fire," says Bengel. "With the spirit or breath of His lips, He will slay the wicked." His eyes were like a flame of fire, searching in their consuming omniscience, piercing through the mask of hypocritical deceit to discern the sin, and penetrating the darkness to discover its hidden foulness. Before His all-seeing gaze, His foes might well tremble in dread.

Many diadems upon His head revealed the absolute sovereignty and authority of this mighty Conqueror. An ineffable and unknowable name was His, of which He alone had knowledge.

A garment dipped in blood was His clothing. As one writer says, "This conquering Hero is not now for the first time to try His capacities for war. Who but He was the vanquisher of the six great blasphemous world-powers already dead and gone? And as the seventh and last and worst of all is now to be overwhelmed, and the same almighty Conqueror comes forth to execute the doom, He properly comes in the same garments, worn and stained on so many battlefields, indicating that He comes in the same capacity and with the same invincible power." His bloody robe is the witness of impending judgment, thorough and decisive.

Armies clad in white and pure fine linen followed Him upon white horses. The mighty Conqueror, who led the expedition against the rebellious world, rode forth on a white horse. The cohorts of believers who followed Him rode likewise on white horses. Unlike their Leader, they were clad in pure and spotless linen. An earlier verse had already explained that fine linen garments were the righteousnesses of the saints. No armour was theirs: they were not the executive agents of the judgment about to fall—that was solely the work of Christ. Enoch prophesied of the revelation of Christ and His saints from heaven to take vengeance upon those that know not God, when he said, "Behold the Lord cometh with ten thousands of His saints to execute judgment upon all."[1]

The armies who swelled the train of their Captain were unarmed. He alone bore a weapon. Out of His mouth went a sharp two-edged sword, with which He was to smite the nations. The sword issued out of His mouth. No ordinary weapon did He wield. He spoke and it was done; He slew His foes by the breath of His mouth. When, for example, Jesus declared to those who came to seize Him, "I am," they fell backward upon the ground.[2] The armies of the Beast and the kings of the earth were to experience the withering destruction of the Almighty's breath. With *that* sword, He was to smite the heathen.

A rod of iron to rule His enemies was also in the hands of the mighty Warrior. As Psalm 2 indicates, this iron staff is a further symbol of the dashing in pieces of those who dared to oppose Him.

A third judicial figure was added: He trod the wine-press of the fury of the wrath of Almighty God. "As in the wine-press the grapes are crushed to nothing," says Hengstenberg, "so are the heathen by the wrath of God." Rev. 14. 20 indicates that it is the rebellious hosts who are trodden down in the wine-press and that the "wine" which flows out is nothing less than their blood. Whilst the language is figurative, it does at least suggest the awfulness of the judgment of God. In relentless fury, the Divine wrath is poured out upon the unregenerate, and vengeance is satiated in their doom.

[1]Jude 14, 15 [2]John 18. 5, 6

As the armies rode forth, John perceived that upon His garment and thigh (*i.e.*, upon the garment in the region of the thigh—where the sword is commonly hung), the Lord bore the name of "King of kings and Lord of lords." The name took the place of the absent sword and conveyed the same import. "The sword of the warrior and ruler," says one commentator, "is everywhere the symbol of his personality and of his whole position." In Psalm 45, for example, the sword is associated with the thigh, and also with Messiah's glory and majesty. He is the absolute Sovereign and supreme Ruler. All other kings, governors, and potentates are subservient to Him. He is the universal Sovereign and all authority has been committed to Him.

The Great Supper

"And I saw an angel standing in the sun; and he cried with a loud voice, saying to all the birds that fly in mid-heaven, Come, gather yourselves together to the great supper of God, that ye may eat the flesh of kings, and the flesh of chiliarchs, and the flesh of strong men, and the flesh of horses, and of those that sit on them, and the flesh of all, both free and bond, and small and great" (19. 17-18).

An angel stationed in the sun anticipated the outcome of the battle which was about to take place. The Spirit of God has striven and pleaded with men to turn to Christ for salvation: the invitation to His great supper has been pressed home through the Gospel for over nineteen centuries, but the blind and insensate race has refused to heed the call. In the day described by the seer, the tables were turned, and those who had previously been invited to the feast now became the food of the ravening birds.

The angel who, from his central position in the sun, can only be identified with the central authority, summoned all the birds that flew in the mid-heaven to the great supper of God. The bodies of kings, captains, and mighty men and their horses, freemen and slaves, small and great, were seen prophetically, lying slain and unburied on the battlefield, the food of the gathering vultures. The closing verse of the chapter declares that the birds were filled with their flesh. So great was the number of the slain that it was impossible to contemplate their burial and their carcases were left to the attacks of the feathered hosts.

The Doom of the Beast and the False Prophet

"And I saw the beast and the kings of the earth and their armies gathered together to make war against Him that sat upon the horse and against His army. And the beast was taken and with him the false prophet, who wrought the signs before him, by which he deceived them that received the mark of the beast and those who worshipped his image. Both were cast alive into the lake of fire which burns with brimstone; and the rest were slain with the sword of Him Who sat upon the horse, which sword goes out of His mouth; and all the birds were filled with their flesh" (19. 19-21).

The ten kings who had given their power and authority to the Roman Emperor[1] were now seen for the last time. Their mighty leader gathered his forces together for the final onslaught upon Jerusalem[2]—an attack which the Apocalypse (detecting the inspiring motives) describes as war against Christ and His army. In their arrogant pride they thought it possible to fight against God.

As foretold,[3] the Lord of hosts now issued forth in vengeance. The description given by Seiss is deserving of quotation *in extenso:* "The Great Conqueror bows the heavens and comes down. He rides upon the cherub horse, and flies upon the wings of the wind. Smoke goes up from His nostrils, and devouring fire out of His mouth. He moves amid storms and darkness, from which the lightnings hurl their bolts, and hailstones mingle with the fire. He roars out of Zion and utters His voice from Jerusalem, till the heavens and the earth shake. He dashes forth in the fury of His incensed greatness amid clouds and fire and pillars of smoke. The sun frowns. The day is neither light nor dark. The mountains melt and cleave asunder at His presence. The hills bound from their seats and skip like lambs. The waters are dislodged from their channels. The sea rolls back with howling trepidation. The sky is rent and folds upon itself like a collapsed tent. It is the day for executing an armed world—a world in covenant with hell to overthrow the authority and throne of God—and everything in terrified Nature joins to signalise the deserved vengeance. So the Scriptures everywhere represent. John saw it, but does not describe it. He only tells the result he beheld."

Judgment fell first upon the rebel leader. The Sitter upon the white horse seized the Beast and snatched him away for condign punishment. Together with the false prophet, who had performed miracles before him and who had caused the peoples of the empire to worship the beast and his image, he was cast alive into the lake of fire. No corporeal death was ever theirs: their eternal doom was in that sea of flame.

It is scarcely necessary to state that the lake of fire burning with brimstone is simply symbolic, but if it be only the symbol, how

[1]Rev. 17. 13 [2]Zech. 14. 2 [3]Zech. 14

dreadful must be the actual condition. Well merited was the judgment of those two men, however, and they were consigned to that awful sea.

The armies which followed them were slain with the sword of Christ's mouth. No natural weapon was wielded against them. The Word of the living God was their condemnation—what Bengel terms "a spiritual weapon of resistless might."

The scene closes with the picture of the birds of prey swooping down upon the battlefield and finally resting, gorged to repletion, and the curtain falls upon one of the most terrible events of history.

Chapter XXIII

The Millennium and After

The Binding of Satan

"And I saw an angel descending from heaven, having the key of the abyss, and a great chain in his hand. And he laid hold of the dragon, that old serpent, who is the devil and Satan, and bound him a thousand years, and cast him into the abyss, and shut it and sealed it over him, that he should deceive the nations no more until the thousand years were completed; after these things he must be loosed for a little time" (20. 1-3).

THE sphere of Satan on earth is restricted to the human agencies who yield to his control, and the two principal enemies, the Beast and the False Prophet, having been removed, his dominion was broken and he himself was now imprisoned. An angel descended from heaven, with the key of the abyss, bound the devil with a great chain, and cast him into the abyss. Once the "son of the morning" (Lucifer) and the anointed covering cherub, the mighty spirit was now degraded in ignominious fetters and shame. The very height from which he fell only accentuated his new abasement.

Seizing hold of the devil, the angel bound him with the great chain which he carried coiled around his hand—a chain whose import Bousset describes as "the inviolable orders of God and the impress of His eternal will"—and then confined him to the mysterious prison referred to as "the abyss." The precise location of this unfathomable pit has been a subject of considerable speculation. Some have stated confidently that it was situated in the centre of the earth, but this would clearly dispose of any question of *bottomless* profundity. It is more probable that the implication of the term is rather of moral distance from God and that, if there is a material site, it is somewhere in space, immeasurably remote from the presence of holiness and truth. The word *abyss* occurs seven times in the Revelation and always as the abode or prison of demons or evil spirits.[1]

Then the devil was shut up and sealed for a thousand years. "The career of Satan from his first connexion with the human race[2] till his imprisonment in the abyss has been one of cruel, heartless

[1] *See also* Luke 8. 31 [2] Gen. 3

deception. He has falsified the character of God; he has blinded the minds of men to the nature of sin and to its eternal consequences" (Scott). Now, for a thousand years, he was prohibited from further deception of the nations. No more would he seduce from God and draw aside to absolute heathenism.

Lest there be any doubt as to the identity of the mighty spirit, his names are again stated in full and in the same order as in chap. 12. 9 (possibly suggesting that the imprisonment of chap. 20 was based upon the victory in chap. 12). He is the dragon, the personification of cruelty; the old serpent, the sinister and subtle enemy of man from the very first; the devil, the deceiver and tempter; and Satan, the constant adversary of the human race.

The historical interpreter still relates this section to the past and declares that the thousand years commenced in A.D. 800, with the inauguration of the Western Christian Empire when Charlemagne was crowned by the Pope and proclaimed "Charles Augustus, crowned by God, the great and peaceful Roman Emperor." How it can be contended that the devil was absent for the following thousand years, however, is difficult to understand. Any unprejudiced reader must be forced to the conclusion that the events described still lie in the future and that earth's day of freedom from its subtle foe has not yet dawned.

The Millennial Reign

"And I saw thrones, and they sat upon them, and judgment was given unto them; and I saw the souls of those who were beheaded for the witness of Jesus and for the word of God; and those who had not worshipped the beast nor his image, and had not received his mark on their foreheads or in their hands; and they lived and reigned with Christ a thousand years. The rest of the dead lived not till the thousand years had been completed. This is the first resurrection. Blessed and holy is he he who has part in the first resurrection: over these the second death has no power, but they shall be priests of God and of Christ, and shall reign with Him a thousand years" (20. 4-6).

With the binding of the forces of evil, the glorious period of the millennium will be ushered in, and John was given a brief glimpse of the heavenly scene during that era. No details were given of the millennial earth, that having already been dealt with clearly by the Old Testament prophets.

The Apostle beheld thrones, to the occupants of which judgment was given. Whilst it is not expressly stated who the occupants were, it is clear from chap. 4. 4 that they were the 24 elders, *i.e.*, the representatives of the redeemed up to the time of the rapture of 1 Thess. 4.

A second group was also seen—"those who were beheaded for the witness of Jesus and of the word of God." After scourging a criminal with the lictor's rods, it was the Roman practice to execute with a hatchet. Those whom John beheld had been killed after the Roman fashion—they were the martyrs who had died after the rapture but prior to the setting up of the image of the Beast, and were identical with those referred to in chap. 6. 9.

The third class were those who, during the Great Tribulation, steadfastly refused to pay homage to the Beast or his image, or to receive his mark in their foreheads or hands, and who paid by martyrdom for their fidelity.

All these had (at different stages) been raised from the dead and the first resurrection was now complete. The reference to "souls" in verse 4 is a little confusing, but it is quite clear that it is not bodiless spirits of whom the passage speaks. They *lived*, and De Wette explains the word as signifying that "they returned again to full life, received a body again."

Whilst there were evidently different degrees of blessedness and of relationship to Christ, all of the three groups shared with Him in the glory of His millennial reign. "They lived and reigned with Christ a thousand years."

It is emphasized by the inspired writer that it is not a general resurrection that is in view, for "the rest of the dead lived not till the thousand years had been completed." The ungodly would be dealt with at the end of that blissful period, but believers would reign in association with Christ. The first resurrection occurs in stages but is not regarded as complete until the last group of martyrs has been raised from the dead.

The blessing of the one who participated in the first resurrection is then coupled with the fact of his sanctification, as if to emphasize that his separation to God and His will found the true basis of his present bliss. The second death had no power over such. Our Lord declared that the one who kept His saying should never see death,[1] *i.e.*, not, of course, that physical death should not touch him, but that the second death should have no hold upon him. Free from all threat of the final death, the risen saints reigned with Christ as priests. He will reign as the great King-priest and those who were separated from the profane world will be bound to Him in sacerdotal loyalty and responsibility. The verse, as Hengstenberg says, "possesses a hortatory character. It calls upon us to regard the troubles and sufferings of this present life as nothing, if we may but attain to the glorious good of the first resurrection."

[1] John 8. 51

The Final Revolt

"And when the thousand years are expired, Satan shall be loosed from his prison, and shall go out to deceive the nations which are in the four corners of the earth, Gog and Magog, to gather them together to battle, whose number is as the sand of the sea. And they went up on the breadth of the earth, and surrounded the camp of the saints and the beloved city; and fire came down from God out of heaven and devoured them. And the devil who deceived them was cast into the lake of fire and brimstone, where the beast and the false prophet are; and they shall be tormented day and night for the ages of ages" (20. 7-10).

During the millennium, the earth will know freedom from strife and universal blessing will be the result of divine beneficence. The glory of God will so pervade the scene that the earth will be as filled with its knowledge as the waters cover the sea. Righteousness and equity will be the principles of government, and evil will be trampled underfoot. The curse removed from the land, it will burst forth into plenty and even the desert will blossom as the rose. Yet, amid all the tokens of God's goodness, amid prosperity and fruitfulness, human nature will remain unchanged. Unrepentant still, masses will shrink from the holiness of God's earthly centre and gravitate to the "four corners of the earth"—as far away from the central glory as it is possible to travel—there to share their antipathy to the Messianic rule and their antagonism to righteousness and holiness. As the centuries roll by, there will doubtless be large accretions to the numbers until, at the close of the dispensation, vast numbers will be in a state of incipient revolt against the rule of Christ and His people.

It is at that period that the seer takes up the narrative again. The thousand years had run their course, and Satan was once more released from his prison. He can only work in the children of disobedience, and he accordingly sought out those whose hearts were opposed to God. Why should God afford him another opportunity of bringing misery and destruction upon the world? At least one primary purpose seems to be that it should be conclusively demonstrated that human nature is incurably evil and incapable of self-improvement. Under every dispensation and and in every circumstance of God's testing, man has completely failed, and it will be made abundantly clear in the final analysis that only divine grace can eradicate sin and impart a new nature.

Hengstenberg maintains that those who succumbed to the Satanic temptation were not only those who had retreated from Jerusalem's centre, but the whole world—all who were comprised in the compass of its four corners. "The deceptive influence exercised by Satan," he writes, "is represented as one that is not to be confined to some one particular land or people, but one that was to possess an entirely œcumenical character. To the four corners of the earth corresponds the *breadth* of the earth in verse 9. The territory on which the cause operates here is the same as that on which the operation appears there." Whether this is so or not, it is evident that great multitudes were led astray by their hatred of divine things.

The nations who were seduced by Satan are described as Gog and Magog. It is hardly necessary to point out that these powers are not identical with the Gog of the land of Magog, whose invasion of Israel is described in Ezek. 38 and 39, since those events were pre-millennial, whereas the final revolt is post-millennial. Jennings writes: "In the Gog and Magog of Ezekiel may be recognized the armies of Russia and her dependencies making the last attack upon Israel at the beginning of the millennium, while in the Gog and Magog of Revelation, we have the last enemies—not of one earthly nation, but of all to whom the term 'saints' can be applied." The Gog of Ezekiel is a prototype of the Apocalyptic people of Gog.

It is probable that the Satanic appeal to these nations was to establish their own government and to overthrow that of Messiah. Galled by the superior position of Israel and their own subordination, they would readily respond to such an appeal, and Satan gathered together to battle a host as numberless as the sand of the sea. The mighty armies surrounded Jerusalem and "the camp of the saints" (possibly intended to indicate a stronghold within the city as in the case of the Romans in Acts 21 and 22).

During the millennium all nations will be required to go up to Jerusalem at the Feast of Tabernacles,[1] and Govett suggests that the attack will take place at that time since less suspicion would attach to the gathering of such vast multitudes and since most of Israel would be assembled at the temple. The obligation to go up to Jerusalem at that period would serve to emphasize the Gentiles' subjection to Israel and would increase the provocation.

Ere the attack was made, however, God intervened. Not a sword was unsheathed and not a weapon used, but fire fell from heaven upon the rebellious host and completely destroyed them. "For the offence of not coming up to Jerusalem to worship, God threatens the withholding of rain: a slow punishment, which would, at any time, admit of repentance on the nation's part.

[1]Zech. 14. 16

But for the crime of coming up in warlike array against His city and king, the stroke of wrath is instant, and there is no room for penitence. Offenders are cut off in their sin in a moment" (Govett).

At the end of his long career of opposition to his Creator, the devil was finally cast into the lake of fire, to join his two human coadjutors, the beast and the false prophet, who had already endured a thousand years of torment in that awful place. In chap. 12. 9, he was ejected from heaven and cast down to earth; in chap. 20. 3, he was confined to the abyss; now he was cast for ever into the lake of fire and brimstone.

Eternal torment in the place prepared for the devil and his angels[1] was the lot of the three principals in the intrigues of evil. No remission is visualized, no relief is intimated. The one who has brought such untold suffering and sorrow to the millions of earth right down the ages, must himself bear the penalty of his folly "day and night for the ages of the ages." Human mind fails to grasp the immensity of the expression, but the awful tragedy of Lucifer's fall can only emphasize the grace meted out to the human sinner.

The Final Assize

"And I saw a great white throne, and Him that sat on it, from whose face the earth and the heaven fled, and place was not found for them. And I saw the dead, great and small, standing before the throne, and books were opened; and another book was opened, which is that of life. And the dead were judged out of the things written in the books according to their works. And the sea gave up the dead which were in it, and death and hades gave up the dead which were in them; and they were judged each according to his works; and death and hades were cast into the lake of fire. This is the second death, even the lake of fire. And if anyone was not found written in the book of life, he was cast into the lake of fire" (20. 11-15).

Dispensations had now come to an end and the final and irrevocable decision was to be taken regarding the fate of all the dead. John saw, poised in air, a great white throne. "The throne is white," says Bengel, "as an emblem of the glory of the Judge, and great as befits His great and infinite majesty." Its purity declared His holiness and the perfect righteousness and justice of its decisions. There could be no appeal from this court: its verdict was final.

The Apostle makes no attempt to delineate the dreadful majesty of the Judge. His own Gospel narrative had already indicated that the Person could be none other than Christ.[2] Before His face, the earth and the heaven were dissolved. Foretelling that day, Peter wrote: "The heavens will pass away with a rushing noise, and the elements, burning with heat, shall be dissolved,

[1]Matt. 25. 41 [2]John 5. 22

and the earth and the works in it shall be burnt up."[1] The inflammable gases of the atmosphere ignited and the earth as a sheet of fire rolled away out of its orbit to destruction. The sin-stained earth disappeared completely and those who were arraigned before the throne were suspended there by almighty power.

All the impenitent—dead spiritually and, in most cases, physically—were summoned for the final judgment. Earthly distinctions appeared for the last time; all were now in the same position. Great and small stood before their Judge.

In absolute equity, the records of human life were unrolled—the books were opened—and each individual dealt with on the basis of his deeds. No verbal evidence was required, as in human courts. The infallible record of the centuries bore its unerring witness against them. How dreadful the fact that not an action in life escapes recording, not a word is lost on the air, not a thought is for ever buried. Every detail is held in the divine records.

Each person was judged according to his works, plainly indicative of the fact that there are degrees of punishment and also that it is a fitting requital. Memory was only able to confirm the witness of the books and to concur in the sentence passed.

Lest any question could be raised, it is also stated that the book of life was opened. If a man's name was in that book it could not appear in the records of unforgiven sins. The final condemnation must be the absence of the name from the book of life and, in that event, the individual was cast into the lake of fire, into the second death. The awful condition of the lost might well awaken the evangelist to the need of those around him and energize him to seek the salvation of those otherwise doomed to the long dark eternity of exile from God.

The sea, death, and Hades are described as yielding up their dead. The number of physically dead held in the literal sea is relatively small and it seems clear that the reference is to the metaphorical sea of people (which agrees with previous uses of the word in the book). The living (but spiritually dead) and those who were physically dead were delivered up. The grave gave up the body, and Hades surrendered the spirit. Death and Hades, no longer required, were cast into the lake of fire. Since sin would no longer mar creation, death would never again intervene and, in guarantee thereof, death and its companion, Hades, were cast into the place of eternal wrath.

[1] 2 Pet. 3. 10

CHAPTER XXIV

The Eternal State

"And I saw a new heaven and a new earth, for the first heaven and the first earth had passed away, and there was no more sea. And I saw the holy city, new Jerusalem, coming down out of heaven from God, prepared as a bride adorned for her husband. And I heard a loud voice out of heaven saying, Behold, the tabernacle of God is with men, and He shall tabernacle with them, and they shall be His people, and God Himself shall be with them, and be their God. And He shall wipe away every tear from their eyes, and death shall not exist any more, nor grief, nor cry, nor distress shall exist any more, for the former things have passed away. And He that sat on the throne said, Behold, I make all things new. And He said to me, Write, for these words are true and faithful. And He said to me, It is done. I am the Alpha and the Omega, the beginning and the end. I will give to him that thirsts of the fountain of the water of life freely. He that overcometh shall inherit these things, and I will be to him God and he shall be to Me son. But to the fearful and unbelieving, and those who make themselves abominable, and murderers, and fornicators, and sorcerers, and idolaters, and all liars, their part is in the lake which burns with fire and brimstone; which is the second death" (21. 1-8).

THE Apostle now stood on the threshold of the eternal day and a new heaven and a new earth appeared before his eyes. The first heaven and earth had passed through the flames and the long-anticipated "new heavens and new earth wherein dwells righteousness"[1] now came into view. The millennial reign had been completed, Christ had "annulled all rule and all authority and power" and "put all enemies under His feet," and the kingdom had been given up to God the Father.[2]

"The new heaven is for the raised and changed saints," says Scott, and "the new earth is to form the habitation of those who, during the millennial reign, were alive on earth—those companies described in chapters 7 and 14," but it is by no means clear that the inhabitants of the new-made world will be limited to the believers of the millennial era. This view is tenable only if it can be maintained that the first resurrection is the dividing line, and that all who participate in the first resurrection (at whatever stage) are destined for a heavenly habitat, whilst all other believers will find their eternal home on the new earth. There is much in support of such a contention, but the Scriptures are not sufficiently explicit on the subject for any view to be put forward dogmatically.

[1] 2 Pet. 3. 10-13 [2] 1 Cor. 15. 24-26

Vitringa, following the historical line of interpretation, suggests that the new heaven and earth refer to the "renewal of the state of the Church" at the completion of the Reformation, but the picture is so plainly of the future that criticism of the historical view would be superfluous. The references in Isa. 65. 17 and 66. 22, for example, have clearly no relation to the Church.

Three quarters of the globe at present is occupied by sea. The feature of the new earth which impressed John the fisherman was the complete absence of sea. The restless and ruthless oceans retreated to provide a world which was completely habitable. The troubled sea is a frequent figure in Scripture of the masses of mankind, and its destructive and separative character is strikingly symbolic of the effects of sin upon the human race. "The wicked are like the troubled sea, which cannot rest, and whose waters cast up mire and dirt."[1] Every trace of the troublous waters was removed from the final scene of peace.

Several references are made in the New Testament to a heavenly Jerusalem. Paul spoke of "Jerusalem which is above,"[2] the writer to the Hebrews of "the heavenly Jerusalem,"[3] and the Apocalypse itself of "new Jerusalem."[4] As his eyes feasted on the sight of the new heaven and earth, John beheld the holy city, new Jerusalem, descending out of heaven from God. Since national distinctions have no place in eternity, the centre of divine government could no longer be an earthly Jerusalem, but in its place a heavenly Jerusalem descended from the glory. This was no literal city, however, since it was described as "prepared as a bride adorned for her husband."

That the Church is included in the symbol of the city there can be no doubt, but Jennings is not without some reason when he states that "this heavenly Jerusalem is not exactly equivalent or co-terminous with the Church, but includes all who, partakers of grace, have no earthly place." In the administration of the world and in the diffusion of divine principles, full use will undoubtedly be made of all heavenly saints, and there seems, at first sight, no reason to narrow down the interpretation of the type merely to the Church.

On the other hand, the city was prepared as a bride adorned for her husband—shining in all the lustre of the glories bestowed upon her by God and resplendent in all the righteous virtues which were her own. If Israel is the wife of Jehovah, and the Church is the Bride of Christ, is it possible for there to be a third company

[1]Isa. 57. 20 [2]Gal. 4. 26 [3]Heb. 12. 22 [4]Rev. 3. 12

described as a bride? Of all whom God has blessed, the Church will stand in closest intimacy with Him. She is the Bride of His Son and the company in which He purposes to glorify Himself before the world. However great the difficulties, it would seem that the primary interpretation of the city can be only the Church. What other attendants there may be, how others may engage in heavenly ministry, we do not know. The details given of the eternal state are remarkable for their sparseness.

As the city descended, a loud voice from heaven declared that God's tabernacle was with men and that He would dwell among them as their God. It has ever been God's delight to dwell among men, and the tabernacle in the midst of Israel was an evidence of His presence. So, when dispensations and ages dissolved into the eternal day, the tabernacle of God was again seen among men. As Israel were His peculiar people in a previous day, the human race would yet be in a special sense His people, and He would be their God. It is perhaps deserving of notice that the figure of the *tabernacle* and not that of the *temple* is used. The former was a temporary and movable structure; the latter was a permanent abode. It may, therefore, be deduced that the messengers of God will not reside permanently on earth but will travel to execute His commissions in various parts of the universe.

Pindar sang of a tearless scene, "where the sun is ever shining and where the souls of the just spend a tearless eternity," and many another poet has voiced the age-long human longing for peace and freedom from sorrow. In the Apocalyptic picture of eternity, God wipes away all tears from His people's eyes. The hopeless and pitiful misery of the race wells up and expresses itself in the flowing tear, but in the glad day pictured in the Revelation, the very cause of misery is disposed of and the loving hand of the Almighty removes all trace of sorrow.

Death itself was banished, and grief, crying, and distress (or pain) were for ever dismissed. Never again should life be marred or blighted; the former days had been swallowed up in the joy of eternity. In this life, as Shakespeare has truly said, "When sorrows come, they come not single spies, but in battalions." As a result of sin there is universal grief, pain, and distress. Jennings well describes it: "the suffering body, the pain-racked frame, the restlessness of fever till the end; and then the pang of broken heart-strings, the long-drawn-out grief of bereavement, with its tears." All that clouded the life of man was to be dispelled; never again should they exist.

The Occupant of the throne itself declared that He made all things new. Here was no flimsy cover drawn over the tragedies of history; no obscuring cloak to hide the diseases and disfigurements of the centuries, but a re-creation in which corruption and mortality found no place. And in token of the absolute credibility of the words, the seer was commanded to write, for the words were faithful and true.

"It is done," declared the Divine Speaker. "I am the Alpha and the Omega, the beginning and the end." Says Bengel, "Twice it is said in this book, 'It is done.' First at the completion of the wrath of God in chap. 16. 17, and here again at the making of all things new." The work was finished and the purposes of God were fulfilled.

Just as, in the beginning, God created, so He now renewed. He could, with justification, claim to be the Alpha and the Omega, the beginning and the ending. In Him was everything comprised: all might, power, glory, wisdom, and honour, the whole range of comprehensible attributes and traits in their full essence were in Him. "God is Himself called the beginning and the end," writes Hengstenberg, "because, as the beginning, so the end yields Him unconditional obedience. His decrees are assuredly carried into effect, on all the seal of His nature is impressed, all bears witness to His glory." Indeed, the creature might well bow down in worship at the revelation of all that God is and all that He has done. He is truly the beginning and the ending. He was before all things, and nothing can reach beyond Him.

The very declaration of His almightiness and all-sufficiency led quite naturally to a promise to the thirsty to satisfy him freely from the fountain of the water of life. Breaking through the scenes of eternal glory, the evangelistic cry rings down to the present day with all its need. It is a re-echo of the appeal of the prophet Isaiah: "Ho, every one that thirsteth, come ye to the waters,"[1] and again of our Lord's words to the Samaritan woman by the well.[2] If God is truly the all-sufficient, the beginning and the ending, in Him alone can the yearnings of the human soul be fully met. Only there can life's raging thirst be assuaged, and He offered to all who thirst the life-giving water from Heaven's fount.

To the suffering Church, with the fires of persecution already passing over her, came a further message. Eternal glory had been depicted. The overcomer would inherit that and God would

[1]Isa. 55. 1 [2]John 4. 14

become his God and he should be His son. The one who, in fidelity to his Master, acknowledged Him in face of danger and potential suffering, would be openly acknowledged by God as son, and during the time of his trial and tribulation, God would prove Himself verily his God.

By contrast, the lot of the unregenerate should be the second death, described here as the lake which burns with fire and brimstone. This is no purgatory, but eternal and irrevocable judgment. The figures used are grim but apt. "Fire stands opposed to water," writes Govett, "a pool to a fountain; life to death. The one quenches thirst, the other heats it to intolerable fury." The awful agony of the lost has already been referred to, and the dreadfulness of their future can only stir the Christian to greater effort on their behalf.

Eight different classes of the unregenerate are mentioned:

(1) *The fearful*, the faint-hearted or cowardly: afraid of the danger of allying themselves with Christ or His cause, these shrank back to perdition.

(2) *Unbelieving:* knowing God's will, these offenders deliberately refused to believe His Word or bow to His claims; without fear of God or faith in Him.

(3) *Those who made themselves abominable;* the reference in this case is clearly to those culpable of unnatural crimes (cf. Lev. 18. 26). As one commentator remarks: "Of such sins, Sodom was guilty, and her doom of fire from heaven, and the plain turned into a lake, was a foretaste of the destiny of those condemned because of such offences."

(4) *Murderers.* The Noahic covenant required the death of any who wittingly took the life of his fellow, "but there is another sentence beyond the death of the body, which is here disclosed, to deter all from that treasonable defacement of their Maker's image" (Govett).

(5) *Fornicators.* Heb. 13. 4 indicates that a special judgment is reserved for the seducer and the one who ruins female virtue. The Biblical warnings against the sins of fornication and adultery were probably never more necessary than in the present day, and the Apocalypse plainly emphasizes the inevitable end of those who deliberately indulge in such sins.

(6) *Sorcerers.* The Mosaic law proscribed the death penalty for those who practised intercourse with spirits.[1] Commerce with evil spirits is no longer a covert practice. Séances and spiritu-

[1]Deut. 18. 10-12

alistic meetings are advertised openly, and the number of adherents to Spiritism is increasing rapidly. The doom of the one who thus ignores the Word of God is none other than the second death.

(7) *Idolaters.* God is intolerant of any object of worship other than Himself. The substitution of any object or being for Him is idolatry and punishable by eternal suffering.

(8) *Liars.* Satan was the first liar. Antichrist denies both the Father and the Son.[1] Those who follow in the steps of the great adversary find their end also in the lake of fire.

The list might well cause heart-searching on the part of the true believer. As Jennings writes: "If a look may be the evidence of 'adultery' in the heart;[2] if hatred is but 'murder' in embryo;[3] if longing or coveting for anything else than God is 'idolatry';[4] if any denial of the alone sufficiency of Christ is a 'lie';[5] where should we be on the ground of self-justification?" Alas, we find in our own hearts only too frequently the reflections of the very sins which God condemns, and it is only the sovereign mercy of Christ which has preserved us from complete failure. But let us judge our own lives and, by divine help, maintain that loyalty, purity, and practical holiness for which our Lord so longs.

[1] I John 2. 22 [2] Matt. 5. 28 [3] I John 3. 15 [4] Col. 3. 5 [5] I John 2. 22

Chapter XXV

Jerusalem the Holy City

"And there came one of the seven angels who had the seven bowls full of the seven last plagues, and spoke with me, saying, Come hither, I will shew thee the bride, the Lamb's wife. And he carried me away in the Spirit, and set me on a great and high mountain, and shewed me the holy city, Jerusalem, coming down out of the heaven from God, having the glory of God. Her brightness was like a most precious stone, as a crystal-like jasper stone; having a great and high wall; having twelve gates, and at the gates twelve angels, and names inscribed, which are those of the twelve tribes of the children of Israel. On the east three gates; and on the north three gates; and on the south three gates; and on the west three gates. And the wall of the city had twelve foundations, and on them the names of the twelve apostles of the Lamb" (21. 9-14).

THE first eight verses of chapter 21 relate to the eternal state, but the narrative then reverts to the millennium, and a detailed picture is given of the Bride, the Lamb's wife.

One of the seven angels who had earlier poured out the bowls of wrath now carried the seer away to a great and lofty mountain to behold the descent of the Bride from heaven in the form of a dazzling city, scintillating like a precious stone. As has previously been indicated, the Bride of the Lamb is not to be confused with the wife of Jehovah. Dr. A. H. Burton remarks that "the Old Testament bride[1] is associated with Christ as triumphant Messiah with girded sword, riding in majestic glory, His enemies falling before Him. But the Bride of Revelation is one associated with a rejected and suffering Lamb. The one is earthly, the other heavenly." F. W. Grant's note on the same subject is worth quoting *in extenso:* "Israel was Jehovah's married wife,[2] now divorced indeed for her unfaithfulness, but yet to return,[3] and be received and reinstated. Her Maker will be then once more her husband and more than the old blessing be restored. In Psa. 45, Israel's king, Messiah, is the Bridegroom; the Song of Solomon is the mystic song of His espousals. The land too shall be married.[4] In the New Testament the same figure is still used in the same way. The Baptist speaks of his joy as 'the friend of the Bridegroom' in hearing the

[1] Psa. 45 [2] Isa. 54. 1; Jer. 31. 32 [3] Hosea 2 [4] Isa. 62. 4

Bridegroom's voice,[1] and in the parable of the virgins,[2] where Christians are those who go forth to meet the Bridegroom, they are by that very fact not regarded as the Bride, which is still Israel. All this, therefore, is in that earthly sphere in which Israel's blessings lie; our own are in *heavenly* places,[3] and here it is we find, not the Bride of Messiah simply, but distinctively, 'the Bride of the Lamb.' The 'Lamb' as a title always keeps before us His death. The 'Bride of the Lamb' is thus one espoused to Him in His rejection and shares in His reproach and sorrow."

The Bride was seen in the guise of a city, conveying, as another writer says, "the thoughts of an organized system of social life and activity of government, of united interests, of mutual goodwill." The centre of earthly blessing was named Jerusalem, and upon this heavenly city the same name was bestowed.

The glory of God filled the city as it descended like a heavenly luminary from the sky. The blazing light streamed from it, reflected as from the facets of a crystalline jasper. The blue or green jasper appears three times in the description of the city—in verse 11 in connection with its glory, in verse 18 as the superstructure of the wall, and in verse 19 as one of the foundations of the wall.

A great wall, 116 feet high, surrounded the city—a reminder of Jehovah's words regarding an earthly Jerusalem: "I will be unto her a wall of fire round about, and will be the glory in the midst of her."[4] Twelve gates, which stood constantly open (verse 25), provided a means of ingress. (The earthly Jerusalem of the millennium is also stated to have twelve gates.)[5] As in the case of the metropolis of the millennial earth, the gates were named after the twelve tribes of Israel, and three stood on each of the four sides of the wall. Twelve angels were entrusted with the charge of the gates. Divine protection was thus provided against all hostile forces. The security of the wall and the guard of the angels at the gates afforded adequate safety to the city. The administration of Israel, and, through them, of the earth will be conducted from the city, the behests being carried out by the angels of the gates, under the authority of the twelve apostles.[6]

The symmetrical arrangement of the gates indicates that the city was an exact square (see also verse 16), suggesting the ecumenical character of its administration.

The wall was apparently composed of two parts—a superstructure and the foundation. There were actually twelve foundations,

[1]John 3. 29 [2]Matt. 25 [3]Eph. 1. 3 [4]Zech. 2. 5
[5]Ezek. 48. 31-34 [6]Matt. 19. 28

which must have elevated the city to a prodigious height, and on the foundations were inscribed the names of the twelve apostles of the Lamb. It is impossible to avoid recalling that the Church has been "built upon the foundation of the apostles and prophets, Jesus Christ Himself being the chief corner-stone",[1] and this additional detail carries one stage further the identification of the city with the Church.

The Measurements of the City

"And he that spoke with me had a golden reed as a measure, that he might measure the city, and its gates, and its wall. And the city lies foursquare, and its length is as much as the breadth. And he measured the city with the reed—twelve thousand stadia; the length and the breadth and height of it are equal. And he measured its wall, a hundred and forty-four cubits, a man's measure, that is, the angel's" (21. 15-17).

When Ezekiel saw the millennial temple measured, it was with a reed and a flaxen cord.[2] John beheld the holy city measured with a golden reed. The standards of Ezekiel's temple might have some intimate connection with earth and its needs and a cord of *flax* might be adequate with which to measure it, but in this city the measurements were by the standard of God's glory and only a *golden* reed would suffice.

The city formed a perfect square and, as the angel measured it, he found the height equal to the length and to the breadth, each being 12,000 stadia or approximately 1,500 miles. This does not, of course, indicate that the city was an enormous cube. Govett undoubtedly takes the correct view when he says, "The city towers above the walls on every side, street above street, and terrace above terrace, till its highest point is attained in the great square in which stand the throne of God and the tree of life." The height was measured from the foundations to the highest point.

The repetition of the number 12 is not without significance. There were twelve gates, twelve tribes, twelve angels, twelve foundations, twelve apostles; the length, height and breadth were each 12,000 stadia; the wall was 144 cubits (the square of twelve). "Twelve is a perfect number," says Bullinger, "signifying governmental perfection. It is found as a multiple in all that has to do with rule. The sun which rules the day, and the moon and stars which govern the night, do so by their passage through the twelve signs of the zodiac, which completes the great circle of the heavens of 360 (12 by 30) degrees or divisions, and thus govern the year." It is symbolic of order and organization.

[1]Eph. 2. 20 [2]Ezek. 40. 3

The city was measured by the Greek stadium, but the wall by the Jewish cubit, the length of the wall being 144 cubits, as measured by the normal man's forearm.

Materials of the City

"And the building of its wall was jasper; and the city was pure gold, like pure glass: the foundations of the wall of the city were adorned with every precious stone; the first foundation, jasper; the second, sapphire; the third, chalcedony; the fourth, emerald; the fifth, sardonyx; the sixth, sardius; the seventh, chrysolite; the eighth, beryl; the ninth, topaz; the tenth, chrysoprasus; the eleventh, jacinth; the twelfth, amethyst. And the twelve gates were twelve pearls; each one of the gates respectively was of one pearl; and the street of the city was pure gold, as transparent glass" (21. 18-21).

The superstructure of the wall was of jasper but the foundations were adorned with—and possibly constructed of—other precious stones. Whereas Solomon's magnificent temple was covered with gold, this city was constructed of solid gold, but the gold was not opaque but as transparent as pure glass. The splendour and incomparable magnificence of the city are beyond human comprehension. God's glory was manifested through His Church.

Twelve different stones adorned the foundations. The stones were identical in nature with those which were set in the breastplate of Israel's high priest,[1] and the order of arrangement was not dissimilar to that of the colours of the rainbow. Each of the gems had its own peculiar beauty. The *jasper* was a dark green opaque stone with veins of various colours; it is thought to have been a species of quartz. The *sapphire* was an azure blue—a deeper colour than lapis lazuli—and was almost completely transparent. The *chalcedony* derived its name from Chalcedon in Bithynia, where it was originally found. It was bluish white in colour and was a kind of onyx. The *emerald* was a vivid green in colour. The *sardonyx* was a flesh-coloured stone of flinty texture, containing the characteristic features of the sardian and the onyx. The *sardius* is usually identified with the blood-red cornelian. The *chrysolite*, literally the "golden stone," was a yellowish-green stone with a gold lustre, obtained mainly from the Levant. The transparent *beryl* was probably the sea-green aquamarine. The *topaz* was a pale green gem, often found in veins of tin. Pliny says that it originated in Arabia and derived its name from the island of Topazos. The *chrysoprasus* (the Greek means "green as a leek") was an apple-green or leek-green stone, often with a tinge of yellow in it. The

[1]Exod. 28. 17-20

jacinth, or hyacinth, was probably a variety of amethyst, violet in colour. The *amethyst* itself was a beautiful purple-violet jewel. Although the colours do not occur in the exact prismatic order, they obviously blended together in a resplendent whole, before which the glory of the rainbow faded into insignificance.

In *The Harmony of History with Prophecy*, Josiah Conder remarks: "In its general plan, the symbolical city presents a striking resemblance to the description of Ecbatana, furnished by the Father of secular history. 'Of this city, one wall encompassed another, and each rose by the height of its battlement above the one beyond it. The orbicular walls were seven in number: within the last stood the royal palace and the treasuries. The largest of the walls nearly equalled the circumference of Athens. The battlements of this outer wall were white; those of the second, black; of the third, purple; of the fourth, blue; of the fifth, orange; all the battlements being thus covered with a pigment. Of the two last walls, the battlements of the one were plated with silver, those of the other with gold.' Thus the Median city consisted of seven circular terraces, each distinguished by the colour of its wall, whereas the Apocalyptic city is described as a quadrangle of twelve stages or foundations. The precious stones of which the walls of the holy city appeared to consist are obviously intended to describe the colour of each resplendent elevation." The city was probably pyramidical in shape, the lowest foundations being larger than those above it. As in many of the ancient buildings of Babylon and other countries, it is likely that a broad path ran along the top of each of the foundations, forming a road along which the travellers could make their way into the city.

Each of the gates was a massive pearl, the reminder of beauty born out of suffering. The pearl finds its origin in some tiny irritant within the living tissue of the mollusc; around the irritating particle, layer after layer of nacre is deposited, until the tiny foreign body is completely obscured by a precious and beautiful stone. The gates of the city were of pearl. That which was unlovely has been beautified by the work of Christ; sin has been put away and an access made to the very throne of God.

The street (or, perhaps, more literally, the large central square or open space) of the city was of pure gold as translucent as glass. The radiant glory of precious stones and of the gold must have proved a dazzling sight as the city descended from the heavens to the centre of universal administration.

The Light and Glory

"And I saw no temple in it; for the Lord God Almighty is its temple, and the Lamb. And the city has no need of the sun nor of the moon, that they should shine for it; for the glory of God had enlightened it, and the lamp thereof is the Lamb. And the nations shall walk by its light; and the kings of the earth shall bring their glory to it. And its gates shall not be shut at all by day, for night shall not be there. And they shall bring the glory and the honour of the nations to it. And nothing common, nor that maketh an abomination and a lie, shall at all enter into it; but those only who are written in the Lamb's book of life" (21. 22-27).

In all sacred cities of the past and present, the temple occupies the place of supreme honour; to it the pilgrim wends his way, and at it the worshipper pays his vows. In the glorious city beheld by John, however, there was no temple to be seen. The temple was merely a shrine in which God might dwell, but here, the Lord God Almighty and the Lamb were revealed in all their glory. God burst out from the limits of sacred buildings and became Himself the temple. Full and unlimited access to God was thus available to the worshipper. No priest stood to minister at an altar of approach; no mediator interceded on behalf of his fellows. God was available to all who wished to approach Him. It is difficult to realize the full significance of the picture, and the blessing of the day portrayed can only be feebly grasped.

No light of sun or moon was required in the city. The Shekinah itself was its light and the Lamb the One through whom the light shone. The words of the prophet Isaiah found their fulfilment: "The sun shall be no more thy light by day, neither for brightness shall the moon give light unto thee; but Jehovah shall be thine everlasting light, and thy God thy glory."[1] The darkness of sin had been dispelled and the light of the glory of God—seen through a veil during the life of Christ—now shone out unhinderedly in that blessed One. Surpassing the light of sun and moon, that radiance illumined the whole city, and even the nations of earth were able to walk in its light (cf. Isa. 60. 3).

No night fell in that scene. The rule of heaven was universally acknowledged and the dark night of sin and rebellion had faded away. The night is the symbol of sorrow and lack of blessing; the gloom spells out its trials and troubles. All these were banished and the beneficence of heaven told itself out in the lasting day.

The gates to the city were therefore never shut.[2] God was always accessible to those who made their way up its terraced slopes. His light guided them and at all times might they come to Him.

[1]Isa. 60. 19 [2]Isa. 60. 11

The earthly sovereigns brought their glory to the city, and the glory and honour of the nations were brought to it. The adoration of monarchs and peoples found its expression in the gifts of their treasures and wealth.

Space forbids a detailed exposition of the glory of the city, but the corresponding Old Testament prophecy in Isa. 60 is well deserving of study in connection with the subject.

From the city were excluded the common, those who made an abomination, and liars. Those who would defile the purity of the city by their presence therein, who held the glory of God in little repute, who would make everything common, could have no part in that city. The immoral and the idolater (for both seem to be comprehended in the makers of abominations) were forbidden to enter. Sin could find no ingress into that place of light; the righteousness of God might not be contaminated by contact with the filthy; the jealousy of the Almighty would tolerate no other object of worship. The liar found no place in that scene of truth and reality. The very thought of duplicity, insincerity, unreality and untruthfulness is abhorrent to God. The liar was excluded.

Only those whose names were written in the Lamb's book of life were allowed to enter. Communion with God is possible only to the regenerate. The unregenerate could never be happy in His presence. Even during the millennium, the work of grace will continue and souls will be born again. The unrepentant sinner will die under the curse (Isa. 65. 20), but the delight of God will ever be in those whom He has called to Himself as new creatures.

The Centre of the City

"And he shewed me a river of water of life, bright as crystal, proceeding out of the throne of God and of the Lamb. In the midst of its street, and of the river, on this side and on that side, was the tree of life, producing twelve fruits, in each month yielding its fruit; and the leaves of the tree were for healing of the nations. And no curse shall be any more; and the throne of God and of the Lamb shall be in it; and His servants shall serve Him, and they shall see His face; and His name is on their foreheads. And night shall not be any more, and there is no need of a lamp and light of the sun; for the Lord God shall shine upon them, and they shall reign to the ages of ages" (22. 1-5).

From the exterior of the city, the Apostle was carried into the centre, where he saw a mighty river issuing out of the very throne. (The fact that the throne is described as "of God and of the Lamb," is a clear indication that the Kingdom had not yet been given up by the Son to the Father, and that the period under review is still the millennium and not the eternal state.) The river was the water of life and was as bright as crystal. In Ezekiel's vision of the millennial temple on earth, waters poured out of the temple to run down through the court and out of the gate.[1] In the Apocalyptic city, the river took its rise in the very throne, plainly suggesting that life and the fulness of blessing originate only in God. "It is no muddy nor turgid stream," says Scott, "but bright and pellucid as the beautiful crystal." Life abundant poured out from the throne. If God had descended to His creatures, it was for the purpose of shedding blessing in all its fulness upon them.

The river flowed through the central square ("the street") of the city. In the square and on both sides of the river stood the tree of life, like an immense banyan tree, sending down fibres to become three huge trunks and thus standing in the square and on the sides of the river. "Here," says Harper, "we may compare the homa-tree of the Persians, growing at the spring Ardvisura, which comes from the throne of God; the kalpasoma-tree of the Hindus, which furnished the water of immortality, the libation of the gods; the tuba-tree of the Arabs; the lotus-tree of the Greeks; the tree of Assyrian sculpture, adorned by royal figures, and guarded by genii, just as, in the Bible story, it is guarded by the cherubim." Adam was ejected from Eden lest he should partake of the tree of life,[2] but access to the tree in this holy city was open to all.

A different variety of fruit was produced by the tree each month. Not only was there no cessation in fruit-bearing, but enjoyment of life continued with the utmost variety of delight and without interruption. Constant joy and pleasure were afforded to the inhabitants of the city.

Whilst the luscious fruit became the food of the saints, the leaves of the tree were medicine for the nations. As in Ezekiel's vision, health came from their eating. (The details of Ezek. 47 are so similar that the chapter should be studied at the same time as Rev. 22).

Since life flowed out in its fulness, the curse was banished (cf. Zech. 14. 11). Hengstenberg writes: "The idea of cursing is always that of the forced consecration to God of those who had obstinately refused to consecrate themselves voluntarily to Him—of the manifestation of the divine glory in the destruction of those who, during their lifetime, would not reflect it, and therefore would not realize the general destination of man, the design of all creation. God sanctifies Himself *upon* all those, *in* whom He is not sanctified. The destruction of everything on earth, which will not serve Him,

[1] Ezek. 47 [2] Gen. 3. 22-24

proclaims His praise." In the holy city, however, there was no object for the penal justice of God, and in place of the curse, there was unrestrained love and life and blessing.

The throne of God and of the Lamb stood in the central square—the centre of the city, as the holy of holies was formerly the centre of the temple. No temple now hid the Almighty from the view of His loved ones. His servants willingly rendered service to Him. There they beheld His face and received His behests direct and His name was impressed upon their foreheads. From that scene of light and glory, His messengers would issue to carry out His commands and to be the executors of His administration, their authority manifest to all in their foreheads. As one realizes that those who are to fulfil those divine commissions are the redeemed of this present age, the marvel of divine grace is only emphasized the more. Unworthy sinners, redeemed by the precious blood of Christ, might well rejoice in the fact of salvation, but that they should become the shrine in which the Almighty God will dwell and from whence He will radiate His glory, might indeed bow the heart in worship. In that wonderful scene they are destined to be His ministers, wearing the sign of His authority upon their heads, ever seeing His face and dwelling in the light of His glory. The Eternal God Himself will shine upon them and unto the ages of the ages they will reign on His behalf.

The absence of night and of any need for lamp or for sunlight was again emphasized to the seer. God was the light of that city. With that scene of bliss and glory, the prophecy virtually concludes. What follows forms an epilogue to the book. The last prophetic picture is the blessing and joy of the millennial day.

Chapter XXVI

The Epilogue

The Imprimatur

"And he said to me, These words are faithful and true; and the Lord God of the spirits of the prophets has sent His angel to shew to His servants the things which must soon come to pass. Behold, I come quickly. Blessed is he who keeps the worcs of the prophecy of this book. And I, John, heard and saw these things. And when I heard and saw, I fell down to worship before the feet of the angel who shewed me these things. And he says to me, See thou do it not. I am thy fellow-servant, and the fellow-servant of thy brethren the prophets, and of those who keep the words of this book. Worship God" (22. 6-9).

As a divine imprimatur stamped upon the pages of the book which John had been commanded to write, came the declaration from the angel that the words were faithful and true. The revelation of soon-coming events had been made by the One who was the Lord God of the spirits of the prophets. All prophecy in previous ages had been inspired by Him, and He had spoken previously through the mouth of prophet and seer. The final unfolding of prophecy had also been made by Him, through the instrumentality of the angel whom He had sent to reveal these things. The speaker was obviously the Lord Himself, accrediting His agent and setting His seal upon the book. He it was who spoke through the prophets and who could rightly assume the title of the Lord God.

Suddenly, there burst forth the glorious promise, "Behold I come quickly." If there is one fact above all others which thrills the heart of the believer, it is the soon-coming of our blessed Lord. Then, faith will give place to sight, shadows to substance, symbols to reality. The sorrows and griefs, the trials and troubles, the problems and perplexities, the sins and mistakes of this life will then be for ever banished, and His people shall see the One they love. He is surely coming. The One who loved her unto death is soon returning to rapture away His blood-bought Church. Yet that second advent has already been delayed over 1,900 years. True it is that a thousand years are as one day with Him, but the long anticipated event cannot much longer be delayed. "Behold, I come quickly."

A blessing was pronounced upon the one who kept the words of the prophecy of the book. They were to be guarded as a treasure since they concerned the unveiling of Jesus Christ. No light estimate was to be placed upon this book, and the one who rightly treasured it would find an especial reward.

After all that he had seen and heard, John prostrated himself before the angel as he had done previously,[1] only to receive a similar admonition to worship God and not one who was after all only a fellow-servant.

The Unsealed Book

"And he says to me, Seal not the words of the prophecy of this book. The time is at hand. Let him that does unrighteously do unrighteously still; and let the filthy make himself filthy still; and let him that is righteous practise righteousness still; and he that is holy, let him be sanctified still. Behold, I come quickly, and My reward is with Me, to render to every one as his work shall be. I am the Alpha and the Omega, the first and the last, the beginning and the end" (22. 10-13).

When Daniel's prophecy was complete, he was commanded to "close the words, and seal the book, till the time of the end."[2] John was specifically commanded, however, not to seal the words of the prophecy of this book since the time was at hand. Centuries were to roll by before Daniel's prophecy neared its fulfilment, but the Revelation began to be fulfilled immediately, and the first three chapters now belong very largely to the past (although, of course, not without their application to the present). No impenetrable mystery attaches to the Apocalypse; the book is open for all to read and for the Spirit-taught to understand. The time of fulfilment of the events foretold was then at hand; some have since seen fruition. How imminent must be the remaining events of which the book speaks!

Bullinger points out that, in the statement of verse 11, the present participle of condition is followed by the aorist tense, relating to acts and not condition. The present condition of the individual is indicative of a deliberate life-choice; therefore, declared the Speaker, let him continue to practise that which he had deliberately chosen. It is not so much an eternal petrification of character or a sentence of finality on the state of the soul, although it is true, as Scott points out, that "habits fix character, and character fixes destiny." The words give the real reason for the command

[1]Rev. 19. 10 [2]Dan. 12. 4

to refrain from sealing the book. The Revelation becomes a savour of death unto death to the ungodly. The unrighteous and the filthy were bidden to continue to practise unrighteousness and filthiness. The righteous and the holy were to continue to practise righteousness and holiness.

Again the Lord declared, "Behold, I come quickly," and added that He brought a reward with Him to render to every man in accordance with his work. The Second Advent connotes not only blessing but also examination of life and works. An individual and appropriate reward is reserved for all His people. The measure of fidelity and loyal service will be the measure of the reward. All the deeds of life will be brought under review at the judgment-seat of Christ, that everyone "may receive the things done in the body."[1]

Once more He used of Himself the title of Alpha and Omega, the first and the last, the beginning and the ending, as if to emphasize the complete summation of everything in Himself. All is comprehended in Him. He is the first and the last.

Saved and Lost

"Blessed are they that wash their robes, that they may have right to the tree of life, and that they should go in by the gates into the city. Without are the dogs, and the sorcerers, and the fornicators, and the murderers, and the idolaters, and everyone that loves and makes a lie" (22. 14, 15).

Adam's fall debarred him from the tree of life, but the Lord declared that those who washed their robes should be blessed and entitled to the tree of life. The blood of Calvary had cleansed them from the stain and defilement of sin and with cleansed robes, they entered by the gates into the holy city, to gaze upon the face of God and to eat of the tree of life. The sinner has been so graced in Christ that nothing is withheld from him. Unbounded blessing is poured out and everlasting life is his enjoyed portion.

Outside the city, however, were the dogs, sorcerers, fornicators, murderers, idolaters and liars. With the exception of the first-named, these classes had already been mentioned in chap. 21. 8 and have been commented on in that connection. The list is headed by *dogs*, that is, says Bengel, "the unholy and impure who, by their rough behaviour, show that they are quite unlike the Lamb. In the language of the world, the rabble are called, by way of contempt, *canaille*, that is, dog." It is the symbol of the contemptible, impure, and shameless (cf. Prov. 26. 11; Matt. 7. 6; 2 Pet. 2. 22).

[1] 2 Cor. 5. 10

Such as these were excluded from the holy city and had no part in the blessing of God. Grace had been spurned and they had chosen their own path.

The Cry of "Come."

"I Jesus have sent Mine angel to testify these things to you in the churches. I am the root and offspring of David, the bright and morning star. And the Spirit and the bride say, Come. And let him that hears say, Come. And let him that is athirst come; he that will, let him take the water of life freely" (22. 16, 17).

The Lord again accredited the angelic messenger as His agent, sent to bear witness to the Churches of Asia of what had been seen and heard. There may be some ground for accepting the view that it was to John himself, as the Lord's sent messenger, that reference was made.

"I am the root and offspring of David," He added. "The *root* of David is the *product* of the root," writes Hengstenberg, "the sprout from the root, that in which the family of David, that had sunk into the lowest depression, again bloomed forth. Because Jesus is the root, He is also the *race* of David. In Him alone is the race preserved." The One who descended from David was a sprout from a withered root, and all the vitality of a new life flowed through Him. The pledge of a new race lay in that fresh shoot. He was the "root" and the "offspring."

He was also the "bright and morning star," the harbinger of the coming day, the herald of the dawn. The title is in a peculiar sense appropriate to His relation to the Church. As the Sun of righteousness arising with healing in His wings[1] will He appear to Israel, but before the Sun rises, the bright and morning Star shines out in the sky. His coming draws near. He is the bright and morning Star. Faith sees the gleam of light and patiently awaits the dawn.

The very title of the bright and morning star seems to touch the Church of God, for immediately the cry rang out from the Bride and from the Spirit who taught her thus to cry—the yearning cry of "Come." Through all the centuries, the Church has longed for her Lord's return and the very reminder of His Advent draws forth that desire afresh. The fact that He would return was lost to view by the great majority of Christians until the beginning of the nineteenth century, but revival of prophetic study and teaching since then has deepened the world-wide yearning of God's people for that blessed event. With deeper earnestness and eager antici-

[1]Mal. 4. 2

pation, the Church is taught by the Spirit to voice her longings in the cry of "Come."

An exhortation followed to the hearer, that is, to the one who read or heard the words of the prophecy, and who had perhaps previously been uninstructed. The hearer also was enjoined to unite with the Spirit and the Bride in beseeching the Lord to come.

With a curious transition, the word was then suddenly converted into a last evangelistic appeal, and the thirsty was bidden to come and whoever desired, to take of the water of life freely. The very imminence of the Lord's return served to emphasize the appeal and to reinforce its urgency. Grace freely offered life and salvation to all who thirsted for the water of life. If the Christian to-day realized all the implications of his Lord's return, the desperate need of the unconverted would stir him to fresh effort and new zeal, in order that by any means he might bring some thirsty soul into contact with the springs of eternal life. The powerlessness and lifelessness of much Gospel preaching may perhaps be due to blindness to the fact of our Lord's soon-coming, and we might well pray for an awakening on the part of God's people.

Final Messages

"I testify to every one who hears the words of the prophecy of this book, If any one shall add to these things, God shall add to him the plagues which are written in this book. And if any one take from the words of this book of the prophecy, God shall take away his part from the tree of life, and out of the holy city, and from the things which are written in this book. He that testifies these things says, Yea, I come quickly. Amen; come, Lord Jesus. The grace of the Lord Jesus Christ be with all the saints" (22. 18-21).

For his sin in cutting and burning the prophetic roll of Jeremiah, the wicked king Jehoiakim met with condign punishment.[1] This book of the Revelation was not given by the hand of an earthly prophet, but rather handed by God to His Son. A dread warning was therefore given to any who tampered with the words of this book. To the one who added to the words, God would mete out the plagues described in the prophecy. To the one who took away from the book, God would take away his part in the tree of life and the holy city and the blessings described in the book. The words are most solemn, but "the fear of man, which always evokes the latitudinarian spirit, could only be expelled by the fear of God."

The intention of the warning was, of course, to prevent any tampering with the Apocalypse; it did not relate primarily to the

[1]Jer. 36

other canonical books, although similar injunctions appear.[1] "The curse denounced," says Simcox, "is on those who interpolate unauthorized doctrines in the prophecy, or who neglect essential ones, not on transcribers who might unadvisedly interpolate or omit something in the true text. The curse is designed to guard the integrity of *this* book of the Revelation, and not to *close* the New Testament canon. It is not even certain that this was the last written of the canonical books." Expositors have been prone to detract from the meaning of the curse and to suggest that it signifies something less than what is plainly stated, but there appears no justification for taking the words otherwise than literally.

The final message to the Church is a reiterated assurance that the Lord will come quickly. Just as the Old Testament closed with the announcement of His coming, so the New Testament concludes with a similar intimation. It is the third mention in the chapter of His speedy return. Nothing awaits fulfilment before that transcendent event. Assuredly, He will come quickly.

Voicing the cry of the expectant Church, John cried out, "Amen; come, Lord Jesus." No human plans or purposes, no earth-born ambitions or motives, not even a concern for the lost, hold back the intense desire. In all the deep-seated love and yearning of his soul; the Lord's return was the greatest desire of his heart. Is it so with all God's people? Only too frequently the mundane pursuit, the materialistic ambition, and the temporal object usurp the place of Christ. May God reawaken the fervour of our first love for Christ and inspire us too to cry, "Come, Lord Jesus."

Whereas the Old Testament closed with a threatened curse, the New Testament concludes with a benediction. "The grace of the Lord Jesus Christ be with all the saints." His illimitable favour reaches out to grace every one of His own.

[1]Deut. 4. 2; 12. 32

Chapter XXVII

The Prophetic Outline

IT may assist to a better understanding of the message of the Apocalypse if an outline is given of the prophetic programme, and this chapter is added for that reason.

It should, of course, be appreciated that all prophecy is centred in the Person of the Lord Jesus Christ and revolves about Him. He is the Hope of the Church and the Desire of Israel; He is the Redeemer for whom creation groans, and the Deliverer for whom the nations wait; He is the coming One who is yet to set all things in order.

The Davidic Kingdom

When David was settled upon the throne of Israel, Jehovah entered into a covenant with him to establish his house and his kingdom for ever.[1] The Davidic Covenant has not yet been completely fulfilled, but has never been abrogated, and in a future day the divine purpose will yet be realized. When the Christ of God descends again to earth, all promises will find their satisfaction and fulfilment in Himself, and the long-expected kingdom will at last be set up.

On the death of Solomon, the kingdom was divided into the two kingdoms of Israel and Judah, the former crowning Jeroboam king, and the latter retaining their loyalty to Rehoboam, Solomon's son. In 721 B.C., the sins of Israel resulted in the ten tribes being carried away captive into Assyria.[2] Judah, however, proved no less guilty, and in 598 B.C., Nebuchadnezzar carried into Mesopotamia Jehoiachin and the chief people of Judah.[3] As a result of Zedekiah's rebellion nine years later, Jerusalem was burnt and the majority of the people carried away. God thus removed the testimony of Israel as a whole, and the sword of government passed to the Gentiles in the person of Nebuchadnezzar, and to this heathen monarch God committed the potential dominion of the world.[4]

Gentile Rule

It was revealed to Nebuchadnezzar (in the vision of the great

[1] 2 Sam. 7 [2] 2 Kings 17 [3] 2 Kings 24 [4] Dan. 2. 37-38

image of four metals)[1] and also to Daniel (in the vision of the four beasts)[2] that, from the rise of the Babylonian monarchy to the end of the age, the sword of world-government should pass through the hands of four great empires, following upon which was to come the establishment of "the kingdom of the heavens." The first of these empires is stated to be the Babylonian and history makes it clear that the three successive empires were those of Medo-Persia, Greece and Rome. The last of these, however, has disappeared as an empire before reaching the final condition foretold in Dan. 2 and 7. If God's Word, therefore, is to be fulfilled, the Roman empire must yet be revived, and other prophecies definitely point to such a revival.

The Seventy Weeks

In a further revelation to Daniel,[3] it was made known that "seventy weeks" were determined upon his people (*i.e.*, the Jews). It is clear that the "weeks" (lit. "sevens") were weeks of years, and that each week is the equivalent of seven years. The period of these prophetic weeks commenced with "the going forth of the commandment to restore and to build Jerusalem",[4] which, as Neh. 2 makes clear, was in the twentieth year of Artaxerxes, or 445 B.C.

The seventy weeks were divided into three sections, viz.:

(1) 7 weeks, or 49 years, were to be spent in the rebuilding of the city.

(2) 62 weeks, or 434 years, were to elapse from then until Messiah the Prince.

(3) After the cutting-off of Messiah, the last week of 7 years was to run its course.

The first era of 49 years was exactly fulfilled, and, as Sir Robert Anderson has proved conclusively in *The Coming Prince*, the second period of 434 years expired on the very day of our Lord's triumphal entry into Jerusalem.[5] After the 69th "week" (actually during the same *literal* week), Messiah was cut off, as foretold by the prophecy. The 70th "week" of Dan. 9, which had yet to run its course, must either have followed immediately upon the previous 69 "weeks" or have been separated from them by some intervening period. Since the first 69 "weeks" were weeks of years, it naturally follows that the final "week" was the equivalent of 7 years, and any interpretation which converts Daniel's seventieth "week" into a long, indeterminate period does violence to the rules of Biblical exegesis.

[1]Dan. 2 [2]Dan. 7 [3]Dan. 9. [4]Dan. 9. 25 [5]Matt. 21

The events which were to occur during that final period of 7 years are carefully detailed in Dan. 9. 27, and it is perfectly clear from history that these events have not yet all taken place. It is a legitimate assumption, therefore, that a break occurred in the continuity of the "weeks," and that the whole of the present dispensation falls as a parenthesis between the end of the 69th "week" and the beginning of the 70th "week." Humanly speaking, had Israel accepted the Messiah after His entry into Jerusalem, the 70th "week" would have commenced at once, but their rejection of Christ resulted in the postponement of the divine purpose.

The Church

When the Jews rejected the Lord Jesus Christ, God suspended His dealings with an earthly people and commenced to call out a heavenly people—a Church composed of all those born of, and indwelt by, the Holy Spirit. Until Calvary, God had dealt with individuals and peoples as Israelites or Gentiles, but that difference has been abolished during the present age,[1] and He now deals with individuals as saints or sinners, as members or non-members of the Church of God. The Church was a mystery hidden in previous ages until the time came for its revelation.[2] Hence there is no mention either of the Church or the Church-age in the Old Testament. When the Church-age comes to a close, judgment and blessing will again be dispensed on a national basis, and Israel will occupy her former position of the favoured nation, and Daniel's postponed 70th "week" will at last run its course.

The length of the present dispensation is not stated in Scripture, but its history, so far as the Church is concerned, is delineated in Rev. 2 and 3. In the letters to the seven churches of Asia, the spiritual history of the Church from its early days to the end is carefully mapped out. In the letter to *Ephesus* is clearly seen the condition of the Church during the sub-apostolic era; *Smyrna* evidently refers to the period of persecutions of pagan Rome; *Pergamos* indicates the union of Church and State which commenced with Constantine; *Thyatira* suggests the rise of Papacy; *Sardis* forecasts the Reformation; *Philadelphia* probably points to Nonconformist efforts of the last century; whilst *Laodicea* outlines the condition of the lukewarm Church of to-day. The history of Christendom is also forecast in a wonderful way in the seven parables of the Kingdom.[3]

The present age, which commenced with the descent of the Holy

[1]Eph. 2. 14 [2]Eph. 3. 5-6 [3]Matt. 13

Spirit,[1] is peculiarly the age of the Spirit,[2] and will end at His removal from the world.[3] This event will apparently coincide with the rapture of the true Church.

The glorious future which awaits the Church is to be united to her risen Head, and every true believer consequently waits for the second advent of Christ. The date of the coming has been withheld, but all events of the present day indicate the imminence of the event. 1 Thess. 4. 15-17 reveals that the Lord Jesus Christ will personally descend into the air, the dead in Christ be raised and, together with the living saints, be caught up to meet Him in the air, never again to be separated from Him or from each other. Every member of the Church will be caught away and not a single one left behind. 1 Cor. 15. 51-53 unfolds the additional facts that the dead will be raised incorruptible and that the living will be changed from mortality into immortality. The theory of a partial rapture is without Scriptural support, as is indicated by 1 Thess. 5. 10, the literal significance of which is: "Whether we watch or slumber (spiritually), we should live together with Him."[4]

After the rapture there will appropriately follow the individual examination of the saints at the *bema*, or judgment seat, of Christ,[5] where each will receive reward or suffer loss according to deeds done in the body. All misunderstandings will be removed, all mistakes rectified, and all shortcomings forgiven. Then, when every blemish has been removed, and the saints have been arrayed in the fine linen of their righteous deeds, the Church will be united to the Lamb in marriage,[6] prior to her manifestation with Him in glory.[7] The glorious future of the Church surpasses human comprehension, and can only be vaguely realized by faith.

After the Rapture

The full display of Satan's activities on earth is at present hindered by the two influences described in 2 Thess. 2, as "what withholdeth" (v. 6) and "He who now letteth" (v. 7), that is, respectively, the Church and the Holy Spirit who indwells it. Both these restraining influences will be removed at the rapture, and Satan will then be at liberty to produce his masterpiece, "the man of sin."

Prophecy indicates that, at the end of the present dispensation, the Jews will return to their own land in unbelief, under the protection and with the assistance of a great seafaring nation.[8] The Zionist movement and the British mandate in Palestine have great significance in this connection. Established again in Palestine,

[1]Acts 2 [2]John 14, etc. [3]2 Thess. 2. 7 [4]Rev. 3. 10, etc.
[5]2 Cor. 5. 10 [6]Rev. 19 [7]2 Thess. 1. 10, etc. [8]Isa. 18

the Jews will rebuild the temple and restore the old Mosaic ritual, and will ultimately be reigned over by a Jewish king at Jerusalem.[1] This king will afterwards be manifested as the "false prophet."[2] Rev. 13. 11-18 reveals that this man (who is identical with the second beast of that chapter) has a twofold authority (indicated by the two horns), and is not only a political ruler but also an ecclesiastical authority.

The great image of Nebuchadnezzar's vision ended in ten toes,[3] and the fourth beast of Daniel's vision possessed ten horns.[4] In these prophecies is indicated a phase of Roman history which has not yet been realized, and other passages clearly show that the Roman Empire is yet to be revived in the new form of a confederacy, or league, of ten kingdoms,[5] with a great emperor at the head. This monarch (spoken of in the prophetic word as "the Beast") commences his career with the subjugation of three kingdoms,[6] after which seven other kings give their power into his hand.[7] To this man, Satan will give the supreme power or world authority, which he offered the Lord Jesus Christ.[8]

Among other characters in God's prophetic programme are the kings of the North and South. Dan. 11 describes the wars, intrigues, and alliances of the kingdoms of Syria and Egypt down to the day of Antiochus Epiphanes, but from verse 40 (verses 36-39 are really parenthetic and refer to the king of the Jews) the future activities of these two powers are brought under review. The King of the South, of course, is Egypt. The King of the North is apparently one ruling in Asia Minor, who is under the protection of the great northern confederacy of Joel 2, the Gog of Ezek. 38, or the Assyrian of Isa. 10.

After the removal of the Church, its travesty will be produced in the great Whore or Harlot, who sits upon many waters,[9] *i.e.*, rules ecclesiastically over multitudes and nations with a power surpassing even Papal hopes and expectations.

This religious Babylon will probably cover all sects and denominations of Christendom, and possibly other religious systems as well. When the process of welding the nations together by this impressive unity has been completed, the ten horns of the Roman Empire will destroy the whole system and organization.[10]

The Jewish State, situated as it will be in Palestine, will be in continual dread of the tremendous power of Russia, and in order to preserve the little country as a buffer state, the Roman Emperor will make a seven-year covenant with the Jews, guaranteeing

[1]Dan. 11. 36-39 [2]Rev. 16. 13, etc. [3]Dan. 2 [4]Dan. 7 [5]Rev. 13. 1-3 ; Dan. 7, etc. [6]Dan. 7. 24 [7]Rev. 17. 13 [8]Rev. 13. 4 [9]Rev. 17 [10]Rev. 17. 16

protection from Assyria and Russia, and promising the preservation of the people in their religious observances.[1] The strength of the northern power, however, will be so great that Rome will be powerless to prevent the threatened invasions of the enemy. Time after time will the Russian hordes sweep down upon the defenceless land, laying Jerusalem in heaps, shedding blood like water,[2] and sweeping through to plunder and devastate Egypt and her glories.

The Great Tribulation

The seven-year treaty, which synchronizes with the 70th "week" of Dan. 9, will be broken after 3½ years,[3] probably at the instigation of the devil, who will at that time be cast out of heaven.[4] The Beast will suddenly put a stop to the revived Mosaic ritual and worship, and force idolatry upon the Jews and the Roman Empire.

The false prophet, or king of the Jews, will enter into the temple, claiming to be God[5] and seeking divine honours for himself and the Beast,[6] an image of the Beast, "the abomination of desolation," Dan. 12. 11) being set up in the temple itself. At this sign the godly will flee to the mountains, as foretold and directed by the Lord Himself.[7] This is the commencement of the terrible period known in Scripture as the time of Jacob's trouble, or the Great Tribulation. The subsequent 3½ years represent the same period as the 1,260 days of Rev. 12. 6, the time, times and half a time of Rev. 12. 14, and the 42 months of Rev. 13. 5. During these few years, Palestine will be the scene of warfare and of terrible slaughter, the horror of which is not exaggerated by the language of the Psalms which allude to it. Throughout the Roman Empire, as well as in Palestine, all will be compelled on pain of death to worship the Beast and to receive his mark in their right hand or in their forehead, no trading being allowed without the mark, the name, or number of the name.[8] The Great Tribulation will also be characterized by God's judgment of guilty Judah and by the outpouring upon earth of the divine judgments of the seals, trumpets and vials of Rev. 6 to 16, with the ultimate result of universal chaos, and the complete disruption of civil and political society. Even during this period, God will have His witnesses,[9] and many will be converted.[10]

In the last days, Satan will gather together the western hosts in the plain of Megiddo to besiege the godly remnant in Jerusalem.[11] Suddenly Christ will come with all His saints to make war upon His enemies. The Mount of Olives will cleave in the midst at His descent.[12] The mighty Conqueror will ride forth in majesty

[1]Dan. 9. 27 [2]Psa. 74, 79, 83, etc. [3]Dan. 9. 27 [4]Rev. 12. 9 [5]2 Thess. 2. 4
[6]Rev. 13. 15 [7]Matt. 24. 16 [8]Rev. 13. 16, 17 [9]Rev. 11 [10]Rev. 7 and 14
[11]Zech. 12; Rev. 16. 16, etc. [12]Zech. 14

and power to destroy the armies of the Beast with the sword, and to give their flesh to the fowls to eat.[1] The Beast (the Roman Emperor) and the False Prophet (the Jewish king) will be cast alive into the lake of fire,[2] the first inhabitants of that awful place.

It appears that, at that time, the King of the North will be conducting a war in the south against Egypt,[3] but the tidings of Christ's return will come to him "out of the east and out of the north" (*i.e.*, from the north-east, or Palestine), and he will promptly return in great fury to destroy and make war on the Lamb.[4] Seeking to fight against the Omnipotent One, he and his armies will perish on the mountains of Israel. with none to help,[5] and it will take seven months to bury the dead in the valley of Hamongog.[6]

Satan, the author of evil, will himself be taken and bound and then cast into the bottomless pit, there to remain for a thousand years.[7]

Apparently only a part of Israel will return to Palestine at the end of the present dispensation. After the battle of Armageddon, therefore, the remainder of Israel will be divinely gathered out from the nations of the world,[8] and brought into the wilderness,[9] where Jehovah will plead with them, and after passing them under the rod, will eventually restore them to the land.[10] The two kingdoms of Israel and Judah, after centuries of division, will be reunited under one head, as pictured in the two sticks of Ezek. 37, and will rejoice in a national conversion.[11]

His enemies overthrown, the Lord Jesus Christ will proceed to set up His earthly tribunal, and the living nations will be summoned before Him for judgment, to be rewarded or punished according to their treatment of His brethren, the Jews.[12] The result will be a tremendous depopulation of the earth, which will, to some extent, be repaired by means of longevity of life and human fruitfulness during the millennium.

THE MILLENNIUM

When all disorder has been removed and judgment has been carried out, the Kingdom of God will at last be established upon the earth. The Davidic covenant will find its complete fulfilment, with Israel as the head of the nations[13] and the centre of blessing, a prince of the house of David sitting on the throne of Jerusalem,

[1]Rev. 19. 11-21 [2]Rev. 19. 20 [3]Dan. 11. 42-43 [4]Dan. 11. 44
[5]Dan. 11. 45; Ezek. 38, 39; Isa. 30 [6]Ezek. 39. 12 [7]Rev. 20. 1-3
[8]Isa. 11. 11-12; Ezek. 20 and 34 [9]Hosea 12, 13, etc.
[10]Amos. 9. 15; Zeph. 3. 14-20 [11]Jer. 31. 33-34; Ezek. 36. 24-31; Zech. 13. 1
[12]Matt. 25 [13]Micah 4. 8

and the Kingdom established for the remainder of earthly history until the ages of time give place to the eternal state. The twelve tribes of Israel will spread in parallel bands across the country from the Euphrates to the Mediterranean.[1] The glory of Jehovah will again fill the temple (that millennial building of splendour described by Ezekiel) and Levitical priests will again minister before Him. For a thousand years Christ will reign in righteousness and equity;[2] peace and joy will pervade the scene. The millennium is the period of the "restitution of all things"—an age in which "the eyes of the blind shall be opened, and the ears of the deaf be unstopped; then shall the lame man leap as an hart, and the tongue of the dumb sing."[3] In that day, all creation will be at peace, and "the wolf and the lamb shall feed together, and the lion shall eat straw like an ox."[4] The prophets are full of the rest, tranquillity and happiness of that age, and it is impossible to comprehend the incomparable glories of those millennial days.

The Final Rebellion

During the millennium, there will be universal submission to Christ and He will be outwardly acknowledged as supreme Lord. Since the human heart is ever sinful, in many cases the subjection will be but a feigned obedience, and lip-service will hide inward opposition and enmity. At the close of this glorious dispensation, the true character of man will be manifested. Satan will be loosed from his bondage for a little season, and will go forth to deceive the nations, gathering them together against the city of Jerusalem in a final desperate effort to overthrow the King and the Kingdom, but fire will come down from God, out of heaven and destroy the rebellious hosts.[5] Satan will be cast for ever into the lake of fire, never again to issue forth on his evil missions. Heaven and earth removed,[6] "the dead, small and great," will stand before the Great White Throne to be judged according to the things written in the books, and all whose names are not found written in the book of life will be cast into the lake of fire.[7] Death and Hades (the resting-place of departed spirits), neither of which will then be any longer required, will also find their end in the lake of fire.[8]

Eternity

2 Pet. 3 reveals that heaven and earth are to be purged with fire, and that God is yet going to bring into existence "new heavens

[1]Ezek. 48 [2]Jer. 23. 5, 6; Zech. 6. 12, 13 [3]Isa. 35. 5 [4]Isa. 65. 25
[5]Rev. 20 [6]Rev. 20. 11 [7]Rev. 20. 15 [8]Rev. 20. 14

and a new earth, wherein dwelleth righteousness."[1] Ages and dispensations will no longer have any part in divine dealings, but all will give place to the eternal state, in which everything is confirmed and consolidated. The abolition of the sea from the world[2] will give an enormously larger scope for the earth-dwellers, who will presumably be the people converted during the millennium. The holy city, New Jerusalem, will descend from heaven as a bride adorned for her husband, and God will dwell with men, removing sorrow, sin and sickness. Everything on earth and in heaven will be perfect and holy, and God will be all and in all.

[1] 2 Pet. 3. 10-13 [2] Rev. 21. 1

Chapter XXVIII

Conclusion

THE study of eschatology can never fail to appeal to the true believer, but whilst the details of the prophetic programme may attract and intrigue, the hope of the Christian is nothing less than the personal return of his Lord. As John McNicol says, his attitude is represented by the closing words of John in the Apocalypse: "Visions of heavenly glory and millennial peace have passed before him. He has seen the new heaven and the new earth wherein dwelleth righteousness, and the Holy City, New Jerusalem, whose light was like a stone most precious. But, at the end of it all, the longing of the aged apostle is not for these things to come. Greater than all these glories is the Master Himself, and the prayer that rises from his heart as he closes his book is simply, 'Come, Lord Jesus.'" Says John Wesley, "The spirit of adoption in the bride says, with earnest desire and expectation, 'Come and accomplish all the words of this prophecy.'"

When our Lord departed from this world at Bethany, the watching disciples returned to Jerusalem radiant with the assurance that, as He went, so He would return, and the New Testament constantly sets before the reader the hope of His return. The details of the prophetic programme unfolded in the Revelation are of far less importance than the crucial fact that the One who ascended to heaven nineteen centuries ago will soon descend into the air to rapture His loved ones to Himself. "We hunger after Christ," said Calvin, "till the dawning of that great day."

All through the centuries the cry of God's people has been, "Come, Lord Jesus." Milton wrote: "Come forth out of Thy royal chambers, O Prince of all the kings of the earth; put on the visible robes of Thy imperial majesty; take up that unlimited sceptre which Thy Almighty Father hath bequeathed Thee. For now the voice of Thy bride calls Thee, and all creatures sigh to be renewed."

In the midst of strife and trouble, Martin Luther voiced his inner desire when he said: "I ardently hope that, amidst these internal dissensions on the earth, Jesus Christ will hasten the day of His coming." And the saintly Rutherford cried: "Oh, that Christ would remove the covering, draw aside the curtains of time and come down. Oh, that the shadows and the night were gone."

If the Revelation has no other message, it does at least warm the heart again toward Christ and reawaken the longing to see His blessed face. May it have that effect upon the readers of this book.

Hark! the song of Jubilee,
Loud as mighty thunders roar,
Or the fulness of the sea,
When it breaks upon the shore.
Hallelujah! for the Lord
God Omnipotent shall reign.
Hallelujah! let the word
Echo round the earth and main.

Hallelujah! hark! the sound,
From the abysses to the skies,
Wakes above, beneath, around,
All creation's harmonies.
See Jehovah's banner furled,
Sheathed His sword: He speaks—'tis done;
And the kingdoms of this world
Are the kingdoms of His Son.

He shall reign from pole to pole,
With illimitable sway.
He shall reign when, like a scroll,
Yonder heavens have passed away.
Then the end: beneath His rod,
Man's last enemy shall fall.
Hallelujah! Christ in God,
God in Christ, is all in all.

JAMES MONTGOMERY

List of Authors Quoted

Atkinson, B. F. C. -	*The War With Satan*
Baines, T. B. - -	*The Revelation of Jesus Christ*
Bengel, J. A. - -	*Exposition of the Revelation*
Bullinger, E. W. -	*The Apocalypse*
"	*Number in Scripture*
Burton, A. H. - -	*The Apocalypse Expounded*
Cumming, J. - - -	*Apocalyptic Sketches*
Darby, J. N. - - -	*Lectures on the Addresses to the Seven Churches*
Elliott, E. B. - -	*Horæ Apocalypticæ*
Farrar, F. W. - -	*The Early Days of Christianity*
Gaebelein, A. C. - -	*The Revelation*
Govett, R. - - -	*The Apocalypse Expounded*
Hengstenberg, E. W. -	*The Revelation of St. John*
Hislop, A. - - -	*The Two Babylons*
Hoste, W. - - -	*Visions of John the Divine*
Ironside, H. A - -	*Lectures on the Revelation*
Jennings, F. C. - -	*Studies in Revelation*
Kelly, W. - - -	*Lectures on the Book of the Revelation*
Newell, W. R. - -	*The Revelation*
Newton, B. W. -	*Thoughts on the Apocalypse*
Plumptre, E. H. -	*The Epistles to the Seven Churches of Asia*
Ramsay, W. M. - -	*The Letters to the Seven Churches of Asia*
Sargent H. N. - -	*The Marvels of Bible Prophecy*
Scott, W. - - -	*Exposition of the Revelation of Jesus Christ*
Seiss, J. A. - - -	*The Prophecies of the Revelation*
Stuart, M. - - -	*A Commentary on the Apocalypse*
Trench, R. C. - -	*Commentary on the Epistles to the Seven Churches of Asia*

Scripture Index

General Index